The Adventures of
RICHARD O'BOY

Other books by the author

WITCH OF SALEM

THE SWORD AND THE PROMISE

A KIND OF JUSTICE

THE PRINCIPAL

DOCTORS AND WIVES

THE JURORS

CASE HISTORY

FOUR DOCTORS

THIS HEALING PASSION

STRANGERS, HEALERS

The Adventures of
RICHARD O'BOY

A Novel by

Benjamin Siegel

Lippincott & Crowell, Publishers
New York

THE ADVENTURES OF RICHARD O'BOY. Copyright © 1980 by Benjamin Siegel. All rights reserved. Printed in the United States of America. No part of this book may be used or reproduced in any manner whatsoever without written permission, except in the case of brief quotations embodied in critical articles and reviews. For information address Lippincott & Crowell, Publishers, 521 Fifth Avenue, New York, N.Y. 10017.

FIRST EDITION

Designed by Michael Flanagan

U.S. Library of Congress Cataloging in Publication Data
Siegel, Benjamin, birth date
  The adventures of Richard O'Boy.
  I. Title.
PZ4.S57AD 1980   (PS3569.I37)
813'.5'4   79-25146
ISBN-0-690-01860-6

80 81 82 83 84 10 9 8 7 6 5 4 3 2 1

To Fran and Joanna,
Edward and Matthew

The Adventures of
RICHARD O'BOY

Chapter One

I have never lived an ordinary quiet life.

SOCRATES

I was born at considerable stress to my mother, who vowed my father would henceforth sleep in a separate chamber. He must have ceased his attentions upon her, because I remained an only child. I was expected to do the work of those unborn, since my father was a farmer and had hoped to have a number of sons.

My mother, born Marie Au'Bois, hated all things English. She had been sent against her will to work as a servant girl in London, where her life was so harsh that when the tall Englishman offered to share his fortune with her she did not stop to think of going home again. My mother wept over Waterloo. I have her gray eyes and a certain harshness about the mouth.

The farm that my father rented from Sir James Nott-Playsaunt consisted of one hundred acres outside the village of Dire-Toombley, in Suffolk. Five miles away is the market town of Clamford, where there is a circulating library; I was there as often as I could manage, sometimes finishing the book as I walked home. I read Byron, puzzled over Browning, was fond of the silver fork novels, read *Oliver Twist* three times, and wished that more books had come from the Brontë family.

On Sundays the village turned out to worship together, mainly because the insistence of Sir James that the service be attended was a higher directive than the call from the pulpit. The church was pleasantly old with gray stone and flint work and a graveyard with hawthorns and elms. It smelled cool and whispered with history. Any of the Henrys could have stopped there, even Elizabeth, certainly both Charleses.

Awe and obedience go together; authority, to exist, requires submission. How then could I both revere and question? It was a vice of mine to question everything, perhaps because Satan had assigned an imp to me. I tried to talk to mine, asked that he show himself, but I think imps melt in the light. Or that failing of mine might have come from my mother's blood, although I did not like to think of being other than wholly English.

The Squire's wife and a daughter had died of the Yellow Jack ten years before; another daughter was married and lived in Scotland, so only Sir James and Peter sat in the big square pew. Sir James had earned the right to suffer with the gout and wore a wide shoe on the afflicted foot, having come into church by cane on one side and son on the other, setting an example that infirmity was no excuse for neglecting the Lord's worship.

Precedence in the church seating was strict. Behind Sir James, although not in a pew, were my father and mother and I, and behind us the tradesmen and shopkeepers and village artisans. My mother sat like a stone while my father slept with his eyes open. I studied the back of the head of Sir James's son and dreamed of heaving a hymnal at it.

To one side of the pulpit was a row of benches without backs where the poor sat. They would each receive a loaf of bread after the service. Among them were the Raffertys, who worked for my father. My father said the Raffertys were grateful for a bit of meat and a roof (which leaked) over their head; anything was better than what they had endured during the famine.

Maureen Rafferty was hidden between the hulking shoulders of two brothers. She was ten or eleven and thin enough for six, all eyes and silence. Where I walked there she was. I would find some scrap in my pocket saved from the table, like keeping a carrot for a favorite pony. She would accept the crumb and bob her head and turn away. I never heard her speak.

It was a warm day, the kind called St. Luke's Little Summer. The vicar droned about sin and repentance, about death and eternal punishment. I saw the Squire shake his head; the sermon was dangerously evangelical. His son turned his head and yawned, delicately tapping one finger to his lips.

After the service Sir James held mini-court for a few moments on the church steps, then went with Peter's aid to their barouche.

The Ramsey family walked homeward, my father with hands clasped in back, eyes on the ground, impressing all with his Sunday solemnity, although I knew he had not heard a word inside. My mother walked a step behind him, I even with her but not speaking. When we reached our home she went inside to take care of her own rites. She had a prie-dieu in her room to counteract the vulgarity of the Church of England.

My father and I doffed Sunday clothes for more practical gear and went behind the barn. It was there on Sundays that my father relived his best years and tried to pass virtue on to me.

As a young man my father had been a prizefighter of the second rank and once had been in the ring with Bendigo of Nottingham before Bendigo took the championship from Deaf Jemmy Burke. My father was the biggest man in Dire-Toombley. I had not yet reached his height but was beginning to feel my shoulders pushing against my shirt, which would not stay buttoned across my chest.

He bore the marks of his trade. His eyebrows were interlaced with thick scars, and his nose went now east, now west. Withal it was a kindly face. My father deserved better than he got.

"My God, she was pretty once!"

As if I was old enough to be ignored if a thought like that needed to come out.

"That's all I saw, her looks. I didn't ask if she'd be a proper wife to me. There's them as would force her, our own vicar wouldn't condemn me for it, but that's not my nature. You understand me, boy?"

I was curious about most things, but I didn't want to know this much about my parents.

"You're grown now," my father said.

He put his arms out straight from his shoulders and stretched. Once, standing like that before me, he had blocked out the sun. He began to rotate stiff arms, twenty turns one way, twenty the other. Always twenty. In the beginning I had counted them.

"You would not be wanting to try the Fancy yourself, would you, Dick?"

"No, Father."

"Mind, I didn't say you were good enough. I was just asking."

I stretched my arms out and emulated him.

"I would have on knee breeches and I'd be stripped to the waist. The ring—the ring, Dick, had to be twenty-four feet square."

Dreaming, his face came alive.

"We had to make the hands and face tough, not to bleed. We soaked and we pickled, I was elbow deep in brine like a mackerel. We wouldn't slog until late, else the knuckles could shatter. Only three times did I have to throw up the castor."

He was happy in memory, even if the memories were bad.

"It's no disgrace to lose, Dick, if you done your best."

My father had learned his maxims and lived by them.

"Even if you don't want the prize ring, Dick, you still need to be able to stand up against the villains. You'll meet enough of those in your lifetime. Come at me now. If you strike me fair, you get a penny. If you knock me down, it's ten minutes' extra sleep in the morning."

"Ah, knock you down indeed. Knock down my own—father?"—half turning from him and shaking my head and then moving in suddenly.

He had taught me well, but he had not taught me to be as good as he was. He caught my hand in his armpit and locked it there while he shoved up at my belly, using my own forward motion, and I went over his head and into the midden.

I said, calmly sitting on the dung heap like Job, "I'll tell you who I'd like to knock down. Peter, that's who."

"The Squire's son? Have I raised an idiot?"

"He says I am born inferior to him and always will be."

"That's true enough. He's of the gentry and you are not. Now get down here and let's be at it. You must wait for your chance and strike quick and exact. A straight blow with your shoulder behind it."

"Peter is above me, the Raffertys are below. Yet there are Irishmen in Parliament and bankrupt lords."

"Everyone's freedom is safe when each man knows his place."

"That means your place is safe, not your freedom."

4

"Don't twist things, Dick. You're a freeborn Englishman."
"And yet—"
"And yet if you don't hit first I will."

We went at it until the sweat flowed, then washed at the horse trough and went to a hollow tree before the tilled land, where the sun was cupped and held, and lay side by side, drying.

"You've taught me to fight. And you say I'm grown. Yet there is much I need to know."

"You've learned all there is to know from me."

"Mother—"

"Mother. Yes."

"She's not happy, is she, Father?"

"It's not her country, lad."

"But when a woman marries—"

"When you were born, Dick, she saw an Englishman, not a Frenchman. That was the end of it for her. And I took myself elsewhere, if you want the truth. There's women enough to solace a man."

I lay in the sun listening to my father admit he was a sinner. I remembered the catechism in the dame school where I had learned to read and write.

What shall become of you if you die in your sin?

"I must go to hell with the wicked."

What kind of place is hell?

"A place of endless torment, being a lake that burns with fire and brimstone."

Who are the wicked that go to hell at death?

"Such as refuse Christ, neglect to read God's word and pray to him; or who lie, steal, curse, swear, profane the Sabbath and disobey their parents. . . ."

My father said, "I should have given her passage back to France years ago."

What chance had a boy raised without the loving counsel of his mother? What chance for a boy whose father was a sinner? The hollow, filled by the sunlight, felt cold.

There was a decaying grammar school in the village to which my father had been willing to send me, after I convinced him of the advantages to the farm in my eventually learning such things as the new chemical agriculture or at least computations to calculate our production. The bargain included my rising earlier and working later.

Not that my father was in great need of my services. The labor of the Rafferty family, for which he paid a pittance, kept the farm going, and when further help was necessary there was always a gang master to hire all the children needed for a penny a day.

After a time my father found out that our textbooks were Facciolati's *Lexicon* and the *Anabasis* of Xenophon and that I was not learning tables to estimate the yield of corn in a field. "Speak to the pig in Latin, boy. See if he will grow fat from listening." Yet my father allowed me to continue at the school.

Instruction was based on fear. I knew this to be true of the schools I had been to, and those I had heard about. Samuel Johnson had stated it for all schoolmasters when he said that children, not being reasonable creatures, could respond only to the rod. An eager adherent to that philosophy was our own teacher, a man named Fudd, a failed scholar, a sour-smelling spindleshanks with a yard and a half of ferule. He used it on me often because I was often late, coming to school with cow pie still marking my boots. I don't know which Fudd hated more, my tardiness or my aromatic reminder of country life. The truth was, his chastising rod held little terror for me since I had been weaned on the taws at the dame school—that terrible great leather belt thirty inches long and two and a half inches wide, split halfway up with six thongs, the ends of which had been burned to harden them.

We were having a respite in the field in front of the schoolhouse because Fudd was late, suffering from some minor illness I hoped would prove terminal. The younger children were playing Hoop and Hide and Harry Racket. One little girl, escaping to a place of concealment, blundered into a new arrival, a boy my age but markedly apart, with shiny buckled shoes and breeches and jacket having known no wear save careful servant fingers on a clothes brush.

He held the girl for a moment and then seized the lobe of her ear and twisted it cruelly; the girl gasped and did not cry out only from the shock of being so unexpectedly punished.

He let her go and I studied him. His face was without flaw

and manly, if manliness comes from imperious gold-flecked Caesarean eyes and fine nose and firm chin. Such a face would have irked me for the sake of contrast alone, since my own looks were, I thought, more pudding than marble.

"Must you," he said, returning my stare, "walk through the fields to come here?"

I looked down at my boots.

"I suggest you clean yourself off before tracking inside."

I reached down and pulled off the offending shoe and then I advanced on him with it, intending to clean it where it would give me the most pleasure, which was against his new waistcoat. Blinking more in surprise than anxiety, he stepped back. Then Fudd appeared, cackling aggrievedly that he had given us time in which to be idle and driving us inside.

I have a weakness. I have a great capacity for hating, even a talent, and one clings to those aspects of character, even if disreputable, that prove individuality. Mere irritants, like Fudd, did not merit a place on my list. But already I knew that this new boy would retain a firm position there, perhaps at the very top.

"We have," Fudd said, peering over the spectacles he never seemed to look through, "an addition. Peter Nott-Playsaunt, I bid you welcome."

He had never welcomed me. Or anyone else for that matter. I admired the way Fudd was able to rearrange his aspect from his usual glowering meanness into toadying respect for the landowner's son.

"I take it you spent some time at Harrow before coming here?"

"Some time, yes, Mr. Fudd." Crisply spoken, the accent purer than the schoolmaster's, more than clothes or bearing the mark of class. "Also Winchester and Mr. Larkin's school in Somerset."

"I knew Mr. Larkin," said Fudd happily. "I had the honor of attending certain institutions of higher learning with him myself."

"I have," said Peter, "been cast out of all those places, and my father gives me no more than a month at your own gracious establishment."

"Oh," Fudd said, "I hardly think—"

"That was the trouble with most of my teachers," Peter said.

I laughed. Hating was one thing, but fair was fair.

Mr. Fudd was relieved to turn his attention to me. He picked up his ferule and stood in front of me. I sat lumpishly on the bench and thought of destroying him. He bent over and looked for some sign of my wish in my eyes but I frustrated him by thinking about mud. If you think about mud you can bear anything.

Fudd said, "We have certain precepts which it is our aim to instill at this establishment, such as courtesy, attentiveness, and a desire for improvement. Do you agree, Master Nott-Playsaunt, that these are desirable traits?"

"I do indeed, sir," Peter said.

"Well, then, with a view to improving the character of Master Ramsey, you may make a suggestion, if you like."

He looked at me and I glared back and he said, "Why, sir, I think the stick would be appropriate."

School was for learning. I had no quarrel with that. The lesson for that day was that one can be punished for another's crime if there is sufficient difference in your birth. I barely felt the rod, knowing Fudd's pleasure in wielding it, considering how much better it was then dismissal. I could not hop from school to school as Peter had done; this was all I had.

After school a carriage came for Peter, in it a girl. I went as close as I dared to look at her.

I knew then that no matter what Peter would do to me I had to encourage his company so that I could see this girl again. I could not then say what she looked like because I saw her through an effulgence.

Peter said, "How good of you to come for me, Cousin."

Cousin!

Use her name, I begged him silently. And he obliged me.

"What shall we do this afternoon, Alethea?"

I took her home with me. I slopped the pigs and was knee deep in muck and cleaned out the barn and said her name while asking her forgiveness for the circumstances. At supper I forwent an extra helping of frumenty because my own bed in my own corner was the only place to be truly alone. My mother had learned to make a few English dishes after my father complained of the concealing sauces which was my mother's version of her heritage. "Honest meat and a potato, that's all an Englishman needs."

My room had been carved out of a section of the old stone

house seemingly to accommodate a dwarf. The bed was put in cater-cornered and I had to enter sideways. I took off my boots and lay down and had Alethea all to myself.

The next morning Maureen Rafferty was waiting for me on the path from house to barn, and I was ashamed that I had not anything for her in my pocket. I spread my hands in apology. She turned from me silently and went to the barn, where she picked up a milking stool. I went on and saw Rafferty backing a horse into a plow lead. Rafferty was a short man with long arms always a little bowed, as if ready to encircle a tree trunk or a boulder. It had taken me a long time to understand his speech, not just the Irish of it but because he talked with a hoarseness that came up from his chest.

"Is Maureen all right?" I said. "She never speaks."

"She was raised during the bad time. A child suffers more than a man."

"The famine?"

"Aye."

"I know the potato crop failed. But there were other things to eat? Meat, bread? How is it the loss of the potato crop alone meant famine?"

"It was the potato or naught."

He was not a man to seize the opportunity to rest. If he could not show the value of his labor, the farmer might turn him out. The risk of idleness burned in him. He was backing the horse and pulling on the reins and making, I thought, unnecessary show of his dedication. He and his family lived in one room. He made me ashamed of my princely pallet. And how did Peter Nott-Playsaunt sleep compared to me? Each in his place to guarantee our freedom, said my father.

"Tell me about Ireland and the potato," I said. "Please, Mr. Rafferty, tell me the history of it."

"What do I know of the history, Master Ramsey?"

"As you were part of it."

"Ah, yes, I was part of it. The Irish, you see, are the poorest people in Europe."

The *est* of anything, I thought, confers distinction.

Rafferty stopped now. He wiped his lips as if he had just downed a draft and folded his long arms across his front, and they looked as if they could go yet another time around him.

"You want to know how we lived, is that it? In mud huts, four, five feet high, with a roof of boughs and sod. No chimney, no window, no furniture, our animals sleeping among us on the mud floor."

Perhaps, I thought, he was exaggerating.

"You would think, then, would you not, that a people living like animals would die out? Instead we grew, our people grew. In some mysterious way we grew at a rate never known to happen before. That's what was told to me, that's what the scholars said. There was no room for four and suddenly we were eight, and before we knew what to do with the eight we were twelve. All in the same mud hut."

"Ah," I said.

"My own county—Mayo—was the worst. Sligo, Roscommon, Leitrim were almost as bad. All of Connaught was bad."

I didn't know what to say. I shook my head.

"No," Rafferty said, "what would you know about that, a grand farm like this. You want to know the rest of it?"

Rafferty's manner had changed. It was almost hostile. Tentatively taunting. Like telling a horror story to some impressionable child and waiting between each development to assess the degree of shock.

"And what kept us alive, you say? Why, the potato."

"We eat potatoes—"

"We ate the potato only," Rafferty said. He stared at me.

On our own table that day had been a stuffed pike, and last week a neck of pork roasted with applesauce and some boiled capons. We had eggs and bacon and fried rabbit and a cold saddle of mutton. We had consumed apricot tartlets, syllabub, Stilton cheese, and celery. Even without a holiday I often ate filberts and walnuts and William pears.

"The potato only?" I said.

"Are we lazy, my sons and I? Do we not work hard enough to the satisfaction of your father?"

"Indeed you do."

He nodded. "You wouldn't say we were a lazy people—"

"I wouldn't say that," I said.

"The potato," Rafferty said. "You could throw the seed on top of a bed and cover it with earth; it don't need much in the way of care. Then you could store it in the ground and you could share it with your pigs."

"Ah," I said.

"More and more people piled up. We boiled the potato and it kept us alive. We didn't know about greens or bread—there weren't even ovens, you see. Nobody was a butcher or a baker or a grocer. We didn't use tea or candles or coals."

"I don't understand," I said.

"Maybe you weren't listening to me, boy."

I wondered what had happened to "Master Ramsey."

"There wasn't room enough or food enough. If a woman was thirty she was already a grandmother. What we had was a plague of people. There was no work, only the land, so you took a farm and divided it and divided it again and a whole family lived on a plot the size of your smallest garden."

I stared at him.

"You don't believe what I'm saying?" Rafferty said.

"I do," I said. "I do."

"We were eight millions, they said, and we all lived on the potato. And then one year we dug the crop and the disease appeared and in a month everything was gone. You know what your Duke said, the Duke of Norfolk?"

I didn't know the Duke of Norfolk.

"He said we should use curry powder instead of the potato and nourish ourselves with curry powder mixed with water."

I tried to look incredulous.

"Wait, if you want the rest of it. When a crop is bad one year, the next year is a good one, so we waited with hope, you see; we had seen crops fail before. The new plants came up strong but then there was a brown spot on the leaf here and there and the spots spread and the leaves dried up and the stems snapped off and in two days—two days, you see—the fields were filled with black plants that stank of decay."

Rafferty's eyes were hooked on mine like Coleridge's Ancient Mariner. He wanted me to see the horror. He wanted my belly to feel the pangs of famine.

"And Maureen?" I said.

"She was the youngest, maybe she felt it most. In May they were dying. Not just hungry, the way you get touchy if you miss a meal. Dying. You looked in a hallway and there was a body.

You walked abroad and there were bodies in the lanes."

"Can Maureen speak?"

"She can if she wants. But she had this hunger. She will always feel it."

Peter Nott-Playsaunt and I were of an age. Until his father decided what to do with him, he was caught in the web of village school and long empty hours. Out of boredom he seized on me for companionship, not that he would have called it that. I was cat-and-mouse amusement, a toy to cuff while he held out promise of friendship. I was willing to play bumpkin. I cared nothing for Peter's cutting tongue, for his primping superior ways, because sooner or later through him I would see Alethea again. He came to the farm and pulled me away from my labors. My father complained to my mother and me but said nothing to the son of the landowner. I took a hackney and rode clumsily after Peter's spirited mare. I think he found me of some interest because of my strangeness. My life was as foreign to him as Rafferty's was to me.

He dismounted in a copse and threw himself on the ground. Sideways on one elbow, he took a blade of grass to his teeth. I stood before him.

He said, "What kind of man are you, Richard?"

"A man like yourself," I said.

"Are you? Do you have anything like my power? A word to my father and I could have you thrown off this land."

Peter Nott-Playsaunt was not someone you could like. "Your father has need of my father," I said.

"Dick—are you a virgin?"

I stood silent but could not prevent the reddening of my cheeks. I knew I was backward in that area. There were boys younger than I in the village who had already fathered bastards, or so it was whispered.

"I have known women," Peter said. "Sit down and I will tell you about it."

"I do not wish to hear," I said stiffly.

I thought of a most unlikely concurrence. Peter's sly probing was somehow akin to the manner of Rafferty when he had told me of the famine. As if each were testing my innocence. As if my inexperience was in some way a challenge to those who had known the best and worst of life.

"It was after I had been released of my obligations to Mr. Larkin's establishment in Somerset, and I stopped in London on my way home. A surprisingly pretty lady of the evening in the Haymarket approached me and, seeing my embarrassment—I admit I was embarrassed, Dick—asked me if I had attained manhood. I confessed my cunctation and she said that she would be willing, for the sake of furthering my education as well as satisfying my curiosity, to enlighten me. I went along with her to a room off Regent Street. It was surprisingly clean and comfortable and—"

He wanted to see me panting for the rest of it but I foiled him by showing no interest, although I wanted him to go on. He shook his head at my dullness, but not hard enough to wipe off the sneer that he wore like a defect of birth.

"You've never seen a woman naked, then, have you, Dick? Lord, it's a miracle."

How long would I have to suffer this association before seeing Alethea again? I sat cross-legged. Peter sat up and copied my position. He looked at me and the sneer faded.

"On the question of superiority," he said. "Sometimes I joke."

"You do not joke," I said.

"It is true that I treasure my lineage. The nobility of my line might not make a duke envious, but there is a baronet or two and even a viscount. But I also recognize the democracy of intellect. I regard you as my intellectual equal, Dick."

"Do you," I said.

"I have noticed it before," Peter said. "When I try to raise you up, you resist me. You're too rigid. It's a lack of trust, I suppose. Well, I don't blame you."

"What is it you want of me?" I said.

"That you speak freely, without hindrance. Not—always. I mean here, now, truth between the two of us. It might be interesting for a change."

"If you like," I said.

"On the question of superiority, where we left off."

"Well, then," I said, "I am stronger than you, and my mind I think works as quickly as yours and has probably stored more. Who, then, is superior?"

He considered that through a lip-chewing moment. "If that were truly so, then I would fall back upon my progenitorial advantage."

He smiled. Without the sneer his face was appealing. Yet I recalled his suggesting I be whipped, and I remembered all the contempt he had put upon me, and how cruel he had been to the child in the schoolyard. I was accustomed to making up my mind about people so that I could fix them and assign merit or lack of it. It was not comfortable to have an amorphous acquaintance.

"Your plans, Dick. What are your plans?"

"Plans? About what?"

"About your life, man. That's what I am always being asked."

"And what do you answer?" I said.

"Sooner or later, of course, I have to take up my place. I have done my best to disappoint my father—getting into the proper schools, as I have, and then being sent down. I could never understand why my father was so singularly free of dismay when that happened. Now I think I understand him. I understand that he has understood me. He knew the time would come when I would tire of childish things, when blood would tell."

"Tell what? How?"

"You wouldn't know about that, Dick."

"I suppose not. What are the signs? Is there a tingling in the feet? Some hotting up of the belly, chest, a telltale flush around the nose?"

"Mind your manners, boy!" said Peter, getting to his feet.

I continued sitting, looking up at him. "The playacting of friend to friend is over now, is that it?"

"Where did you get the insolence to presume friendship with me, Ramsey?"

I said to myself, Remember Alethea.

"Ah," he said with a sweep of his hand, forgiving me. He squatted, plunged his hand into the soft loam, and came up with a handful. "The difference between us is here, Richard Ramsey. Land. You can ride for hours and still be on my father's land. One day it will be mine. That's the difference between us, Ramsey. We own the land. The land does not change. From father to firstborn forever."

"A man can buy land."

"Can your father buy land?"

"No."

Peter had discovered an ant in the pile of dirt in his palm.

He blocked it with his forefinger and again rapidly as the insect frantically looked to escape.

"Your cousin—"

"Alethea?" He was intent on thwarting the ant.

"How old is she?"

"Alethea is of an age with Shakespeare's Juliet," he said absently. And then, sharply, "Why? What's that to you?"

I shrugged.

"The cat can look at the queen, is that it?" The sneer was back.

"I saw her once in the carriage—" Then I pretended to want him talking of other things. "So what is it you will do with your life, Peter?"

He had tired of preventing the ant's escape and was now using his finger as a spear. I jostled him and the dirt spilled.

"I say!" he said.

"Sorry," I said.

"You want to know what I will do. My choices are limited."

"Limited?"

"A gentleman can exercise his talents in certain directions and not in others."

"I see."

"First there is the church. My father has certain livings at his disposal. I have thought of being an imposing vicar thundering sermons from the pulpit. And perhaps, one day, a bishop. Does that appeal to you, Richard?"

"I think not."

"The next choice open is the law. A barrister, perhaps, rather than a solicitor. I fancy myself in a wig freeing, with my eloquence, some beautiful poisoner. Would you be a lawyer, Dick?"

"I like the learning implied in the term."

"Ah, yes, Ramsey the scholar. And then there is medicine. I could be a surgeon whipping off legs as fast as one could pull the wings from a fly. My God, Dick, it's you who have the hands for it. You could hold down a squirming victim with one hand and gut him with the other."

"That does not appeal to me, but I can see that you would like it."

It was the mark of Peter's insufferable manner that he could ignore a barb as he pleased. "Finally there is the army. My father would buy me a commission if I wished. I would not mind a regiment of my own—cavalry, of course. Of all the professions there is the one you could never attain, Ramsey. You might, with luck, study for medicine or law. But all you could ever be is a foot soldier. How would you like that?"

"Not at all. What I have in mind—" I considered the risk in being open with Peter, but I had never been able to tell this to anyone. "I would like to go to the University and leave my final choice of profession to whatever circumstances I encounter there."

"University? You?" He coughed a laugh and it assumed control of him. He lay on his back holding his belly. "Ah, Ramsey, how very humorous you are."

"I fail to see—"

"A farmer's son, even one exposed to poor old Fudd's Latin, dreaming of the University. How do you think you would be welcome, with the stable air forever surrounding you?"

"There are scholarships," I said weakly.

"True. I should not laugh. You may someday be a Member of Parliament while I, having gambled away my inheritance, am forced to drive a stagecoach." But he was still stifling his laughter.

At which point a girl called out, "Peter? Where are you, Peter?" and she appeared, hair wondrously disarrayed, cheeks flushed, mouth half open to show small white teeth. "There you are, then. I have been looking for you for half an hour. Your father wants you to drive him to Clamford for some jellies. Oh. Who—?"

"May I present my schoolmate and tenant farmer's son, Richard Ramsey," Peter said grandly.

I ached for wit and could not find even my voice.

Chapter Two

So began my eager and willing enslavement. Since I could not hope to appeal to Alethea as gentleman acquaintance, I accepted the part of plaything. Alethea used me to test the limits of coquetry, moving from bewitching availability to cold denial, playing me like a horse, reins loose, at a gallop, almost at the goal, to be then bruisingly checked, hurt calculatedly inflicted to the point where I might in self-defense deny the game, whereupon the shy smile and touch of hand to indicate there was hope, if of the slightest.

I was in thrall but I was not fooled. I accepted the indignity because it was the price of being with her. And, alone at night, my fantasy was not under her control.

One day I saw Peter Nott-Playsaunt on horseback talking to Maureen Rafferty, who, piteously thin and silent, looked up at him in a manner which even at a distance looked like supplicant to invading warrior. Peter got off the horse and reached into his pocket and handed Maureen something. It had to have been more precious than the poor scraps I donated. Then he secured the horse and took her to a place I had discovered and shown him, a spinney ringed by thorn and bramble with an opening I had cut out. I had used it as a place of retreat though I no longer needed it, having learned the art of withdrawing while upright among others.

I looked after them, wondering at so strange an association, but then I saw Alethea on the lane winding down from the eminence on which the landowner's house sat, so I put Peter and Maureen out of my mind. Alethea was far away yet I knew her from silhouette alone. As she came closer I took advantage of the space between us to study her coming without the need for the sidelong glance which was all I permitted myself in her presence. I had time to note she was not truly graceful, yet the promise of grace to come was in her carriage. When we were close enough, without greeting she said, "Have you seen Peter?"

I lied that I had not.

"He promised to meet me here so I could have a companion for a walk."

I did not offer myself, but waited.

"Ask, then," Alethea said.

There were two Aletheas. If I knew her longer I was sure there would be more. The Alethea I took home each night was gentle and loving and without features, more presence and glow than person. This close she was haughty and imperious but a child, real, with dots of perspiration where the hair began at her forehead and what was surely a pimple beginning under one cheekbone. It was the realness that excited me, the smell and saltiness and warm breath.

"I would be honored to—"

"Fairly said but too halting. A little more roundness of tone."

"If I could accompany you—"

"Not direct enough."

"May I walk with you, Alethea?"

"You're very familiar, sir."

"You have called me—Richard."

"You think that gives you the right to intimacy? I use the first name of our groom."

"Say what it is I may or may not do, then," I said coldly.

She considered whether to dismiss me. "Well, then, if it means so much to you."

As we walked she let her hand graze against mine, but when I tried to hook little fingers she frowned and moved away. We came to a flat rock next to a stream and she bade me dust it. I had no kerchief and used my hand, but she considered that not clean enough and had me remove my jacket so she could sit upon it. She sat and I stood until she said I might sit on the ground beside her.

"It is a pity, Richard, that you can never be more than a farmer. Could you not have selected your place in life more carefully?"

"It is possible," I said, "that a man's worth is what he makes it."

She studied me with a frankness of manner she could never have shown a peer. "You are not unattractive, Richard. It is just that your face is too—fierce. Could you not soften your look a little?"

I tried. She said, "Now you look doltish." She leaned toward me, her face inches away. "You would like to kiss me, would you not, Richard?"

I began to tremble. She laughed and stood up. "Now see me home but walk behind me, like a proper retainer."

I promised myself I would, from then on, ignore her. A man was more than a trifle. Near to the manor house she said, "You may kiss my hand. But drop to one knee first. I am a princess, you know."

She waited until I knelt, then, laughing, ran to the house.

The next morning I was about to be whipped again. True, I was late but it was hardly my fault. Sometimes a small mishap draws strength from itself to foster another one and one is helpless to break the chain. The muck in the pigsty sucked the Wellington right off my foot, and in attempting to retrieve it I fell to one knee and, seeking a handhold to rise again, a slat of the fence came apart in my fingers and I was thoroughly besmirched. I had to change breeches and stockings and the class was assembled when I arrived.

There was no art to Fudd's beating. He lacked the strength and skill to snap the rod at the end of the downstroke for the extra cut, and there was little apprehension in me.

But as I bent over I saw Alethea's face at the window. Out of boredom she had come to see how we passed our mornings. I could abase myself in a hundred ways before Alethea, but I would not let her see me whipped. I straightened up. I said I was truly sorry to be late and would try to do better.

"Bend over, sir."

I said I would not. Further, I said that Fudd had flogged me enough the last time. My weals had not yet healed over.

There were *ahs* of shock from the pupils and also some sounds of admiration, and I found myself basking in that. I had never before been a hero.

"Master Ramsey," said Fudd, in a tone so reasonable that despite experience I began to hope, "I ask you pleasantly, sir. I ask you to consider your own future. You are here to obey without question because you are here to be educated. Not to obey is not to be educated. Not to obey is to lose your position here. Is that what you want, sir?"

"No," I said. "But I will not be whipped this morning. If you like you may whip me twice as hard tomorrow."

I looked at the window without turning my head; it seemed to me there was disappointment on Alethea's face.

Fudd, to whom this poor school was his last chance at survival, was, in his own way, willing to fight for it. The top of his head came barely to my breastbone, but if I could not be subdued then his hold on his school would be gone since without fear from all there could be no institution. I knew all this and did not wish to destroy him, nor cast away my own chance for learning, but I would not be flogged in Alethea's sight.

"For the last time," Fudd said.

I shook my head. He raised his arm to strike me and I caught his fist. I said again I was sorry to be late, and as I apologized I squeezed without making a show of it so it appeared I was doing no more than holding him. When his face went white I let go, having crushed his knuckles, and that was the end of my formal education. Which was the first of the two results of my knowing Alethea.

The spinney I had discovered lay just beyond the boundaries of our own rented land in the area that Sir James let go untended. I was there to mend a fence, and again I saw Peter with Maureen. Again he offered her something which she accepted and they disappeared together.

I was upset and did not know why. I didn't know what they *did* there. I had been around farm animals enough to have witnessed the mechanics of it, and I knew the strange wildness that overcame me when I was with Alethea, but I could not translate any of that into an image of what took place within that spinney. Certainly Maureen was not yet formed for lovemaking.

Later Peter came boldly to the farm to preempt me.

"Why were you not in school today, Dick?"

"I have been expelled."

"Has that anything to do with the enormous bandage Fudd wears on his hand?"

"He can still flog with the other."

"Oh, to have chosen that morning to be late abed. Climb up behind. Alethea is bringing a horse for you. We are going to race, practice for chasing the hounds. *Sans* fox and riding clothes, but a taste. Who knows, Dick, someday I might even invite you to my house."

We went to where Alethea waited on horseback, leading a hunter. He was a big horse and did not mind my weight, testing me first with a sideways dance or two and then letting me settle in so I felt like a centaur.

"We begin here," Peter said. "It's the kind of course a fox might take. It will be up Breakbottom Hill and down and through the woods at the Two Georges, across the steam, alongside Gilson's Pond and up Twofaces Hill and down through Farmer Greenwood's land to Barrows Crossing. The winner gets a kiss from Alethea."

"I never said—" Alethea said.

"Girls give prizes," Peter said. "That's the way of the world."

"And if I win?" Alethea said.

"Ah."

"It's possible," I said.

"Then think of a prize for her."

"She can have anything just for the naming of it."

"Listen to the man," Peter said. "I offer him a taste of a gentleman's sport and at once he takes on the guise of a gallant."

Someday, I said to myself, I shall see you flat, Peter Nott-Playsaunt.

Peter yelled "Go!" after he had a length on us. I took after him. In a moment I heard a piteous "I can't keep up" behind me. I almost waited, she was more to me than Peter, but there was a new feeling in me, the need to beat the landowner's son.

I had done things in rages before without considering my neck because fury cloaks its consequences. The horse was new to me, and it looked as if Peter had selected terrain he had already tested. He was beautiful to watch. Hatred did not blind me to his magnificence. He was one with his horse, as if his were the four legs; the wind painted his hair behind him; his shoulders were up and forward and his head thrusting. I went thundering after him but soon knew I could not match him, let alone overtake him. He took a stile and I after him, but I had no experience in jumping and was almost dislodged; frantic to retain my seat I leaned too far back and the horse reared. By then Peter was out of sight. When I reached the end of the course I found Peter lying on the ground with the back of his head against a tree, sucking on a blade of grass, as if to present a picture of having been waiting a long time.

"Two minutes," I said. "You didn't beat me by more than two minutes."

"You belong in the heavy brigade, Dick. Big horse, lots of armor. You're just not built for speed."

"You cheated."

"I beg your pardon."

"You didn't go through the wood as you said."

"I did."

"You did not, you skirted it."

"Did you go through, then?"

"No, I followed you."

"Then you cheated too."

"Alethea will go into the wood and be lost."

"I think you fancy her," Peter said.

"Nonsense," I said.

"I suppose it's a human failing to yearn for the unobtainable. You're as suited for Alethea as I am for Queen Victoria. You'd best find yourself some dairymaid, Dick."

"I saw you and Maureen," I said.

"Spying?"

It was a gift; he could, with a word, make me hot and heady like the contents of a wine barrel.

He smiled. "What do you want to know, Dick?"

"She's a child."

"She is old enough."

I shook my head in irritation. I felt like a bear with one persistent buzzing fly circling my head. "I should never have told you about—"

"Her hunger? There is nothing she would not do for a crust. Believe me, nothing."

When he teased it was as if he were using the sense of taste. I could have stopped it with a quip as he would have. Instead I assumed the role he had sketched for me—the blundering lout, overgrown, above whose head the nuances and implications flew unrecognized.

"You must speak up, Dick, clearly and to the point. Is it that you want to know exactly what happened between us? Or is it just that you cannot find the words to express your disapprobation? Or is it that you want me to cease and desist because of your prior interest? You must be clear. Anger and disappointment muddle the tongue."

What I wanted to do was put his head between my two hands and bring them together.

"Actually," Peter said, "the main thing is that you want to know what we did. I know how you virgins are. You dream and rub yourself but you don't *know* anything. Because who is to tell you? If there are books on the subject you don't know where to find them. What you need is an experienced friend. Like me, Dick. So I will tell you what it is Maureen and I do inside that cave you discovered for us."

"I don't want to know," I said.

"Of course you want to know. It's her hunger, you see. Yesterday I brought her a leg of pheasant, roasted. You should have seen her demolish it. After that I suggested—"

"A baby," I said. "She has no flesh on her bones."

"What do you know of flesh, Dick? The main thing is willingness, and Maureen is willing."

"I truly believe you are a monster," I said.

Peter laughed. "I am—a man. You, Dick, are not yet a man. And that gulf between us is greater even than the gulf between a farmer's son and the lord of the manor's son. But I will teach you. Sit down, now, and listen."

"I will not listen," I said.

"Why?" The question was honest, not taunting. So was the answer.

"I don't want to learn," I said, "from you."

Then Alethea, panting, came up to us and slid off her horse and sat down, making sounds of exasperation. "I went into the wood. There was no path. Why did you not say there was no path, Peter?"

"How could I know?" Peter said.

"I see," Alethea said. "Neither of you went through the wood."

"It was good of you to take your time, Alethea, since Richard and I were talking of matters hardly fitting for young female ears."

"Indeed," Alethea said.

"Yes. We were talking of the French."

He was too devious for me, too unexpected. When he set out to prick my own standing in life I knew if I kept silent he would tire of it. But now the sneering smile was on his face and he would be going as far as he dared and my being silent would not stop him because he could play off Alethea.

"Some races," Peter said, "are by their nature inferior. Such, of course, are the French. Napoleon was successful only insofar as he encountered those races as morally deficient as his own. When, however, he attacked the English the results were foreordained."

"It's a boring subject," Alethea said. "Really, Peter, it's a boring subject."

"Boring? Do you think it's boring, Dick?"

"I think it not worth pursuing," I said.

Not that Peter could be stopped. Alethea often went as close to the edge as she dared with me and I often did the same with Peter, with the titillation of possible danger or at least explosive reaction, but it was beyond that sort of game now with Peter; there was mania in his eyes. "The French are not only an inferior race but their lack of morals is known all over the world."

Alethea stood up. "Let's find something to do."

"We are doing something," Peter said.

"Is it a game, then?"

"If it is I've had enough of it," I said. I went to my horse and untied its reins.

"Wait," Peter said. "The best part is coming." He got up and faced me, smiling. "Take, as an example, those French serving girls in England. Was not your mother one, Richard?"

"Yes."

"Well, take your own mother. How fortunate for her to have found an English yeoman to take her out of her kitchen servitude."

"Alethea is right," I said. "You are boring."

"Fortunate and—necessary? They are all of them hot for the English, so I have heard."

"You bastard," I said.

"Ah, you see my point."

I hit him as my father had taught me, straight from the shoulder, and Peter crumpled with no sign of life.

"Oh my God," said Alethea, kneeling beside him. She

touched his face, then called me murderer and mounted and rode off. After a while Peter opened his eyes. I reached to help him up but he refused my hand.

My father and Rafferty between them were trying to uproot a small tree, the roots of which they had loosened. I added my weight to theirs and finally there was a satisfying tearing sound. My father said, "This could have been done an hour ago if the farmer's son was where he should have been."

"I have to talk to you, Father," I said.

"And it's time I talked to you. Rafferty, trim it and cut it into sections for the stove and fill in the hole."

We went behind the house to our jousting ground and locutory.

"Now mind me, Richard. No good can come of your running after the master's son every time he wiggles his ears."

"Sir James is landlord, not master."

"A term of speech. Now that you've thrown away your chance of an education—"

We had not talked about it, except as I had explained I had caught and hurt Fudd's hand when I was objecting to being unfairly beaten and as a consequence he had denied me the school.

"It's hard to know how a freeman is entitled to behave," I said.

"I never hit you, not even when you were young."

"I know."

"I've never held with whippings."

"Nor me."

"I'm not saying you did well. A schoolmaster has the right to beat you for being late and also, if I guess right, for your looking down your nose. I've seen you looking down your nose at people, Richard."

"Well, it's done."

"There's other schools—"

"Not for me. Not for a while, anyway."

"Well, then, I can use you here."

It seemed safe then to tell him what I had done to Peter. With caution, however. "A man insults you and maybe you can let it pass. But when he insults your mother and father, then what?"

"A man does that to me? I guess I would have to hit him."

"Good, Father. That's what I did."

"You hit—who?"

"Peter Nott-Playsaunt."

My father's fist slashed, and I went back five feet and down. He said, "Get up so I can knock you down again."

I got up and he knocked me down again.

"Now you may get up and stay up."

I stood rubbing my chin.

"You hit—the son? Sir James's son?"

I nodded. He looked as if he were going to hit me again and I stepped back.

"But why? You fool. Why?"

"You told me you would have done the same."

"But not to the son of Sir James."

"I could not let it rest."

"He said—what did he say?"

"He said my mother carried me before you were married."

"He said that? And you hit him?"

"Yes."

"Richard, you will suffer for it, but you did well."

"Suffer?" I said.

"Do you think Sir James will allow this to pass? Perhaps he will force us to leave. I have no right to this land except as I pay him; he can have me off at any time. Well, now we must wait."

"You say I did well, but you struck me for it. You say an Englishman is freeborn, yet you worry now that the landowner will evict you. I don't know where the truth lies, Father."

"You've been to school, I haven't," my father said.

That night I slept poorly. It is the mark of a man that he defend himself and his family against insult. So how could harm come from that? Sir James would understand that the provocation had come from Peter. Surely nothing more would be made of it. But then I saw again the look on Alethea's face as she called me murderer. Even if Sir James could overlook my offense, would Alethea? And perhaps it was she who needed my forgiveness. Was it not because of her that I was no longer a scholar? I practiced hating her but I could not succeed. She had found a place in my blood as it went up and around and down according to William Harvey.

In the morning came a summons from Sir James that we call upon him. My father did not change to Sunday best but from used work clothes to clean work clothes, and he had me do the same. "We will appear as what we are."

He walked beside me, his face solemn. We did not discuss what was about to confront us. My father had on the gaiters of the countryside, but his kerchief was bright and his hat set a little to the side as it might have been in the days of his prizefighting. He was big again, as in the days when I could walk between his legs. He was never to appear that big to me again.

A servant showed us to the library, where Sir James sat with foot wrapped in flannel high on a pillowed hassock. He waved us to two chairs placed before him. I looked around the room with interest and admiration and envy. To think one entire room had been set aside for books. On the table was Mrs. Gaskell's *Cranford* with the Mudie wrapper around it. There was an enormous globe on a floor stand, and I would have given much to travel around it with my finger.

I had never been this close to Sir James, and I studied his face. His nose had no shape at all left and went from deep red to purple, with pores so large you could fix a straw in them. I thought about that for a while, the way his face would be turned into that of a porcupine. He had lost two teeth on his right side and cultivated a droop in the lip there to conceal the space. It troubled me that he was deemed superior to my father, who was obviously superior to him in all ways save birth.

"How are you, John?" Sir James said.
"Fine, thank you, sir."
"I am not happy to see you in these circumstances."
"No, sir."
"Shall we get to it, then?"

I didn't know what it was we were about to get to, but suddenly I knew I didn't like it. The black wainscoting of the paneled walls seemed to come closer.

Sir James said, "Your son, Richard, John Ramsey, is accused of attacking my son, Peter Nott-Playsaunt."

Beneath the official language the two fathers nodded at each other. Sons.

"Attacked?" I said.

Both fathers looked at me admonishingly.

"I will tell you when it is time for you to speak," Sir James said. He cleared his throat loudly and took a handkerchief from his sleeve and spat into it. Since it was out anyway, he blew his nose.

"A boy has a scuffle with another lad," my father said. "Surely there's no seriousness to that, is there?"

"Ordinarily not, John. I would go along with you there and say ordinarily not. But this is not an ordinary circumstance. You follow that, don't you, John? You must admit there is a difference between your son and mine. In lineage, that is. You do see the difference, John?"

"I do, sir."

"And therefore it is not the same thing as, say, your son fighting with some other farmer's boy."

"Definitely not the same thing," my father said.

"So when your son takes his fist to the son of—if you will allow me—the lord of the manor, it is not a thing to be taken lightly, or dismissed."

"Certainly not," said my father.

"And even if that were all, an altercation, an exchange of blows—"

"There was no exchange," I said under my breath. "Just the one blow."

"What is that mumbling?" Sir James said.

"He does that," my father said. "It means nothing."

"Well, stop it anyway. Now. Yes. So even if that were all, some punishment would be in order."

"Some punishment, yes," my father said.

"If that were all," Sir James said. "A simple shove and shove back, a disagreement. We could settle that at once, and simply, but the evidence says otherwise. The evidence says this was an attack, a deadly attack."

"No," I said loudly. "It wasn't like that."

Sir James did not look at me, he looked at my father. And my father brought his face close to mine and said between clenched teeth—in a tone so murderous that I was suddenly almost frightened to death—that if I opened my mouth again, that if I said anything at all without being asked, he would reduce me

28

to a bloody puddle right there on the floor.

"If," Sir James said, "if there is to be consideration given to mercy—"

"Mercy, yes," my father said.

"Then we must see if there was incitement, some reason strong enough to—"

"Reason," my father said.

"Who would know the truth, then, better than my own son? I asked Peter if he had done anything to provoke your son in this unforgivable action. I asked him sharply, mind you, I asked him in a manner to convince him of the seriousness of his reply if he had done anything to inflame your son. And he said—"

My father and I leaned forward.

"My son assured me—I did not ask him to give me his oath but I am sure he spoke the truth—he assured me there was nothing in his speech or behavior that could have in any way incited the regrettable violence perpetrated by your son—"

I jumped up. I said that was a lie, and I will always be ashamed that as I said it my voice broke. My father put his hand on my shoulder and pressed. I sat down and waited for my arm to fall off. "That is the last time, Richard, you understand me?"

I nodded. I could not trust speech.

"So there we have it," Sir James said.

I bit my lip not to speak. Truly bit it; I could taste the blood.

Then my father spoke up. "With all respect, Sir James. With all due respect. There is the way your boy tells it, and there is the way my boy tells it. They are not the same."

"Are you saying you agree with your son that my son lies?"

"No! Of course not, Sir James. All I mean to do is point out, sir, that there are two sides to this."

"If my son tells me a thing is so then I must believe him."

You have that right also, Father. But he was silent.

"If one cancels the other we are at the beginning," Sir James said, "and thus settling nothing. So we are fortunate to have a witness—"

"Witness," my father said.

"A third party. So we need not rely only on Peter's word, or Richard's. I have asked this witness to come forward." He picked up his cane and banged with it on the floor. The liveried servant opened the door and Sir James gestured to him that he step aside to let Alethea come into the room.

"Come, my dear, come forward now. Here, stand beside me. You know the Ramseys."

Alethea closed her eyes and opened them, which was as good as a nod. She looked pale. She was composed and distant and beautiful, and she looked only at her uncle.

"Now, my dear. You were present at this unfortunate occurrence—"

"Yes, Uncle."

"You saw this boy, Richard Ramsey, attack Peter?"

"Yes, Uncle."

"Now this is the nub of it, my dear. This is the very nub. I want you to think carefully. Did Peter say anything to Richard, before the attack, anything in any way provoking?"

"We were just—talking. I think Peter was discussing Napoleon and the battle at Waterloo. That's all I remember."

"He said nothing to Richard to—to excite him, to anger him?"

"Nothing. That is, I heard nothing in any way insulting, anything like that. Of course—"

"Of course?"

"If he were French—well, Richard's mother is French—and if he were upset that Wellington won—"

"So Peter said nothing—nothing that could possibly cause—"

"I didn't hear anything. As I said, just the history of it, Napoleon's defeat. Then—"

"Then?" Sir James said. "Do not be afraid, Alethea. Speak out, just as it happened."

"Richard struck out—like a madman."

I will hate you forever for this, Alethea, I thought.

"You may go now," Sir James said.

She walked out without looking at me.

Sir James said, "You see now, do you not, John, that this is a most serious offense?"

"Oh, yes," my father said.

"We will let Richard speak now. Have you anything to say for yourself?"

"Only this," I said. "Only that it did not happen that way."

"Peter lied? And also this young woman, my niece Alethea, she also lies?"

The Squire's question hung in the air between us like an

executioner's blade temporarily arrested. My father's mouth was half open as if wanting to guide my reply.

I shook my head. Not naysaying but in frustration and disbelief. My father looked relieved. Sir James said, "This is a most serious crime. Your boy could be jailed or even transported."

Having been given my one chance to speak I was back to not being noticed. It was between the magistrate and my father. My attention wandered. Surely Sir James was exaggerating the importance of the affair.

"Yes," Sir James said. "Even transported. We can't send our criminals to America any more since the stupidity of their independence, but there is still New Zealand."

Sir James reached to touch gingerly the bandage over his foot. My father looked thoughtful. I tried to keep my mind still but the thought formed, about to rise into action, that for my salvation I must run now, out of the house and away from the land as far as I could. Because in this quiet room my future was being destroyed.

"It may be," Sir James said after a silence of several minutes, "that I have a solution."

"Yes?" my father said.

Perhaps another beating, I thought. I could tolerate that.

"As you know we have gone to war in the Crimea. Why not send Richard to expiate his offense by serving his country?"

"He's barely sixteen," my father said.

"I'm sure they would overlook that, considering his size."

"Hmm," my father said. "Better a soldier son than a son in prison."

"Exactly," Sir James said.

Chapter Three

Perhaps I should have run away then, but I had no practice in running. What I had practice in was in doing what I was told. We walked home in silence. Finally I said, "When do I have to do this thing?"

"Tomorrow. Sir James would not like delay."

Then I said, "You did not speak up for me, Father."

Sir James would be forever on my list, along with Peter and Alethea, but what was I to do with my father?

"The army is not a bad life. And anyway there was no choice for you."

"No choice for a freeborn Englishman?"

"It's a question of law," my father said. "Will you never understand that, Richard?"

My mother was waiting at the door.

"We've lost him now," my father said. "Not that you care. Were you ever a mother to him?"

I hardly knew whom they were talking about. Some waif, some accident of the household. My mother looked at me. Usually—like setting a plate before me—it was always with head averted. It occurred to me then that I had always been a little afraid of her. She was a dark woman. Sometimes I was wary of my father's arm, or if that was not enough, then a stick, but I had never been afraid of him.

"Come inside and sit with me, Richard." On her lips it came out *Reeshard.*

In the parlor she sat on her rocking chair and I sat on a bench.

"Lost you how?" she said.

"I am going into the army."

"That is what you want?"

32

"No. It is what Sir James says I must do. Else, he said, I would be jailed for striking Peter."

"That is your English law?"

"That is Sir James's law."

I looked at her mouth, which was my mouth. She was a small woman made smaller by the way she pulled herself together. She had long dark-brown hair that would have appeared luxuriant except for the cruel way she pinned it close to her head. I could see what had attracted my father, I was old enough to see. She might once have been pert and gay.

"I never wanted a child," my mother said.

"I know that, Mother."

"I will be punished for that."

"Punished?"

"God does not like mothers like me."

I didn't know about mothers, so I kept silent. I tried to find something good to think of her.

"When will you leave?"

"Tomorrow."

"There is no time then."

"For what, Mother?"

She made an irritable and somehow piteous gesture. It called attention to her hand, which despite the farmwoman's toil looked soft and well shaped.

"When you were little, Richard—you would not remember—I tried to teach you French. But you would not learn. You wanted to be English. You are English."

"Yes."

"I loved your father."

I did not understand. I did not know what she was saying.

"A life slips through your fingers. You want this and that; you think, you hope. But then you grow empty. Your mother is a monster, Richard."

"No," I said. A boy does not want a monster for a mother.

"I have never kissed you, Richard. Not even when you were a babe in my arms."

Stiffly then she extended her arms and I got up and knelt beside her and her arms were like rope and her lips against mine were cold. She was a woman without feeling, and to pretend anything else was useless. Like Alethea. Were they not the same?

33

I went to my room to see if there was anything worth taking with me for the morning. I would not need clothing or food and as I looked around I saw I had nothing of value, nothing I could not do without. I decided to take with me only a book that I had read several times by a woman named Jane Austen, the truth of which I had pondered much about, because she wrote of a large and loving family. I lay down and considered my predicament. I was not loath to go, the world was larger than Dire-Toombley, and there was excitement in that. But there was also anxiety because I would be tested in ways I could not imagine. It could be that I would discover myself to be a coward, or a fool. Out of habit I started to dream about Alethea, but I cast her out of my mind.

I was up early and I had porridge with my father.

"You'll find the recruiting sergeant in the public house at Clamford," my father said.

"Yes."

"You will write, then," he said, getting up.

"Yes, Father."

"You'll remember what I told you?"

"Yes, Father," I said, wondering what he had told me—outside of the rights of an Englishman, which I had not discovered to be true, and how to strike a fast, straight blow, which so far had not been to my advantage, except for the satisfaction of it.

"Well, then," he said, standing awkwardly for a moment, then patting me on the shoulder and going out.

My mother, looking down and brushing some crumbs from her apron, said, "Well, Richard."

I looked at her, thinking there ought to be tears. I had read about such things, the grief of a mother parting from her child. It was true that the English were chary of demonstrating feeling, but my mother was French.

"Keep yourself clean," she said.

"I will," I said.

"Clean and—"

"Yes?"

She was struggling to be motherly, and it was more painful to watch than our parting. I kissed her on the cheek to put an end to it and picked up the small pack, which contained little except the book by Jane Austen, and I went out. I walked about saying good-bye to the farm, but that did not take long nor did it grieve me. I would hardly miss the muck of the pigs' residence or the pond on which the stupid geese lived or the fields which were to me only reminders of my toil. I saw Rafferty wrestling with a broken fence. I went up to him and said, "Mr. Rafferty, I'm off to join the army."

"Are you now," he said.

"I'll be saying good-bye," I said.

"Is it the army or is there a war?"

"There's a war in the Crimea, they say."

"Where is that?"

"I don't know."

"The world's a big place."

"Yes."

I considered telling him about Maureen so he could keep an eye on her. But Rafferty was going about his business and I had to go about mine.

"You've got a good morning for it," he said, holding up the fence with one shoulder while he looked for a nail.

I set off and did not look back. The sun warmed my head and shoulders while the faint breeze set the trees along the dirt road to dancing. I felt strong, and while there was an unease somewhere in my belly, I thought I should not be ashamed of myself in whatever I was about to face.

After I had walked a mile my thoughts grew darker. Once I had seen an ex-soldier without legs begging in the public square at Clamford. He had worn a scarlet coatee with a dangling, dirty ribbon. I was walking freely and alone. According to the magistrate this was in lieu of punishment, but why need I go through with it? I could go to London, where a man could lose himself for a lifetime. Or to one of the channel ports and across to France—was I not half French? The more I thought of it the more it seemed like a sensible course of action. Why plod on and join the army because an idiot had decided so and my father had acquiesced? Why should I not remain free?

I was not comfortable with such thoughts. Freedom to go where I would without having been told what to do was a new and dangerous idea.

I heard a cart behind me and without turning to look I moved to the side of the road. It drew abreast of me and slowed. Peter Nott-Playsaunt held the reins and Alethea sat beside him.

He called out, "On your way to Clamford, are you? Jump in and I will take you there."

I said nothing.

Alethea said, "Richard! Come."

I ignored her also.

She said to Peter, "If he will not ride then I will walk along with him for a bit."

Peter stopped the cart and Alethea climbed down. She walked alongside and I did not look at her. She said, "I did not know this would happen, Richard."

From the cart Peter said, "I would come down myself but he might strike me again."

"I might," I said.

"He is incorrigible," Alethea said. "I said he was incorrigible."

"You've done enough harm," I said.

"Sir James said I had to say what I did. He said you were an upstart. He said upstarts could bring this country down if they were not put in their place."

"So you lied," I said.

"I did not think anything could come of it. And you *are* an upstart, aren't you, Richard?"

"Alethea," I said, looking straight ahead.

"Yes, Richard?"

"I want you to know something."

"Yes, Richard?"

"I want you to know that I will take out the thought of you at night before I go to sleep or during the day when there is time and I will consider how much I hate you."

"Oh, Richard. You are telling me how I will always be with you. You will never stop thinking of me."

"I will never stop hating you."

"You do not hate me, Richard. I know about such things. I know how you look at me and I know how you feel when I am close to you." She put her arm through mine and pressed against me. "Like this."

"I admit that you can turn me into water. But it will not dilute my hatred."

"Will it not? Then stop." She tugged at me and I stopped and standing on tiptoe she kissed me as high as she could reach, which was the tip of my chin. "Now tell me you hate me."

"I do," I said, rubbing the place with the back of my hand.

"Then I hate you too for the dolt that you are."

And Alethea signaled to Peter and clambered back into the cart with a furious display of petticoat.

Peter let the horse's pace match mine. "You know why you are in this fix," he said. "It's your nature to embroil yourself into needless mischief. If you wanted the satisfaction of hitting me, had you gone about it the right way, had we squared off, you might have said you were teaching me as your father had taught you. You don't know how to be devious, Dick, and that's your trouble."

"I'll remember you," I said. "I'll remember the feel of your chin against my knuckles."

"I pushed you a little hard, I admit that."

"You might have admitted that to your father."

"He was just playing at being magistrate, I was sure he would just tease you a bit and let you go. But this nonsense about going into the army. Really, Dick, do you think you're cut out to be a common soldier?"

"It was all a sorry game, is that it?"

"Well, you did strike me. But now, if you show some remorse, I'm sure I can speak to my father and—"

"Remorse?"

"All you have to do is say you're sorry.

"That's all I have to do?"

"Say it now, before Alethea, so she can be a witness. Then I guarantee that we can all go back to the way things were."

"Say it," Alethea said.

"Alethea the witness," I said. "She has already given me the Judas kiss." I spat on my fingers and rubbed by chin.

"You can't make a silk purse—" Alethea said.

"Come now, Dick," Peter said. "I beg you, I really do."

"That's all I have to do? Apologize?"

"That's all."

"I don't understand," I said. "Come down and make it clear to me."

"You'd best not," Alethea said.

"Even Richard would not make the same mistake twice," Peter said, climbing down.

I grabbed him by the silk ruffled front of his shirt with my left hand and crashed him back against the wheel of the cart. I raised my other hand to club him and I might have killed him then. Peter made no effort to resist me, which I think is the reason he lived. Had he struggled, had he perhaps tried to hit me, I think I would have brought my fist down on him.

With sparkling slits of eyes and small red mouth he said, "Go off and get yourself killed then, Richard Ramsey. I lied about wanting to help you. Had you said you were sorry I would have laughed and turned my back and Alethea would have lied as she lied before. Would you not, dear cousin? Tell him how you would have lied."

"A liar lies," I said. "It is part of her nature."

I let him go and resumed my walk. He called out after me, "They will kill you, Ramsey. You hear me? And who will care? Do you have one soul who will care?"

I didn't answer. After a while I heard the cart go back the other way.

At Clamford I knew my way to the public house although I had never been inside it. I saw the sergeant who was recruiting right off. He was trimmed all over with silver and lace and wore an officer's cap. He was engaged with another, and I stood a distance apart until he was finished.

This other recruit was a strange-looking fellow. He was very tall and very thin and everything about him stuck out, from his arms to his chin and nose, and this angled impression was helped by the way he naturally leaned forward so that he looked like some great land bird obsessed with the memory of once having been able to fly.

He was protesting to the sergeant that his name was Jarvis, with an *a*. The sergeant, laboriously writing in a ledger, stopped with every other word to refresh himself from a tankard.

"Don't tell me my business, lad. There an't no *a* in Jervis."

"There is in my name, sir. Jarvis, Jarvis with an *a*."

"I can't put down anything here which an't true. This here is official. I have to put down your age and your name, and I've got to spell it all right. This is the Queen's business, you understand that? Now, how old are you?"

"Twenty."

"What's your reason for joining the Queen's forces?"

"I awoke this morning with a terrible desire to do my patriotic duty."

"Then here's the Queen's shilling, and now stand aside while I look to this other lad."

"You've not spelled my name right."

"Stand aside and don't tell me my business."

Jarvis shrugged, went up to the counter and got a pot, and brought it back to the table. He sat down, lifting the drink to his mouth with his eyes above it half hooded so he looked more than ever like some strange bird.

"How old are you?" the sergeant said to me.

"Eighteen."

"You're big enough but your years an't reached your face yet. But I'll put it down if you say so. What's your name?"

"Richard—"

The sergeant fumbled for his beer and, in doing so, knocked his ledger to the ground. Reaching down for it, he almost fell off the bench. He came up, face flushed, and said, "What's your mother's name?"

"She enlisting too?" Jarvis said.

"Au'Bois."

"Eh?"

"Not eh, oh," Jarvis said.

"Bois," I said.

"Boy," Jarvis said.

"Once more," said the sergeant.

"O'Boy," Jarvis said.

"First name?" said the sergeant.

"Richard," I said.

"Richard O'Boy," the sergeant said. He wrote it down.

I thought, Why not? A new name for a new life. Richard O'Boy. I tried it in my head.

"The Queen's shilling for you"—handing it to me—"but don't be boasting you're part of the Queen's own. Not yet. It's still up to the doctor. You don't come in with the clap or if you don't have a tooth top and bottom. You two poor sods. The mamas who whelped you will weep over this day." His head fell on the table with a clunk.

"I'll buy you a drink," Jarvis said, "that is, if you're old enough." He put his bowed head close to mine and grinned. I was surprised to see a human nose instead of a beak. "I'll keep your secret."

The sergeant, in a startlingly loud parade-ground voice, said, "All right, men, on your feet." We were, but he wasn't. He tried to get up and fell back on the bench. Jarvis took his one arm and I took the other and we stood him up.

"Forward march, now. To the barracks."

"Where the hell are the barracks?" Jarvis said.

"Look sharp now," said the sergeant, going limp between us. We got him outside and saw another sergeant with a group and we followed them. They seemed a dirty, ragged lot. Then we were in a large hall with no one to tell us what to do.

"Peregrine," Jarvis said.

"What?"

"Peregrine Jarvis."

"Richard. Richard Ram—"

"That's not what he wrote down."

"O'Boy," I said. "Richard O'Boy."

"Comrades-in-arms, then, Dick." He held out his hand and I shook it. After a while came in a colonel so bright and polished he looked like the sun coming up.

"His cohorts were gleaming in purple and gold," Jarvis said.

Someone brought the officer a stool and he stood on it. "Welcome to the Fifty-seventh Foot, men. Ours is a glorious history, and we expect that you will add luster to it. Do as you're told and you will be proud soldiers of the Queen. Disobey an order and we'll take the skin off you. March them over to the hospital, sergeant."

As we straggled along with the others, Peregrine Jarvis said, "Maybe it's not too late."

"For what?"

"That's the question."

"Why follow at all?"

"That's another question. But I have this premonition of evil. You ever get premonitions of evil, O'Boy?"

"No."

"You're lucky, then. I see blood. Shattered bodies. I think I'd be better off at home in the arms of my loved ones."

"Why did you leave them, then?"

"They didn't exist, to tell you the truth. How about yours, do they exist?"

"No," I said.

We stood in line waiting our turn at the doctor, who, wearing a long white coat, sat on a chair with a bowl of disinfectant at his side in which he kept dipping his fingers. He had us open our mouths and then bend over so he could look up our arses.

"I've always been a fellow who prized his dignity," Peregrine Jarvis said, straightening up after having his rear orifice inspected.

As for me it was all a great circus. I had never seen so many men under one roof, and it was amazing to consider in how many sizes men came, with what degrees of hair on their bodies, and lengths of arms, and protuberances of various sorts. The air was filled with talk so foul there was almost a blue tinge to it, and while I knew some of the words there were others I had not heard before and only in context could I follow their meaning. Most of the new soldiers were Irish. The army was the last resort for the impoverished male, and the famine had filled our shores with more men eager to work than there were jobs for.

Next we stood in line waiting to be shorn. A huge Yorkshire fellow with an enormous pair of scissors worked steadily with the facility of a sheepshearer. He swore that now no recruits could desert because they'd be known like barbershops by their bare polls.

"A thief gets sent to prison," Jarvis said, "and the first thing they do is cut his locks. In the army the same thing is done. Ergo, is the army the same as jail?"

"Not having been in either one before I cannot say."

"More similarity. You are dressed in a style distinctive enough to be separate from that of the populace. To demonstrate that you are different. Of course, jail is much safer. No one fires grapeshot at you in prison."

"Then why choose the army?"

"It's bars versus clean air. An Englishman needs air and space. You can shoot him in a field, that's all right, but you must not confine him. At least, speaking for myself, that is the choice I made."

"You were a—?"

"Criminal. Thief, to be precise."

I had never known a thief. Or, to my knowledge, seen one.

Especially one so evidently well born and educated as this new friend. Friend? How could I be a friend to a thief?

"Ah," Peregrine Jarvis said. "I see the nose is up. I expected some dearth of civilized company here but hardly disapproval of my former way of life. Why are you here, then, Richard O'Boy?"

"Must everyone here be—"

"Look about you. Eliminate the dull-witted and the cloddish. But the others, those with a modicum of intelligence, if they were not criminals, why would they be here?"

"To protect their land?"

"All rushing to arms because there is a threat to the safety of the realm? An enemy in the Crimea? Do you know who that enemy is?"

"No."

"Do you know where the Crimea is?"

"No."

"Well, then."

"Tell me of your crimes," I said.

"With pleasure. Will you then tell me how you came to be here?"

"I will."

"I am a man," said Peregrine Jarvis, "who sees things clearly. I am not and have never been impressed with homily, injunction, or catechism. As soon as I was old enough to think for myself— I believe it was at the age of two—I decided it was all bombast nonsense and no more than a device to keep off the animals. What man in his right mind would love his neighbor as himself? If the meek inherit the earth it will be because the earth has become worthless. Honor thy father and thy mother? My father and mother despised me and beat me. Do not covet they neighbor's wife? My neighbor's wife coveted me at the age of thirteen and took me into her bed. Should I go on, or do you see my point?"

"I am afraid I do not."

"You do not." Jarvis shook his head sadly. "Of all these worthy types, whom have I selected for confidant?"

"I am trying," I said. "I might not be quick, but I am trying."

"All right, then. You do not see that the world lives on humbug."

"I have little experience of the world," I said humbly.

"Attend me, then. I said I was a thief. I learned that if you needed something and took it and were not found out there was great benefit to you. Providing of course that you were not afflicted with that holy invention, conscience. But now you say to me how could I be so evil, why was I not edified by the examples around me?"

"I was certainly about to say that," I said.

"Whom," Jarvis said, "would you suggest that I should have used for examples? The successful and the wealthy? Clergymen, for instance. Our rector at home filled his stomach and covered his back from the tithes the church demanded. Lawyers? The ones I knew had no interest in the guilt or innocence of their clients and supported those laws which favored the skillful interpreter, such skill to be unavailable, of course, to the ordinary man. Doctors? The ones who pressed for fees in the cure of ailments which Nature healed except insofar as medical intervention delayed or prevented the process? In which sad eventuality the bill, notwithstanding the failure, was duly presented. And so, Richard—"

"And so, Peregrine?"

"It was apparent to me that I lived in a knavish world where the rewards went to the slick and the cunning, all hiding behind pretensions of rectitude which, by dulling the rest of us, made their own thievery more secure."

"And so you joined them."

"Not successfully," Jarvis admitted. "I did not wish to become politician or manufacturer, nor did I wish to join the Church or Medicine or Law. Moreover, I lacked ambition. All I did was satisfy my own lack of standard morality by taking what I needed. And often enough I was caught out because I had no real talent for it. My philosophy pleased me but my implementation was crude."

"And yet," I said, "you found the time to become educated."

"You say that as if education and propriety went hand in hand. I read for a while at Oxford but was dismissed when I was found out to have helped myself to the purse of a don who was careless enough to have left it on his desk while he attended the castigation of a sizar who had confused Ben Jonson with Marlowe."

"But why the army?" I said.

"They were at my heels out there."

"I don't know how much of what you told me I am to believe."

"Oh, you are sharper than you look, Richard O'Boy. It is true that thievery and lying are brothers."

"And if you are truly a thief by nature, then it would be foolish of me to let you near."

"My argument is with the morality of a society. I did not say that rules of behavior are not necessary. Such as not stealing from a friend."

By then it was his turn to be shorn, and upon completion with bald head he looked more than ever like some great eagle or condor. I gave up my own locks with little regret, having at that time in my life little personal vanity. We then went to the tailor shop to be measured for our clothes. Again we took our place in a long, snaking line; it appeared that Her Majesty had little difficulty in achieving her military quotas.

"When I mentioned Oxford back there," Jarvis said, "your face lit up and then turned wistful like a child denied his bit of plumcake. How is it a boy from the country dreams of Oxford?"

"Why do you say I am from the country?"

"Why? When we uncovered for the doctor there was a line across the back of your neck, brick red above and milk white below. Where else but the countryside could one achieve such varied colors? And then I noted your hands when you signed for the recruiting sergeant. Your fingers were twenty times the size of the quill and your palm rough to boot, as I noticed when you shook my hand. It is also in your voice. And your trousers and your shoes."

"I am not ashamed of it," I said.

"Of course you are ashamed of it. We are all ashamed of where we come from."

A soldier with a marked string measured chest and length of leg, and another soldier pulled articles from a bin and threw them at us. We stacked up shako and red coatee, ammunition pouch and canvas pack, greatcoat, water bottle, and forage cap.

"Now you," Jarvis said. "I mean to say, why? You're not a thief like me or a ruffian or emigrant. Looking at that guileless face, I could almost believe you enlisted for your country's sake."

I shook my head and recounted the events that had brought me here. Peregrine put his head back and laughed. He had sharp strong teeth and the bird image disappeared to be replaced with something feral, oddly dangerous. "You're a gull, boy. More—a robin, a lark, a rabbit. This is the year 1854. We are the most powerful country in the world, the most advanced in the marvels of this mechanical age. Trains travel so fast across the country as to take your breath away. The Crystal Palace—have you seen the marvel of the exhibition?"

I shook my head.

"England. Victoria's England—not William or George's, but the noble Victoria. You are no longer hanged for stealing a crust. Nor can a nobleman have you whipped for refusing to doff your hat. Did you truly think a country magistrate could have you jailed or transported because you knocked down his son?"

"My father believed it."

"Let me tell you a secret, Dick. You're not to whisper this to a living human being, do you hear me?"

I nodded.

"I'm the bastard son of a duke. There are things I know. You've been gulled."

"I had to agree else my father would lose his farm."

"Gulled again. My father had many times the amount of land your little squire owned, and he had many tenants. A good tenant was someone to cosset and be grateful for. Did your father pay his rent?"

"Yes."

"On time, in the full amount?"

"Yes."

"My good little O'Boy, how you were diddled."

"Because Sir James played at being emperor and my father was too weak to protest?"

"As you tell it, that would be the sense of it."

"Then I have learned something," I said.

"You're a lucky man, O'Boy. Of all the scoundrels you might have attached yourself to, you found Peregrine Jarvis. I shall take you under my wing, my boy—my boy, O'Boy—and we shall take your innocence and turn it into cunning." He put his long arm around my shoulder. I thought how appropriate was the term—under his wing.

"Cunning," I said. "Not wisdom?"

"For that you would need a soldier sage, which I am not."

"Put shoulder in."

"A sage soldier's shoulder."

My uniform was tight and Jarvis's was loose so we effected a change of some items. A man trundled a wheelbarrow through the hall calling out that he would buy our old clothes.

"It's either sell them or send them home," Jarvis said. "Have you anybody to send them home to?"

I hesitated, then shook my head.

"Might as well pick up a few pence, then. It'll be a long time before we need civilian clothing again." He signaled to the man, who offered him fourpence for trousers and jacket and cravat. Jarvis threw his pile into the barrow. The man offered me twopence for my shirt and trousers, and when I objected Peregrine said, "Take it. It's twopence more than you will ever see for them."

"That's a good pair of homespun. It cost—"

"No matter, Richard. It's the last tie. Cut it. As for my own clothes and what they remind me of, I'd as soon throw them down a bunghole."

I watched my clothes being cast away and that was the end to it, the warmth of my body dissipating in the heavy garments. My mother had sewn the buttons on. I had gone to school in those trousers and had brushed them for Sunday wear.

Peregrine said, "Clothes make the man, according to our friend W.S. With this jacket I dub thee warrior. You know that now you may kill? Without this uniform you faced the gibbet if you did. All because of a change of clothing. Would you still argue that this is a rational world?"

Our names were read off and I answered to the name O'Boy. We were dispatched to our various depots, and I was relieved that Jarvis was sent along with me. Despite his talk of having been a thief, despite his attitude toward the institutions I had been taught to respect, I thought I could learn much from him. And, more important, I thought I could depend upon him if the need for that should arise.

There were fifteen beds in the room, none with sheets. A wizened man who looked too old for soldiering, with a bad scar swelled with proud flesh almost completely around his neck, explained, "Took them all away. Just came in and stripped them off and sold them, most likely."

"Thieves?" said Peregrine, with professional interest.

"Well, they said the sheets could spread the French disease.

The troops in London use sheets and one out of four has the syphilis."

"I'd rather catch it in the regular fashion," Jarvis said. "What's your name, friend?"

"Crabwart. I've been a soldier for eighteen years. Three more to go and I kiss the colors good-bye."

Peregrine appeared fascinated by Crabwart's scar. "I don't suppose you were ever beheaded?"

"Eh?"

"Were you ever in Afghanistan?"

"Never left the bleeding country."

"I think it happened in Afghanistan," Jarvis said. "One of the pasha's swordsmen—"

"Pasha's Turkish," I said. "That is, according to the last schoolmaster I had."

"Emir. Sultan. He had such skill with the blade that one day, faced with one who doubted him, he had his detractor stand before him while the swordsman whirled his weapon so quickly it could not be followed by the eye. A thin red line showed around the man's neck."

"So?" I asked.

"That's what the man said, completely unimpressed. Then the swordsman said, 'Try turning your head.'"

"I never cared for stories," Crabwart said. "I could never get the moral. You'd best pick out beds for yourselves."

I dropped my gear on a bed next to the wall for the privacy. Up came a northern Irishman, taller than Peregrine and as broad as myself.

"I'm O'Malley," he said, "in charge of this depot."

"Yes, sir," I said.

"You can't have that one."

"Why not?" I said.

"I say who gets the beds here. Take one more to the middle. Do you have a watch?"

"Shake out the beds before you use them," Crabwart said. "They're like the continent of Asia. You'll see black, brown, and white residents."

"I don't have a watch," I said.

He turned to Peregrine. "How about you. You got a watch?"

"Yes," Jarvis said.

"Hand it over."

"Why should I do that?"

" 'Cruities an't allowed to hold watches. I'll take care of it for you."

"I don't think so," Jarvis said.

The Irishman had black brows that almost met in a straight line. He frowned and they did meet. "You'd best learn to do as you're told. You're in the army now."

"Are you a corporal?" Jarvis said.

"No."

"Sergeant?"

"No."

"Officer of any kind?"

"For the last time, hand over your watch."

"Bugger off," Peregrine said.

The black Irishman balled up a fist that looked the size of a rugby ball and went for Jarvis, who stood perfectly still until the Irishman was close enough and then shot up a bony knee, and as the soldier bent forward, grunting, his Adam's apple met the edge of Jarvis's forearm, in position and waiting. It was beautifully executed. The kind of thing never taught to me by my father.

O'Malley lay on the floor retching. There were a dozen men in the room, all carefully ignoring him. Finally Crabwart called another man and they dragged the Irishman into a corner.

"He'll recover," Peregrine said.

"How do you know that?" I said.

"It depends on how hard I hit."

"You've done it before, then."

"More than once," Jarvis said. "He'll have a sore throat and he won't walk easily for a while but he'll recover. He won't, I should imagine, collect watches for a while."

"You think we should just leave him lie there?"

"He's the enemy. You do not love your enemies. I thought I told you that."

"Christians—"

"You can't be a Christian and a soldier at the same time. They tell us we can. Armies going to war parading as Christians. Christian Englishmen killing Christian Frenchmen and vice versa. You ever wonder how that can be?"

"Rendering unto Caesar?"

"Eighteen," Jarvis said. "You're never eighteen."

We were marched into an adjoining room for dinner of stringy meat and overboiled potatoes and then dismissed. I wanted to be alone, and the only way to do that was to lie down and close my eyes. I covered myself with my greatcoat and gave myself up to the blackest melancholy I had ever known. I was so sick from it that I shivered. I thought of my bed at home in that strange little cater-cornered room. I thought of the cold water coming from the pump in which I washed. I thought of the pigs waiting for the slop I fed them, and the feel of the earth when I put the seeds down, and the dust of the road as I walked to school. My father teaching me prizefighting and my mother putting food before me, silently, but it was hot with good smells and nothing like I had just been given for dinner. I had never considered any of those things, certainly not with longing or affection, and now everything conspired to form a band around my throat and I wanted it all back again. I thought of Peter and how there were times he spoke to me as an equal. I even thought of Fudd with some regret because despite his lack of worth as a person he had knowledge, some of which had been transferred to me.

And, saving it for the last, I thought of Alethea as I had in bed at home in the special way that took her essence and separated it from her mocking ways. Remember, I told myself, how you hate her. Then there was something hot and moist in my eyes and I opened them and Peregrine Jarvis was standing looking down at me. I was ashamed and turned my face to the side.

He put his hand on my shoulder and was silent for a while and then said softly, "I would not cheer you if I could. What I will tell you is that all feelings are good, even pain is as good as joy, because those things remind us that we are alive. This first night will be your worst, but do not try to forget anything. We're both bound for new experiences which will try to crowd out the old, but we have to remember everything."

I didn't see how one could sleep in a room filled with snorting, gargling, snoring men, but I did.

Chapter Four

We were up at five in the morning, which was no hardship for me but rather a taste of home, while from the expletives and groans of the men around me you would think they had been lie-abeds all their lives. We had to make our cots, attend to our cleanliness, and at six o'clock were on the drill field, where it was right turn and left turn until a quarter to eight. The drilling of the awkward squad was under the direction of a corporal named Greenbriar. He was of medium height, and when he stood at parade rest he formed a perfect rectangle, from his high square shoulders to his planted heavy shoes. His hair was almost orange, which he tried to make inconspicuous by cropping in the manner of the recruits; the tint, however, went all the way down and in a crowd of a thousand hatless men on a cloudy day you could at once distinguish Greenbriar. He had been at Chilianwala, and whatever his disposition had been before he was now gloomy about the bravery of raw soldiers, without faith in the intelligence of their officers, and suspicious of a war department that withheld arms, clothing, and medical supplies. So he considered it his task to hold the army together. He was close enough to the men to keep them from desperation or revolt and enough of an officer to receive instant obedience. Peregrine and I learned the drill quickly enough, but periodically and on purpose Peregrine would turn the wrong way or find himself out of step.

He explained to me, "The object of the army and my object are not always the same."

"The object of the army," I said, "is to turn you into a fighting man."

"I have always been a fighting man."

"The army would prefer that you fight in conjunction with others and not as an individual bloody screaming Indian with a tomahawk."

"I have never seen sheep fight, have you?"

Although I hated the endless drilling and obeying what often seemed to be mindless orders, I began to see that men without necessarily moral worth or self-appreciation or individual courage could be trained to advance without question into enemy fire.

"You're right, of course," Peregrine said. "If you can induce men to obey an order—any order—without flinching or examination, then you have an army, which is superior as a fighting force to a ragged mob."

I was beginning, I thought, to learn when not to believe him. When Peregrine made general worthy statements, it was usually to use them as a blanket beneath which he could pursue whatever he considered to his advantage.

Surprisingly, considering Peregrine's occasional disruptive behavior, he and Corporal Greenbriar became friendly. I think Jarvis was attracted by the soldier's pessimism, and the fact that he did not like his job as instructor. Peregrine liked the perverse and the ill accommodated. It affirmed his own feeling of the lopsidedness of the universe.

At eight o'clock we had breakfast of coffee and tommy—a sort of brown bread—and from ten to twelve we drilled again; then dinner at one, to be drilled again from two to four.

Flogging was common. Hardly a day passed without one soldier or more getting from three to seven hundred lashes. One stormy cold morning a young man was stripped and tied to the halberts. He had spat in the face of a sergeant who had been dissatisfied with the soldier's cleaning of a latrine and directed him to do it again. The beating commenced. There were more than one of us taking some delight from the spectacle. Another's blood is pleasing when it does not splash on yourself. Then the drum major struck the drummer to the ground for not using his strength sufficiently. Sometimes a sympathetic wielder of the lash would make a great show of plying it while laying it on as gently as possible, but mostly this was discovered. Finally the surgeon, noting how black and swelled was the victim's back, moved to interfere. He picked up the cat and said, "You can see they're too thick, they don't cut. That makes the punishment too severe." The soldier was taken down and carried to the hospital, where within eight days he was dead.

The sergeant who had reported the original offense said that it must have been from the cold.

It was a thoughtful thing to see a man flogged so. The officers considered it as much for the edification of the men as for the culprit.

Greenbriar was sitting with Peregrine and myself outside the barracks the evening the soldier died. "Christ," Peregrine said. "A man beats a horse in the streets of London and he's set upon, and if he survives the fists of some gentle passerby he could find himself before a magistrate for abusing a poor dumb animal. A soldier, it seems, is something less than a poor dumb animal."

Greenbriar said, "You can't have discipline without punishment. That horse you mention, Jarvis, learns what he must do from what he must not by the use of the rod. Is that not the way of things?"

"Schools are run that way," I said. "If a student, why not a soldier?"

"Pain is a reminder," Peregrine said. "As the father of Cellini swatted his son across the face when a salamander appeared in the fireplace, to make him remember what he had seen. But enough lashes to kill a man? Who benefits from that?"

"I do," I said. "I have learned that spitting in the face of an officer is against the rules."

"Not that I'm *for* flogging," said Greenbriar. "Someday I think the army will do without it. That is when there will be enough honor in the wearing of the Queen's colors, and the misfits and the brainless will not be allowed to use the army as a place of refuge."

"Is it not a haven for you, Corporal?" Peregrine said.

"My father was an army man. I went in the army as a lad like you two with the thought of rising in the ranks. I've soldiered all over the Empire."

"How long have you been a corporal?"

"Ten years."

"You think that fair?" Jarvis said.

I knew his methods by now. Peregrine was a troublemaker. He was unhappy unless he could irritate. We were haters, both of us, but whereas I cherished the few names on my list and hoped one day to effect a balance between wrongs and villains, Peregrine hated the world, the state, the government, and especially the contented.

Some cavalry officers rode past, laughing and making their horses dance.

"Damned plungers," Greenbriar muttered.

"Plungers?" I said.

"Swells. So superior, yawning, speaking their gammon talk."

"Elegantly bored," Peregrine said.

Greenbriar dangled a limp wrist. "Wewwy, wewwy howwid, haw haw."

"They wear corsets," Peregrine said.

"The British cavalry—" I said, with some notion of protesting.

"Oh, brave," Greenbriar said. "The bastards are brave in battle. I've seen them. They'll ride into a cannon with their silly swords waving. It's just that I don't like to be looked down on, you see."

"All your time and devotion," Peregrine said. "Should you not have risen higher? You think that fair?"

"We're going to war. I'll look for my chance then and take it."

"What kind of chance would that be?" I said.

"Some battlefield action, hoping someone will notice. Maybe Raglan himself."

"Raglan?"

"Lord Raglan, he's commanding general."

"I heard about him," Peregrine said. "He's got only the one arm, an't he?"

"Lost it at Waterloo. Right elbow smashed by a musket ball. He walked back to the cottage they were using for a hospital and they whacked off the arm, and when the surgeon tossed it away Raglan said, 'I say, bring that arm back, I want the ring my wife gave me on that finger.'"

Greenbriar filled a short black pipe, stuck it in his mouth, and lit it, puffing so hard the air took the smoke to me and made me cough.

Peregrine pounded me unnecessarily on the back. "It's not only his having one arm. I hear he never commanded in battle, and he's sixty-six years old."

"Married Wellington's niece," Greenbriar said.

"If I'm in a war," Peregrine said, "if I'm getting shot at and all, I would like the people in charge to have a certain amount of experience. I mean I wouldn't want them to be as ignorant as myself."

"We don't talk that way about our superiors," said Greenbriar.

"Of course not. Just a bit of speculation. Being English, our generals would be the best, of course. Buying their commissions would, naturally, make them superior tacticians."

"Buying?" I said.

"Raglan's father bought him his commission when he was fifteen years old."

I glanced at the corporal to see if this was more dangerous talk, but he said calmly, "That's the way it's done." His pipe had gone out and he lit it again, keeping it alive so vigorously it looked like the smokestack of a locomotive. (So far, I had seen that only in a magazine illustration.)

"Still, Jarvis, how do you know about buying commissions and matters like that?"

"Just common knowledge."

"Wait," I said. "I don't understand. I thought an officer would have to have superior ability. Otherwise, when he gives an order—"

"One would think that superior people were superior for other reasons than having been birthed by superior people," Peregrine said.

"Hold on now!" Greenbriar said. "You're not a damned Chartist, are you, boy?"

"Heavens, no," Peregrine said. "I'm not a damned anything except a damned human being. Or a damned Englishman." He smiled. "On the other hand I don't believe in Lordolatry either." He reached behind the corporal and pushed my head. "Thackeray."

"Thackeray," said Greenbriar.

"Some writer. He was commenting on the way common man deferred constantly to the nobility."

"I see nothing wrong in that. I mean there may be stupid people in every class, but England has nobles, always had, and ordinary folk, and that's all right with me."

"When you know your own place, that's freedom," I said. "My father told me that."

"I never had recruits like you two," Greenbriar said. "Come drill period tomorrow I think I'll make a special effort to work your arses off."

"And serve us both right," Jarvis said. "Meanwhile I'll tell you about the practice of buying your commission in the army.

It's not all that venal—I mean unreasonable. You see, in the time of Cromwell we were ruled by professional soldiers and people came to hate the very name *army*."

"Cromwell," said Greenbriar. "He did some good things."

"He certainly did," said Peregrine. "But after the Restoration we decided—we the people of England—that power should never again be in the hands of military men. So when we established a standing army—back in sixteen hundred something—the only way you could become an officer was to pay for it, a largish sum, too. Therefore who became officers? Men of property with a stake in the country instead of military adventurers. And the purchase price was a guarantee of good behavior—if you were dismissed from the service you lost what you paid in. So the officer class had everything to lose and nothing to gain from a military revolution."

"He's educated," I said to Greenbriar.

"He's only saying what everybody knows."

"That's what I mean. That's what education is."

"The war," Peregrine said. "You mentioned the war?"

"We'll all be in it."

"How much time?"

"You'll be trained in another month."

"You would think they would tell us," I said.

Jarvis said, "Would you tell a horse where you're thinking of riding him?"

"War against whom?" I said.

"We'll be going to the Crimea," Greenbriar said.

"Where's that?"

Greenbriar waved his hand vaguely. "Russia, Turkey, someplace around there."

"Who's on our side and who's against us?" Peregrine said.

"Well, the Turks—"

"We're fighting them?"

"No, we're helping them. Then there's the Russians—"

"Also on our side?"

"No. We're fighting Russia."

"That's a terribly big country," I said.

"And there's the French—" said Greenbriar.

"Helping the Russians?"

"No, the French will be on our side."

"How can that be?" I said. "We've always been fighting the French."

"The Russians," Peregrine said. "They have the largest army in the world."

"Have they threatened the Empire?" I said. "Is it that?"

"I told you too much already," Corporal Greenbriar said. He worked on his pipe. I sniffed at the smoke to be reminded of the smells of home.

Peregrine said reflectively, "If I'm going to fight somebody it's because he has offended me, or just because I don't like him, or I feel something has to be avenged. I need a reason. If I fight an enemy of my country, then I want to know what that enemy has done. I don't see how you can fight unless you have a reason, unless you can feel angry."

"Soldiers don't have to be angry," the corporal said. "Being angry has nothing to do with it. I might even go so far as to say that often enough being angry can be an interference. What's required is coolness and good judgment."

"I don't see that," I said. "You're saying you can kill someone without being angry?"

"Certainly, if you know he's trying to kill you."

"And he thinks you're trying to kill him and thus—"

"That's the way it works," said Corporal Greenbriar.

We fell into a silence for a while, and I felt uneasy, especially because I wasn't being told enough. I needed to understand all these new experiences. "What's war like, Corporal Greenbriar?" I said.

"Ha," he said.

"You've been in battles—"

"I have."

"Can't you tell me?"

"Mostly it's being tired. You never get enough sleep when you're in a war."

"Talking of sleep—" Jarvis said.

He and I went inside, and the corporal went off to his own quarters. Inside, O'Malley must have been waiting in a corner. Then Peregrine was down and O'Malley was standing over him with the weapon he'd used, it looked like a block of wood, and O'Malley had raised it for the coup de grace, and everyone watching in that frozen state which is a combination of fear and disbelief.

I reached across Peregrine's bed to shove O'Malley out of line, and then I jumped over the bed and was close enough for a blow as Peregrine tried to get up and I had to push him out of my way when O'Malley used the block on my right arm, so I had to hit him with my left. He went back and back until the wall stopped him. Peregrine was up and rubbing the back of his head.

Crabwart was standing in front of O'Malley, hands out flat, placatingly, but O'Malley wasn't looking to fight, his expression puzzled and even a little ashamed.

"What do you say?" said Crabwart over his shoulder to me and Peregrine. "Any harm done?"

"Dick settled my score," Peregrine said. "All I've got's a headache. How about your champion?"

"He says it's settled," said Crabwart, leaning toward O'Malley to listen.

"So long as there's no more sneaking up behind me," Peregrine said.

"No report, then," Crabwart said. "No need for a flogging, right, boys?"

O'Malley, not without wariness, came to us. He put out his hand and Peregrine took it and I did the same. O'Malley said hoarsely, "I used to be able to sing "Country Garden," all the way up to the high notes."

"You'll get your voice back," Peregrine said. "I've seen it happen before."

"Is that right?" O'Malley said.

"You have my word on it. You'll be singing high C like a canary."

"All right, then," said O'Malley, nodding once to Peregrine and once to me and going to his own bed.

"Now I've got our future planned," Peregrine said. "As soon as we can get out of the army we'll put you in the ring. I take care of all the details for one half the proceeds. My God, man, I never saw a blow like that. If you weren't off balance you'd have taken his head off."

"My father said I was not good enough for the prize ring."

"Fathers. Mine said I would never learn to wipe my own arse, and now I can do it with either hand."

My bed was next to the wall and Jarvis's beside mine. One

of the soldiers, named Hitch, had his wife with him. The army let her share his bed in a corner of the barracks which they had screened off with a blanket. In return for the lodging she kept the room clean, washed and mended all our clothes, and helped with the meals. By now we had one brown blanket, never washed, and one sheet issued a month, and straw for the mattress once every three months.

There were sounds of activity from behind the blanket screen.

"I wish they'd stop that," Peregrine said.

"Stop what?" I said.

"We definitely have to see Miss Loopy."

"Who?"

"She's Mexican. You know where Mexico is?"

"Certainly I know where Mexico is. What's Miss Loopy?"

"She has a cottage near here, I have been informed, with three skilled associates. Tomorrow night we shall pay them a visit. Do you have any money?"

"Two shillings."

"Never mind. I shall dig into my own hoard. And you can learn to dig into yours."

"Sometimes I know what you're talking about, and sometimes, as now, I don't know what you're talking about."

"I told you, did I not, that I was a duke's bastard. But my mother was married at the time. Her husband, who thought himself my father, was a great admirer of mechanical progress. He bought a cage which he fitted over my genitals at night and locked. Attached to it was a device whereby any erection was made to ring an electric bell in his bedroom."

"Sometimes I can almost tell when you're lying," I said.

"It's the truth, that's how I was brought up. Later I understood that a man with that attitude toward the expression of natural phenomena would have driven his wife to agree to the attentions of another. And oddly he was part of the group that tried to get Parliament to legislate a death sentence for adultery. How surprised he would have been had his wife turned out to be the victim of such legislation."

"Where is Miss—Loopy?"

"On the other side of the village."

"I thought we may not leave the barracks."

"The call of the flesh is stronger than the laceration thereof."

Peregrine shivered. "That poor lad on the halberts. I think if they tried to flog me I should insist on the firing squad instead."

Some of the recruits were playing cards, others were practicing pitch and toss, and most were lying on their beds staring up at the ceiling. On the other side of the curtain the activity had ceased and in a while the wife came out, her husband's greatcoat over her shift. She was a short, fat woman with a cast in one eye. Barefooted she went outside and in a few moments returned and none of the men spoke or looked at her.

"How could you bring a wife to stay here," I said.

"Desperate measures for desperate situations. I would not condemn a man's behavior if he has not affronted me. I do not expect any man to act as I would act. I would never offer a man advice."

"You offer me advice all the time."

"I do, don't I." Peregrine was sitting on the edge of his bed facing me. He tried to bring the soles of his feet together. "That is because you are such a fledgling. A bare slate to be written upon. A *tabula rasa*. I knew I had to be responsible for you. The moment that recruiting sergeant elected to change your name I felt like a midwife. I heard a voice saying, Jarvis, henceforth you and O'Boy shall be linked."

In the morning we were given fifteen minutes to turn out with full pack for a forced march. That meant eighty rounds of ball cartridge in a pouch, canteen filled with water, hatchet, rifle, and bayonet, haversack with two days' provisions, blankets to be rolled on top of that, and greatcoat rolled on top of that. Greenbriar had instructed us how to fold everything and where to hang everything and how everything was to be attached, and I had made a mess of it then. Now I began to roll the blanket and I made a further mess of it. Strapped on top of the haversack, it fell limply on both sides to my waist. Added to that was the onset of panic because time was running out, and besides I felt like a fool because there were others who knew how to do it properly.

One of those, of course, was Jarvis. Having secured all his own equipment neatly, he unrolled mine and rolled it up again and settled it in place. The whistle blew and we had to fall out on the parade ground, the men ready in varying degrees. The sergeant major screamed us into some semblance of formation and off we went, through the village and into the countryside.

Peregrine whispered, "That cottage there, the one with the red roof, you see it?"

"I see it, what about it?"

"That's Miss Loopy's."

It looked ordinary enough, hardly a place to house harem delights.

We marched and the sun came up and it looked as if the exercise had been arranged to watch the sun's exacerbation. After a while a man here and a man there collapsed and they were pushed or dragged to the side and left.

"Now it begins," Peregrine said.

"What?"

"The weeding out."

Ahead of us struggled Hitch, the soldier whose wife lived with him in the barracks. His figure was much like hers—below medium height and larded. He was struggling under the weight and height of his pack, which, with greatcoat and blanket, came a foot above his head.

"Why doesn't the poor bastard just drop out?" I said.

"He can't afford to."

"He looks as if he'll die in this heat."

"Better for the army that he die here than there. There are hotter places in the Empire than East Anglia."

"The way he lives is degrading. A wife in an army barracks. Surely he would do better as a civilian."

"Would he? You don't know much about poverty, do you, Dick. Here they both get food and a dry roof."

The colonel, out in front, fresh on a horse, increased the pace. More soldiers dropped. It was a great temptation to follow them, to slip off the pack and life flat-backed on the earth. A piece of grit, too small for a pebble, insinuated its way through my sock and lodged just above the nail of my little toe on my left foot. With each step it worked in a little more, going from irritant to agony. Peregrine, seeing me limp, said, "Drop out, then."

"Not me."

"I love your spirit. It has conquered mountains and seas for the Empire. How fair it is to be English born."

After eleven miles we were allowed to rest for five minutes.

Crabwart, the oldest soldier among us, lying on his back, said, "A fair beginning to a day's march. I mind the time we considered fifty miles just a brisk walk." He barely had breath enough for the end of the sentence, leaving his mouth open and closing his eyes.

A recruit barely older than myself, a boy from the south whose English was so heavy with Cornwall that few could understand him, said something that sounded like: "Fifty miles is a cruel thing, would they want us to go so far?"

Greenbriar was not on his back but had slipped off his haversack and was leaning against a tree. "A march like this is a small part of your training. At the end of it you will find yourself ready for food and bed. But suppose this were a forced march—twice the pace and three times the distance—and at the end of it you were walking into enemy guns?"

I was busy searching for the damned bit of grit in my sock when the order came to resume march. No one asked me if I was ready. The others scrambled to their feet, not to be reprimanded. I noted that with an intimation of terror. When it's time for an army to move, no one stops for a dilatory soldier.

Except Jarvis. He stood by while I frantically worked at getting my shoe on. I said he ought not to tarry on my account, and he said friendship was more important than marching. At which point Corporal Greenbriar came by and told us to move, and Peregrine said grandly he would be along in a moment, he was waiting for me.

"Move out," said the corporal.

This was not a fellow soldier smoking a pipe and sitting with us outside the barracks. This was a command, and his own father would have had to jump. I considered that interesting. It meant that a man could be more than one thing.

Peregrine said, "Surely there's no harm in my waiting another moment for O'Boy here."

"Move, and that's the last time you'll hear me say it."

Jarvis weighed his disposition to be himself against the consequences. I was afraid the consequences would win. I said quickly, "I'm ready," although I hadn't had time to tie up my boot. I got up, half standing on it, and got my haversack on.

"You'd best take another minute to get yourself in order," Peregrine said.

Greenbriar opened his mouth and I was afraid of what would

issue. I grabbed Peregrine's arm and went hopping with him to the ranks, which were already on the move. Peregrine was thoughtful. He motioned to Greenbriar. "If I'd taken another moment would you have—?"

"I would," Greenbriar said. "And your back would have been sore for many a day."

Peregrine shook his head as if in sorrow.

"Look at it this way, Jarvis," Greenbriar said. "Suppose I have to tell you to get up that hill and bayonet a Muscovite who is sitting there minding a cannon. Are you going to stop and think about it? Are you going to consider if you ought to obey my order or not? Because if that's the way it's going to be, Jarvis, do me a favor. Come down with the cholera or break a foot or tell the colonel you have proof his wife's been sleeping with his adjutant. Anything, but don't come to the Crimea with me."

"I see your point," Peregrine said.

We went on for a mile or so and I was shuffling half out of my shoe, when Peregrine suddenly grabbed his belly, bent over, and fell to the side of the road, at the same time dragging me with him. The line moved on. Peregrine fixed my laces and we both got back. Greenbriar had seen us.

"I got a sudden stitch," Peregrine said. "A bit of wind but I'm all right now, thank you, sir."

"And you?"

"I tripped," I said.

"A few cuts and the two of you will be the better for it."

"I'm doing the best I can," whined Peregrine. "I wasn't cut out for this life but I'm trying. You've got to give me credit for trying, Corporal."

"The trouble is that you're friends. A man oughtn't to have friends in the army." Greenbriar, shaking his head, left us and went forward.

"What does he mean by that?" I said.

"He means one of us could get his head blown off and the other will feel sorry."

On we slogged, without bands or cheering crowds, and some too proud to drop in the first half now went to the side of the road and sat, not collapsing because the body had failed but just for the sake of sitting, because it was insane to keep moving when it was just an exercise and there was no siege to lift, no enemy to encounter, just the colonel in front tiring on his horse.

"Is this the way Alexander conquered the world?" Peregrine said. "Is this how the legions of Rome did it? Shall we two become part of history?"

"I'm tired," I said.

"What I mean to say," Peregrine said, because he would find something to say at the door of heaven, "is that every foot soldier in every army has to be the same. He groans under the weight of his pack and complains because the soles of his shoes are too thin and watches the officer in front on his horse and wishes the animal would stumble and send the master down with a broken neck. Nothing changes, not even the thoughts. To get back to camp and plunge the poor feet into a stream. Hot tea and tommy and maybe a bit of marmalade. And then, with the ache somewhat soothed, perhaps a quick visit to Miss Loopy. Was there ever a soldier who did not think along those lines?"

"I wasn't thinking along any of those lines," I said.

"Of what, then?"

"I was thinking of a girl I knew."

"The one you told me of. She who was the witness against you."

"You've known girls."

"Oh, my, yes. Not being an Adonis it has always been my practice to be brotherly. It is amazing how many young ladies were not loath to a bit of incest."

"What I don't understand is, how can you feel love and hate at the same time?"

Ahead of us the married soldier stumbled and fell. He tried to get up and could not, lying like a turtle on his back. We grabbed him up between us and got him in line.

"I can't do any more," he said. "I've worn off the bottoms of my feet, I'm walking on the bones."

"You've got to finish," Peregrine said. "You want your wife on the parish?"

When we saw the barracks in the distance, Peregrine said, "Are you learning, then?"

"Learning what?"

"The end of the journey has its roots in the beginning, and man is always stronger than he thinks."

We threw off our impedimenta and lay down. The room was at once filled with the sounds of snoring.

"For this relief much thanks," Peregrine said. And, after a moment, "Well, it's us for Miss Loopy's." He tried to come to a sitting position, but all he could do was raise his head a few inches. He tried again and fell back. "Another time, then. Miss Loppy will wait, nor will her charms wither in twenty-four hours."

I said nothing.

He said, "Are you disappointed, Dick? If so I will make the effort if it kills me."

"I wasn't going anyway."

"I thought we had an arrangement?"

"You were just talking."

"But you need instruction. I do the best I can with you, but there are areas beyond my capability."

Jocaren, the boy from Cornwall, came over holding a stub of pencil and a sheet of paper. I didn't understand him, and Peregrine, head cocked listening intently, said, "He wants to ask a favor."

Jocaren nodded, and this time I was able to follow his accent. "You or Jarvis, either one, I'll pay."

"What do you want?"

"If you'll just write a letter for me."

"You can't write?"

"Bravo," said Peregrine.

"Nobody here can write except you and Jarvis."

"And you're not so sure about Jarvis," I said. "Well, give it here and tell me what you want to say."

" 'Dear Mum and Da.' "

"Da?"

"That's my father."

"Go on."

" 'I am all right, I am fine. I get plenty to eat. We have good beds and my uniform is smashing as you will see when I take a picture.' "

I looked up. He said, "How could you write so fast?"

"You didn't say much. Anything else?"

"Well, if there's room. 'Best wishes to you and also Gram and Timmy and Charles. Also Dingy and Muffin and Corrinne.' "

He thanked me after I had refused his offer of a penny. Peregrine said, "I wonder who is Dingy?"

"Probably his cat."

"No, Muffin's the cat."

There was a thumping behind the drawn blanket in the corner.

"I'll be damned," Peregrine said. "He didn't have enough strength to finish the march."

I got my shoes off and lay spread-eagled on the bed and thought of nothing.

"About poverty," Peregrine said.

"I'm asleep."

"I promised myself to tell you about this."

"Not now."

"Please," Peregrine said, and he sounded serious. "There are things I have learned and I have no one to pass them on to except you. Nor can I delay instructing you, because I am going to die ahead of you."

I was almost asleep and then what he was saying overcame me like a vast sad wave and I said, "Damn you for saying that."

"No reason to get upset."

"You soothsaying bastard," I said.

"Will you listen to me for a while?"

"It's so important?"

"No, it's not."

"Then get on with it," I said.

"We never had a revolution in England. It was happening in the countries around us, so Parliament passed the reform bills in a panic. You know about that?"

"I suppose."

"Thomas Malthus—he died about twenty years ago—he wrote about the problems of population. He thought the poor should be suppressed because otherwise the entire earth would be peopled with paupers."

"Like us," I said. "You with your university education and me with whatever I gleaned from grammar school in the same position as Jocaren, there, who cannot read or write."

"It's social history I want to tell you about."

I closed my eyes.

"Don't fall asleep when I'm educating you."

"I merely closed my eyes the better to concentrate."

"An enlightened country like England does not let its people starve, especially since starving people can take up arms and overthrow a government. But people like Martineau warn that there is great danger in helping the poor because, using Malthus's thinking, you then develop a great congregation of the impoverished. The poor begin to take for granted that they are to be supplied with medicine and advice gratis, all their lives. She said the evil was increasing every day. Even to looking for assistance in childbirth as their due."

"Being poor isn't desirable, I think, even with assistance in childbirth."

"However, she said that the blind and the deaf should be cared for in asylums, and she agreed that accidents should be treated free."

Suppose, I thought, that Alethea had stood up before Sir James and said that I had been provoked, that it was only to be expected that a man of sensibility and honor, like myself, should have struck out at someone vulgarly impugning the status of his birth. And suppose then that Sir James had demanded that his son apologize to me. And Peter had then humbly asked my pardon and I had graciously granted it, and then Alethea and I had gone off together hand in hand to seek the bower which Peter had used with Maureen (somehow it had not been sullied) and—

"Harriet Martineau did not believe," Peregrine said, "in making provision for the elderly poor."

"Why not?" I said.

"I am glad you are interested, Richard. She said if the state were to provide for the old, that would encourage people to marry and have children at too young an age and thus shrug off the burden of caring for their aged relations."

I wanted to get back to the bower, but I had lost the way.

"Malthus left his mark, Richard. Certainly we must provide for the poor because no country can allow its citizens to die of hunger. But make the provision onerous and undesirable, so that the poor themselves will prefer a life of honest toil to charity."

For a moment I was back with Alethea. I don't know what we did—exactly. I had no experience to place it against. We were together and she looked at me in a soft yet tantalizing way and she touched me and encouraged me to look at her and to touch her.

"A man named Engels, a philosopher," Peregrine said, "said in a book called *The Condition of the Working Class,* that the workhouse has been made into the most repulsive residence which the refined ingenuity of the Malthusian can invent."

I did not hate her, I thought. She was young and had no choice.

"The food—in the workhouse—is that of the most ill-paid working man, and the work is harder. Otherwise they might prefer the workhouse to their own wretched existence outside. You take the poorest and the most downtrodden and the most miserable of men and women, and none would prefer the workhouse to what they have."

If I could not have Alethea, I thought, then I would be recluse and celibate.

"Are you paying attention?" Peregrine said.

"I am, of course."

"Criminals in prison are better treated than paupers, and often a pauper will commit an offense so he can go to jail rather than the workhouse."

"Or even go into the army," I said.

"Yes."

"And so?" I said.

"Why am I telling you this? There is another world underneath the world we know. Men like Hitch know and fear it. If you should have to go into that world, I have prepared you a little for it, at least in theory."

"Why should I ever have anything to do with that underworld?"

"One never knows, Richard."

The drilling became harder, almost frantic, as if there was not enough time to turn us into soldiers. We learned to snap the bayonet into position and thrust with it. Into the soft parts. "Don't waste it on bone!" roared the instructor. We learned to load the smoothbore musket and sight and fire and reload. It had a name—Brown Bess. I learned to fire it accurately and reload it quickly. It was the part of the training I liked.

Each night Peregrine talked of going to Miss Loopy's as fatigue overcame us both. Then one morning, without warning, ready or not, we put everything we owned on our backs and made ready for the trip to Plymouth, whence we would board the ship to Bulgaria.

"They can't send a virgin to war," Peregrine protested. "If I let it be known they will surely leave you behind."

I was frightened and at the same time filled with a strange eagerness to be tested.

Chapter Five

Some of the officers assigned to share our ancient sailing vessel came aboard with their wives, as if this were a voyage of pleasure to take the sea air. Some wives brought along their maids. One wife, elegantly attired for war in a long gown and slippers with sun hat and kid gloves, supervised an endless succession of boxes which were taken by some impressed soldier to the officers' quarters, selected to be as far as possible from the horses and the men of the infantry.

The men were not permitted the marital indulgences of the officers, and last night I had witnessed a touching farewell between Hitch and his wife. I listened unabashed, for their relationship was of great interest to me. I had thought romantic love restricted to the beauty of such as Alethea, and older prosaic unions were more convenience and habit than ardor. The Hitches were not verbal people, communicating more with touch and look than the fencing sentences in the novels I had read. They held hands and sat on the cot with their shoulders together, comforting each other as if comfort could be stored. Then Mrs. Hitch said, shaking her head, "I will not permit it. I will not leave you." Her husband smiled sadly and said nothing. She said, "I will find a way."

Now, as we went below to claim possession of a hammock—they were stretched one above the other six high—I noted that walking behind Hitch, corpulent and harassed as he, came a soldier not with pack and musket but embracing a bedroll; as if in imitation of Hitch, walking as he did in shoes too tight, taking possession of a low hammock with Hitch immediately throwing his belongings in the one above. Although no one's uniform fit well enough, this second Hitch's fell in particularly unsoldierly folds, and a coil of long hair was beginning to escape the shako.

I said to Peregrine, "How dare he bring her along to God

knows what dangers? How could he place his own wife in jeopardy?"

"Before you judge the actions of others," said Peregrine, "unless those actions hurt you, you would do well first to gain some experience of the human condition."

"I was just making a comment to you," I said, aggrieved.

"I know, and I do not want to seem harsh, but sometimes, Richard, you are so much in need of instruction that my life's work toward that end is appalling in its difficulty. Take a look at Jocaren there."

The boy from Cornwall was sitting on his hammock looking lost and frightened. He was staring straight ahead at nothing, listening to the slow roll of the ship under our feet as if it were the tread of beastly things advancing to rip him asunder.

"Now observe Crabwart, the soldier with experience."

Crabwart, whistling through his teeth, appeared to be making up his bed as in the barracks, turning under the corners and smoothing out the sheet. Except that there was no sheet, just a piece of canvas attached by rings to the stanchion. He glanced right and left and, shoulders hunched for concealment, reached inside his jacket for a flask, from which he took two or three choking swallows, and secreted it again.

"A quiet, settled man?"

"I would say not," I said.

"Now look at O'Malley, O'Malley the brawler."

The big Irishman took three paces up and three paces back, all the room there was, pausing at each turn to put his palms together and link fingers and shake them up and down as if wringing out a wet shirt.

"Who is at ease here, anyone?"

"You, Peregrine."

"I do not count. I am made of sterner stuff."

"I, then. Because I have you to lean upon."

"Then, you foolish boy, look again on a pair of lovers."

They sat holding hands and talking together quietly.

"How many women do you know who could do what that woman has done? Concealed in a soldier's uniform to be with her husband on his way to war. And not an officer's war, not toward the best of quarters with serving men in attendance. She will share his lot, the mud and the cold and the danger."

"How do you know there will be mud?"

"There is always mud in war."

"What would I do without you, Peregrine? To whom would I turn for all this wisdom?"

Peregrine nodded solemnly. "You think you are scoffing but you are not."

"I know I am not," I said.

Mrs. Hitch was hardly beautiful or voluptuous or as far as I could see desirable in any way. Yet there was proof enough of love. I thought of Alethea's shining face. It was fitting that a man longed for her, fought for her, had her fill his dreams. (Not that I stopped hating her, of course I still hated her.) I could not understand that a person like Mrs. Hitch could have found someone who thought of her as I thought of Alethea. And, incomprehensible as it was, it was somehow warming to know that love was universal, and not limited by snobbery or the fancies of poets. If it came to that, perhaps Mrs. Hitch was superior to the delicate loveliness of someone like Alethea. Would Alethea have followed me into this noxious hold?

We had fair winds and soon were out of sight of land. Not that we saw much of either land or water, since our presence on deck was not encouraged. I found the pitching of the ship not unpleasant—how could an Englishman not feel at home on the sea? There were others, however, to whom the long slow shifting of the timbers was sickening, and among those was Peregrine. He lay like death in his hammock, staring at the outline of the figure above him inches from his face, and his quick philosophy was mute and for days he did not eat. I offered him some of my salt pork and biscuit and he turned a green face to me and said that, were he able, he would toss me overboard. I looked about me and thought of the hibernation cycle of bears, except that the smell in that hold was worse, I was sure, than that of any den. Lacking information, without a fact or even a rumor on which to base speculation, not knowing where we were bound or how long it would take, one wrapped around him his own living space and sank into a self-created morass. No one bothered to tell us anything. If the officers knew, that was considered sufficient. Ordinary soldiers were not needed for decisions; when the time came they would be told what to do.

I had to get away from the miasma of spirit and the noisome atmosphere. I took my blanket and went up on deck and sought a corner where I might be unobserved. I found such a place near where the horses were packed together in stalls on the deck. The area had not been hosed for several days, and with the wind in my direction I had not bettered my condition by coming up into the sea air.

Horses are bad sailors and suffer from confinement at sea. Whenever the ship rolled the animals became frantic, stamping and screaming. Sometimes an animal broke his leg from kicking out at the barriers, and he was then shot and thrown overboard. I wondered how much difference there was between the condition of the horses above and the troops below. Both were brought along on this mission to submit to orders, to go where they were driven. Then I cautioned myself that this path of thinking led to the darkness of anarchy. An Englishman was proud to defend his monarch and the kingdom, and it was a mockery of decent British values to compare his lot with that of animals. So having chastised myself I lay in my burrow contemplating the sea and the sky.

One morning the sea had turned rough and the horses were frightened and kicking. Every living thing should be able to protest intolerable living conditions, if unable to change them. A horse could either run or kick, and there was no place on the ship for him to run. The sound of their screaming was especially unpleasant. One could live with horses on a farm and never hear it. This morning I observed an officer, a captain, coming from the elysian section and going up to a horse he called by name, Sultan. It was evident the horse was his. The horse could not be quieted, and the officer climbed over the barricade. Through the slats I could see him slip in the slime underfoot at the same time that the crazed animal brought up his knee and cracked the officer alongside his head.

I went up to the stall and tried to take hold of the horse's bridle. His eyes were wide and rolling, which made me properly respectful and glad the barrier was between us. He pulled his head away and his feet lashed out, barely missing the officer's head.

I said, "Sir, can you move?"

He had one hand to his temple, and blood was coming

through between his fingers. "No," he mumbled.

"Try," I said. "If you can get to your feet I can pull you over."

"I can't."

I had curried horses and fed them and worked with them and ridden them, but I didn't know what to do with a horse this taken by terror. There was very little space between the horse, the barrier, and the fallen officer. I climbed on top of the railing and leaned down to grab his hand, but I couldn't get a purchase and in a moment the horse's hooves was going to make jelly of his head. I had to turn the horse around and I could not do it from the outside, so I took hold of the horse's bridle and lowered myself to the floor, but I could not find footing there because of the muck and kept myself from falling only by holding on to the horse's head. Now I tried to maneuver the animal around. He was trying to rear but my weight was too much for him. I sought for a dry spot with my feet but it was all slippery, and should my hands slide off the bridle I would be on the floor and as likely as the officer to have my head mashed. So of course my palms began to sweat, making my hold weaker, and of course the horse then pulled away harder, because in moments of peril all things conspire to increase the danger.

The officer, his voice thin and distant as if his spirit was considering departure, said, "What's got into you, Sultan? Be quiet, that's a good boy."

"Sultan?" I said. "Are you Arabian? I don't know anything about Arabians, I know about quiet ordinary domestic beasts who do their work and don't try to murder their masters. Listen to me, Sultan. I'm a farm boy. We help each other, animals and farm boys, and neither one has anything to fear from the other. You hear me, Sultan? I'm just as far away from home as you are. I don't like to be on a ship either. I don't like the feel of it moving under my feet and I don't like the sea when it's dark and cold, the way it brings death close. Now turn, just back up and turn around. That's a good boy."

Sultan paid no attention to me at all. He did not find my voice soothing or reassuring, and he did not care much for my philosophy. I was just another irritant adding to his displeasure, and he pulled violently to get away from my grasp.

"Well, then," I said. "One way or the other." I put all my

weight on his head and forced him to lower it and I shoved back and made him take the one step I needed to give me room so I was between the horse and the fallen officer.

I got my left hand wrapped inside the bridle and with my right took hold of the officer's jacket and heaved. As strong as I was, I could not accomplish a feat like that. I had raised him a little, but at once he sank back into the fecal mud.

"You've got to help," I said. "The next time move with me, try to get your hands onto the top. Now, ready, go." I heaved again and he pushed down and reached up and got the fingers of one hand on the top of the barrier.

"Hold on," I said, "while I get another grip." I repeated the movement with my hand on his bum and got him up a little and a little more, and he fell over the other side onto the deck. I let go of the animal and vaulted over. I picked the officer up. We were both covered with filth. He was holding his head and I took his hand away to look at the wound. Most of the bleeding had stopped. The skin was opened by the horse's knee, but there did not seem to be any distortion.

"I'm Captain Terence Bright. What's your name?"

"O'Boy, sir."

"Of the Fifty-seventh?"

"Yes, sir."

A pair of handlers came on deck with a hose and at Captain Bright's directions they washed us off, leaving us clean but shivering.

"It's a change of clothes for both of us, son," Captain Bright said. "O'Boy, is it? I am in your debt, sir."

I went below for some dry clothes. Peregrine, who was beginning to feel better, was chewing on a biscuit. He asked me if I had fallen overboard, and I told him what had happened. He said thoughtfully, "Be careful around that officer, Dick. Better if you had nothing at all to do with him."

"I did him a good turn. He said he is indebted to me."

"Will he not, then, resent you? Common soldiers and officers must stay apart. He will do you harm even without intending it. Try to have nothing to do with him."

"This is another of those many times, Peregrine, when I do not understand you. First, he will probably have already forgotten that I saved his life. And if he does not, if he wishes to do something for me in return, should I spurn him? You and I, Peregrine, owe much to each other. Are we enemies, then, or friends?"

"There is a difference but I do not wish to go into it now. Just remember what I say, Dick. It may be that he will try to be your friend. As he is an officer that will be impossible. So be careful of him, Dick. Promise me."

I promised, not knowing what I was promising.

Day followed monotonous day, with sea and sky the limits of the world. In the hold the stench was frozen.

"Has it ever occurred to you," Peregrine said, "how it is that the unwashed poor can tolerate the unfortunate conditions of their life?"

"By learning patience?"

"Not patience, adaptability. The first thing they do is lose the sense of smell. Do you think otherwise they could live as they do? Take a deep breath now, what do you smell?"

"A horrible stink."

"Exactly. But I no longer smell it. I have not joined you on deck for fear that the sight of the rolling sea would bring back my mal de mer, and by remaining down here I have finally lost my abililty to distinguish odor. And soon I shall lose my capacity for indignation, faced with the fact that there is no one to whom to complain and no chance of amelioration. We are here forever, stuck in amber. Perhaps we have all died and this is one of the seven circles—"

"What we voyage toward might be worse," I said.

As the horses kicked out in frustration, so a man denied a target picks either on himself or on his fellow sufferers. A soldier named Cochran—as I said, most were Irish—a short, compact, red-cheeked man whose head was half bald, with huge freckles compensating for the hairless part, decided that the Hitches had become an affront to him. He was, he said loudly in their hearing but pointedly not directly at them, sick of the way a wife donned a uniform to which she was not entitled and forsook her wifely duties ashore to preempt the place of honest soldiers.

"I've got a wife at home myself. Would I let her join me here in this pigsty? Not as I value her well-being. When I married her I swore to honor her and do all I could to keep her well."

"Did she ask to come with you?" said Mrs. Hitch. "Did she offer to, and did you refuse her?"

"Are you speaking to me?" said Cochran, face superciliously averted.

"That I am, as you have been speaking of my husband and myself. Will you answer me, then?"

"Sure, it was never considered," Cochran said.

"Then keep your criticism to yourself. That I chose to be here with my husband is his business and mine and none of yours."

"Mind your tongue, woman," Cochran said. "Since you wear men's clothing you should not think to be treated as anything but a man."

"You're a bag of wind," Mrs. Hitch said. "It smells bad enough in here without your adding to it. I'll thank you to go off by yourself and be quiet."

Hitch was sitting quietly, listening to his wife and nodding his head slowly as if he could not himself improve on her rhetoric. Cochran grew red and began to swell up.

"If you were a man—"

"What would you do then?" said Mrs. Hitch. "You said I was dressed like a man and responsible like a man. If you've got something to say then say it, and if there's something you want to do then do it."

"I'll take no abuse from you, madam."

"And I'll not listen to your blather. So put a cork in it and be off."

"My own wife would not dare to talk to me like that—" and Cochran balled a fist and raised it over his head, whereupon Mrs. Hitch, rapidly rummaging through her belongings at the foot of her hammock, extracted a frying pan and hit Cochran over the head.

He looked more surprised than hurt and his knees gave but he remained standing. Mrs. Hitch with two fingers pushed him in the chest, and he slowly fell to the floor.

"Well done, old lady," said Mr. Hitch, not having moved from his place.

"I was saving him the pain of having to deal with you," Mrs. Hitch said.

"I had no fear it would go so far," said Hitch, kissing her on the cheek and then setting to mending some socks.

Mrs. Hitch knelt beside Cochran and shook him a little, saw that he was going to be all right, and patted him on the cheek.

It became so that each day one did as little as possible to stay alive because existence had turned into minimal preservative stupor. One ate the rations, crouched as briefly as possible over the trough, and for the balance of the day went, as Peregrine put it, to picking the lint out of one's navel.

"As long as we remain in this floating cocoon," said Peregrine, "we are at least safe. But is safety so lacking in the sparkle of life preferable to the risk of death and destruction? Is apathy preferable to pain? If one by wishing could sail these empty seas forever, would one so choose? What about you, Corporal?"

I had agreed to share my corner on deck with four or five men, away from the bustle of the sailors, who went back and forth to stand or pull a rope or turn a crank in incomprehensible patterns.

"I'm a soldier," said Greenbriar. "My job is to fight."

Jocaren said, "It would be a question of being killed or hurt bad for certain. I mean to say, if the chances were one could live through it, I would certainly want to leave this place."

Crabwart said, "I'd just as soon stay here and count the days until my time is up. It would be a sad thing if old Crabwart, just a few years away from his pension, were to stop a ball not even aimed at him. I do what I'm told, always have, and I was told to be here on this ship, and here I am and I'm taken care of. There's food, it's dry below, and God alone knows what's ahead."

"And there is the point," said Peregrine. "What God alone knows, man is desperate to find out. He could live forever in his shelter but he suffers from two sinful attributes, without which he could be spared much discomfort—boredom and curiosity. So he must stick his head up and peer about and finally take a closer look at the creature with the gaping mouth and terrible sharp claws."

One morning there was a darker patch on the horizon. As the sun came up the patch grew closer, and suddenly there were toy ships in a harbor. The word *Varna* flew around the ship, and uncertainly and without orders we took up our muskets because we had come this distance to meet the enemy. As we drew nearer to the ships in the harbor, we wondered if they were Russian and, if so, were they about to fire upon us and, if so, why were we so openly approaching? Still no orders to crouch and load and be ready to fire. Our officers and their wives came out to line the rail as if on a pleasure boat on the Thames. Now we could see the flags, and they were British. Dozens of ships, and that was a brave thing, and we gulped and felt English pride. There were other ships with other flags, and Greenbriar said that was the tricolor, that was the French.

Where, then, was the enemy?

"Peregrine, the sea is filled with swimmers!"

"But how strangely they float."

Head and shoulders out of the water: I had seen no one swim like that. Scores of them, bobbing.

And then, hard on *Varna,* another word swept the ship: *cholera.* The worst disease known. A man alert and cheerful at noon could be dead and buried by evening. A man would show a blue tinge around his mouth, cry out for water; he would begin vomiting and in a moment collapse. What made it terrifying above all other ailments was its mysteriousness. The doctors knew nothing about its causes or how to cure it. Some recovered, most died.

"They're all dead," I said to Peregrine.

"They put weights on their feet and throw them into the sea. Then the bodies decompose and the weights keep them upright."

Bodies rotting in the sun.

The soldiers clustered, seeking comfort in each other's ignorance. They asked questions of themselves, knowing no one had the answers. If there was cholera on that shore, why should they land?

The orders came to disembark. British soldiers had to obey, there was no revolt in them. We marched out onto the deadly land.

There was no enemy. The Russians had not come down to fight. The British and their allies, the French, set up camp and awaited orders from a field staff who had no notion of what should be done, what they wanted to do, or why they were there in the first place. In a short time we were known as the army of no occupation—except that of burying our own dead. Cholera marched through the ranks, taking the high and the low.

We scooped out holes in the sand to make a place to sleep. We envied the French their *tentes d'abri* shared by three men, each carrying one part. Peregrine found a bit of canvas and some sticks and made a lean-to and invited me to share it. It was like a palace.

"What kind of war is this?" I said.

"We are certainly not knights. There's no nobility to it." Peregrine had found a pan and was washing his feet.

"I suppose they will just send us home and that will be the end of it," I said.

"They can't do that."

"Why not?"

"It is easy to unleash the dogs of war but difficult to kennel them up again."

"Who said that?"

"I don't know. Shakespeare said something like it, but not exactly."

"Is there any sense to it at all?" I said.

"Never," Peregrine said.

"I don't want to be a part of something if there's no sense to it."

I had a sudden feeling of uneasiness and then a burning inside, and I had a craving for something cold to drink.

"It's nothing," Peregrine said.

"Cramps. I'm getting cramps."

"Everybody's got that. It comes from all the salt meat and sleeping on the bare ground."

I had never been sick in my life. I didn't know anything about sickness.

"Oh, Jesus," I said, and I got a few stumbling steps away before I vomited.

"It's nothing," Peregrine said, fingers squeezing the back of my head. "Some bad meat, that's all it is, some bad meat."

"Tell me," I said, "tell me if my skin looks blue to you."

"You're talking nonsense," Peregrine said.

Then the contractions hit me, not only stomach and bowels but the muscles of my arms and legs. It was like being held in the grip of a huge remorseless hand that was slowly closing. I got my trousers down just in time. I forced myself to look. Pure rice water. Classic. Then I vomited again and then the cramps again. I remember looking at my fingers. Shriveled and bone hard.

Peregrine was spooning some burning stuff down my throat. "Brandy. Brandy works fine."

"Where did you—"

"Never mind. It should be champagne. The officers have crates of champagne which they believe protects them from—"

"Say it," I said.

"Say what?"

"Cholera."

"You have a fine imagination, Dick."

But I had been watching others die and helping to bury them. What they died from is what I was suffering from. It was ridiculous.

"It's ridiculous," I said to Peregrine.

"What's ridiculous?"

"I haven't even decided what to make of my life."

"Plenty of time for that."

"I'm dying, Peregrine."

"Don't be a fool."

"A dying man deserves more respect."

"You've forgotten what I said. I am going to die ahead of you."

I had protested his saying that before. Now I began to castigate him and the hand clutched my bowels in the middle of a word and I tried to get outside but I was too weak. Peregrine cleansed me.

I wanted my mother. A mother. Not the one I had had but the one I should have had. I wanted to be taken care of, tenderly, to be told to close my eyes. The hand was soft on my forehead. I was fed some peppery mixture.

"I never even got to fire a musket at the enemy. It's a silliness."

"Hush now. Take some more of this."

The voice was feminine, the touch soothing. "Mother," I said.

"Yes, that's right. Swallow it all down."

Mrs. Hitch put my head against her bosom, and her fingers stroked my hair.

Peregrine went for the surgeon, who said, "What do you want of me, a diagnosis? He's got cholera. They say champagne helps. Do you have champagne?"

"No," Peregrine said.

"Pity." The surgeon poked at me, held my eyelids up, and let them go. "Another hour, maybe two."

"He's not going to die," Peregrine said. You could tell from his tone that it was not simply a pious hope but a certainty.

"How do you know?" said the surgeon, sounding honestly curious.

"Because I will go ahead of him," Peregrine said.

The surgeon shook his head. Either medical people know what to do and they don't have the proper medicines or they don't know what to do and they won't admit it. Since he was not going to keep me from dying, I wanted to know if he had some comfort for my soul.

"I am not a priest," the surgeon said.

"Give him something for the pain, then," said Peregrine.

"Here is some laudanum."

I was at a ball. Alethea, with her back to me, was dancing with one beau after another. Everyone was dressed in shining white while I wore my cow-pie–stained farm clothes. Whoever found themselves dancing too close to me veered off in disgust. I could not dance but I could fight. I challenged each swain in turn and whipped him. When all were vanquished I turned to Alethea for my reward. She turned her head and there was no face, merely blankness.

The cramps came again, which meant they would be followed by the rice-water stools. I was swaddled in some cloth like an infant. I could not stand the smell of myself, so I did not know how any dared come near me. But Mrs. Hitch did.

"He's just a wee lad."

"A lad, yes, but hardly wee," Peregrine said.

"We've been married long enough to have one his size, Hiram."

Mr. Hitch nodded. I had not known his name was Hiram.

"You could catch it from him," Peregrine said.

"So could you," Mrs. Hitch said.

"Hurry and teach me something more, Peregrine," I said. "There is not much time."

Mrs. Hitch bathed my bottom. My throat was swollen with gratitude toward her and her quiet husband. Would Alethea have cleansed me and nursed me? I admired Hitch, who did not senselessly require beauty of face and slenderness of ankle.

He died, I thought. In Bulgaria. In Her Majesty's Service. That sounded better that if he had died of the putrid fever in Dire-Toombley. I was already ennobled. For whom? My father, perhaps, talking solemnly in a resting moment to Rafferty. Not my mother, she spoke to no one. Alethea? Said without tears, perhaps to a friend as they dressed for a dance, an obiter dictum to show that one accepted the demise of past admirers philosophically. Peter to Maureen as they did whatever they did in their bower. "A deserved fate. He never should have struck me."

I lay with fantasy and with pain. I was ignorant and uncaring of what went on around me. That there were others dying was no concern of mine. That an army had landed to do battle and found no enemy to fight was a farce played out on a stage in Southwark.

"The situation," Peregrine said, "is this. The allies—that is to say Britain and France and the Turks—have decided that the Ottoman Empire must be protected against the Czar. Here at Varna the Russians have drawn back their army, while cholera does their work for them. The sensible course would be to return home because we appear to have lost our casus belli."

"How long have I been sick? Weeks?"

"You're going into the sixth hour."

"And I have not died."

"As I said."

"I wonder," I said, "if I am not somewhat better."

The cramps came as sickeningly and agonizingly, but their duration, I thought, was less, and they were not at once followed by that watery discharge.

"There is now talk," said Peregrine, "of invading the Crimean Peninsula to get at the Russian naval base at Sevastopol."

"I have never heard of those places."

"Nor have our masters. It is even said that the French have consulted Napoleon by means of a planchette."

"How do you know these things, Peregrine? You may be an uncommon man but you are just a common soldier."

"I have been out ferreting information. I have many sources. Like the boy who assists the cook who serves the valet of Raglan."

"I want to get up."

"You are still too weak."

"Please, help me up."

Peregrine took me under the arm and helped me stand. The earth spun; by clenching my teeth I made it stand still.

"You have turned into a stick, Richard. Your face is nothing but bone."

"But I am alive."

Mrs. Hitch came by with her husband. "Praise the Lord, he is on his feet. I will make him some soup."

"From what?" I said.

Hitch said, "If need be, from a stone. Mrs. Hitch always finds a way."

They walked up to shake my hand. First Jocaren, then O'Malley and Crabwart and Cochran and others whose names I did not know. Corporal Greenbriar said, "When a man catches the cholera and lives he is a man to stay close to; he has the secret of survival."

Mrs. Hitch brought me her soup. It tasted of earth and I drank it all and slowly felt my strength returning.

I learned more from Peregrine. Some of the men wanted to grow beards but Raglan would not permit it, saying an Englishman ought to look like an Englishman and beards were foreign. Russell of the *Times* decried this as parade-ground nonsense and wrote about it in his newspaper. He himself had a huge beard and may have taken Raglan's order as a personal insult.

When I felt stronger I went to look at the town. It stank. Everywhere stretcher parties carried the stricken fever cases to the hospitals. Luckily I had evaded that; Peregrine said the sewers were cleaner than the hospitals where they dumped the patients to die.

We received orders to embark. I could not carry all my equipment and Peregrine took half of it on top of his own pack. When we got on board the ship rocked at anchor for days while the men fought for space at the rail to spew. Once again the horses objected to their cramped stalls. Over everything was the appalling odor as the corpses danced in the water. Finally the huge fleet took to sea—60,000 men, Peregrine said—and he talked of the Armada, only this time the numbers were on our side.

"It was quality, not size, that won for us," I said.

"Look out there," he said, pointing to the gray water. "It looks like any other but we call it the Black Sea. In time to come you will point it out on the maps to your children. A farm boy from East Anglia, how could you have dreamed that one day you'd be sailing on the Black Sea?"

Finally a landing area was decided upon, and it took five days to move everyone ashore. In welcome the skies opened up for us. An unbelievable amount of guns and stores and rubbish grew on the beach. Over four miles of us, all testifying to the variety of British might, from the Highlanders in their dark green tartans to the scarlet Guards. Now for the first time we saw the enemy, a long line of horsemen up on the crest, lances glistening in the sun. We stared at them. How strangely quiet they sat in their shaggy fur caps. I feared their strangeness. I would not have feared a man like myself whose vulnerability I understood, whose points of weakness I could attack. I did not know if those Muscovites were like me.

Chapter Six

We marched inland, with the great mass of the Russians visible on the heights. They did nothing but watch and menace by their numbers. Our cavalry deployed with great dashing up and down, the purpose of which I could not fathom. There were occasional Russian shells to which our artillery boomed reply. It was more exercise than war.

We rolled down the coast, choking with heat by day and shivering by our campfires at night. Then, in our way at the bottom of a long slope, was a river and beyond it a great bluff with the Russians waiting atop it. We stopped and dug in while the general staff pondered what to do next. We sat looking across the river at the Russian fires dotting the night like fireflies.

"By morning," Peregrine said, "Raglan and his advisers will have made up their minds. My guess is we're going to advance across the river while the Russians practice British decapitation."

"There's a lot more of them than us," I said.

"It would seem so, Dick."

"I don't feel very heroic, Peregrine."

"You took the Queen's shilling. That doesn't guarantee heroism, just obedience and a vain effort to keep one's underwear clean."

I waited for more. I always expected, with Peregrine, that he was about to say the one word that would clarify my life and give purpose to it.

"A silly business, being a soldier," he said. "Well, we'll know by tomorrow what we're made of." Whereupon he wrapped himself in his greatcoat and lay down by the fire and in a moment was asleep.

It was disappointing. The night before a battle, the first battle, when one could not be sure if he were to prove coward or knave, there was a need for Peregrine's apothegms. Then it occurred to me that perhaps Peregrine needed some reassurances from me, some calmative to allay his own fears, but as I tried to consider for him how simple it was to be brave I could hear him snoring. Perhaps that was his message. We were going to need all the strength we had.

I was entitled, I thought, to more. Some inspiring invitation to valor, an indication that all the kingdom was watching. So I learned for the first time that the great events are impressive only in the perspective of history, and exhortation does not appear on a dusty battlefield except in a play by Shakespeare.

I listened to Peregrine snoring and the susurration and raspings and clinkings that came from thousands of men and horses up and down our side of the river, and I sat with my hands clasped around my knees and stared out at the twinkling lights across the river. Perhaps some Russian lad was sitting just so staring at me. He would be sixteen, like me, whether or not he had had to lie, like me, and he would by now have learned many things, as I had, and tomorrow I would kill him, or he would kill me. All in the name of his sovereign, or mine. I needed Peregrine then, to explain this, but he had shown it was time I learned by myself. It was too much to grasp, and I rested my head on my knees and slept.

In the morning there was a great bustle but no one knew what it was we were preparing to do. The river Alma sparkled in the valley; on the opposite slopes the Russians waited for their officers to make up their minds as we were waiting for ours. Horsemen dashed furiously from their regiments up to Raglan's tent and dismounted and in a moment came out again and jumped on their horses and dashed madly away as others rode up as madly.

We were told to keep ourselves in readiness.

"Don't eat anything," Peregrine said to me as I reached for a ration can.

"I haven't had breakfast."

"Forget about breakfast. You shouldn't have anything in your stomach in case you are wounded there."

I tried not to consider that.

Finally Raglan and his aides and the French and their staff

appeared to have come to a decision, and we were told to advance to the river in abreast formation. No one was sure how deep the water was, or how cold or how strong the current. To the staff officers, watching us through their glasses on the hill behind, all we had to do was ford the river and slaughter the enemy. The advance could be plotted simply on a map, using cardboard cutouts and a croupier's stick to push them with. Why, then, were we hesitating?

The slender straggling line of British infantry, each man with musket held high above the water, began to move forward. Peregrine, to my left, slowly keeping pace with me, kept up an irritable muttering. "Incompetence and insanity, I don't know which they have more of. Sending soldiers against enemy positions like this. There the Muscovites sit, a few hundred yards off, with all those heavy guns to blow us out of the water. On the map the river Alma is shown to be in direct line to Sevastopol, and we want to get to Sevastopol so we cross here. The fact that the Russians have many times our troops and guns—that's not considered. Raglan will sit back there on his horse with that special telescope of his attached to a rifle stock so he can use it with the one arm he has left, and he will observe us getting killed while Nolan, his ambitious assistant, will say, 'God, I wish I were down there.'"

"They are not firing yet. Why are they not firing?"

"Because they have yet to overcome their amazement that we are actually advancing on them. They can't believe it. The elephant sits and watches as a line of mice approaches. His first problem is to overcome his astonishment."

I lost contact with Peregrine as the current grew stronger and the enemy began to shell us—geysers going up as the balls struck—and the man to my right stepped in a deep hole and I tried to snatch him free but I was too late and soon his drowned body with floating pack drifted away. By this effort I was turned around and for a while I walked backward, compounding the dreadfulness of frontal attack. Here and there a soldier was taken out by grapeshot or cannon ball and we tried to close the gap because shoulder-to-shoulder formation produced a continuous life of fire, except that we were not firing; it was taking all our effort to remain upright and advancing. Some soldiers, thirst-crazed from fever, walked with heads down to the water level, scooping in mouthfuls. I called to Peregrine, but the crash of the Russian guns reverberating from the cliffs made all other sound impossible.

We reached the other shore—those still able—and climbed frantically up the slope toward the enemy, shouting more from hysteria than battle cry. Corporal Greenbriar, having located a patch of beach from which his orange-colored hair could be visible, established himself and began to shout commands. I remembered what he had said about distinguishing himself in battle to gain promotion, and now the glasses of the high command would be on him.

Halfway up the rise I looked toward him and he was no longer there; that is, he was there but his head was not. The rest of him stood still for a moment with one arm still lifted. I stood transfixed that a body should end at the shoulders, and as I watched it fell. Then I was up the hill with the others, shouting I know not what, with musket at the ready though I did not stop to load. The smoke in the air made me choke and tears started but there were none for Corporal Greenbriar or for the bodies I stepped over and around to continue the climb. Because I remember that I was not thinking of anything, and grief needs thought. Sounds came from my throat as if my vocal cords were on loan to another, a steady shrieking, a killing sound.

The fortunate ones died quickly; the others were mangled, as round shot, grapeshot shells, and musketry volleys made the air unsafe. And then the Russians took their guns and dragged them away. Which meant the scraggly stumbling men of the infantry were invincible.

Now the second line should have come in to make good the achievement of the first. That was an axiom of war. But no second line was brought in, and the enemy was spared to fight again. We could have turned the Russian defeat into a rout then, taken Sevastopol, and a year of torment might have been averted, but the generals hesitated.

I stopped now to see where I was, not having looked about me before. A wide street of dead and wounded stretched the whole length from the river upward. The ground was littered with muskets, clothing, equipment of all sorts. The wounded—Russian and British and French—sobbed and screamed and called out for help. I did not see any doctors.

I examined myself, starting at my head and working downward, and I appeared to be whole. Then I went looking for Peregrine. I stepped over bodies, resisting pleas for help. I saw an officer sitting with his back to a rock, hands on his knees. There were no limbs below. "They might have left me one," he said fretfully. There were groans and cries for water. The artillery had scattered headless trunks, arms, and legs. There were broken weapons, bugles, helmets, trampled rations. Blood filled the hollows and stained the river.

Then I saw Peregrine, back to me, sitting with one elbow on a cartridge box, and above my relief at having found him I thought how characteristic it was that in the midst of the carnage Peregrine was taking his rest. I called and when he did not answer I went around to face him, and my stomach heaved and there was a pain in my heart so sharp I will never feel its like again, despite the enormity of any tragedy that might befall me. Peregrine's lower jaw and the front of his throat had been torn away. Yet his eyes showed that there was still life in him; they lighted up upon seeing me and I said nothing because there was nothing to say and he said nothing because he had nothing left with which to speak. I thought that it was a sin that he still lived. He could not move and all communication came from his eyes, which now fastened on mine with a terrifying insistence as if he had taken what life was left and concentrated it.

"What should I do, Peregrine?"

He looked at me, down to my musket, and back to my face. There was no question what it was he wanted and no question that I had to do it. I put a ball in and primed it and he watched approvingly and I put the barrel against his head and pulled the trigger. It was the first shot I had fired in the war.

I turned cold after that. I saw sights to tear hearts apart and I was unmoved. The dead lay in heaps. The wounded lay without succor. There were no bandages or splints, no chloroform or laudanum. So had the government prepared for war, forgetting the price that had to be paid for victories. The wounded were stacked on soiled straw or old doors. Since the cries made sleep impossible, I, along with some others, spent the night fetching water for those still living. Not one man in five saw a doctor. When one appeared it was to perform an amputation—on the ground and without sedation—because Dr. Hall, principal medical officer of the army, did not believe in anesthesia. I heard one officer say, "Now I believe Wellington. He said that next to a battle lost there is nothing so dreadful as a battle won."

The doctors poured cold water in the faces of their victims and took off legs. I saw four amputations, and each man died immediately upon the removal of the limb. In the morning I helped dig pits to bury the dead. The sick and wounded were jolted in litters and arabas to the river mouth to be lifted into boats for Scutari.

We saw strange birds appear in the sky. "Vultures," someone said. "There have never been vultures before in this part of the world."

The siege was laid before Sevastopol, supplies being brought up from Balaclava eight miles away. By day it rained and at night it turned bitter cold. There was scurvy, dysentery, skin disease, the ever-present cholera. The army was disintegrating, and the enemy had nothing to do with it. Except that we could estimate that their rate of attrition could not be less than ours, keeping our comparative strength the same. We were never wholly dry, never clean. Scabies and fleas and lice made their abodes on our bodies. There were times when I envied the fate of Corporal Greenbriar, so smoothly had he been toppled.

I would not let myself think of Alethea, as I would not bring even the thought of her into all this suffering and degradation. I talked little and sought no man's company. As I would not think of Alethea so I would not think of Peregrine Jarvis, who had made life brighter for me. The loss of him could not be borne (except were he present to make it bearable).

The Turks took the opportunity to loot. One tried Hitch's tent, to come shrieking out in flight pursued by Mrs. Hitch wielding her lethal frying pan. Hitch had acquired some grapeshot in his backside which Mrs. Hitch was extracting at a slow rate, figuring to keep him an invalid and out of combat as long as possible. O'Malley had disappeared, whether dead, and his body lost, or captured. Jocaren, the boy from Cornwall, had lost a hand and was in one of the makeshift hospitals in Balaclava. Cochran, who had railed at the Hitches for combining marital and military, would take no pleasure again in a return to his own hearthside, having received a wound in his groin, *de nihilo nihil*. I had come through outwardly unscathed, but there was a wound in my mind. It was as if an extra layer of air stood between myself and the world. I was as before in that I responded to hunger and thirst and conversation, but I felt a calcification of the spirit. I walked about pretending to be a soldier, and no one noticed that I had become a stone.

One morning some pale sunlight appeared and everyone rushed to spread out their sodden clothing. I was basking, face up and eyes closed, when I heard, "Isn't that O'Boy?" I opened my eyes to see standing over me the officer who owned Sultan. He was not muddied and unwashed and filthily garbed as I was, as all the common soldiers were. I did not resent that. Peregrine had taught me humility. Officers deserved more than infantrymen because they were of superior intelligence and breeding and had been able to afford their commissions.

"Sir," I said, starting to get up.

Terence Bright put his hand on my shoulder. "No need for that. If you don't mind, I'd like to sit and talk to you for a moment."

"I don't mind, sir."

There was no place for him to sit. He hunkered down, keeping his bottom well clear of the mud. "I've been thinking of seeking you out, O'Boy, but we've been in the middle of a gallimaufry, haven't we."

"I've heard it called worse." And quickly, "Sir."

"You were at the Alma?"

"Yes, sir."

"You came through all right, then."

"I was lucky, sir."

"You were indeed. With the cholera at Varna, besides."

"How did you know that, sir?"

"I inquired." Bright smiled.

He was not a handsome man. There was a self-indulgence about his face, excess flesh under his jaw, and a slight prissiness about his mouth.

Although Bright had prevented me from rising, I sat with a stiffness in my shoulders since there was no way for a man from the ranks and a commissioned officer to relax together, even squatting in the mud.

"Can I tell you something straight out, O'Boy?"

"Certainly, sir."

"I'd like to be your friend."

I smiled weakly, wondering what he was talking about.

"Of course, the army doesn't permit that sort of thing, I mean officers associate with officers and the enlisted rank with themselves and never the twain shall meet except when orders are given. We both understand that."

"Of course," I said.

"It's not alone that you saved my life, you really did, you know, and my gratitude—" He blinked and turned away. "If ever— well, you have only to call upon me."

"Thank you, sir."

"It's not that alone, you see. I just feel that we can be friends." He put his hand on my shoulder. "Richard, isn't it?"

"Yes, sir." I didn't need a friend. Especially not one wearing the insignia of a captain.

"Good." He smiled and nodded in satisfaction as if I had indicated approval. "You must call me Terence. That is, when no one is about to hear. You understand that it would not do for you to use my first name if anyone is about."

"Yes, sir." I assumed he had been drinking. Officers consumed cases of champagne, especially because of its therapeutic value against the cholera.

"The sad truth is, Richard, I have no friends at all. It's a dreadful thing to be in a war and have no friends. Wouldn't you say?"

"Yes, sir," I said.

"I was determined on an army career since I was a child. I used to cut out pictures of officers from the magazines and put them up on the wall of my room. I never wanted to be anything but an officer. But my father is in trade, not a very successful man. You understand how it is, Richard."

"Yes, sir," I said.

"So buying a commission was quite out of the question, and besides one needed a private income to live as a gentleman, but I managed an appointment to Sandhurst and that made me an officer, without purchase, and I must live on my allowances. That is not only difficult, but my fellow officers hold me in contempt, and for that reason. Can you understand that, Richard?"

"Yes, sir. I mean, no, sir."

"I'm certainly as well educated as any man on the staff, probably better than most. I believe I know more about military tactics. But there are no nobles in my lineage, no knights, no baronets, not even a landowner. The long and short of it, Richard, is that I don't belong."

I tried to look sympathetic. I even felt—slightly—understanding. I remembered what Corporal Greenbriar had said, headless Corporal Greenbriar. "We're in a war, now, sir, and that's different from the army in peacetime. An officer can distinguish himself in a war."

Bright nodded eagerly, not so much at what I said as at the fact that we were at least holding a conversation.

"What you said is true enough, Richard. They're striking a new medal now; it is to be in the Queen's name. The Victoria Cross. I think a man who winds up with one of those need never be concerned about his family tree."

"Exactly, sir," I said.

"It isn't necessary to call me sir when we are talking together like this. We can pretend that we're just two friends talking."

"I don't know how I can do that, sir," I said. "I appreciate what you have told me, but I don't think I could forget the respect that is due your position."

"That is admirable of you, Richard. I would want you to think that way, yet at the same time I would like you to understand that despite my rank I'm a person like yourself. So let's try, shall we?"

I didn't know what it was he wanted me to try. I did not want to be his friend; I could not pretend that a captain and a soldier like myself could be friends. And I remembered what Peregrine had said about not letting this man come too close, and although I didn't know what Peregrine had meant, he had practiced sortilege well enough to know which of us was first to die.

"How is it you come to the army, Richard?"

I shrugged and did not answer.

"It wasn't for the food and a uniform as it was for the others. I suspect you've had schooling. University?"

If I answered his questions we might be on the way to the friendship he wanted. If I were unresponsive I might offend him, and one did not give offense to one's captain. Yet I resented his offer. If I had gone up to him and suggested friendship I would have been lashed for familiarity.

"Latin? You studied Latin?"

I shrugged.

"And Greek?"

"Some," I said.

Captain Bright nodded happily. "I might have been a scholar myself but the army came first. If it weren't for my love of the military I would have gone to Oxford and read history. Do you like the study of history?"

"I do," I said. "I've read Suetonius—"

"I'm just so happy that we can talk together like this. It's been so long—" He shook his head. "They either ignore me or—once I heard two of them discussing my accent. Do you find anything strange in my accent, Richard?"

"You sound like Oxford or Cambridge to me, sir."

Bright beamed.

"What happened to Sultan?" I said.

"He broke both legs on the ship from Varna. I never even got to ride him in the field."

"I'm sorry to hear that." I had left out the *sir*. I was still wary, but perhaps I was as much in need of fellowship as he. Hitch smoked a pipe and said little, Mrs. Hitch was reminder that sanity still existed, but Peregrine had left an awful chasm.

"I'm in command of your company now," Bright said.

"Why?" I said. "We're foot soldiers."

"They said we're half strength, what with Alma and the cholera, heavy losses in officers as well as men. We know the real reason, of course. But I'll make the best of it. Perhaps with your help, Richard."

How could I help him?

"Where is your home, Richard?"

I told him.

"I'm from Sussex myself. I miss the trees and the fields. No place in the world is as green as England."

"I agree with that."

He stood up, stretching his hands on the small of his back. "I've seen the Turks squat like that for hours. I suppose you have to be born to it. Richard, do you play chess?"

"Well, I know how but—"

"Excellent. I carry a small case. It's in my tent; why don't you go and fetch it for me?"

"Yes, sir," I said, rising smartly.

He apologized with a turn of his hand. "That wasn't an order, of course. I'll get it myself and we can meet near the bluff there, there are some flat rocks and—" He smiled. "We won't be seen."

I needed Peregrine so we could laugh together. Of course we would be seen, and Bright would be derided (except his state of ostracism already existed), and I would be seen as a toady (except there was no one whose opinion mattered). It was better, however, than the nothingness into which I had sunk, as anything would have been better.

We found a spot beyond the encampment, and the captain brought out the traveling set with the miniature pieces and we set up the board. Heretofore my only opponent had been myself, as I had taught myself to play from a book I had taken from the library at Clamford and practiced with pieces I had fashioned. I opened tentatively and soon discovered that Bright played cautiously and with little flair. I found myself tearing into him joyously and watched his play become confused.

"An excellent situation for chess play, wouldn't you say, Richard? Here we have the ground troops and the cavalry and all we lack are the bishops. The castle is Sevastopol. Raglan and the French general—I can never pronounce his name—they're me, and you're Menshiko. You don't mind being the Russian?"

"No, sir."

He made a disappointed face. "Call me Terence."

"All right," I said, but I could not.

The sun came out a little stronger and dried the mud on me. I could feel the caking. Bright looked as if he had just been turned out by a solicitous batman. The circumstance was incongruous, false, and perhaps dangerous.

I made a mistake and Bright gleefully captured my bishop. He was preening; he cared about winning. I casually brought up a knight to back up my queen and in my next move checked him.

"Ah," he said, pulling at his lower lip.

"I think, Captain," I said, "it won't do."

"Your move? Too late to change it, you know."

"I meant that we'll be noticed."

"Don't you worry, Richard. Nothing will happen to you."

The Russian guns sounded and ours answered. A horse whinnied and there was the sound of musketry in the distance. A war was being fought out there. I wanted to believe that I was apart from it. A pair of chess players in the sun. Some of the stone in me began to flake and I began to feel my body was whole, if still somewhat weakened by the cholera, and the cloud which had settled in my head began to disperse. Bright moved in a rook to counter the threat from my queen and I pointed out that it was unprotected. He quickly moved it away. I was the better chess player. A dirty mud-covered soldier was superior to the resplendent officer. I grinned to myself and thought how Peregrine would have been pleased.

"This damned stupid war," said Bright.

Peregrine would have pointed out that all wars were damned and stupid.

"They have no notion what they're about. After Alma we could have put them to rout, but Raglan, as always, hesitated and Cardigan would not commit his brigade. We might have pushed them out of Sevastopol and the war would have been over. Raglan diddles, balancing that damned glass of his with one hand. You know what saves us, Richard? Only that the Russians plan as stupidly as we. Do you have a girl at home?"

It came too suddenly not to have been calculated. There was a girl always in my thoughts, I said to myself.

Bright began to talk quickly. "I was married for two years. And then one morning she walked out. Not a word, not a note, she was just gone. You know what I did, Richard? I sat in the bed-sitter that we had near the camp and I cried. Would you believe that, Richard? A grown man and a soldier. And then I laughed, because the truth of it was I was glad to get rid of her. Of all girls, if you want the truth. Which of them are worth the trouble they cause? She was pretty—beneath me, of course; her father had a small shop; he sold bric-a-brac. She was very young. We had an arrangement, her father and I. When I graduated from Sandhurst we were to be married. She was a child, I decided to raise her to my own level. I gave her books to read, taught her manners. She was cold in bed, so pretty and cold in bed."

What man could speak of his life to another man in this fashion? I decided he had been drinking. He proved it, taking out a flask and offering it to me. I shook my head.

"Come," he said, "two men together, friends." He handed the flask to me.

I choked, the liquid burned.

"Aqua ardente. One should always sample the wine of the country." He took a long drink. "Tell me about your girl, Richard. Did she let you touch her? I suppose she did, a strapping fellow like you. Do you like girls, Richard? I mean really like them, or is it just that you think a man is supposed to?" He put his hand on my knee. "No great crime if you don't. They waste a man's time, and they have a tendency to be unfeeling. Have you ever felt that, Richard?"

"I don't know," I said. "Perhaps."

"I knew it," he said. He stood up. "Duty calls and all that. By the way Richard, your corporal—what was his name?"

"Greenbriar."

"Yes. I'll be needing a replacement for him, won't I. I'll have to think about that. Well, I've enjoyed our little talk, Richard. I hope we can have another soon." He waved and was off, picking his way fastidiously over the rough ground.

Peregrine, who had warned me about this man, had not known him. Bright was an earnest friendly fellow who was honestly in need of someone with whom he could talk freely. As Peregrine and I had talked. There was certainly no harm in it. In a day or two he sought me out again, again offering me his flask. This time I sipped more cautiously and found the instant warming effect more agreeable.

"Richard, have you tried the Turks' hubble-bubble pipe?"

"Yes. I do not care for it."

"Nor do I. But I like their style of rolling tobacco in paper. Have you tried that?"

"No, I have not."

"I've got some here." He took out some bits of paper and gave me one to hold while he extracted some finely ground tobacco from a pouch and put a pinch in his paper and mine. I tried to emulate the way he held it between his fingers. He rolled it back and forth and made a cone and I tried the same thing. He lit his fat cylinder and my loose one and mine went up in flame and I spat it out.

"It takes a while to learn the art." He took his from between his lips and offered it to me. I took a puff and gave it back.

"I'll tell you what I don't like, Richard. I don't like sleeping alone."

There were many French tarts following the army. I was going to bring that to his attention but decided I had better not. It began to rain and a wind sprang up and we went into the lean-to I had constructed in poor imitation of the one Peregrine had fashioned.

"You live like this, do you?" said Bright, sitting on my pack and folding his arms around his knees. "A man needs more comfort than this."

"I think I have learned that the army does not want its soldiers to be comfortable. Who would want to leave a place that's warm and dry to answer an alarm?" I had forgotten who my listener was. Was that what Peregrine had meant, that I might say something injudicious and find myself painfully disciplined?

Bright did not appear affronted. He said, "You haven't called me Terence."

"Terence," I said.

"I like the sound of my name on your lips. Have you no special friend, Richard?"

"I had one."

"And—?"

I saw Peregrine with his throat open and then I saw a stranger raise a musket and shoot him. To an unobservant watcher that boy could have been I.

"He's dead," I said.

"Ah," Bright said. Death in the Crimea was a natural condition. "We're all part of a ghastly mistake. We shouldn't be here, but no one has the courage to send us home. I want to tell you something, Richard. May I tell you something?"

"Certainly."

"I'm sick of the army," Bright said. "The ambition of a lifetime tarnished and diminished. I think, as soon as this is over, I am going to resign my commission. I'm going to live someplace where it's warm. Italy or Spain. Perhaps I'll paint."

"I wish I had a talent like that," I said.

"What are you talented at, Richard?"

"Nothing, I suppose."

"I can't believe that. You *look* like a talented person. What did your father do?"

"He's a farmer. But before that—"

"Yes?"

"My father used to be in the prize ring."

"Really?"

"Yes, he's a man of great strength. And quick, too. He taught me something of the art—"

"Well, well," Bright said, reaching over and feeling my arm. "You are strong yourself, aren't you. Of course it was evident when you saved me from Sultan on the ship. So your father taught you to fight."

"We practiced together every Sunday afternoon." Who takes advantage of your instruction now, Father? Peter? Why should not you and he become friends, you have so much in common. Differences in position don't matter. Look at me, taking my ease with an officer. Then I was sick of hating, and I felt grateful to Terence Bright. I smiled at him, and he began to squeeze my arm in little movements. It made me uncomfortable and I straightened up but he did not let go.

"What's going to happen with this war?" I said.

"Terence. You must be able to use my name—*sans souci*? My French is not of the best. Try, will you?"

"Terence," I said.

"Good. The war? I've already expressed my opinion about that. What can you expect when it's being run by old men? Do you know most of the general staff is over sixty? And they can't see, only Lord Lucan doesn't need glasses."

"I think I would like to go home," I said.

"To whom?" Bright said.

To Alethea, who was probably thinking of me at that moment, worrying about me, probably weeping at night at the thought that she had helped send me here. I would come home and in her gratitude she would—

"Tell me about your girl," said Bright, moving his fingers down my arm and taking my hand. "Girls are all right, when they're available. But when they are not—"

The alarm sounded and I jumped for my musket.

"Sentries get bored and frightened," Bright said. "They see ghosts."

I still had to report. We milled around uncertainly because there were no orders. After a while most of us dispersed. Bright was gone. The last person to have held my hand was my father, and he had stopped when I was five. I had wanted the touch of Alethea's hand. But men did not sit with their hands together.

Terence Bright was a mystery to me, but he was antidote to the cold and the dirt and the danger. I had tried isolation and the suspension of thought to recover from the salty coldness of Peregrine's death and it had not worked well. My misery had not diminished.

The next time I saw Bright, he said, smiling, "War makes strange bedfellows, does it not? But for a Turkish and Russian disagreement across the world we would never have met. And here we are of an age, but I have the commission and you have not. Have you ever considered the awesome power that gives me over you?" He smiled again; it was not pleasant but rather somewhat disturbing.

Of an age. He considered I had to be at least eighteen else the army would have rejected me. And he was probably as old as Peregrine.

"You never told me why you became a soldier, Richard. And if you wanted to, why not have tried for a commission? Had your father no wealthy friends? Had you none?"

I almost told him. Of Peter and Alethea and Sir James and my father. I said, "Did not the country need troops? England was going to war."

"Are you pulling my leg, Richard? Patriotism?"

I looked blandly back at him.

"No matter. The time has come, Richard, for perhaps a little more directness. You appeal to me mightily. So tonight—let us say at midnight—I would like you to come to my tent."

"I'm on guard duty."

"I can take care of that."

"I would rather not," I said, leaving it open whether I meant his taking me off guard or my going to visit him.

"Rather not?" while he considered my meaning, and *"Rather not!"* when he decided I referred to his invitation.

I watched his choler rise and then subside as he gained control. "I have some respectable things to eat, Richard, and there's some wine and we can forget this damned war."

I knew that when I came off guard duty there would be nothing I wanted so much as sleep. So I told him that. There were a number of things about Bright I did not understand, but I knew that despite his insistence on our Terence and Richard association he was never completely forgetful that we were officer and common soldier. Nor was I. I was sixteen and fresh from the farm and I did not know what he wanted.

"I could order you," he said, smiling.

"Then I would have to obey," I said.

"But I want you to come of your own free will."

It seemed like a lot of fuss over one friend going to see another.

"Let's leave it at this, Richard. I want you to join me, and I shall expect to see you. If you prefer not to, that's of course your own affair, isn't it." And with the smile set on his face he left.

The corporal of the guard looked puzzled. "I have you on my list for guard tonight but I was told to excuse you, I don't know for what reason. Now what is it? Are you excused or are you assigned?"

"I'm assigned," I said.

I took my musket and gear and went forward to spend the night looking at the watch fires of Sevastopol. No Russians attacked. A sleety rain began to fall and my greatcoat proved little protection against the creeping cold. It was not yet winter, by the calendar, and I wondered how one could withstand the cold then, and I decided it was bootless to worry about it because by winter I would be either out of the Crimea or dead.

I heard snatches of a mournful strain coming from the Russian encampment. Without understanding the words or having heard the melody before, I knew what they were singing about. If only the war were over, if only they were home again. Since each of us felt the same, was it not the height of absurdity that we faced each other for the purpose of mutual destruction?

The rain came down the back of my forage cap into my neck, then between my shoulder blades, there to collect in an icy puddle. Perhaps, I thought, I would die this night. Not from an enemy ball or from a fever but from misery alone. I walked up and down for a while and flailed my arms, and when that brought little relief I bowed my head to turn myself into a farm animal. I had seen horses and cows standing that way in the rain, not moving, withstanding by acceptance. Then I thought that the only thing one can learn from an animal is how to be an animal. So I got up and walked back and forth again and I dared the Russians to attack because I was capable of killing—had I not killed my one friend in the world?

I begged you to, old friend. I would have done it for you. I was dead anyway, and you saved me pain.

I miss you, Peregrine.

I miss you, too.

What is it like where you are?

I cannot tell you. I would like to tell you but there are no words. Just one thing, Richard.

What is that?

Do not be afraid of death.

Should it be welcomed, then?

No. There are many things you have to do.

Peregrine, what sort of man is Captain Bright? Why did you warn me about him?

He is not your friend, and he must not become your friend.

Then I have no friends.

Stop being so solemn. Enjoy the evening.

Enjoy it? The rain is so cold it burns. My bones are awash. My feet are sloshing. I want to be warm and dry. Will I ever be warm and dry again, Peregrine?

Do not be so concerned with the trivial.

What is important, then?

Listen to the singing. How clear is the message. Queen Victoria is warm and dry. Will she ever know how you feel this night?

She is the Queen.

The Czar is warm and dry. Will he ever know how that singer feels?

I know you now, Peregrine. You are an anarchist.

No. I think, therefore I am. I want you to do that. Where is Greenbriar?

Dead.

O'Malley?

Dead or taken prisoner.

Hitch?

Wounded.

Jocaren?

Lost his hand.

And on his yacht Cardigan is sitting down to a late supper prepared by the French chef he brought along.

Peregrine, you left too soon. There are things I don't understand. What must I do with the captain?

Shun him.

Will you watch over me for a while yet?

Not for much longer. You can't be a boy, you know. You must turn into a man quickly.

What about fear? At the Alma I saw a ball come bounding toward me and my trousers were wet.

You're brave enough.

Will I see Alethea again?

Oh, yes.

Thank you, Peregrine.

Chapter Seven

When I was relieved as sentry I stumbled back in the direction of my tent, and it wasn't important that I be clean again, or safe and warm, or even a man exercising his brain with ideas. I didn't want those things since they were never going to be possible anyway, and what I wanted now more than anything was sleep, because sleep was a little death.

So that the horse prancing now in front of me was a nuisance, and when I went to walk around it it got in my way again, and such was my need for some temporary unconsciousness that, forgetting that atop the horse would be someone of superior rank, in a moment I would have ripped my bayonet up into the animal's belly. With effort I raised my head to warn the horseman, seeing only that he was all in blue and pink and a member of Cardigan's Light Cavalry Brigade. He was as clean as I was filthy, and he wheeled his horse with little showy movements of feet as if he were performing on Rotten Row for the benefit of the great ladies out for a ride.

I stepped out, and I was blocked again; this time it was obviously done on purpose, and I said, "Out of my way, damn you," but slurring the words. I was not so poisoned by fatigue that I forgot the consequences of so addressing an officer.

"What?" he said in his mightiness, his face in shadow.

I said, "You're in my way, sir," but the *sir* I handed him was the sort one gives to equals before a challenge.

"You're dirty," the horseman said. "You're as dirty as a guttersnipe. Where's your pride in yourself, where's your pride in your regiment?" And the horse pranced some more and I could not get by.

"Sir," I said, "I live in mud. My friends have died in the mud. I have no horse to separate me from the mud."

"He's just the same," said the rider. "Just as cross-grained and hard-bitten as ever."

He? As ever?

He turned his head, taking the shadow from it.

"No," I said. "It is not possible."

"I agree, but it is still so."

"I'll be damned," I said. "How did you—?"

"It is certainly a strange thing. Cardigan sought to fill out his brigade and I was sitting at Aldershot, waiting. And here I am. And there you are. Richard, I did not expect to see you again."

"Nor I you, Peter."

At first, and despite the circumstances of our parting, I was glad to see him. He was reminder of home, and of Alethea. And at first he must surely have felt the same, except that he would have recalled our last meeting more sharply than I. So there was no leaping from horse for embrace of joy.

"Excuse me, Peter. I have been up all night at sentry duty and I must sleep. Can I arrange to see you later?"

He surveyed me from his eminence and considered what role he should adopt. He might have forgiven my handling of him and played at being friends; after all, we two were from the same small corner of England, met by chance on this most foreign of shores.

"Peter?" he said. "I am Lieutenant Nott-Playsaunt. And you are a foot soldier. Ramsey, isn't it?"

"My name," I said, "is O'Boy."

"Indeed?"

"A change was offered through error. I decided to keep it."

"The new life, is it? Can one start anew and ignore the old?"

"I must get some sleep now," I said, feeling my limbs turning to treacle and his words stretching out in my head.

"You, tired? Richard the Lion Heart? He of the mighty fist?"

"Another time, Peter," I said.

"And will you not ask of Alethea?"

"Is she all right?"

"She misses you."

I had dared not hope for that.

"Before I left she mentioned you. How amusing it had been

to toy with you. You were so serious and doltish. Her favorite word for you—doltish."

I could not believe that here in the stench of the dying Peter could play at his favorite game. His smile was cautiously taunting. His eyes were narrowly assessing which way the cornered animal would jump. One jabbed in needle by needle without knowing whether this torture or the next would turn the domestic beast feral. He had played the game with me often enough until the consequences had brought me to this place. Now he played it again and toward what end?

With great skill he maneuvered his mount to keep me in one place.

"Really, Peter," I said.

"You are insolent—O'Boy. Do you not know the difference between you and an officer?"

"Let me go," I said.

"The last time we met—do you recall the last time we met, Richard?"

"I remember."

"You had me by the throat with that ham of a hand of yours raised to strike me."

"What do you want of me?" I said.

"Sir."

"Sir," I said.

He was using the horse now to make me move backward. I was ready to fall on my face with exhaustion. I was still not what I had been before the cholera. To look up at Peter I had to look into the sun, and I was beginning to see double images. I was at the state in which Peter would need only one prick more.

Don't you see what he's about, I heard Peregrine say. His aim is to make you lose control. He knows if he can achieve that you will oblige him by destroying yourself.

I am calm. I have never been calmer.

I could hear Campbell talking to his Highlanders fifty yards away. "Soldiers have nothing to do with the cause of quarrels, their duty is to fight; but in this instance you have a noble cause to fight for: the protection of the weak by the strong." He had the best disciplined unit in the army, maybe because each of them knew that if they did commit a serious offense his name would be written up on the porch of the local kirk at home for all to see. "You will stand shoulder to shoulder, you men of the Ninety-third, and if anybody is wounded he must lie where he falls until the bandsmen come to attend to him. No soldiers are to go carrying off wounded men."

"So you changed your name," said Peter. "One can hardly blame you. Richard Ramsey was certainly not a name of which to be proud."

I thought that if I could take him by the one leg and pull him from the horse and roll him in the mud it would afford me all the pleasure I needed. Just to roll his elegance in the mud.

"Nothing to say, Richard? I have never known you to be short of words."

I was silent, and he blocked me with his horse.

"Now you can see the great gulf between us, Richard. You down there, muddy and disgusting-looking and myself mounted and, if I may say so, quite well turned out in this cherrypicker garb. So now if you will salute me—I do not insist on obeisance—I will let you depart."

He did not disturb me. Who cared about the affectations of a Peter Nott-Playsaunt?

"By the way, Richard, I bring you tidings of your family. Your mother and father have been quarreling so over your joining the army that the entire village can quote them, they scream so at each other. Your father said your mother never was a mother to you—I don't know how he could say that; surely a woman would know if she birthed her own child. If, however, he had questioned his own fatherhood I would understand that better."

"Enough," I said.

"Of course a gentleman does not speak of such matters, I was merely recounting what is public knowledge. So although they have turned your little farm into Billingsgate with their squabbling, I will say no more. Meanwhile, Alethea—"

"What about Alethea?"

"It is piteous to hear her name coming from your mouth. I told her you had a passion for her, which made her laugh. But she did say she misses you."

I had to close my ears to the other things he said to annoy me, I had to tell myself that he would make up any wild tale toward that end. But Alethea—from whom else could I get news of her? "What of Alethea?" I said.

"She misses you, she told me so. Her boots, she said, have never been so clean as when you were about."

"Peter," I said. "Hear me. I know now the mistake I made. I did not hit you hard enough. One day the time will come, and your nose and mouth will know my fist and your nose will be spread over your face like a second skin and you will have no teeth left."

"You bastard," he said, his voice rising shrilly. He looked about as if for a witness. "How dare you, how dare you—"

And then coming toward us was Captain Terence Bright, my friend, who would not let harm come to me, and so I pulled Peter from his horse and hit him with the back of my hand, just hard enough to knock him into the mud. That was all I wanted. He came up spluttering and reached for his sword and came at me. I had to counter with my bayonet. We squared off and perhaps, had Bright not been there, perhaps this would have been the ultimate confrontation between Peter Nott-Playsaunt and myself. As it was, foot soldier to officer, I would pay for this before a firing squad.

Bright said, "Hold on, now. Hold on."

"Captain," Peter said. "You saw it. You saw it all."

"Did you fall from your horse?" Bright said.

I laughed to myself. I was secure then in his protection.

"Dragged, sir," Peter said.

Then I looked up at the Causeway heights and gulped and without words pointed. Like that bit from mythology, it was as if soldiers sprang up from seed cast on the ground. Russian cavalry, coming toward us. They had found the weak point to break through to Balaclava, from which all our supplies came. Our main forces were deployed on the flank; only Campbell's few hundred Highlanders faced the Russians.

Cursing, Peter leaped to his saddle and rode off. Terence Bright, who did not allow military affairs to interfere with his personal concerns, said, "You did not come to me last night, Richard. I waited for you."

I could not reply; his disappointment was too monstrously insignificant. I looked at the advancing Russians, moving their horses at a walk, their might designed to strike terror by numbers alone. When they were a half mile away Campbell shouted an order and the long scarlet double rank formed, their kilts moving in the wind. The front rank knelt, the second stood behind. "No retreat," shouted Campbell. "Here you stand."

"I won't ask you again," Bright said.

The Russian guns fired ahead of their horsemen. When a scarlet figure fell, the space was closed by the men on either side. The Russians moved to a trot, sabers drawn. Then the Scotsmen fired, a concentrated volley, and the ranks of the Russians wavered, then broke. Men screamed, horses reared, and there was a great tangled bloody mass. The Russians re-formed. The men of the 93rd fired again. The Russians moved back toward the heights.

"Do you have a reason, a good reason for not having come?" Bright said.

I almost turned to call him an idiot. Was he not aware of the miracle we had just witnessed? The thin red line of marksmen had stood firm against enemy cavalry many times their number.

"You can't expect me to keep making the offer again and again," Bright said.

What offer was he talking about? I watched Surgeon Munro go among the men, using chloroform if he had to operate despite the injunction of his senior medical officer.

"So be it then," Bright said.

Peter Nott-Playsaunt came dashing back, riding magnificently, his pelisse flaring behind him. He was, I thought, born to the cavalry. They seemed to ride at random, except when formed for attack, those peacocks of horsemen, always at top speed; and I could never understand what they were supposed to be accomplishing.

Peter brought his horse up sharply and said, "Well? Well, Captain?"

"Well, what?" I said.

"Do you hear his insolence, sir? In addition to having assaulted an officer, do you hear his insolence?"

"He's insolent, well enough," Bright said.

We had just seen one of the great heroic feats, the isolated action to be remembered when the war itself would be forgotten. And the two officers discussed my insolence, immune to the dead and wounded so short a distance away.

"I want him punished," Peter said.

"And so he shall be," said Bright.

Ah, no, I protested silently. You spoke of our being friends. A friend doesn't speak of punishment.

"I knew him in England," Peter said. "For the sake of his father and mother who farmed on my father's land, I would spare his life."

Peter, I thought, I've misjudged you.

"But I would suggest at the very least he should be flogged."

Again? Where are you now, Schoolmaster Fudd?

"That seems fitting," said Bright.

Friendship? Had he not come to me decrying the gap between us, insisting that we could overcome it?

Bright said, "What, in the army, is more important than the maintaining of discipline?"

What, indeed. I was not yet fully grown but I was almost completely educated. And in the morning when they stripped me and I waited for the drum major to lay on the strokes, I said to myself, Is it not fitting that one pay for education?

Pain can be borne more easily than degradation. It is the nature of such punishment that it attacks the soul as well as the body. Hatred feeds upon it. No one can come through a whipping feeling benevolent or instructed. The mind flutters. They would turn me into a dog or a horse but I would neither neigh nor bark.

I was given fifty strokes, I counted the first fifteen, after which there was a red miasma before my eyes and I carefully, thoroughly, dismembered Peter Nott-Playsaunt and Terence Bright in my head.

When they cut me down I could not stand at first, and a soldier on either side helped me for a few paces until I shook them off. After that I walked very straight—it was not so much the pride as the pain of bending my back—and Peter came after me and, leaning down from his horse, whispered, "Damn you, Richard, do you finally understand? All this has happened because you are inferior."

When I next saw him he was one of the acolytes attending Lord Cardigan. If one had to go to war, I thought, was not that the proper way for an English gentleman? His accouterments flashed in the sunlight and as yet he had suffered no insult to his uniform. He could have been attending a fancy ball or sitting on an anxious charger waiting for the huntsman's horn—a hard exhilarating ride, followed by ale and a pipe and stories of chasms leaped and brambles defeated. If a rider sometimes broke a limb or sometimes his back, that was part of the excitement.

A foot soldier sees no more of a battle than an ant. But Russell of *The Times* was there, and he sent his dispatches home. I saw what I saw, and later I learned what was not there for me to see.

Cardigan's Light Brigade was churning with disappointment because they had not yet been committed. Scarlett's Heavies had charged uphill against a large Russian force and routed them, and had Cardigan then taken the enemy in the flank there would have been a great victory. But the "noble yachtsman"—thoroughly inexperienced as he was in war—would not move without precise orders, and Raglan's orders were notoriously vague.

The Russians had overrun the Turks' artillery positions and were beginning to move off the guns. Wellington had never lost a gun. Raglan was not going to allow a gun to be lost either. He would have committed all the British forces rather than suffer that humiliation. So he sent his firebrand aide, Nolan, to Cardigan with orders to rescue the guns. The redoubts were visible from where I was standing, and not so far into the fortified valley as to make the task impossible.

Nolan went tearing down to the plain with the orders. He had been chafing at his own inactivity, he believed the Light Brigade should have been in action before this, and he was delighted now to have a hand in it. The orders he carried, if one is to believe Raglan's intentions, were to take back those Turkish guns and nothing more.

Nolan delivered the orders and Cardigan, after perusing them, dressed his troops, 673 of them, and led them slowly forward. They moved up into that valley at the end of which were placed the heaviest of the Russian guns, while all the terrain was covered by enemy artillery on both sides. It was, as Lord Tennyson later put it, a valley of death. As we watched they reached the point at which they should have begun to wheel in a right turn toward the height from which the Turkish guns were being hauled away, but there was no sign of their changing directions. Instead, they continued toward the mouth of the valley, toward the Russian gunners. Steadily, not yet at full gallop.

No one believed what he was seeing. Not us, and not the Russians. Any soldier knows that the cavalry never advances into gun positions—horses are too valuable; one uses the infantry for that. If I had then been on the Russian side watching those immaculate horsemen coming at me, I would have suspected some trick, albeit one with the characteristic insanity of the British. True, at Alma the Russians could not believe that British troops would be ordered to ford a river into strongly held enemy positions, moving upright and exposed. True, the Russians had not believed Scarlett's charge, five hundred troops uphill into thousands of enemy forces. So now they watched this idiotic, suicidal advance and did not believe what they were seeing, but it worried them.

The message Nolan carried might have been altered by verbal additions of his own, but he was killed almost immediately, his testimony forever lost. Cardigan, up to then so cautious and dilatory, may have felt shame in having taken no part in the fighting and determined on an act so stupendously daring as to secure his name in history. His name surely is there, whether attached to heroism or idiocy.

Cardigan gave the order for the charge. That martinet of the playground, the yachtsman playing at war, was coolly out in front, and suddenly one loved him for it. Those lisping epicenes with their corseted waists were fighting like madmen, blunting their swords against the thick coats of the Russians, and one loved them for it. A man can be despised for what he appears to be and admired for what he is capable of.

The Russian gunners furiously poured shot into the crazed British horsemen, so careless of death. The screams of the horses could be heard above the sounds of battle. The ground shook from the cannonading; periodically, smoke obscured the scene and then lifted and with surprise one saw Englishmen still on horseback, still advancing, sabers forward over their charges' ears, shouting in a killing frenzy; and although shot scattered the brigade, the Russians must have been in terror of those decimated but still advancing British.

There was James Shegog of the 5th Dragoon Guards, a giant who, when his mount was killed by a carbine shot, scrambled to his feet, cursing, dragged a Russian from his saddle, killed him, vaulted onto the horse's back, and continued after his regiment. Private John Veigh of the Lancers, a butcher, grabbed the weapons of a dead comrade and went off wielding two swords, his shirt sleeves rolled up and already smeared with the blood of his trade. He cut down six Russians and lost his horse but he was unwounded and came back still wearing his butcher's smock and still smoking the short black pipe he had had in his mouth when he left.

Sergeant Talbot had his head carried off by a round shot while for another thirty yards his body continued to ride forward.

In our own ranks the infantrymen, spectators only, picked out enemy guns and gave them names—Bessie, Maggie, Anne— after the wives of unpopular officers. Obscene gibes were shouted at the balls as they came bouncing over the plain.

Once I spotted Peter as he met a large gray-coated Muscovite and unseated him. I felt a throb of pleasure. I wanted Peter between my hands so I could pluck him apart, but I did not want him hurt in battle.

Now all order was gone as riderless horses, mad with fear, impeded those still trying to move ahead; the squadron was shattered; each second another horse or rider went furrowing into the ground; and still there were those protected maniacs who fought their way through the battery with sabers and lances and the hooves of their own horses on the Russian gun crews, and a handful fought their way back through again and reached our lines, straggling in with dragging plumes and busbies, torn jackets and overalls, ripped sleeves and jackets, the gold lace torn off their backs. I admired their blundering unswerving courage, although some members of the infantry were heard to say, "Served them bloody right, the silly peacock bastards." Perhaps Wellington himself might have agreed. He hated unnecessary heroics. "There is nothing," he once said, "so stupid as a gallant officer."

Of 673 that started, 195 returned.

I did not see Peter again. Since the commonness of each day's killing and dying was dulling sensibility, if I had come across Peter I might have killed him. Why should that act have been of more consequence than the bodies rotting on the ground whose lives, up to that point, might have been passed in total innocence and purity? Since we have become no better than the Romans, and infinitely inferior to the Greeks, with the millenniums between graced principally by railroads and corsets, it is more important to develop resilience than outrage.

I was next sent as part of a supply train to Balaclava, an assignment I eagerly accepted, both to get away from the pounding of the Russian guns and because there was some slight promise of finding a piece of sky one could look up at without cowering. My shoulders now were almost always defensively hunched and the eye did not look out openly and directly but in a slightly squinting manner, to give full opportunity of ascertaining the periphery. I had never before appreciated the luxury of stretching one's own neck in the security of one's own countryside.

Balaclava proved to be worse than Varna or the battlefield after the Alma crossing or the plain before Sevastopol. It was repository for all the ghastly detritus of a war ill conceived and poorly supported. It was as if we had been gaily outfitted in military finery to be paraded before the public and then sent across the seas to be dropped in a huge cesspool.

Balaclava was a swamp dotted with hovels into which the sick, mostly from cholera, were crammed. Each day hundreds were buried with barely enough dirt to cover the bodies. On the beach where our supplies were unloaded were camels and horses and bullocks which, through sickness or exhaustion, had reached the point of uselessness and were left there to die. The ships in the harbor floated in a sea where parts of bodies bobbed. Dante Alighieri's levels of hell were scrubbed prettification compared to the reality of that Crimean town.

I thought that I had not seen anyone having anything to do with the course of this war, no decision-maker or speechifier, who had come to see and smell for himself. I thought that of old the British kings rode ahead of their troops into battle. Even Richard the First, who might better have remained at home to govern his people, spent most of his reign abroad to fight the infidels. But fight he did and smell the stink of the aftermath of war he did and see the result of steel and tooth and claw on frail flesh. Victoria would never see this, nor her ministers, nor Parliament. But I was not yet seventeen, and what did I know of government?

At Inkerman we fought the soldier's battle because the field of action was so concealed in fog that our officers on the heights could not see what was happening and so could give no orders. The Russians came down in gray waves, blending with the haze, and often we did not know if we were striking at man or mist. Their overcoats were like armor; we thrust at them, feeling our bayonets dulled, yet with a sigh or shriek the soldier dropped. I don't know how many I killed or wounded and there was no pleasure in it, not even the joy of hatred, because I did not know what harm the enemy had brought to the Empire. I was a soldier and told to fight and I did.

Sometimes it happened that I saw a face in the uniform, a human being staring back at me, but I confess it was no more difficult for me to shoot or stab than if he had been made of clay.

I did not care for the army which had flogged me, or the Whitehall warriors who had sent me here; but I had not been tied by force into the uniform, nor had I refused my training or declined the food. If I had become coarsened and immune to the suffering of others, I added the experience to the store of happenings as one adds to one's learning Caesar's *Commentaries* or irregular French verbs or the pursuit of astronomy.

The Russians had no more support from their officers at Inkerman than we, so when they finally withdrew it was as individuals tired of the fighting. I dropped to the ground and thought of Alethea. I was, I told her, still whole. I had recovered from the cholera when most victims did not, so there had to be a charm on my life. Had I not come through the Alma crossing unmarked and the same during the siege and here at Inkerman?

I thought of Alethea to obscure the cries of the wounded. I tried to recall the smell of her and the fields, the sun, and the grass.

My education went on. Near me a boy was frantically tearing open his jacket to reveal the hole in his body. I thought, If he begs me for a bullet I will not oblige him. I had done it for Peregrine but I was not a battlefield executioner. Near me was a shoe with a foot in it. It was hard to think of Alethea. I could close my eyes but I could not block off the stink. A Russian grabbed at me. He lay spread out as if he were taking his ease in his own bed. I saw no holes in him, no blood. I took up my bayonet and held it at his throat. He gabbled some more.

I said, "What do you want, damn you?"

Then, staring up at me, his eyes held no more life. I kicked him over and there was a hole in his back the size of a melon.

Then there was a buzzing of a half-spent bullet wearily searching out someone's flesh as a butterfly seeks a flower, and the buzzing grew louder and then triumphant with relief as it found a target in the back of my right leg, where it exploded like a minié ball.

I shouted in my head, How could this have happened? and I took the wound in both my hands to hold myself together.

Now I was being mocked by all the wounded I had ignored. *He* would not bring us water. *He* would not weep for us. *He* cannot move, he must wait to be helped, and the surgeons are very slow in coming. Now the bastard is one of us.

It was only pain. I remembered the strokes of the rod on my back. I had not cried out then. But this was worse because I did not know the extent of it; a flogging leaves scars only. I had no wish to be maimed or to die. I considered one versus the other. As I would not be a cripple so I would not give up life. I grew weaker. Soon I would be begging for succor. Like us, said the others. Let him know what it feels like to be ignored by such as he. As he was. As he is no longer.

In a while two figures appeared on the battlefield wearing long coats and talking together quietly as if traversing the corridors of a hospital. One was old and one was young. I raised my hand as if hailing an omnibus.

"What have we here?" said the old one.

With my chin I indicated my leg. The young one stretched it out for examination, taking out a blade to slit the trousers. I let go long enough for the cut and grabbed hold again.

"Tell me your diagnosis," said the old one.

He was teaching. I did not want a student. I would not let go.

"Is it your hand that is wounded?" said the old one.

"My leg."

"Then take your hand away so that it may be looked at."

"I am holding back the blood."

"We have to look at it, don't we?"

I felt if I released my leg I might lose it. I could not let go.

The young one said, "There are others who perhaps need us more than you do." He stood up. He had a small beard trimmed to a point. The older one had a larger beard, untrimmed. The old one bent over and took my fingers and pulled them back, and I knew if I had not let go he would have broken them. Then he stepped aside and the young one got his fingers in the wound and rooted about. I would have fainted then but I needed to watch them both. I had seen what doctors do on a battlefield.

"Well?" the old one said.

"I can't see, there isn't enough light."

"There is enough light. What do your fingers tell you?"

"I think the gastrocnemius is well nigh pulverized."

"Ah."

"Also, I think the tibia is shattered."

"Is it your opinion, doctor, that there is no possibility of repair?"

"Under these conditions?"

"These are the only conditions we have."

"I would like to try."

"Try what?"

"A reconstruction."

"Look about you. Does this look like the Royal Infirmary?"

"I heard that Surgeon Munro did a Syme's operation of the ankle joint, the first time it had ever been done in the field."

"Munro is not in favor," said the old one. "He insists on the use of chloroform when Sir John Hall believes that men disabled by the shock of gunshot wounds cannot survive the aftereffects of the drug."

The old one had been carrying a bag. He set it down and pulled it open. There were shiny things inside that clinked together.

"No, I'll do it," said the young one.

"Yes, that is best. A battlefield is the best place to learn. More bodies here in a day than one sees in the lecture halls for years."

I used my musket to prop myself into a sitting position. As they took out their instruments I said, "Brown Bess here is loaded. A man must reload each time he fires, else all he carries into battle is a useless stick."

"Why are you telling us that?" asked the young one, deciding between one tool and another.

"His mental faculties are disordered," said the old one, taking out a saw and whipping it in the air.

"No wonder. He has a terrible wound."

117

"I do not consider that a proper medical observation."

"Interesting. An interesting wound. I still say that were there time, an available hospital, I would like to try to save that leg."

"Of all commodities time is in the shortest supply here. And the nearest proper hospital is at Scutari, and that is three hundred miles. Unless you consider Balaclava available, which it is not, with no room under roof for the casualties already there."

"I would not take a wounded hog to Balaclava."

"Ergo—"

"You want me to do it, then."

"I thought you might like to try. I shall, of course, be watching."

"Should I use skin flaps?"

"I should think a circular is enough."

"Gentlemen," I said. "I am not delirious, although I am nearly so from listening to you. You are not paying attention to me. I was talking about my musket. It is loaded, I believe I said that? Should you attempt to amputate I will shoot one of you. I cannot shoot both but I cannot promise which of you will be first."

"How ungrateful," said the young one. "There are many wounded calling for us, begging that we attend to them. We came to your first; how can you be so ungrateful?"

"I have but two legs," I said, my voice conciliatory. "I am fond of them both." To the young one I said, "You say if you had time you could help me keep both."

From the boy with his guts exposed came a sound of air issuing from a small opening.

"If I had time," said the young one.

"Can you bind me up, then?"

The old one shook his head but the young one took out bandage and wrapped it around my leg. He started toward the boy but the old one said, "Not him. There is nothing you can do for him."

"Thank you, sir," I said.

The old one said, "There is locked jaw waiting for you, soldier. Maybe something worse. If you live to be taken to the hospital, they will only remove your leg there. And the intervening time will only decrease your chance of life."

"So you would amputate," I said.

"At once."

"But I have seen field amputations, and all the patients die."

"That is in the hands of God."

The young one said, "Would you really have shot one of us?"

"Yes," I said.

In the harbor floated piles of arms and legs, sleeves and trousers still on them; corpses rose from the mud and entangled ropes and anchor chains. I fell into a nightmare without falling asleep. I looked for Peregrine to guide me, but he was gone as he had warned he would be. The hasty bandage the young doctor had put on was soon asop with blood. I sat clutching it, holding in my life. We were taking the middle passage to Scutari, three hundred miles across the Black Sea. We wounded lay on the deck, side by side like sacks of flour. The fortunate ones were feverish enough not to know what was happening. Few of us had blankets, some were barely clothed. The ones with dysentery lay in their own filth. We were fed the ordinary salt ration of the ship diet. There were one or two surgeons aboard who occasionally walked about looking at us to see if we were still alive. Each morning those who had succumbed were dragged out of place and thrown overboard with no words said.

This was my third sea voyage, each worse than the last. I engaged myself in conversation. Richard, if you live will you ever travel again? Dick, I promise you, I will not even salt water to boil my eggs.

The ship was so small there was no sense of security between the deck and the rough sea. I went in and out of awareness as if, like the ship, I bounced in the waters.

Next to me a soldier with arm bandaged and suspended from a string around his neck said, "You ever been to Manchester?"

"No, I haven't," I said.

"You wouldn't know it, the way it's changed."

His head was as evenly round as a ball but the rest of him was thin. "They saved my elbow. That was a bit of luck. When you've got the elbow they can attach something and you can move it. Only now they say the mortification is spreading and they have to take more off. You in the Fifty-seventh?"

"Yes."

"I was a cook."

"What did you cook? I never had anything but biscuit and salt pork."

"I cooked for the officers."

"Were you a cook before you came into the army?"

"I was a tailor's apprentice. Manchester way. You never been there?"

"Never."

"You wouldn't—"

"Know the place," I said.

"I'd have been better off without a leg, like you."

"I'm not without a leg," I said.

"Sooner or later, then. But with one hand I can't do no sewing. And that's a shame because I had the neatest smallest stitch you ever saw."

"Why'd you go in the army, then?"

"For a bit of change. I was tired of sitting on a bench. You ever sit on a bench twelve, fourteen hours?"

At the other end of the deck two sailors pulled a body clear by the ankles, scraping it along the planking.

"God rest his soul," said my neighbor.

I lay flat to have in my vision only the spars of the ship and the sky. At first I had raised myself on one elbow to look about me, but now I wanted to spare myself the sights.

"Shall I tell you about Martin and the Jew?" the man said.

"Yes," I said. "Tell me."

"Martin was a tailor. A Jew came in with a pair of trousers he wanted treated special because one of their holy days was coming up, you know Jews have all those special holy days."

"I didn't know that."

"Yes, they consider certain days very special. I think it was the Jew's only decent pair of trousers, and he wanted it ready in time. Martin said he was busy and couldn't guarantee just when it would be ready but he absolutely promised it would be ready in time for the Jew's holy day. The Jew had to be satisfied with that and he went away. Then every few days he came back to see if the trousers were ready and each time Martin said no, not ready yet, but not to worry because he gave his promise it would be ready in time."

"Was Martin just leading him on?"

"No, his promise was as good as gold."

Some large bird had come to rest in the rigging.

"Get on with the rest of your story because we're near land," I said.

"How do you know that?"

"Because there's a land bird up there"—remembering the nautical information I had got from Peregrine during the first voyage.

"So as I was saying, every week the Jew comes in for his trousers and Martin says it's not ready yet, and the Jew is more and more worried but Martin says he gave his word. Well, finally it's about two days or so before the Jew's holy day and the Jew comes in very nervous and Martin brings out the trousers; they're all finished and a marvelous job it was, too. All mended and pressed and looked as good as new. The Jew's face was shining, he looked so pleased. And he told Martin so: it was the best job of mending and pressing he had ever seen, and Martin said he was pleased himself that the Jew was so pleased. But then the Jew says, Really now, Mr. Martin, why did it take you so long? It was just a pair of trousers, you weren't making them up from cloth, and of course you did a wonderful job, but it took weeks. It seems to me that a job like that could have been done sooner, considering that God only took six days to make all the earth. So Martin said, Look around you. Don't you think God should have taken a little longer?"

Chapter Eight

Cursing, my stretcher bearers picked their way through amputated human arms and legs which had been flung out the windows onto the pavement. They also had to circumvent the rotting carcass of an army mule.

We had sailed into the harbor of Constantinople, the golden horn with the city curled around it. Facing the Bosphorus lay Scutari, the silver city venerated by the Greeks. On the tallest hill was the immense yellow quadrangle of the barrack hospital with its square towers on four corners which the Turks had given to the British. As a painting of a slaughterhouse from a distance can be pleasant with color and design before one comes close enough for the excruciating detail, so for a moment before being taken off the ship it was possible to appreciate that at last here we would not be touched by the war. It was a quarter of a mile up a slope to the hospital. I was carried. I was one of the lucky ones; there were those who were dragged.

In this least prepared for of all wars, with food and clothing and medical supplies insufficiently supplied, how could the wounded have been other than brutally ignored. Englishmen would conquer the enemy quickly. Therefore, casualties would mostly belong to the Russians. That so many were British was an embarrassment. The army did not like to have wounded men who not only could take no further part in the fighting but required the unproductive expenditure of money and personnel. And then they would have to be returned home to have the public look upon blinded and legless and armless men who did not at all resemble the smiling indomitable fighters the newspaper dispatches lauded.

When we got to the doors of the hospital, the fetor was so

overwhelming that one put up an arm to guard against it. Over the door in letters of fire I imagined the words which had greeted Dante: *Lasciate ogni speranza voi ch'entrate.*

I was tossed on a canvas bed and left there. I decided I would henceforth breathe only through my mouth. I had known the appalling smells of the battlefield but at least they were in the open air; here they were constantly added to and undispersed. There were four miles of beds not eighteen inches apart. The floors were so rotten they could not be scrubbed, if anyone thought of so treating them; the walls were thick with dirt and there were vermin everywhere.

Those were observations I made later. Now I was concerned with pain. My leg had been severely jolted in leaving the ship, and I lay making holes in my palms with my fingernails to keep from groaning. Most of the wretches around me made no such effort. The silent ones were those awaiting death. I raised myself a little to see who my immediate neighbors were. On my left side was a mummy with only an opening for his mouth. No sound came from him. I turned to my other side. A boy lay there with his leg loosely and poorly bandaged; it was bloody and suppurating. His face was as muddy white as the canvas. He was sobbing.

"O'Boy," I said.

"What?"

"My name."

"Oh. Jamie Notch."

"How long have you been here?"

"Since early this morning."

"Where did you get yours?"

"Inkerman."

"So did I."

He blinked and tried to smile. "I come from London."

"East Anglia."

"We licked them good, didn't we?"

I was thinking they had licked us good. "Since this morning? Have you seen a doctor?"

"No."

"It's a devil of a way to treat heroes," I said.

"Heroes?"

"You're a hero. Wounded in battle, weren't you?"

"I was that," the boy said.

"Her Majesty ought to be along in a day or so with the medals."

"You think so?" Then he couldn't ignore his suffering any longer and turned away. I lay looking up at the rafters, where some rats scampered, and I wished them surefootedness because they were directly over my head.

In the aisles some soldiers came and went wearing armbands to indicate their status as nurse. Some were themselves wounded but, being ambulatory, had been pressed into service. One brought over a bowl and offered it to Jamie, who shook his head. Shrugging, the man passed it to me. I took it and waited for a spoon that was not forthcoming so I drank some of it and where it was curdled I spooned it in with my fingers. It tasted like lard flavored with loam, but since it was supposed to be food I ate it all, hoping my stomach would hold it.

The nurse, back with another bowl, stood over the bandaged man to my left and surveyed him for a bit and said, "Hey, mate, can you hear me?" There was no answer and the nurse said, "I'll be putting some mush in your mouth." He applied some to the hole with his finger. He leaned down to see if it was going anywhere and he shoved in a little more and then he straightened up and shook his head.

"Where are the doctors?" I said.

"You'll see them soon enough. Maybe too soon."

"What do you mean by that?"

"Your game is to keep what you got, and their game is to take it away. You follow me?"

"No."

"The longer it takes one of them to see you, the longer you are what you are."

I studied that for a moment without making sense of it. I said of the bandaged one, "Is he dead?"

"Looks that way. Of course you can never tell, can you. I seen them lay like rocks two–three days and suddenly start yelling for their supper."

He reached over the body with his bowl and passed it to the next man.

No one came to claim the body, nor did any come to tend to the living. I lay back and considered my plight. If the experience of battle was worse than the rigors of training, and lying wounded on the battlefield certainly was worse than being whole, then being here at this hospital was worse than any of those because of the unrealized expectation which went with the name—hospital—that one would be taken care of.

I tried to think of Alethea but I was losing her. Her features were beginning to dim and I could not recall the sound of her voice. I was left with more hatred than love, because hatred was a much easier emotion to experience in this setting. I hated Alethea and Peter, I hated Terence Bright and Lord Raglan. I hated Sir James and my father and soon I lay hating myself. Why had I agreed so spinelessly to place my life in the hands of the army? That Sir James could have had me transported because of one blow to his son was, according to Peregrine, manifestly false. Why had my father not seen that his value as a tenant was greater than the misbehavior of his son, and why had I not seen that even jail or being sent to Australia would have been preferable to what I had since experienced? Who would not be a felon on two legs rather than an ex-soldier on one?

I was suddenly irritated with the sobbing of Jamie Notch, and I bade him harshly to be done with it. His attempt at suppression was pitiable.

"How old are you, Jamie?"

"Eighteen."

"The age of a man, is it not? Then how can you lie there sniveling like a child? What is it that so disturbs you?"

"My leg is mortified."

"How do you know that?"

"I can smell it."

"That is the smell of this place, not your leg alone."

"They will cut it off," Jamie said.

"Don't let them. Stand up to them."

"Is that a joke?"

"Ha, ha."

"Do you want to hear about me, O'Boy?"

"Talking is better than sniveling."

"My father run out on my mother and she become a whore. So I left the house and borrowed some money and bought a barrow and became a costermonger. I hardly made enough to make the payments. What I wanted to be was a clerk in a chandler's but he expected me to keep figures and I'm not good at that. When I get my medal and they send me home do you think it's too late for me to learn to keep figures?"

"You're not stupid, are you?"

"I don't know if I'm stupid."

"You're not stupid," I said.

A doctor came down the aisle attended by two burly men wheeling a cart with a plank over it. The doctor edged in between my bed and Jamie's. He was a gaunt man with a glaze over his eyes like a sleepwalker. He said to Jamie, "How do you feel, son?"

This was the first sign of human kindness I had seen for a long time, and a tear bubbled up from my chest and I all but choked on it.

"I'm fine, sir," Jamie said.

"Let's take a look at your leg, then"—proceeding to unwind the wrappings. The closer he got to the flesh the greater the odor. I could note it, I thought, without minding it as much as I had. From the doctor's face he did not mind it at all. Which meant, I thought, that the world will continue to stink because all noses will eventually grow accustomed to it.

When he had all the bandage off he threw it on the floor. Jamie stiffly looked away. The doctor prodded a little, casually, I thought, and then said to one of his assistants, "Let's get him on the table."

"What for?" said Jamie. "I'm all right here."

"We're going to make you better, son."

This time, although his voice was just as soft, I thought the sentiment no longer kindly.

"I ain't going noplace," Jamie said.

"Now listen to me," the doctor said. "You see how many there are here who need my attention. There are too few doctors and God knows how many wounded, who keep pouring in. Now here I am, ready to take care of you, my boy, and I'm going to do the best I can. So will you have faith in me?"

"You're not going to take off my leg," said Jamie.

"Yes," the doctor said, "I am."

"I can't do without it," Jamie said. "I've got a girl, she won't look at me—"

"I can promise you one thing," said the doctor. "You won't live long if I don't take it off."

The doctor gestured and the assistant scooped up Jamie as if he were weightless and put him on the plank. Jamie began to beg and cry. The men on the nearby beds began to call out, at first in support of the boy and then, hearing their own voices and stimulated by the others, taking the opportunity to let out their complaints, and soon there was bedlam, this one demanding to know why a hospital was placed over a cesspool with open sewers ("the Sanitary Commission will hear of this, mark me, my brother-in-law's an engineer") and one wanted a sheet, the canvas was rubbing sores in him, and several shouted the food could not be eaten while there was an equal number who said, inedible or not, there was not enough of it. There was no ventilation. And what about the rats. The accents were of all Britain but the resentment was unified: how could a country take its wounded, who, next to those already dead, had given so much for the Queen, and instead of rewarding punish them?

The doctor and his aides were unmoved by the commotion and proceeded to go about their business. One stood at the head of the cart and held Jamie's arms. The other held Jamie's feet, the unmarked one dangling over the side and the other straight out in the center.

In the middle of the furor a man appeared with a coterie a half step behind; they slowly walked up the aisle, and as they moved a circle of quietness fell and when he reached the cart most of the jeering ceased. One voice, however, so thin and quavering its source could not be identified, called out, "You'll be taking off another limb without chloroform, will you, Sir John?"

Sir John Hall, principal medical officer of the Crimean forces, was identified by the older patients in sotto voce to the newer. He looked down at Jamie's leg, nodded once in confirmation, and went off followed by the junior surgeons and physicians. He stopped quickly to confer about a case or two. Then, just before exiting, he addressed the ward. "You are all British soldiers, have you forgotten that? This is a Turkish hospital; we are doing the best we can with it. Some of you will recover and be returned to duty, some of you will be returned home." There was a faint cheer at that. "Some of you will die here. Which category you belong in will be between you and your Maker and I suggest you take up your problems with Him."

The ones who were going to die began to boo. I assumed

it was the ones who knew they were dying because the others would have feared his displeasure, and who knew which owners of those limbs in the courtyard had incurred some doctor's displeasure. The dying ones, having nothing further to lose, began obscene catcalls as the chief medical officer hurried from the hospital.

Meanwhile the doctor with knife and saw had taken off Jamie's leg and sewn the stump. The boy had shrieked just once and it was the kind of sound one remembers all one's life because there was nothing of manhood or humanity in it. The assistant took the leg to the nearest open window. Jamie was wrapped and returned to bed, where he lay in blessed unconsciousness.

The doctor came to me. I stared at Jamie's blood on his coat and still on his fingers. He followed my gaze and wiped his hands on the sides of his coat. I said, "You don't have to bother with me."

He began to loosen my bandages. "What do you mean, son?"

"I mean don't take your knife to me."

He gestured to his assistants and they came one on each side of the bed to lift me to the cart. This time I did not have my musket.

"Wait," I said.

"No time," said the doctor.

"Listen to me," I said.

He shook his head, and I saw he was too tired even to complete the motion.

"I won't let you amputate," I said.

"Ah," he said. He sat on the edge of the bed. He spoke more to himself than to me. "It's too much for me. I had a nice quiet practice, not exactly Harley Street but nearby. The Queen requests—I haven't slept for forty-eight hours. No room and still they bring in the wounded. And then a bumpkin tells me I may not get on with my responsibilities."

"Do you do anything besides amputations?" I said.

He glowered and forced himself to his feet. He gestured and the two men attempted to lift me from the bed.

The one taking my left arm was not well balanced and I was able to fling him back to the aisle. The one on my right was heavier and I could do no more than cast him at the first one's feet. The doctor was watching with some interest. He said,

"We can get two more, or four or six, whatever is required. I think it may take six. You shouldn't have all that strength, considering your ordeal."

"At Inkerman a doctor said if he had the time he could save my leg."

"Did he, now?"

"There should be more to your profession than lopping off limbs."

"Now the bumpkin is appealing to my professional pride."

"You could try," I said.

He shook his head. "It's badly smashed up."

"I know that."

"It's a matter of the blood reaching the affected part, do you understand that? Without blood you have gangrene and death. If that's the case with you, you had best not argue with me."

"Well, is it the case?"

He put his hand in my groin. "The main artery begins here and then goes down and branches, one division here and one here." He felt between the first and second toe at the arch. I looked at his face. He didn't show anything. Doctors never do. I had to ask. "Do you feel something?"

"You have a pulse here." Then he felt behind my ankle on the inside and I watched his face again and again no expression but he said, "There's a pulse here, too."

"So my leg can be saved, then."

"It doesn't mean that at all. It means that perhaps we can wait. There's a compound fracture with bone fragments all over. I'm going to debride as much as I can."

I lacked the experience of knowing whether what he was doing hurt more than the amputation I had avoided. I don't think the doctor was punishing me for insolence so much as he was abstracted by fatigue; he was as close to being asleep and still functioning as it was possible to be. How then could he be concerned if he were hurting me?

He put on a fresh bandage and told me to watch my toes.

"What's going to happen to my toes?"

"If they change color or swell up you had best demand to see a doctor."

"You're not coming back to check my progress?"

"I may not see you again at all. I've done more for you than I ought."

"Does the dressing get changed?"

"No. Leave everything as it is. We're asking for Nature's help and we promise not to interfere. Unless you get the Checkers symptom."

"Checkers?"

"Draughts."

"Ah."

"Checkers, I say, because I was for a time in the United States studying their brand of medicine. Several injured hospital patients would meet to play draughts, or checkers, they termed it. When their bandaged parts smelled so bad that no one would play with them then it was time to intervene."

Jamie died the next day and his bed was taken by a man with a stomach wound. The nurse told me that stomach wounds could not be treated and he wondered why the man had been brought in. Usually they were left on the field to die. The nurse, whose name was McWatter, said the hospital was being investigated by the Sanitary Commission, because newspaper reports of the conditions here were outraging the British public. He himself was a bandsman and had served in hospitals in the United Kingdom. He said that this building was not habitable for well folk, let alone the sick and injured. He said there were rumors that women nurses were coming out from England.

We were all, I thought, prone to fantasy.

I worked at trying to bring Alethea to mind but I could not. I did not want to think of either my father or mother. Then for some reason I thought of Fudd, my old schoolmaster, and I was sorry I had injured his hand. People did what they were called upon to do. If he had flogged me it was not entirely because of his own cruelty but because it was considered the proper treatment for a recalcitrant student. Just as the flogging I had received in the army was the proper treatment for a soldier who had behaved as I had to an officer. Surgeons cut off legs because it was simpler to do so rather than take the time at debridement and bandaging as the doctor had done for me. I, too, would do what I was called upon to do if I could ever determine what that calling should be.

Having nothing better to do than lie on my back and stare at the infested ceiling, I wondered what position in life I could find that satisfied these requirements: that at the end of each day's efforts I should have justified the divine spark which was inside me. In molding the multitudes on earth and breathing life into them, God could have overlooked putting the spark in everyone. Like the story about the Jew and the tailor, He liked doing everything in a terrible hurry. But I believed the spark was in me because the sound of a word or the sight of a field or tree or dawn or the quality of a girl's voice or three or four notes in a song or the clasp of a friend's hand—these things and others started a kind of quickening to make me know I was more than a horse or a pig. So my work, whatever it might be, had first to cause that kind of response. But since for all I knew dustmen felt it too, I would need more recognition than that.

Just as I would not like to be wholly a beast of burden, so I would not care to be nothing but a solitary thinker. And finally, I would not like my work to be grandiose. I would not want it commented upon or used as example to be followed or disparaged. I did not want a seat in Parliament but I did not want to be a corner sweeper. I wanted my work to provide excitement, but in secret.

As I considered all this, the first profession to commend itself to my attention was that of thief, with some Robin Hood aspects to provide moral content.

My thoughts never began *If I live*, because I never considered the possibility of my dying. I was prepared for much pain still to be borne and the healing would be slow. (Then in the midst of my confidence I remembered the optimism of my having recovered from the cholera, but the bullet that found my leg at Inkerman had not been instructed I was to be unharmed.)

I went back to considering my fortune. The army would certainly release me, since I would hardly be considered fit to march fifty miles, or perhaps even five. I would not, I thought, seek further traditional schooling. I would not seek knowledge sifted through the mind of some don who had never smelled what I had smelled and never seen what I had seen.

One morning as I opened my eyes there was a woman beside my bed. It took a while to identify her sex, but her hair and bosom were as I remembered womankind from some distant world.

"How long is it since you wore a clean shirt?"

"I've forgotten."

"Can you take it off?"

I took it off gingerly, fearing that some of my skin would adhere to it. She took it and dropped it into a basket at her feet.

"How long is it since you washed yourself?"

"I've forgotten."

"Here is a basin and here is soap and a sponge. Do as well as you can."

The water was warm. Where had she found warm water, since the six or seven shirts that were washed monthly from the thousands of patients were washed in cold water?

After observing for a while she said, "That's not the way to do," and she took the sponge and applied twice the soap I had and begun to scrub me with twice the force I had been using. I had not been in the hands of a woman since Mrs. Hitch had nursed me through the cholera. This woman, who was about my mother's age, twisted me about and my head came close to her bosom and I longed to be held there. She was plain and her hands were red but, lacking competition, she was a goddess.

I said, "I thought there were no women—"

"Miss Florence Nightingale has changed all that."

"Nightingale?"

"All England knows about the horrible conditions you poor boys have been forced to endure."

That was heartening, that all England knew.

We began to enjoy the use of towels and soap, knives and forks, combs and toothbrushes. (What, Dr. Hall had demanded, did a soldier want with a toothbrush?) We managed to get more to eat than the half-raw chunks of meat, and we were even given soups and wines and jellies. (Preposterous luxuries, said Dr. Hall.) Miss Nightingale also saw that we received socks and boots and shirts.

Each day I was stronger, and at last I sat on the edge of the bed staring down at my two legs. The doctor who had wanted to take the leg off came along and said, "Admiring them, are you?"

I had not seen him for a long time.

"Pain?"
"Yes."
"Checkers?"
"No one has objected to my company."
"Can you move it?"
I raised my leg a little.
"Move your toes?"
I was able to.
"You seem to be one of the fortunate ones. Well, then," he said, moving off, as tired-looking as ever.

Would I be a doctor? I thought not. I was not truly concerned with the well-being of others, which is purported to be the purpose of the medical profession, not that the doctors I had seen were over-afflicted with that passion. There were two things I was sure of—I did not want to go back to being a farmer and I did not want to return to school.

I stood up and promptly fell down. The pain, starting in my leg, shot upward to my head, where it exploded. After a while there was a head leaning over the side of the bed next to me and a voice inquiring, "What are you doing down there, sonny?" I reached my hand up, the gesture inviting him to give me his own hand but he had none. I used my good leg and my hands on my own bed and got back in. I lay looking up at the ceiling again. I knew every fissure, the hiding place of every crawling thing, the exercise ground of every rat.

"How long have you been here?" said the man without hands.
"Not sure, I think a few months."
"How is it?"
"How is what?"
"Everything."
"Fine."
"I can't get used to these women," the man said. "They got no feelings. They clean you up, shit and piss and all."

The next time I saw a nurse I asked for a crutch. There wasn't any, she said, and I asked for a cane and she said there wasn't any of those and I asked for a stick. The next time I saw her she said she had found nothing that looked strong enough to bear my weight.

Something, I said.

Finally, she found for me a great piece of wood like a shepherd's crook and I got myself off the bed and tried a step or two. When the pressure hit the bad leg I was close to expiring from the pain, but I thought if I did not train this leg to work for me it would shrivel and be of no use. I practiced until, putting a little weight on my bad leg at a time, I learned to hobble. I went out to see the world. There were miles of corridors, but I wanted to see more than the other wretched patients. One evening—I did this day and night—I followed a light to a small room in which a woman sat at a table covered with papers. She looked up as I approached. I thought I would be berated for keeping everyone awake. The woman said softly, "Good evening."

"You're the Bird," I said.

"They call me that, I know."

"Is it disrespectful?"

"Not at all. Are you well treated?"

"Better since you and your ladies came."

"Would you care to sit down for a while?"

I had not talked to anyone except my ever-changing neighbors, who were mostly in such torment that I found it best to ignore them.

"Miss Nightingale, you do not have to be here. I think about that."

Half her face was in shadow. The half lit by the lamp was drawn with fatigue. But in some manner she was lighted from within. I could feel the force of her as strongly as if she were shaking me by the shoulders.

She asked my name. She asked where I had been wounded and how old I was. I gave her my official age, and she looked at me with complete understanding, knowing my real age and why I had falsified it.

"How long have you been in the army?"

"Something over a year. I'm not sure how long I've been here in the hospital. The days aren't marked and there are no newspapers."

"Would you like some news of the world?"

"I'm disturbing you, you were working." I began the involved procedure of getting to my feet. She stayed me with a gesture.

"I have some Constantia—it's a ladies' wine but it's all I have. And a biscuit?"

I took the wine and the biscuit and I was crying. It didn't show but I was crying.

"But you don't have to be here," I said.

"You want to know why, is that it? God told me to."

"He told you to come here?"

"He told me to devote my life to the relief of suffering."

At first, my education up to this point having induced more cynicism than belief in holiness, I looked for some sign of self-service or delusion. But this woman's calm grandeur, and the results of her intervention that I had seen, made me believe her.

"And you, soldier O'Boy, do you think it is a good thing to relieve the suffering of others?"

"I have been more concerned with bearing my own," I said.

"Of course."

"You brought women here to look at terrible things."

"Not all were able to. There were those who wanted to join me yet would promptly have fainted at a drop of blood and would have run, covering their ears, from a room in which a man lay screaming with pain. Nor did I want those so hardened by their own misfortunes that their capacity for feeling was deadened. You have been helped by our coming, have you not?"

"Yes. I'll go back to my bed now, Miss Nightingale. Thank you."

She watched me struggling to my feet. "O'Boy."

"Yes?"

"Your life will be worthwhile."

I smiled and limped out, not knowing what she meant but feeling warmed.

Each day my leg appeared stronger. After some weeks the doctor came and took off the bandage. My leg was a mass of dried blood and white skin, shriveled and thin. I've lost it, I thought miserably.

"It's a miracle how well it's healed," the doctor said.

"Healed?"

"It will fill in. The life is there. I doubt that you will be able to climb a mountain, and perhaps you will not be able to run as fast as before, but you have your leg and I congratulate you."

"Will you wrap it up again?"

"No need. I think I will recommend your discharge, O'Boy. We need your bed for more important cases."

I applied to be invalided out and more weeks passed as the doctors consulted and the army looked for ways to hold me, but finally it was done and I was aboard ship going back to England. I could walk well enough, if hesitantly; at shipside I had bought a carven stick more for security than need, since I had bad dreams of falling down in some public place.

Soldiers in peacetime were ruffians; now they were heroes, particularly those returning with some inoffensive wound. I enjoyed the few days of attention at Portsmouth and then took the train for London, thence by coach to Clamworth and by cart to Dire-Toombley. Where else should I have gone?

I bade the carter let me out at the foot of the rise leading to the farmhouse. I smelled deeply of the grasses and invited nostalgia because it was nearly two years that I had been away. I sought for the good memories but there were few. Instead I remembered the long walk to school and the humiliation when I arrived there; I thought of the farm chores beginning with daylight and of my mother's coldness and my father's weakness. As I ascended the hill I noted the path was overgrown, whereas it was the duty of one of Rafferty's sons to keep it well scythed.

I noted with some pleasure that my bad leg functioned well enough on the ascent. It had become my habit to assess its rate of recovery under differing conditions. At the top the clearing, like the path, showed signs of lack of attention. There was a strange stillness about the house, not the quiet of inhabitants temporarily away but the hollowness of an uninhabited dwelling. With some dismay I went inside to find that indeed no one lived there.

I dropped my haversack and went off seeking Rafferty, thinking if he and his family were also gone then the home of my boyhood had been stricken with some sort of plague. But I did see Rafferty and he was working as usual, and suddenly I found it offensive that the blight had been selective. He saw me. I stood letting him approach me, leaning on the cane, presenting the image of prodigal hero for practice since I hoped soon to adopt the posture for someone else.

"Master Ramsey, sir!"—coming to attention and bringing hand to the side of his head in an exaggerated salute.

"Where are they?" I said.

"Ah, you look fine. Just fine—and grown."

"My father and mother," I said.

"A sad thing."

"What *happened?*"

"But surely you know—"

"I know nothing."

Rafferty hesitated, because while it is natural to like delivering bad news it is also known that the bearer thereof often assumes a risk. The risk of reticence grew greater because I was advancing on him, cane in hand. He said hurriedly, "Your father is dead."

"How?" I said, because everything has to be known before the effect is felt.

"He was fixing a wall at the south end and it collapsed on him. No one was with him. I fancied it happened so because when I found him he was under a pile of stone."

"You found him?"

"Yes."

"And then?"

"Me and the boys carried him home. He's buried out near the church."

"When? When did it happen?"

"It's almost a year now."

"And no one to tell me?"

"It seemed odd your not being at the funeral."

"My mother," I said, saving all the thinking for later.

"Oh, Sir James was a true gent. He took her up to the house."

"And you, Rafferty. You're still working the farm."

"Well, sir—"

I had never been *sir*. How did a uniform and two years' absence make me *sir?*

"The truth of it is," said Rafferty, "I may be taking over the whole place. Sir James said it was a possibility."

"You?" I said.

"Why not? I was not a farm laborer in Ireland. I had my own farm there."

"Sorry, Rafferty, I did not mean—but I would have first claim here, would I not?"

"That's as may be," he said, head down not to let me see the resentment. "With you in the army—and going to war—nobody thought much of your coming back."

"You're not to worry," I said. "How are Mrs. Rafferty and the boys and Maureen?"

137

"All fine except for Maureen—"

"What happened to her?"

"Nobody knows. Just a short time after you, Maureen left. Packed her clothes one morning without a word, and we heard nothing from her since."

"You haven't tried to find her?"

"Her mother's sure she's gone into service and that would be a good enough life for her."

"No letter? No word, you say?"

"She can't write."

He did not show any regret, so why should I feel anything?

"Sir James took my mother in, you say?"

I turned away and he called, "Your mother's dead too, boy."

I was a block of wood. I couldn't move and I couldn't feel anything. "Both?" I said. "Both dead?"

"Aye."

"And nobody let me know?"

Rafferty shrugged.

"How did my mother die?"

"She was sick."

"I think," I said, "I will talk to Sir James. Is he still up at the big house, or is he dead too, or disappeared?"

"He's there. Where would he go? His foot is as big as an elephant's leg. Sits there snarling."

"I'll let him snarl some at me, then."

I began to walk slowly toward the manor house and I thought that now I was an orphan I should feel some sorrow. But I had seen so much death that it was not more notable than a method of demonstrating life. But a father and a mother needed a child to weep for their passing, else there might be no rest for them.

I remembered my father taking my small hand in his and his lessons in prizefighting and the pride he took in my prowess. Up to the moment of his betrayal I was sure I loved him—and perhaps he trusted and believed in Sir James; why would he not, the Squire was personification on earth of law and justice, the comfort and protection of the mighty, and did he not provide that my father had food for his family and a roof over their heads? Why would my father, who was a simple man, not have been convinced that jail awaited me and that the compromise of my going into the army was a sign of favor from Sir James? How could he have rejected such an offer?

I wept then for my father, and in weeping helped not only him to rest but myself as well, because it is better to weep over a father's death than dry-eyed to dismiss him as unworthy of tears. For my mother my tears had to wait.

The door was opened by a manservant who asked my name, and I said Ramsey. He left me outside the door and in a while came back and asked which Ramsey.

"Sir James will be surprised and no doubt delighted to learn that there is still a living one."

I was shown into the library and stood before a mound of blankets and one leg up on a stool with more bandages on it than had ever been used to keep my leg together. I looked at the lord of the manor and I felt cheated. Had he been all hale, were he a man, I would have wanted to spit out my contempt, but there was nothing left to receive it. This man was grossly fat and his shapeless nose was swollen and covered with red and purple and blue thin worms. Is it not being cheated to hate as a child and wait for growth to take revenge on the giants who have caused such distress only to find the giants diminished and no longer worthy of chastisement?

"Ramsey, is it? There are no Ramseys around here. No longer."

"I was a Ramsey when you sent me away from here."

"You?" he said, peering up at me. "Richard?"

"Tell me about my mother," I said.

"You were in the Crimea? Alma? Inkerman? You saw Raglan? Cardigan? Campbell? Tell me about that."

"What happened to my mother?"

"Richard. Sit, boy. Wine?" He bawled for the manservant. "Is it true what Russell writes to *The Times*? We slapped down the Muscovites, did we not? Oh, you were the lucky one. What would I have given to ride in that charge with Cardigan—"

"Can you not hear me? Do those blankets muffle your ears? I came to find out the truth of my mother's death."

"You say you were in the army. Yet they told me there was no Richard Ramsey there."

"Then you tried to let me know," I said, defeated.

"Your father and mother died, man. Would I have kept that from you?"

"I was not known as Ramsey in the army."

"Who, then?"

"O'Boy."

"Why?"

"My mother's name."

"I took her in, you know. Your father died in the fields."

"I saw Rafferty. He told me. My mother went to work for you, then?"

"She would not take charity."

I did not ask if he had offered any.

"She died of phthisis. The servants nursed her until the end."

"Did she leave any word for me?"

"No one knows. For the last few days of her life she spoke only French."

Chapter Nine

I thought of the woman who had unwillingly borne me, who during my growing up suffered the daily reminder that I was as English as my father, and who—finally free of the weight of both of us—had not been able even to return to France to die.

"I would know something of her time here," I said.

Sir James shrugged; at least something moved under his bulk of blanket.

"May I see her room?"

He rang for a servant. It was a fine house with many fine rooms, and I wondered which of them my mother had died in. We went up the stairs and up and up and at the top there was a room neither fine nor as decently habitable as the one she had shared with my father in the stone house. There was no trace of her in the bare bedstead in that cramped slanted-ceiling attic chamber.

I went back to Sir James, seeking a reason to shed tears for my mother. He had not moved. I doubted if without help he could have changed position. I thought I would recommend poverty if wealth and position caused one at the end to swell up like a toad.

Died, I thought, a servant girl as she had begun.

"There is coming to you," Sir James said, "nineteen pounds, four shillings, and sixpence."

"Coming to me?"

"We found it in a box in her room. There were some Popish beads; we did not save those. A dress or two went to the parish workhouse."

She was as much of a stranger to me as if I had been taken from her at birth.

"Peter," Sir James said. "You remember my son, Peter?"

There was no sign of his mind being less clear than it was. Therefore the question was insulting, a way of seeing me as less than a full man. How could I not have known his son, Peter. Had I been a rock in his fields, a tree lining the path to his house? I could feel the familiar heat rising from my belly but I suppressed it—sometimes I could do that—for against whom was my rage to find expression, an old sick man who could not keep himself warm enough? Ah, yes, I knew his son, Peter.

"He was with Cardigan's Brigade. You may have seen him—from a distance, of course. You may have been able to pick him out. You did know Peter."

"I saw him. I picked him out well enough."

"You did? Well, then, tell me: he rode well, he fought bravely?"

I let him wait, and I thought how I would say to him that Peter turned tail and fled, that he had fallen off his horse, that his comrades had jeered. But if those things had truly occurred then I could never have hated Peter Nott-Playsaunt but pitied and forgotten him. So I said yes, I had seen him, and he had done nothing to disgrace his father.

"He is now in London," Sir James said. "A youth of quality, having fought for Her Majesty, deserves a period of relaxation, deserves, if I may say so, to become a man of the world." Sir James closed his eyes and nodded at his own recollections. "He's at the Clarendon, and he'll visit the night houses of Leicester Square and Charing Cross Road—still there, I warrant—and he'll see the cockfighting at Faultless's Pit in Endell Street; he'll be gaming and drinking and whatever else strikes his fancy, and when the time comes he will return home to assume his responsibilities. As you have, I take it?"

"I don't know what responsibilities are left to me here," I said.

"Ah, perhaps none, that is true."

"You are letting Rafferty take over the farm."

"Yes, I did tell him—you were not here, were you, Richard? And a boy, could you assume the duties your father guaranteed me? Rafferty's a good farmer. Still, you think you have rights here, is that it? Death cancels all obligations of leasing, you know that, don't you? And no one here expected to see you again."

"Why not? You expected to see Peter again."

"This estate will be his, his family is here. This is his home."

"Was it not mine?"

Sir James shook his head at my unwillingness to see the facts. "A boy of your—station—it's the army for life, is it not?"

"Yet I am here."

I was a ghost yearning for corporeality. Now I understood violence, the word usually prefaced with senseless, but it was a way to assert one's being, because a man needed to be noticed, recognized, given his due. My father had known his place and left me with no place. If I lifted that mass on the chair and cast it onto the ground would he still be able to say "No one thought to see you again" or "Did you know my son, Peter?" My inheritance was nineteen pounds, four shillings, and sixpence, but it was not left to me by name. And it was not considered that I might want to farm the land worked by my father.

"I know the farm better than Rafferty," I said. "He was given isolated tasks, day by day."

"Do you want the farm, then?"

"No," I said.

"Then—?"

"No matter," I said.

Sir James directed his servant to bring him a box, which he opened to extract the money—which I took, without counting, thanking him as if it were his gift, because what has hatred to do with comity if one has proper instincts?

"There were," Sir James said, "some pounds and pence more, but since your father had owed me for various sundries my bailiff made the accounting. I will call him with the figures if you wish—"

"It will not be necessary," I said, angry at myself for making the expected rejoinder, but feeling I had passed enough time in this arid place.

There was a knock on the door, which opened, and Sir James said, "Alethea, my dear."

For the first time I was aware of how poorly my uniform fit.

Alethea said, "It's not—can it be—Richard? Is it you?"

Alethea walked around me as if studying a horse she had some interest in purchasing.

"He has grown, has he not, Sir James?"

"Has he?" I said ungraciously. "What else has he done?"

It was she who had grown. She had passed from child to woman. I remembered her hair, carelessly caught up and pinned back. Now she had drawn thick tresses from the center of her forehead in curving waves over the tops of her ears so only the lobes were visible. She had used bandoline to glue it all in one shining surface while the rest was twisted up at the back of her head in a chignon. Her dress was all embroidered and flounced in some gauzy green stuff. She would not, now, race me to a tree we had selected to sit under, nor leap, disdaining aid, to the back of a horse.

Sir James groaned. Alethea went to him at once, all solicitude, straightening his blanket and patting tenderly the bandage on his foot.

"Would you like some brandy, Sir James? Or some more of the draft the doctor left?"

"I'll take no more of that vile stuff. Your touch, Alethea, is all I require. How kind you are to me, child."

"If I am kind, sir, it is kindness I have learned from you."

Finding these expressions of mutual approbation distasteful, and needing mightily the free air, without further word I left the house. I was limping and had to use my stick as I began the walk back to the place that had been my father's house, my home no longer. Too much had happened too soon, and I felt my mind jellied. I needed a quiet place to sit and think. I had not planned for another day. I had thought to come home and be cared for, coddled perhaps for a while; instead, this battering of deprivation. And beyond the happenings themselves was my picture of myself—a shadow figure of no consequence, a son who could not weep for his mother's passing, who could not insist on his rights as his father's heir, if rights there were. A flotsam man who did not know where he belonged.

She said, "Your leg—you've been wounded?"

I said nothing, nor did I slacken my poor pace. I had thought of her for two years in the midst of loneliness and death and carnage. I hated her, but the hatred was impure, tainted by the wish to put my arms around her.

"Will you stop then," said Alethea. "Just for a minute. Let me look at you. Is this a way for old friends to meet after so long a time apart?"

Old friends. I stopped and turned and brought my eyes up to her face as slowly and heavily as if there were weights on my eyelids. She was herself and more. Time had filled her figure, and the child's prettiness had become something richer, deeper, and hence more inaccessible than ever. I had mooned over her, and dreamed of her, and felt unworthy except in fantasy, so even had she not testified against me I would have hated her. If a girl is too beautiful for you should you not feel hostile? Could you nod approval as she keeps herself for one more handsome, wealthy, and of superior birth?

"So," she said. "You run from me."

"Better than the years I spent running after you."

"Did you, Richard? Did you run after me?"

"Until you did your best to send me to prison."

"That is how you saw it? That it was something I wanted? When I saw the hatred in your eyes I would have undone it if I could—but let us not talk of that now. You are back and—I was going to say unhurt, but you have been hurt? You have suffered, Richard? But you are better now? Whatever it was—"

"A difference of opinion between me and the doctors. They would have preferred me legless."

"Oh, my God, Richard."

"However, I have the two. One somewhat marked but still a support to this aging body." She had used some scent; on her forehead, I thought. While pleasant to the nostrils I preferred her with the natural moisture there after running. She was now like the women of great cities, all of a piece with their stylish clothes, desirable and interchangeable. The Alethea I remembered could let her locks fly without dismay, and if her chin was pocked after some excess of rich food she did not take to her bed over it.

"Peter preceded me, did he? Did he speak of our meeting?"

"He said—"

"He said—?"

"He said he had you flogged." Alethea took the stick from my hand and brushed it back and forth through the wild flowers.

"Indeed he did."

"Mostly I see in him kindness. But with you—"

"Peter provides me no abatement. Although I do not forgive,

sometimes I can forget, and so it was beginning to be with Peter, and then he feeds me cause for ill will afresh. It is his way with me, I understand that."

"Would you believe he has always been fond of you?"

"As one loves his victim?"

"He told me once that given the choice of comrade to face the world he could think of no one he would want above you." I began a protest, but Alethea brushed it aside with impatient fingers. "I know him, I know my cousin. He sees you, a farmer's son, excel in school, and Peter boils because no one must excel but himself. He sees you stronger and quicker than he and he boils again, because you lack his family line, his wealth. He sees my eye turn to you and—"

"Never. It never did."

"Oh, but it did. As it does now."

She dropped my stick and put her hands flat against my chest. I could feel their warmth through my shirt. I put my hands over hers, at which she pulled them away.

"I thought of you," I said. "Every day. So I played cat to your queen. Thank God a man can dream as he pleases and by keeping the dream to himself only he is affected."

"But now you have told me."

"No matter. I think I will leave now, Alethea, I have a life to begin."

"Life? Where will you go? What will you do?"

I answered with a shrug and a shake of head.

"Come," she said, reaching down for the stick and handing it to me. I took it to carry only. She guided me toward the summerhouse, taking my hand. The touch sent my heart pounding and there was a wild wish for more, but I would not let myself think of what more there might be. Seated then, side by side, she said, "You've changed, Richard."

"How could one not?"

"I don't mean just the alteration of time. Before, you were often fierce. Now you are awesome."

"How awesome?"

"Dangerous."

I did not feel dangerous. "Am I, then, no longer soft and doltish?"

"Sir James gave me the dispatches of Mr. Russell in *The Times* to read. He has unkind things to say of the generals but he says you are a hero."

"I? Richard?"

"The British soldier."

"Should the British soldier then not be rewarded?"

She kissed me. And drew at once away.

"Your mother and I—she was here for nearly a year. We talked together often."

"You and my mother?"

"At first I wanted practice in my French speaking. And then she was so delighted at hearing her native tongue, no matter how poorly spoken, that we were often together. She read the papers when Sir James was finished with them. She followed the course of the war. She was always so worried for you, Richard."

"Like any mother with a son in a war?"

"She was the most unhappy person I have ever known. She wanted nothing so much as to be in her own country. Came your father, and then you, and years of being in a foreign land which remained always an alien place. When your father died, and what he left added to what she had saved amounted to some thirty pounds—"

"Thirty pounds!"

"Perhaps more. I think she said it was thirty. She could have then returned to her home and lived out her life there. A husband gone, a son swallowed up in the war. She tried to reach you after your father's death—we all did—but the army had no record of you. And still she remained here, a servant to Sir James, all in the hope that one day she might see you again."

"And yet for sixteen years there was no sign of—love."

"Is love a thing you know about, Richard?"

"I confess I am not an expert in it."

"Is there not, Richard, a center in you of coldness never yet reached by anyone?"

"If there is," I said, "how would you know of it?"

"Because it is so with me too."

Of Alethea I could believe it, she had proved it to me often enough. But was it true of myself? Had I not wept for Peregrine and my father? Had I not been saddened at my comrades' being blown apart? But from what depth had the tears come? Was I not always able to move, whistle, fight, talk, and have thoughts unconnected with misery? Was it true that no one—not even Alethea—had been able to penetrate deeply enough to rive me?

"Some call it strength," Alethea said, studying me.

"Better cold at the center than mewling," I said.

"But someday there will be one who will be able to warm it."

"You. You, Alethea, if you but wanted."

And then she was the Alethea of old. Laughing and taunting and holding me away. As I left, she was laughing.

I slept in my old bed for the last time and in the morning left without once looking back. From Clamford I took the coach to London to seek out purpose. My mother's money, plus the bit I had put aside, would see me through until the sign came, so I did not fear beggary.

I had read about the multitudes in the largest of the world's cities, with vehicles coming so fast one after other that to cross a thoroughfare would be an adventure. My first sight of London was no view at all, the coachman setting me down and dropping my box after me in a fog so thick and yellow that I could not believe it was midday. I picked up my box and took a step. The mud underfoot was as bad as Balaclava. I opened my mouth for a breath and the fog rolled in rancidly, oiling my throat. I coughed. I began another step and took it back because left was as good as right. A carriage drove along cautiously, and then another coming from a side street nearly caused a collision. The driver of the first vehicle screamed some imprecations. The other driver answered him in kind and I stood by to watch the combat, since only fists and clubs could follow such invective, but in a moment they were each quietly on his way. A boy lurched into me and excused himself and I reached for him and made his fingers release my handkerchief. When I would have cuffed him he slipped from my grasp and vanished. A woman came out of the mist, appearing so suddenly as to have been freshly formed out of the air. "Hello, luv," she said, "it's a misery, an't it?"

I admitted that it was and she said we could have a bit of brightener in her room if I liked. It was only a step away and one had to get out of this poisoned air. The invitation was tempting. I had been tempted before. I was, at eighteen, and despite the opportunities of army life, a virgin still.

When the woman stepped closer for better persuasion I noted the paint on her face caking and her eyes had the look of hot coals dropped onto unbaked bread to melt its way halfway in before stickily sloughing. I thanked her but said there were matters to which I needed to attend. She took a step and disappeared. I was alone again while the fog swirled tentacles around my face and down the back of my neck. I ventured a step into nothingness. Then there was a heavy tread and I saw with vast relief a member of the Metropolitan Police, solid and comforting in shining hat, stiff stock, greatcoat, stout belt, and white gloves.

He had appeared out of frightening obscurity like a familiar landmark. Standing stolidly with his hands behind his back he was copybook England. He touched his hat with his forefinger and said, "Good evening, sir. Can I be of help?"

"You could tell me where I am," I said.

"Are you lost, then?"

"This is London?"

"Where else in the world would you find a pea soup like this? Where would you be heading for?"

"I don't know."

At which he glanced at me with the suspicion built into his calling. He was a big man and accustomed to looking down at his civilian charges. Since I stood eye to eye with him the effect was lost.

"I've just arrived," I said. "I suppose what I need to get on with is a place to stay."

"You want the army barracks, is it?"

"I'm just out."

"You're too young to be out."

"I was wounded."

"Ah. I may be able to put you on to something. Friend of mine died at Varna. You know Varna?"

"I know it."

"His mother and father run a bread and tart shop not far from here. On top it's a storeroom which I've heard them talk of wanting to rent out. Since you wear the uniform, there's a chance they'd feel kindly toward you. It's better than some low lodging house where you'd share a bed with crawlers. It's just off Oxford Street. If you're willing to try it I'll walk along with you."

"That suits me."

A uniform, especially if you have the brawn to fill it, conceals youth, and as we walked together I noticed that this new acquaintance was no more than a year or two older than I.

"Constable Jeffries."

"Richard O'Boy."

I liked his calmness and assurance, and yet he was free of arrogance. I said, "What's it like, being in the police?"

"Important. Doing what's needed, that's what appeals to me."

"Ah," I said.

"The commissioners are partial to men've had army training."

"When I shed this uniform I won't be anxious to get back into another. But the work's worthwhile, you said?"

"There's jobs and jobs," Constable Jeffries said. "So much per diem for so much of your time. It wouldn't suit me well to sell shirts or tot up figures. I'm a useful man here, doing a useful job."

"That makes sense."

"Not to everybody. My sergeant, who's a man likes his history, says it wasn't too easy getting the force started. The Englishman is careful of his liberty. Police on the streets was thought to interfere with it."

"But it's all right now. I mean, police are well accepted now, wouldn't you say?"

"We have to tread easy, I can tell you that. Sometimes we'll be out directing traffic and people will try to ride us down or lash out with their whips as they go by."

"Criminal types, you mean."

"No, decent citizens."

"Afraid of Cromwell's return," I said. "Is the pay enough?"

"Small. But you can add to it—I, for example, make calls. You get a man wants to be called at five or six in the morning, some pay sixpence a week."

We walked on, with Jeffries growing more companionable.

"You expect danger from the criminal classes; what I can't stand is the costermongers. They hate the police more than anybody. They'll do anything to serve out a crusher."

"Crusher meaning—"

"Bobby. They'll lay in wait and as soon as you pass throw a brick. Or drop something from a rooftop. Or whop you with a stick at your legs and run. Makes them stand high with their fellows if they can put down a constable."

"Miscreants and villains," I said. "Who stands between them and ordinary folk but you?"

"Exactly," Constable Jeffries said.

"Would you say that everybody has to obey the law?"

"Everybody."

"No exceptions?"

"None."

"A toff, an M.P."

"That's the oath I took."

"I'm getting interested. Except for the uniform."

"It's wearing the uniform I like. However, we have another branch, the detectives. They wear their own clothing."

"Whatever they like?"

"Yes."

I remembered then what Plato had said in the *Republic* about the nature of the guardian. That he be keen of perception, quick of pursuit in one apprehended, and strong if he has to fight it out with his captive. Brave and high-spirited. What an irresistible and invincible thing is spirit, said Plato, the presence of which makes every soul in the face of everything fearless and unconquerable.

Was I fearless and unconquerable? I had known fear and I had been conquered. Was I, then, not eligible?

But then, Plato had said, if that be their nature, how would they escape being savage to one another and to the other citizens? We must have them gentle to their friends and harsh to their enemies. Where shall we discover those at once gentle and great-spirited? For there appears to be an opposition between the spirited type and the gentle nature. Yet if one lacks either of these qualities, a good guardian he can never be.

The fog, which had not only closed in the sight but muffled the street sounds, now lifted and I was taken aback by the tumult. People were either buying or selling or delivering goods to be sold, or rushing to work so that they could make something for sale or wait for customers. There were pantechnicons with tires of iron, huge omnibuses painted red or blue or green, with the passengers (all male) climbing from the iron rungs to sit back to back against the knife boards on top with feet against the skirting planks. Open barouches, coal wagons and brewer's drays, cabs loaded with portmanteaus and bandboxes taking their occupants to railroad stations, light carts of fishmongers and hotelkeepers. Here and there a trap open in the pavement for workmen underground repairing gas and water pipes. High chimney towers pouring out thick black smoke. Women running into the street to pick up horse dung with their hands and stuffing it into parcels of cloth. Chemist shops with colored flagons lit behind. Dock laborers, sailors, organ grinders. Street sellers: Chestnuts all hot, a penny a score, buy, buy. Half quire of paper for a penny, twopence-a-pound grapes, three-a-penny Yarmouth bloaters. Who'll buy a bonnet for fourpence, pick them out cheap here. Three-pair-for-a-penny bootlaces, penny-a-lot fine russets.

Street Arabs not more than eight or nine years old with ragged trousers hanging by one brace, old coats too large, without shoes or stockings, some with blacking boxes slung on their back, some running alongside cabs and hansoms turning somersaults or walking on their hands, begging a penny for their efforts.

Clerks in dark cloth suits with billycock hats, women in heavily flounced crinoline skirts with pagoda sleeves.

The constable nudged me, pointing out a boy in a beaver hat with a little surtout, trousers of black cloth, and black silk necktie and collar. "Look at the short hair. Just out of prison, that's the suit they give them."

We turned off Oxford Street and into a series of alleys. The constable pointed out a bakeshop across the street and said he had to get back to his duties but to tell Mrs. Gum that I was sent by Constable Jeffries to ask about the spare room. I thanked him sincerely and as he turned to go back I said, "By the way, if I'm interested in learning more about the police where should I inquire?"

"The Commissioners are at Four Whitehall Place. In back there's a lane known as Scotland Yard. Ask there."

As I hesitated on the curb before trusting myself to the street traffic I felt a slight tug at my back pocket and, reaching behind, enclosed a thin wrist. The owner thereof began to wriggle and moan piteously that he didn't do nothing and it was a terrible world that consigned young children such as he to a life of suspicion, distrust, and persecution simply because he had not the money for a decent suit of clothes or even for a rag to blot his nose and it weren't his fault that he had found no place to wash his face that morning. I thought him not younger than five or older than twelve.

I said, "This is the second time in one hour, the other getting away, and is it that I seem so easy a mark for your family?"

"I didn't try nothing. I was a little faint from hunger since I hadn't nothing to eat today."

"You touched me to keep yourself from falling," I said.

"That's it."

"You are," I said, "the dirtiest boy I've ever seen. Have you ever bathed?"

"It's bad for you."

"Well, I left the constable a moment ago. I think if I called he is still within the sound of my voice."

"Jeffries, that's the one," he said, resigned. "He's got it in for me and he'll have me up before the magistrate. He wouldn't think of letting me go, of giving me another chance. Not Jeffries. You call him and it's Tothill Fields for me."

"Maybe they'll bathe you there."

"Call him, then. I don't care. I'm sick of life anyway."

"Are you," I said.

"Innercent folk getting sent to prison. Like my dad."

"Where's he?"

"The Model."

"I never heard of that."

"Pentonville's the proper name."

"What did he do?"

"Like I said. Nothing. Man breaks a drum—and *he* got away—and my dad was just passing by and they nibbed him. Innercent as a babe, he was."

"How long since you saw him?"

"I don't know."

"You don't know?"

"I mean I can't count the days."

"Where's your mother?"

"She went off with some diddikis."

"English, please. You can't count days and you can't speak your own tongue, either?"

"They have wagons and go out to the country. They tell fortunes and nail chickens and the like."

"Gypsies?"

He shrugged, his shoulders not moving his coat much.

"Where do you live?"

He made a gesture in one direction with four fingers together and the opposite direction with his thumb.

"If I promise to let you go will you at least tell me the truth?"

He blinked and nodded and lifted his face up to mine. His eyeballs were white against his sooty face.

"Your father?" I said.

"God's truth."

"That he's in jail or—innercent?"

"He's in the Model, all right."

"Your mother?"

"She walks the Haymarket."

"And you did try to steal my handkerchief?"

He blinked again but did not take his eyes from mine. "I did think you'd have a wipe on you and you wouldn't miss it, whereas I would get a few pence for it which'd buy me tea and a bun."

"You're not very good at your work. I'm not experienced in these matters, yet I felt your fingers."

"I an't been at the school for a while. I been busy."

"School?"

"Where else'd you learn?"

"What kind of school?"

"Place in the Seven Dials. Man called Bindy."

"Fagin," I said.

"No, Bindy. We have to call him Mister Bindy."

"What's the training like?"

"He stretches a coat on a line with wipes in the pockets and you have to pull one out, and if the line shakes he hits you in the legs with a stick."

It was difficult to tell what he looked like beneath the dirt. He had small square teeth with a space in front and there was a share of intelligence in his manner and a pleasing directness even about his lies. I asked him his name.

"Roger."

"Roger what?"

"Roger."

"People usually have two names."

"Roger's all I got. Say, what's it like being a sojer?"
"I'm out of the army. How old are you?"
"Fifteen."
"Eight."
"Can't be eight. I remember being eight and my dad didn't give me a beating because it were my birthday and that was—well, a time ago."
"Ten?"
"I could be ten. I got a friend he's nine and I'm bigger, and another friend's bigger'n me and he says he's near twelve so I guess ten is about right."

I took out a sixpence and handed it to him. I expected that he would snatch it and run, but he stood regarding it and then me, waiting for me to explain. So I said, "This is for the tea and bun. Would that encourage you to a further life of crime?"

"I don't care for a life of crime. It was the money I was interested in."

"Well, now you have it."

He tipped his hat and said he considered himself in my debt. I watched him walk off in his castoffs and thought of myself at that age—not that long ago—going to school often in clothes that didn't fit better.

As I watched he stopped, turned, and came back. Holding the coin in his outstretched hand he said, "It's not fair and I won't be a party to it. I tried to nail your wipe, and just 'cause I was stupid at it you gave me sixpence anyway. It's not right for a street boy like myself to take 'vantage of a decent type like you, and I'm giving you back your money."

I didn't believe a word of it. I took the money and put it in my pocket without insisting, as I thought he expected, that he keep it.

"Just one thing," Roger said.

Ah, I thought.

"I an't had no 'vantages and if I turned to crime it was 'cause I didn't know no better nor had a friend or family to steer me right. If I could come to a man like you for advice once in a while or run someplace for you to fetch a letter or something like that."

"I'm not in need of a runner. And my advice can't be worth having, else I would be in better circumstances than I am."

At that I went across the street and studied the contents of the bakery window. I found Roger beside me doing the same thing. We were not so far apart in age that both our eyes were not bulging at the sweets. I went inside and said to the woman behind the counter, "Two currant tarts, please," and I handed one to Roger, who began at once to tongue out the center in lingering licks, nostrils quivering as if he were bringing all his senses to bear. I bit into mine and without Roger's discipline ate the rest of it whole.

"Mrs. Gum?" I said.

"Yes? That's me." The woman looked as if, once having been of ordinary height and stature, she had sustained some gross assault of heavy hand on top of her head, causing her to be flattened and broadened. Yet there was a quickness to the face and softness to the voice which was agreeable.

"My name is Richard O'Boy. I met a constable by the name of Jeffries who directed me here, thinking you might rent me a room."

"Jeffries. Yes. You're a soldier?"

"Done with it." I raised my cane to establish my legitimacy.

"You been abroad?"

"The Crimea."

"You knew Tommy Gum?"

I shook my head.

"He died at Varna. You been there?"

"Yes."

"What was it like at Varna?" Mrs. Gum said.

What was the place like in which her son had died. Should I tell her it was a place of quiet greenery and sweet air where death had come to the occasional soldier swiftly and without pain? Or should I tell her of the instant corruption, the maggots in wounds so quickly as if waiting in the flesh for their opportunity.

Mrs. Gum said, "He was taken by the ballot. We didn't have the money to buy him off, Mr.—"

"O'Boy."

"We have money for food, money to buy our flour, money for shoes—if you look down you will see I an't barefoot—so how is it I did not find the money to buy my only son away from death?"

"He died for Queen and country," I said.

Mrs. Gum, tilting her head upward, the top of her gaze lost in underbrush of eyebrow, said sharply, "Do you believe that? Do you believe that, Mr.—"

"O'Boy."

Roger had been inching up to the case, and Mrs. Gum, without looking at him, swung out her short plump arm and caught Roger on the side of his head. "Do you know this boy?" she said to me.

"Not well," I said.

"Watch him, then. He's a thieving little rascal."

"I am not," Roger said. "I lack 'vantages, is all. That's my trouble. But I'm not—"

"He'll steal the hair out of your nose," Mrs. Gum said.

Roger went out the door and disappeared. I didn't actually see him open the door and leave.

"He does that," Mrs. Gum said. "Sometimes it's enough to scare you. He's like a roach gone into a crack before you can get your hand up to swat him."

"How does a boy like that live?" I said.

"How long have you been in London, Mr.—"

"O'Boy."

"There are thousands of children like Roger in this city. They don't have homes. They sleep where they can, they eat what they can beg or steal, and that's the size of it."

"He doesn't strike me as the criminal type."

"Criminal? He's just a homeless, hungry boy."

"But I thought—"

"Because I hit him, called him names? He's a boy. I had a boy of my own. I remember when he was the age of Roger—if you can figure what age Roger is. And he doesn't go hungry as long as I have this shop. There's always a stale roll, or whatever I can spare. You were going to tell me of Varna."

"Not a pleasant place," I said.

"He was twenty. How old are you?"

"Eighteen." It was time to revert to the truth.

"You look older."

"I am older," I said.

"He was not like you and yet—he was a much slimmer boy. He had a quickness in him, you know what I mean, in his face, his movements. He was impatient. He couldn't learn the trade from his father because one has to wait for the bread to rise. With him everything had to happen at once."

A man opened the door to a back room from which came a gust of heat and some heavenly smells. He looked as if all the muscles in his body had been borrowed from to make room for enormous forearms, so from elbow down he was a giant while the rest of him could have dangled from a hook in a doctor's office. He was average height, which put him a foot above his wife.

"This is my husband, Mr. Gum, and he can't hear and he can't speak."

She began to flutter her hands at her husband with exclamation points and flourishes and curves and chopping motions while her face danced along grimacing and frowning, smiling and imploring. Mr. Gum nodded here and there, questioned here and there, appearing to make sense of her gyrations.

"If you talk slow he can read your lips a bit."

I said, "Pleased to make your acquaintance, Mr. Gum," and he nodded and reached out his hand. I was uneasy about letting him take mine for fear he would smash it. Yet I had seen the delicacy of his tarts and I took a chance. He held me firmly, shook my hand up and down once, and let go. I felt relieved. His hands moved questioningly to his wife, and she said to me, "He wants to know if you knew Tommy. I told him you didn't and he don't understand. He thinks soldiers all know one another."

Mrs. Gum was a woman familiar with many topics at once. "My head," she explained to me later, "is never empty. I put aside this to pick up that and go back to this when it's ready. It's like baking. You wait for a crust to appear while you're kneading something else and mixing some jam for tarts in between. (Tommy didn't understand that. He thought it was all waiting.) That's the way my mind is. I don't go from start to finish till the conversation is over and then you sit and stare at one another. Of course it's a tragedy to me that Mr. Gum can't neither hear what I say nor join in himself, but he was like that when we got married. It's not as if I didn't know what to expect."

That was later. What she said now, without pausing, was, "Jeffries comes in for a roll now and then."

Mr. Gum went to the back room.

"Was he like that from birth?"

"The constable?"—snorting a little to show she was teasing. "From birth."

"It's a wonder to me," I said, "a miracle and a source of admiration how he got along in life."

"That's one of the reasons I fell in love with the man. Admiration. And respect. Hard enough for a man with normal senses to find his way in the world. Mr. Gum has always made his living. He's never had to go on the parish and he's never gone with his hand out for help to a living soul, not since he was a boy. A man like that, I decided, with a pride like that, would be a man worth marrying. Not that I didn't worry some about having Tommy, whether he'd be like normal children. Of course, I wanted him anyway."

At this point I knew I had a gift. If I had always had it I had never know it to be worthy of special notice, or to see that it gave me particular advantage. But now I saw how useful it could be, provided that the meeting with Constable Jeffries was the sign I had been seeking. The gift was that people talked to me.

"How does he get along?"

Mr. Gum came in with a tray and set it down.

"Ask him something, anything at all." Mrs. Gum made a gesture with her thumb and her husband turned his attention to me.

I said, "How many kinds of bread do you make here, Mr. Gum?"

He told me, in exquisite detail. That he made everything from tiny breakfast rolls to thick workman's fare for lunch to delicate finger-size sticks for the well-to-do to entertain with and heavy black crusts for the poor. He said it all with dancing hands and eyes and fingers drawing pictures in the air. I understood him perfectly.

"He was at Varna—did you say you were at Varna, Mr.—"

"O'Boy."

"O'Boy."

"I was there," I said.

Mr. Gum pointed to my cane and I limped a step and his wife said, "You were wounded there?"

"At Inkerman."

"I am not so foolish," said Mrs. Gum, "as to resent your

standing here alive while Tommy is dead. I am not so foolish as to feel that."

"If you did it would be natural. When a friend of mine was killed I was glad it was he and not me even though I grieved for him."

"I used to be a mother. I'm not a mother any more."

"I can't help you," I said. "If I could help you, I would."

"I'm a religious woman, so I'm supposed to believe he's gone to a better place. Which gives me less in the way of comfort than I expected. But Mr. Gum, he don't have any religion at all, and he don't have any comfort at all. Look at him, you think he's a man has any comfort?"

"I can't help him either," I said.

"You're a blunt young man."

By now I was willing to leave and seek accommodations elsewhere. I was filled enough with my own hurt and not willing to take on a share of anyone else's. If Tommy had died at Varna, so had hundreds and hundreds of others. I didn't know him and I didn't know most of them. Except for Peregrine the deaths had meant little to me, and so far as Peregrine was concerned I had decided not to think of him again until I could do so without pain.

"You said something about needing a room," Mrs. Gum said.

"Constable Jeffries—"

"I guess he meant our storeroom. That's upstairs." She mimed a question to Mr. Gum, who considered it and looked me up and down in a way to take my skin off, examining all my moral credentials. Finally he nodded and Mrs. Gum said, "You passed him, which means you could pass any man in the world. That goes for Members of Parliament and the royal family. There's a cot up there—at least there used to be"—more gesticulation to Mr. Gum, who nodded again—"it's filled now with some odds and ends. If you'll clean the place up yourself and it's to your liking, the rent will be reasonable enough."

"Does one have to go through the shop here?"

"You want privacy, is it? The room is as private as can be. Follow me and see for yourself."

I went outside with her, and she squeezed through a space between the shop and another building. There didn't seem to be enough room for an undernourished cat and I followed with

160

some trepidation, thinking that to be stuck there was to be forever entombed. There was a courtyard in back with access to another street. She said that this was my private entrance to use for all my secret comings and goings, although there was another door at the back of the bakery.

    She preceded me up a short flight of open wooden stairs and taking a ring of keys from her waist unlocked a huge hasp in the door. We went into a room three times the size of the alcove in which I had slept at home, with a stout wood floor on which I stamped to test its solidity, and Mrs. Gum asked if I was a dancer or acrobat and did I intend tumbling exercises. There was a wide window looking down to the courtyard through which the afternoon sun shone, and there was a plaster and beamed ceiling and the walls were as stoutly wooded as the floor and up came the smells of baking bread, and I certainly had stepped into paradise.

Chapter Ten

My first thought was to see to my nest. I gathered all the crates and racks and bric-a-brac that the Gums had stored here and brought them downstairs, where Mr. Gum, with eloquent gestures, determined which were to be cast on the rubbish pile and which taken back to the bakery for possible use. When all that was left in my room was the bed, I borrowed scrubbing brush and a pail of water and soap from Mrs. Gum. Though the sun sent sufficient light through the window I was not satisfied with the corners—remembering the condition of that hospital at Scutari—and set up rush lights there to make sure my scrubbing was thorough. Finished with the floor I washed the walls, then opened the center part of the bow window—an English invention to allow light to enter from three directions at once—for drying.

I went back to Mr. Gum, who stood kneading bread with such grace and strength that I stood and watched for a while admiringly, when Mrs. Gum behind me said to me sharply, "I don't ever want anybody sneaking up on Mr. Gum."

"I was not—"

"I'm sure you had no such intention in mind. But I don't want him observed like an ox at work without him knowing. Get to the front of him if you have anything to say."

"I was going to ask him for some nails and a hammer." I moved closer to the front of Mr. Gum and spoke to the two of them. "You speak to me roughly, Mrs. Gum, and I am not happy with that, but I am pleased with all else here, and if you will accept my good faith I would be satisfied with a small indication of an apologetic nature."

"Go along with you," said Mrs. Gum. "I have an edge to my tongue, I've been told that often enough, and you said one so I'll say two. A hammer and some nails, you say."

"I want to put up a shelf or two."

Mr. Gum nodded, and wiggled his fingers at Mrs. Gum, who said to me, "Mr. Gum says help yourself at the tool chest in the back. And there's planks there you can use. And he says you're a boy to his liking, you put him in mind of our Tommy, and he says to tell you that I might bark but I don't bite, so you're not to take offense. Not that I don't bite if the occasion arises."

I believed her. I took the materials back to my room and put up some shelves and hooks for some teacups and a milk pot. The shelf near the bed was for several books which would be the beginning of a library. I hoped to acquire some of the works of Charles Dickens, having already read *Dombey and Son* and *Oliver Twist*. I found Mr. Dickens poetical, although I understood his growing fame was due to his ability as a teller of stories. I wanted copies of *Alton Locke, Henry Esmond,* and *Cranford.* Then the sonnets of Elizabeth Browning, to see if she was as incomprehensible as her husband, having enjoyed the comment of a reader who, having failed to understand either of them, said he hoped, upon their marriage and trip to Italy, that they would at least be intelligible to one another. I wanted some of the poetry of Byron and Thomas Carlyle's *Life of Schiller*. Undoubtedly this would take a long time, considering how costly books were, and that I was contemplating a profession that was poorly paid. Still, I should be able to purchase a book now and then and meanwhile I could borrow from Mudie's lending library.

Finally the room looked and smelled clean enough, and I shut the window to keep the soot of the city from returning it to its former condition. There were two things I wanted of a room of my own: a lock on the door and cleanliness. At home my room had been kept clean but there was no door to it, while life in the army had been both doorless and filthy.

Mrs. Gum said she would provide for me a ewer and basin and a stand to keep them on, a chair and a deal table, and sheet and blanket for the bed. The sheet and blanket were to be returned as soon as I could purchase those articles for myself. "I am renting you a room, Mr.—"

"O'Boy."

"Yes, renting a room, but I am not running a rooming house, if you see what I mean."

Some more trips up and down and my lair was secure.

I thought about becoming an officer of the law. A policeman saw that peace was maintained and laws were not broken, and it did not matter the station in life of the lawbreaker. Practically, of course, there would continue to be differences between crime in Belgravia and crime in Whitechapel, but even if there was one law for the rich and one for the poor, Sir James Nott-Playsaunt could hang as well as a Bill Sykes—at least a policeman could arrest them both. My father had said that everybody had to know his place in life, but it seemed to me that a policeman—at least while performing his duty—could claim to have no place at all, and that appealed to me.

Mrs. Gum, standing in front of the bakeshop, caught me as I slipped through the alleyway.

" 'ware the nursemaids now, Mr.—"

"O'Boy."

"Yes. They tend to pick up the scarlet fever, you know—" pointing out the red of my uniform coat.

"If so it's their last opportunity. After today it's a dark suit of clothes like everybody else."

"Pity. Before Tommy was sent abroad I loved the look and so did the girls. I was always one for a uniform myself. Before Mr. Gum caught my eye I lived down near Shadwell and took up with a sailor or two. In a decent way, you understand."

"Naturally, Mrs. Gum."

"Where are you off to now, Mr.—"

"O'Boy."

"Yes. I'm just asking in a friendly way, you understand. I am not a prying person."

"I know that, Mrs. Gum. I thought I'd see a bit of the city and then I'll be trying to make up my mind about some business. I'll walk along Oxford Street, that's just at the corner, and then I'd appreciate your telling me where the Strand is, which I have heard is the first street in Europe, and then I want to see Pall Mall and then Whitehall—"

"From Oxford Street you turn to your right on Charing Cross Road and that will lead you to Whitehall. On the way you'll be close enough to the Strand to take a look at it. For my taste it's just a fancy street with a lot of clubs wouldn't let you or Mr. Gum past the doors. Keep one hand on your handkerchief and one on your money. You've got a country look to you, Mr.—"

"Why do you have such difficulty with my name, Mrs. Gum?"

"I don't know, I'm usually good at names. I just never heard a name like yours."

"Why don't you call me Richard, then?"

"I will, Richard. As I was saying, about your country look. They'll all be out, all the sharpers and bludgers and duffers and the flimps—"

"Those are all bad people, I suppose."

"Bad's the word. That red coat will draw them like flies to treacle."

"I'll be careful, Mrs. Gum," I said, pleased there was someone to say it to.

I thought I would never lose my amazement at this city. I was not prepared for the bustle, the energy, the excitement. The streets were filled with diversions. You could buy almost anything to eat—baked potatoes and ginger beer, treacle rock, toffy, lollipops, peppermint sticks, meat pies, glasses of milk—I found out later that the seller bought skim milk, watered it down, and sold it sweetened with sugar.

I stopped at a coffee stall. The beverage I was given was mixed with chicory, which in turn was mixed with baked carrot, and the result neither looked nor tasted like coffee but it was hot enough and I drank it.

A man stood on a box across which a placard stated he was Dr. Bokanky, the famed herbalist. Waving his hands over his head to attract listeners while not impeding the flow of words from his mouth, he declaimed, "Now then for the kalibonca root that comes from Madras in the East Indies. It will cure toothache, headache, giddiness in the head, dimness of sight, rheumatics in the head, and is highly recommended for the ague. Never known to fail. I have it for the sixth and twenty year from one penny to sixpence the packet, the best article in England."

An old Jew accidentally brushed against a woman wearing a grass-green dress decorated with flowers with an azure blue scarf and golden jewelry, all strapped like a harness onto a body like a superannuated cavalry horse. She spat at the old man. "Can't do that, can you? You spat on Christ, and now all you can do is slobber." The Jew shook his head, spat emphatically on the street, and walked on. The Lord Mayor of London was David Salamons, a Jew. I followed the woman's progress up the street, where shortly she met a man with flabby cheeks and dewlaps, blue eyes, and an enormous trunk in a short jacket. The Frenchman Taine said the regimen and the port that the English drink begin to deform the face, the teeth jut forward, and they have the appearance of a bulldog with purple marks on a brick red face.

This was the most densely populated city in the world. Coming from the lane off Oxford Street, through the stifling alleys, I saw troops of pale children who had spent the night huddling out of doors. In the Strand there were no children, only men and women exquisitely attired with neckbands and immaculately white ruffled fronts. Considering the frequent rain and the black mud underfoot, the pristine linen would have to be changed and replaced several times a day. The women wore heavily flounced crinoline skirts with pagoda sleeves and elaborate mantles. The men wore dull black top hats, dark frock coats above lighter trousers, and dark silk chokers. In the street drays, carts, four-wheel and hansom cabs, saddle horses, broughams, and chaises formed a continuous stream.

A girl said, "Please, sir."

Very young but tall, head almost to my shoulder, she wore no crinoline but a dirty cotton dress and a straw bonnet with a bit of faded ribbon. And dirty of face, the soapless children infesting the streets like sparrows.

"Yes?" I said.

"Help me, sir, please, sir."

"How? What's the matter?"

She clutched a package in crumpled newspaper. "Please, sir. I'm in such terrible trouble, sir. I was sent out to buy the fixin's for my dad's breakfast—a collop of bacon and an egg and some tea and sugar. I was holding the money here in my hand—two shillings it was—and two villains came up on me, one on each side, and they buzzed my money and now I daren't go home."

"Why not? Wasn't your fault."

"My dad's hit me before for less'n this. He'll take my head off for this. Don't need to ball his fist, either, slaps me with his open hand and tumbles me across the room. My ears are still ringing from the last time. I can't go home, I'm too scared. Help me, sir, please, sir."

Big eyes, filling with tears. Like Maureen's, I thought, if Maureen had ever cried.

"If you'd lend me the money, sir. I've put some aside at home and I could get it and be back with it here in a question of minutes, and I'd leave you this to hold, sir." She handed me the parcel, which was heavy enough.

"What's in here?"

"It's my books. I was taking them back to the reverend; he lends me books to read."

"Like what?" I said. "What sort of books?"

I was straining her, the look behind the tears was sharp. "Two shillings, little enough to a sojer like you but a bloody fortune to me if I don't have it nor the breakfast either with my dad raising his hand to me."

"Yet you have it at home, you say, to repay me with."

"I was saving it for a new dress."

"Two shillings—is that what a breakfast costs?"

"Twelve there are of us, all in one room too. Could anybody feed twelve for less?"

"Your mother—"

"Died and gone two years since."

"Who takes care of you, then?"

"Questions. If you don't want to help me that's all right, sir"—holding out her hand for the package. "Time's running out. If I don't get back with the fixin's my dad'll be out looking for me and it'll be worse than just losing the money, it'll be putting him to that extra trouble, you see, which will make him a lot madder. But you don't have to help me, that's all right, sir."

"I didn't say I wouldn't help."

"You will?"—a tremulous smile beginning.

"Twelve," I said. "And you the oldest?"

"Yes."

"How could that be? You're no more than—"

"I'm older'n I look."

"I hold the books?"

"Yes."

"And you'll be coming right back with the money?"

"I promise, sir. Five minutes to get to the store—I'll run all the way there and home—and you stay just here, say, five minutes more and back I come."

"Well, then," I said, taking out two shillings and handing them to her.

"Oh, thank you, sir, you are a saint." And taking the money she ran off.

I walked up and down with the package under my arm, looking

at the store windows, marveling continuously at the sights of London. I watched as a monster wagon crawled through the streets with ropes and hooks for letting enormous barrels down into cavern cellars. A turning led to the hallmark of the city—unbelievable contrasts side by side. Here was a ground-level opening to an underground slaughterhouse. Inside, the walls were inches thick in blood and fat where the sheep were hurled to be knifed and flayed. Nearby were fat boilers, glue renderers, fellmongers, tripe scrapers, and dog skinners. And always the ubiquitous food sellers, no matter if the ingredients were putrid and contaminated by the surroundings. And everywhere the prostitutes. I was accosted five times within a hundred yards, some so young I could not believe the nature of their invitations.

Back I went to stand as close as I remembered to the spot the girl had left me. It seemed half an hour had passed, and then an hour, and I unwrapped the package to let the brick within fall to the cobbles. At first my anger was uppermost, and then I laughed at myself that I had been so easily gulled by a child.

I had looked for a sign and found it as Constable Jeffries appeared out of the fog. Now was this not a further sign that, having myself become a victim, I should now devote myself to the extirpation of such crimes? I saw myself stalking the child and pouncing upon her as she cried out for mercy, the stolen shillings clutched in her hand, hauling her to court and thence to Newgate to be shut up forever while the gentry walked streets made safer by thieftakers like myself.

Still I was not sure. Did I prefer to go to the docks to load cargo, or stand all day behind a counter in some mercer's establishment, or crouch over a high desk to be scrivener to some solicitor? And did I want to stay in this city? That was the easiest of all to answer. There was filth here and danger and terror and great beauty and excitement and promise—yes, I would stay here. I could try the police. They would not, after all, exact from me the twenty-one years the army demanded, to be escaped only by leaving them part of the function of my leg.

I found the way to Whitehall and from there to number 4 Whitehall Place, which backed into the narrow lane to the east called Scotland Yard. I picked one of the metropolitan districts of police divisions at random and, upon presenting myself and stating my purpose, was sent to a room to talk to a sergeant.

His name, he told me, was Buckles. He was tall and thin to the point of resembling a cadaver, yet I found out later he had such strength in his hands he could, with thumb and forefinger, break a man's wrist as easily as cracking a piece of stale bread. He questioned me about my education as closely as my army career, and did I have any reason for wanting to be a policeman other than the poor pay and the danger.

"It's a useful occupation, I think."

"So is dustman and omnibus driver and coffee-stall owner."

"I didn't get a *call*—"

"Who does? It's the size of the living that comes first, wouldn't you say? I'm a dissenter myself, kept me out of Oxford."

No sign of a smile to show he was not to be taken seriously. Yet—a policeman who might have attended Oxford, were he of the established church? And so my father was right again, for I was thinking like a farmer's son.

While we were speaking the door opened and a man came in quietly, taking a chair to the side as if not to interrupt, but following the interview keenly enough to show he was part of the apparatus.

"Inspector Criddle," Buckles said.

At a lull the inspector said, "So you want to wear the uniform, do you?"

He had a square face with high color and a pair of blue eyes so unsympathetic that the sight of them, I thought, by young criminals could alone cause a diminution of their antisocial activities.

"I do not, sir," I said.

"Then what are you doing here?"

"I want to join the police but I do not want to wear a uniform, I've been in one long enough. I heard there's a detective force does their work in plain clothes, and that's what I'm interested in."

"We recruit from the constabulary," Buckles said. "A man gets his experience in the streets, and if he's so minded he can then apply for the plainclothes division. It is not our policy to recruit a man directly out of civilian life into the detectives."

"I'm not in civilian life," I said. "Except for the last week or two."

"Good point," said Buckles, looking at the inspector.

"Would you be ashamed to wear the uniform, is that it?"

"No. That's not it at all. But after two years in the army I want to appear like other men. I do not want to stand out from the population."

"Ashamed," said the inspector.

"No!" I said.

"It would appear that way," said the inspector.

"Then you weren't listening," I said, making to get up.

Buckles held his hand palmside out to me. "Temper," he said.

"A police officer does not let himself be easily provoked," Inspector Criddle said.

I was as stupid here as I had been in the street with the girl who had gulled me. They were testing me for flaws and I was revealing all I had.

The inspector said, "I don't understand why you want to join the police."

I looked to the sergeant to explain what I had already said to him, but he was silent. By now I understood my reasons for being here less than before, as vague as they were then, and I thought that another question or two would overload the already teetering barrow of my tolerance.

Buckles said, "You want a job, is that it?"

"I need to work, yes. But there is more to it. I think the police might even be necessary."

"Might be?" said the inspector. "Even!"

"I don't think the free inhabitants of a city ought to be like an army—that is, having no individual liberty, as a soldier has none who can be ordered to go here and there, and be flogged if his superiors think it necessary, or even executed. So I do not like a government police force in peacetime."

The inspector stared at me and Buckles was clearing his throat.

I tried to salvage something by saying, "What appeals to me about the police is the evenhandedness."

"What do you mean by that?" the inspector said.

"That there be one law for all."

"He's a Chartist," said the inspector coldly. "Were you ever a Chartist?"

The sergeant said, "The movement came and went before he was old enough to spell his name."

The sergeant shrugged in apology for correcting his superior. Criddle said, "I was referring, of course, to certain ideas—"

"I was in mind," I said, "of the Gordon riots in 1780."

"Do you care to ask him why, Sergeant Buckles?"

"Yes?" Buckles said.

"They were burning down the houses of the Catholics, and when a deputation went to the Lord Mayor to protest, that official said, 'The whole mischief seems to be that the mob have got hold of some people and some furniture they do not like and are burning them, and what is the harm in that?'"

"You're Catholic?" said the inspector.

"No, sir."

"Then the point is—?"

"Evenhandedness," I said.

Sergeant Buckles and Inspector Criddle conferred eye to eye without speech. Criddle nodded sharply and went out.

"I'm accepted, then?"

"First to the police surgeon for an examination. And then I would prefer you serving as a constable in uniform—for, perhaps, six months—after which we would consider transfer to the detectives."

"I will not get into uniform again."

Buckles had deep lines of resignation pulling down the corners of his mouth, as if he had seen all the ignorance there was but could never accept new forms of it. "What would be the harm in—"

"The constable keeps the peace, he patrols, he is seen, he is the shepherd. That is not my nature."

Buckles sighed. "See the surgeon, then come back to me here."

I went down the hall to a room where I found a man low in a chair with his feet up on a desk; he was contemplating a pair of shiny bluchers. I stood for a while sharing his admiration of their excellence. He did not let my presence disturb him. I had no cause to find doctors estimable and he was doing nothing to change my mind.

He looked to be in his early twenties, his jacket on the back of his chair, waistcoat and dark trousers as well cared for as his boots. He turned his feet. "Nothing like a good gloss on good leather to give a man satisfaction." He looked down at my own boots stained with London mud.

"I'm here for an examination."

"Ah."

Seconds passed while I entertained the notion of slapping his feet off the desk and on the backswing catching him cross the chops. Reluctantly his gaze left his footwear to rest on me. "Army? Passed their examination, didn't you? You look healthy enough. I don't see that we have to go much further." He scratched around for some official paper and took up a pen.

"Name, age, any past serious illnesses—"

"I had the cholera."

"Ever had the pox, the—" He swung his legs off the desk. "Cholera? Recovered from the cholera?"

"Yes."

"Take off your jacket and shirt. Let me take a look at you. I've never seen anyone recovered from the cholera."

The doctor began to poke and prod me, rolled a cylinder and held one end to my chest and the other to his ear, pulled down my eyelids, had me stick out my tongue, and in general made me feel like a fish that a cook in a fine household was considering for Sunday dinner.

"How did you know it was the cholera?"

"They were dying from it all about me."

"Fascinating. Was it the water?"

"Water?"

"There was an army chap said something about boiling the water. What special thing did you do?"

"I was just waiting to die is all."

"Marvelous, marvelous. Well, let's get on with the rest of it"—going back to his desk and this time putting only one foot up. "Pox? Clap, syphilis? Ever been in the foul ward?"

"No."

"Any drippings, any leaks?"

I shook my head.

"Any sores, chancres?"

"I've never been with a woman," I said.

"How old did you say you were? How long have you been

in the army? A virgin?" He grinned and dropped one eyelid. "Ever feel the urge to paint your face? Or is it the solitary pleasures you prefer. Makes you blind, you know, or takes away your senses. Or is it that you're just not equipped? We may as well see the whole beast, having gone this far. Drop your trousers."

When I was stripped he said, "Built like a ruddy bull. The city's full of dolly-mops, you wouldn't be denying them the pleasure? Are you religious, is that it?"

I shook my head.

"Virgin? *Cum grano salis.* Were you discharged from the army?"

"I was wounded."

"Not where it counts, eh? The whole bleeding city's a brothel. How long have you been in London?"

I told him.

"I give you twenty-four hours and—just remember if you come down with the French disease you'll not be curing it by connection with a young virgin's box. They believe that out there, you know. Damme, cured yourself of the cholera, did you? You can't blame the girls, you know. If they work from early morning to late at night the best they can make is three or four shillings, so no wonder they take to whoring. St. James, Leicester Square—I thought Glasgow was bad, the dirtiest city in the world. Oh, my God, so it's your leg, is it."

I looked down at it, which I did not usually like to do.

"It's much better now."

"What did this?"

"A bullet."

"One bullet?" He whistled. "How did the surgeons ever—"

"They didn't do anything."

The doctor frowned, pressed his lips together, gestured that I could get dressed, and shook his head.

"I'm fine now," I said.

"Xenophon—"

"Yes?"

"You would not have heard of him, but—"

"I heard of him."

"Really. Then you may know what he said: 'Look to the feet in your choice of a horse; should these be faulty reject the animal at once whatever other good qualities he may have.'"

"I am not a horse."

"I'm sorry," said the doctor, "I cannot pronounce you fit."

"Oh, no," I said. "Oh, bloody no."

"Sorry."

"First," I said, "a doctor wants to take my leg off where I was hit in the field, and I didn't let him. Then a doctor wanted to take it off in the hospital, and I didn't let him. And now that I've walked on it this far you will not say I am fit. It is not enough that you looked at it—they all looked at it—or that you touched it and rubbed and pursed your mouth. Test me."

"I have already seen your leg. It has been badly hurt. I must consider if you can keep up with the duties of constable."

"You believe I cannot move as fast as necessary?"

"Well, yes."

"A man can get away from me because of this poor leg?"

"It is likely, is it not?"

"Have you, then, doctor," I said, "two good legs?"

"I—yes."

"Then play the part of a two-legged criminal. We are both equally distant from the door. Moreover, I will let you stand and I will stay seated. I must prevent you from leaving this room, poor leg and all."

"How ridiculous," said the doctor.

"Yet if you cannot leave by that door before I stop you, will you then consider me fit?"

I had not intended to do more than prove I was quick enough. But this bastard, who would not have his judgment questioned, was already cheating, having begun to sidle toward the door. I let him take another step and I was on him and, because of my annoyance, I whipped him toward the desk, harder than I should have, and he toppled over it to the floor. Which should have been the end of my police career before it began, but I had mistaken him as he had mistaken me. He got up, rubbing the back of his neck, and said, "You win, Mr. O'Boy. You are fit enough."

"Thank you. I am sorry that—"

"You're a violent man, Mr. O'Boy."

He made some marks on a card and I took it back to Sergeant Buckles. "Come back in the morning and you'll be sworn in and given a warrant card."

"Good," I said.

"The inspector does not believe in taking someone off the street and immediately assigning him to the detective police. Nor do I believe that to be good policy. I convinced him you would merit a probationary period, during which I would instruct you myself, using the Madras method. Are you familiar with that?"

"No, sir."

"In India they instruct children by putting them in the care of older students."

"You are hardly a student—"

"Wrong, as you shall see tomorrow. No man can know criminal London thoroughly if he takes a lifetime. Would you like to know why I bothered to change the inspector's mind?"

"Yes, sir."

"Because I am sick of ignorance, Mr. O'Boy. You have read the work of Mr. Samuel Smiles?"

"No, sir."

"He writes, 'We hear that knowledge is power but we never hear that ignorance is power, and yet ignorance has always had more power in the world than knowledge. Ignorance dominates because knowledge has obtained access only to the minds of the few.' Mr. O'Boy, do you want to learn?"

"Yes, sir," I said.

"I will teach you then. Do you have civilian clothes?"

"I'm going out to buy some."

"I don't want you dressing like a navvy but not like a swell either. Stay away from shoddy—that's the new cloth they make from rags. Fustian is better than corduroy. A spencer and a neckcloth will do you, and for a hat get a Muller cutdown. And strong boots; your time in the army has taught you the value of those."

"What kind of hat did you say?"

"There was a murderer named Franz Muller who always took his victim's hat and had it cut down to eliminate the part containing the victim's name. Now it has become popular. A top hat is no good for moving quickly when need be, and it's more of a target."

On my way back to my room I avoided those shops with the trousers and jackets dangling on hooks before the door and went into the fashionable store of Marshall and Snelgrove on Oxford Street. I told the clerk I wanted some serviceable trousers and a jacket. At the word serviceable his brow creased and he looked up at the ceiling for guidance.

"Those trousers you're wearing, did you buy them here?" I said.

"Yes."

"They will do. Find a pair in my size."

"We do not sell reach-me-downs, sir."

"How long would it take to fit me, then?"

"Eight to ten days."

"I can't wait," I said.

So I had to repair to one of the establishments with garments hanging in the wind. I was able to find a pair of trousers that fit well enough, changing into them in a back room, but I had difficulty with a jacket since the proprietor could find none that I could button without splitting it across the shoulders. Finally he brought down a surtout which fitted well enough if I did not button it, and to fill in the front I purchased a waistcoat of a flowered pattern which he assured me was favored by the gentry. Carrying my uniform in a bundle, I went into a cookhouse to have a chop wrapped for consumption in my room.

It was getting dark. I noticed a group of ragged boys looking in the window of a small grocery shop at the barley sugar and brandy balls. I saw one insert the point of a knife into the corner of a pane of glass and give it a wrench. The pane cracked and another boy applied a sticking plaster, with which he pulled out enough glass to get his hand through. I came up to them and they scattered without fear, standing a few paces off to stare boldly at me, a civilian without authority even to chastise. I called to the proprietor and he came out, a small man in a half apron. Seeing what had been done he advanced on the boys, shouting; for him they ran away. The owner, at least, had a position which they recognized. Then I saw a flash of dress amid their trousered legs, a tall girl, a familiar-looking girl, and I ran and nabbed her.

"We meet again," I said.

"I don't know you, let go of me."

"I had a package that belonged to you. Wrapped in newspaper. Some books you were returning to a clergyman, wasn't it?"

"Ah," she said, "I an't never seen you before."

"You return my two shillings," I said, "or I march you off to the station house."

"Was it you, then?" She cocked her head to look up at me, impeded somewhat by my fingers at the back of her neck. "The kind gentleman who loaned me the money to buy breakfast for my dad? I went back looking for you, sir. I walked up and down and you wasn't there."

"How fortunate then that we've met again. Let's have the money."

"If you'll wait right here I'll run off home and get it. I've been keeping it, waiting to see you again."

"Why can't we just go along home together and I can ask your father for the money."

"Please, sir, you wouldn't do that. He'd beat me something terrible."

She struggled and twisted and in the process her bosom brushed up against me and she noticed my notice and immediately she dropped the role of wheedling child. She pulled back, hand on hip, and said, "Perhaps we can make an arrangement for the two shillings," and I restrained my desire to laugh, she was doing it so badly. Too, I was somehow pleased that she showed no experience at it.

She had fine eyes, the strangeness of which observation occurred to me even as I thought it. One might notice that of a properly dressed girl met over tea, perhaps at some relative's home, or a stranger getting out of some noble's carriage, glancing up for a moment as you went by. It was hardly a mental comment for a disheveled, smudged girl of the streets.

"What kind of sluttish child are you," I said. "Where have you learned to behave like that? How old are you?"

"I'm fourteen, near fifteen, if you want to know."

Older than Alethea when I had first seen her. I contrasted the sweet elegance in that country field with this hoyden in a muddy lane.

"You like me, don't you, sir," she said.

"Like you! A thief like you? What's your name?"

"Jessie."

"Jessie what?"—thinking that like Roger she'd have no other name, would not know even that people came with two.

"Jessie Marsh."

"You need a licking. I'd like to give it to you myself but you say your father's so good at it I'll put you in his hands. Let's go along, then."

Instead of begging again, she now drew herself up to some

semblance of dignity, the way a misfit cradles his own distinctiveness. "You notice how tall I am, for a girl."

"That you are," I said.

"What good's a tall girl? Men don't like tall girls, they want little cuddly ones. They don't like a girl to be strong, and I'm strong."

"I noticed that."

"I know what a woman's place is in the world."

Place, I thought. My father's definition of freedom.

"You have to be—petite? That's French."

"So it is," I said.

"That's what you have to be. And helpless. Well, I an't helpless, I can take care of myself real good."

"How long have you been a thief?"

"I an't a thief. I just borrowed some money from you and I'll pay it back."

"That was my idea, too. What sort of work is your father in?"

"He works on the docks."

"And you? What do you work at—I mean, when you're not cadging shillings or smash-and-grabbing sweets."

"I've got a craving for sweets. That's why I was hanging about when I seen what the boys was up to. You know what they say about children sucking a sweet?"

"No. What?"

"They say the habit of sucking a sweet starts a craving in the gullet and that can later only be satisfied with drink. You know anything about that?"

"No. You were going to tell me about your work."

"I always been working. Since I was seven; I was a watercress girl then. I'd get up before daybreak and go to Farrington Market, and then you tie up the bunches and you walk the streets and you call out"—she raised her voice in a child's wail—"'Watercress, four bunches a penny.' You're out all day for three or four pence. That's what I done. Then I was a step girl, that's a girl that cleans steps who an't allowed in the house to clean anything else, and I got tuppence a house. You want to know what else I done?"

"No," I said.

"You know anything about being poor?"

"I've never been poor," I said.

"And you're interested in me, an't that right?"

"I'm not at all interested in you," I said.

"I sold matches, and I walked around waiting for a toff to take a fancy to me—that's what I done."

"I don't care. I've heard enough. You're going to keep on talking to me until I forget about my money, is that it?"

"There's been men come round asking questions of the persons where I live, writing things down, all about what kind of work do you do and how much do you pay for your lodgings—you know how they ask them questions? Like they're in a jungle someplace talking to savages doing things they'd never do. You know what I mean?"

"No."

"It's not like your wanting to know the work I done."

"Back to that? I thought I said—"

"Never mind. You really care about me, that's what I think. Anyway, the men come round asking questions, and I hear later it comes out in some one of those papers. Now, a person tells them he's hungry, say. This man writing things down, he understands what being hungry is but not like there's ever been a real pain in his belly, you see? He doesn't know when you've got a pain like that you'll do anything. He doesn't know what cold feels like. He knows what it is, but that's all. He doesn't know what it's like not to have enough clothes to keep off the wind. He doesn't know you can't sleep when you're in a cold room and you don't have proper covers. But when you ask these questions, I know it's because you care about me."

"I didn't ask any questions. Just one or two, that's all, and I'm sorry I started the whole thing."

"But you are interested in me, an't you?"

"No. And stop trying to talk me around. I don't want your life's story, I want my two shillings. I think it's best I get you to a constable."

"No, sir. Please." Back to pleading child in a bewildering change. "I'll return your money. I swear it. Right now. You wait here and—"

"I changed my mind," I said. "Keep the money."

With that I released her and she stood rubbing her neck

where I had been holding her and she took a step away and, just out of my reach, she said, "You're a fool, then, an't you, to be taken in by a young girl like me?"

"Very likely," I said.

"I don't see that you'll be safe in these streets. And I don't see why a sojer like you cares about a girl like me, anyway."

"Who said I cared about you?"

"Well, you talk to me, and you act as if you care about me. But I guess you're off to India or someplace like that."

"I'm finished with the army."

"Lovely. Are you married?"

"No."

"Lovely."

"Go home," I said. "Go—away."

"What will you be doing, then?"

"I'm joining the police."

She blinked and took a step back and then she disappeared among the people in the street as a doe disappears among the trees in a wood.

Chapter Eleven

I was up at first light, not to be late. I washed my face and got into clothes which had become unfamiliar to me, my fingers fumbling at buttons which appeared to be in the wrong place. I went out and had tea and bacon at a stall and walked the awakening streets.

It lacked ten minutes to eight when I presented myself to Sergeant John Buckles. He looked me up and down.

"Inspector Criddle will swear you in."

Criddle came in abstracted, holding papers, frowning. "You going after Tyler?"

"Yes, sir," Buckles said.

"In the rookery?"

"Where else would he be?"

"You'll be taking some constables with you?"

"Uniforms in the Holy Land would not be a good idea."

"You'll not be going in by yourself?"

"I was planning on taking O'Boy, here."

"Ah. O'Boy. Sergeant Buckles has convinced me to stretch the rules for you. Are you worth it?"

"Yes, sir," I said.

"Oh. Well, then. Put up your hand. You'll uphold and defend the laws of the city, the parish, and Her Majesty's realm?"

"Yes, sir."

"Give him his warrant card then, Sergeant."

"Here it is, made out all nice and official."

"Stand to with him, Sergeant."

The men were paraded before going out on their beat. A sergeant read the instructions for those unable to read for themselves.

I asked Buckles if I could forgo carrying the truncheon he offered me.

"You might wish you had it. On the other hand there is a routine caution about its use. Some of the folk out there have skulls as thin as paper."

"If I carry it, does it not show who I am? Isn't the purpose of wearing ordinary clothing to let us go into places where a uniformed constable would be shunned?"

"They'll know you soon enough."

"You don't carry a truncheon," I said.

He reached for his hat and let it drop to the floor. It clanged. Retrieving it he tapped it with his knuckles. "Saved my life more times than I can remember." We went toward the door. "Are you ready then, Probationary Detective Constable O'Boy?"

"Am I all those things? Yes, sir, I am ready."

"No sirring from now on. On the streets I'll be John. At the station house I redeem my rank and will be addressed as Sergeant. Into the fray then, Richard."

Women carried on their heads heavy baskets of fruit on their way to Covent Garden. Buckles stopped at a lane in which had gathered a group of young men. Some wore full-skirted velveteen coats and others long side-pocketed corduroy waistcoats set off with brass, pearl, and carved bone buttons; all wore cord trousers tight at the knees and looser below over heavy ankle boots.

"Costermongers, Richard."

They had formed a ring, within which two of them were squaring off. I considered them with my father's professional prizefighter eye. They were not well matched. The taller and broader one had given his jacket to be held by a shouting supporter. All wore large silk handkerchiefs around their throats.

"The kingsman," Buckles said. "That yellow pattern on a green background is favored by costermongers. Know them."

"Because they are of the criminal class?"

"No. They work at their barrows, selling fruits and vegetables. But they're a race unto themselves, and they're a violent people. The kerchief and their way of dressing are the way they maintain their difference. If you study neckcloths you will learn who walks the streets of London. Look there, crossing the street, the man with the twice-about white one—that's a clergyman. Gissing said the divisions were between those who did and those who did not wear a collar, with each class then endlessly subdivided. The way each folds his neck attire shows his awareness of his own social standing."

"Gissing?" I said.

"George Gissing. You haven't read him?"

"No."

"And I took you for an educated man. George Gissing and Charles Dickens—those are the two writers who know their London."

The smaller costermonger bored in with his head down, and the taller one easily fended him off and with backward step helped the other along with a roundabout swing that caught the shorter man on the side of his head and down he went.

"They admire fighting more than anything," Buckles said. "They believe it's necessary to a boy's education that he work his fists well. And when they tire of fighting amongst themselves they seek out a common enemy—the police."

"Why is that?"

"Few citizens like the police. The costermonger takes more joy in his dislike of us, that's all."

I heard them talking in a language I could not follow. "Are they foreign?"

"As English as you and I. They talk a kind of patois, a backward pronunciation. They say on for no, and say for yes."

"Kool the esclop," said the victorious fighter, pushing through the ring of his fellows to stare at Buckles and me.

"That's 'Look at the police,'" Buckles said. "They know me."

He moved to walk away and I followed.

"The old one's brought his babby with." The fighter came around in front of me and stood chin to chin. "Are you handy? You're a big enough one. You want to go at it with me?"

He had no nose, at least what he had been born with had been flattened, and his eyes could barely be seen because of the swollen flesh over his cheekbones.

"Maybe," I said. "One day."

"I love to bring the big ones down," he said.

"Another time," I said.

"Pearly's my name. You'll remember it?"

"I will," I said.

Pearly bowed low before me and in straightening up somehow

managed to knock off my hat. I bent down for it and a foot kicked it just beyond my reach. I reached for it again and then, realizing I was in the middle of a fool's game, I stood up, leaving the hat on the ground. Buckles was watching. I felt resentfully that this was his London and these his costermongers and I being so fresh on the job should he not have stepped in to help? This was a child's contest impossible to win at, and the victim could only be made to look foolish. I did not want to look foolish. You couldn't be quick enough to grab the hat in motion, and if you did you would be all ascramble and clutching with no dignity left. So you could either wait until the players tired of the game or forgo the hat and walk away. I couldn't do either of those things and Buckles was keeping back, watching, and I thought this a good time to quit the police because what good is a policeman who has been duped and mocked?

"Why don't you give the esclop his topper?" Pearly said.

I felt grateful to him.

"A man can't keep his hat on," said Pearly, his face two inches from mine, "should not be walking the streets instructing others."

I agreed with that. And so, I was sure, did Buckles, standing now well back and out of my sight. I reached down slowly, knowing they would wait until the last moment to move it, and I thought I might then be quick enough but I wasn't. So I straightened and caught Pearly's chin with my left hand while I grabbed his arm and pulled it behind him and began to press it upward. It should have been simple since my movement was unexpected and the surprise should have left him no time to stiffen. I misjudged both the speed of his reaction and his strength. I could not get his arm beyond the parallel. So we stood locked together. And now I was doubly foolish, with Sergeant Buckles observing.

"Knock the crusher down, Pearly."

"Serve him out, Pearly."

We circled, he attempting to break loose and I attempting to bend him. He was amazingly strong.

"O'Boy," Buckles said, "stop dancing with the man."

It was the hint of tired contempt in his voice that made me find a drop more energy, enough to move Pearly's arm above the main limit of his resistance, so that, close to the cracking point, Pearly said, "Let go, curse you," and I said, "As soon as you fetch me my hat."

His friends continued to encourage him but I had him now and in a moment I'd have luxated him; he bent forward and down, I handling him as if he were too fragile to dip unattended, and he picked up my hat and I said, "On my head, please," and he reached back with it and with a shove I let him go.

He turned to face me, rubbing his arm. His friends gathered. Then Buckles stepped forward.

"We won't be doing anything so foolish, now, would we, men?"—taking his hat off and testing the edge of the brim with his fingertips in a gesture they appeared to recognize.

Pearly said, "I want his name."

"Richard," I said. "Richard O'Boy."

"I'll remember," Pearly said.

I walked along with Buckles in silence. After a while I said, "What did I do wrong?"

"I didn't say you did anything wrong."

"You didn't say I did anything right, either."

"Given the provocation, you did right. On the other hand the costermongers are crazed by their feelings about personal honor, especially where the police are concerned. So from now on you're marked and you've got to be doubly careful. Pearly'll get you if he can."

"You were testing me," I said.

"I was watching you being tested. That is not the same thing."

We walked on and I felt uncomfortable. Buckles had neither chastised nor complimented me, and I needed one or the other. I was both myself—a man always boiling to resist affront—and a police detective who had accepted guardianship of the law.

"We're a bit early," Buckles said. "Let's sit in the park for a bit."

The notice read: IT IS HOPED THAT THE PUBLIC WILL ABSTAIN FROM DAMAGING WHAT IS CULTIVATED FOR THE PUBLIC PLEASURE.

There were gigantic horse chestnut trees with pink and white flowers and rhododendrons taller than the tallest man. There were no railings and, outside of the notice at the entrance, no restrictions.

I sat beside Buckles on a bench. He said, "How is it that not a child picks a flower, and common people come here and picnic and never damage anything?"

"Because people are good," I said. "Except for those who are bad. The bad ones don't come here, they don't like parks. What I want to know is, would they have played with your hat as they did with mine?"

"No."

"Why?"

"Because they know me."

"They knew me for a raw detective."

"You have no reputation yet," Buckles said. "What they know about me is that I would never let up. I would have the youngest whipped and the oldest sent to the Hulks. They don't know about you. They'll play with you the way they did with your hat—a little at a time, irritating you to see if it turns into real anger, and then they'll wait to see if you cool and forget about it. They'll want to know how bad an enemy you can be. And then they'll want to see if you can be fair. Remember what the inspector said about not using your position for private ends?"

"But you'd be vindictive, that's what you said."

"That's true," Buckles said. "I'm not perfect. John Stuart Mill said, 'The only purpose for which power can be rightfully exercised over any member of a civilized community against his will is to prevent harm.'"

"Well?"

"He was never a Peeler. Peeler, or Bobby, from Robert Peel, who created us."

I watched a mother with a child just beginning to walk. She held his hand and encouraged him. With her other hand she held her skirt out of the dirt. A boy wobbled a hoop along with a stick. Protectively behind him came Grandfather in yellow waistcoat and Oxonian shoes.

"Time," Buckles said, getting up.

He set off at a good pace and I kept up with him. "Where are we going, John?"

"To the Holy Land."

"Knights Templar, are we?"

"That's what it's called, the Holy Land. St. Giles. There's also places like it behind the Ratcliffe Highway. And there's Lambeth and Southwark, Spital Fields between Union and Thrall streets, Bluegate Fields—you'll get to know them all. Rookeries. You know why we're looking for our man there?"

"Why, John?"

"Because when you're looking for a criminal you go where the criminals live."

"I see, John."

"The man we want knocked down an old woman and stole her purse. Being old and not very well, the old woman never got up again. That's foul, an old woman. There's some crimes I'm easy on, but I'm dead on the scent of the foul ones. I never let up on those."

"Murder," I said.

"Not always. A man kills another man for sneaking into his bed when he's away. Excusable, you see. Or taking a club to your woman in anger, or she to you. Equally excusable."

"It's not the law you're talking about, then."

"You can't go after them all, can you? Forty-two of us?"

I wanted to ask about him, how he had got to be what he was, but this wasn't the time. He was walking too fast for me but I couldn't tell him so.

"We'll be leaving the place where decent folk live and with one step we'll be in the bad section. Now you look at those marks there." Buckles pointed out waist-high smudges against several buildings. "That's where they lean up against, because being poor they're dirty, and their clothes leave a mark. They have no employment and nothing to do so they come out in fair weather and lean and talk. Are you noting all of this, Richard?"

"I'm listening and remembering."

"You don't see the need to write my gems down?"

I smiled and shook my head.

"There's a fellow, Mayhew, he comes into the rookeries and talks to gonophs and magsmen and prostitutes and writes down their stories and puts it all down in books. You want to know the facts of the London poor, you read Mayhew."

"I thought you said Dickens and Gissing?"

"Nobody knows it all. Not Dickens nor Gissing nor Mayhew nor John Buckles. So, where was I? Yes, the poor are dirty. Second, the poor smell bad."

"If you said smell and stink, John, I think it would be clearer."

"You're a mouth, all right. As I said before. Well, then, the poor stink. It's better now, since clothes are made of cotton. You can wash something made of cotton. The woolens took too much work, and they didn't bother. You take the factory children, even the children in school; didn't change their clothes from New Year's to year's end. Slept in them, never took them off.

"Sometimes the poor, being poor, turn to crime. Most are not very good at it, and they remain poor. So you have the poor, and the criminal classes, and they mix one into the other. But they are not the same, you are not to think they are the same. There's honest poor. Like my own father, who died spitting up blood, having toiled all his life. He was a man with pride in his appearance, and he'd go into a barber's shop once in a while when they had fresh bear's grease and have it rubbed into his hair. He'd have been a dandy if he could have afforded it, but he never even had a Sunday suit."

Talking, Buckles was weaving through the crowds, and I close behind. He was a man who could be mum as a rock face for hours on end, and when the talk was on him, as now, it was like the overflowing of conscience. As if he had found someone to leave his memories to, a legacy that would otherwise die along with him.

Buckles stopped to look down at a man in a dreadful state sitting with his back against a building. He had terrible sores all over his face. A young boy stood beside him, holding an upended cap in his hands. I was reaching for some coppers when Buckles slapped my hand down.

"Up to the scaldrum dodge, an't you?" he said to the man. And, to me, "This is a gegor—those wounds are faked." He took the cap from the boy and spat on it and rubbed it in the worst of the man's facial wounds. I protested but Buckles told me to keep quiet and watch. The sore disappeared. "What they do is rub a little soap in and then vinegar on top of it."

"A man's got to live, gov'nor."

"The boy's yours or hired?"

"I gets him for tuppence a day."

"See he gets something to eat. I'll be back to see if you attended to it. You take in enough, see the boy gets a crust."

"Yes, sir, thank you, sir."

Off we went as Buckles said, "Some really disfigure themselves, with gunpowder and vitriol. I don't bother them. I consider beggars useful."

"Useful?"

"A man drops a farthing and propitiates the gods."

"You're a strange policeman, John."

"A man knows he's dying, he gives his shoes to his eldest son. I didn't want them, so I left."

"I'd like to know about that," I said.

"Damn you, Richard, you're drawing me out. I've grown accustomed to this boil, the throbbing is company. Well, then, stop your ears if you're dainty and bruise easily. What I remember is being sent to haul him out of one gin palace or another. Did you know that geneva kept England from revolution? Did you know that, Richard?"

"No, I didn't know that."

"Truth. In the twenties and thirties—before you were born—there were uprisings all over Europe. In England the ruling class trembled in their Wellingtons. But then the poor discovered gin and the country was saved. When my father had a job—sometimes he had a job—he was paid in the public house, so my mother would wait to see if he'd be home on time and if not I had to run and fetch him, hoping there'd be something left of the week's money. If I was late and he hadn't spent it all inside, there was still the bug hunters waiting outside to rob the drunken fools. That's one point of view. The other is that for a penny or two you could escape for a couple of hours. Good-bye to the misery and hopelessness of your life. For a couple of hours. Gin is a comfort, anodyne, and friend. You see anything wrong with gin, Richard?"

He asked the question harshly. I shook my head.

"And what, after all, would he be coming home to?" Buckles said. "A scrap of cold steak left over from the day before, a spongy loaf, a shapeless piece of something in a basin purchased under the name of butter. A pot of tea with the strength taken out of it from two meals before. The tablecloth would be dirty, the cups chipped, the teapot greasy with a damaged spout."

Then we were in the middle of Disraeli's other nation.

Between the two nations there is no intercourse and no sympathy; who are ignorant of each other's habits, thoughts and feelings as if they were dwellers in different zones or inhabited different planets; who are formed by different breeding, fed by a different spoon, ordered by different manners and are not governed by the same laws—the rich and the poor.

I wondered if Buckles had not dredged out the memory of

his own background the better to have me deal with the new world we were entering.

"Hark to me now, Richard. We are after a criminal. The criminal lives in dark holes underground, in the hidden back rooms of dirty houses. Sometimes policemen disappear with no trace in these rookeries. So I want you to watch my back."

Who will watch mine? I thought, but said nothing. *Quis custodiet ipsos custodes?*

"Eh?" Buckles said. I had said the Latin aloud without knowing it.

" 'Who shall keep watch over the guardians?' "

"Indeed," Buckles said.

"Weapons," I said. "Should we not have weapons?"

"I have this"—tapping his hat. "You didn't want to carry a truncheon, remember?"

"You didn't tell me then we were going to invade enemy territory."

"Are you afraid?"

"Certainly. Especially an assault without weapons."

"The constable is only officially unarmed. Many a one hides a dirk in his greatcoat and a short staff of gutta-percha in his pocket."

"I have a feeling," I said, "that I was not properly briefed for this mission."

"Why do you think I am telling you this now? They say that once in this warren a wanted man is safe. These yards and tenements have traps and bolt-holes, one cellar connected to another; there are escape routes through the mazes and over the rooftops. If you chase your quarry here you could find yourself creeping on hands and knees with desperate characters awaiting you as you come up through a two-foot hole. Or you might step on a cesspool covered in such a way that you could be swallowed up."

"If it is that dangerous, why are we proceeding?"

"Why did that question never occur to me?" Buckles said admiringly.

The first yard we came to was covered with night soil from overflowing of the privy to a depth of six inches with bricks for a footpath. Around the walls were coster carts on which some prostitutes lay sleeping. Buckles trod the bricks with neat precision. I followed him with less steadiness, anticipating the trip and fall into the dejecta.

We went through wide green entrance doors into a kitchen filled with smoke, lighted by a hole in the roof. Before a fire were lodgers drying their clothes, some toasting herrings, some drying the ends of cigars picked up in the streets. Men and women of all ages, dressed in clothing that appeared to have come from a costumer's, rented out over and over until, with each successive user adding wear and soil, no longer could a penny be earned for the use thereof, at which time these people obtained them. Smock frocks, long red plush waistcoats with long sleeves, old shooting jackets with wooden buttons, blue flannel sailor shirts—clothes so black and shiny with grease it was difficult to determine the original color.

At our entrance there was first a stillness, then, behind us, a scurrying as of guilty men fleeing or messengers dispatched to warn those deeper within. Buckles did not look left or right but proceeded as if he knew this place well.

We went into sleeping rooms with beds and palliasses jammed close together. The sheets were generally black. There were little boxes separated by boards for those who were married. We went up a flight of stairs. I was having trouble breathing from the effort of not using my nose against the odor. Having lived through Scutari I thought I should have been able to bear this better, but the memory of stink does not erect permanent defenses. I looked in at some of the rooms while Buckles did not appear to, intent on whatever was still ahead of him. I saw a room with a Lascar and his woman on a palliasse on the floor, covered with a single old blanket, the smell of opium barely overlying the stench.

We went through that house and through another courtyard. Broken windows were patched with rags and paper. Here each room was let out to a different family, sometimes more than one. In the cellar were fruit and sweet-stuff manufacturers; in the front parlor were barbers and red-herring vendors; in back were cobblers; a bird fancier was on the first floor; three families on the second; Irishmen in the passage; a musician in the front garden; a charwoman and five hungry children in the back room.

Everywhere was filth. Clothes were drying and slops emptying from the windows; young girls with matted hair walked barefoot, once-white shifts almost their only covering. Boys in coats of all sizes but none fitting the bodies. Some in no coats at all. Men and women in every variety of scanty and dirty apparel—lounging, scolding, drinking, smoking, squabbling, and swearing.

A brick came flying and glanced off Buckles's shoulder. He did not turn or falter. I looked for the thrower, saw only jeering children. I could not stop else Buckles would have left me behind. A naked girl, very young, came out of what looked like a hole in the ground. She stood in front of me with her hands on her hips, arching her thin body. "You can squeeze me for a penny." There were catcalls behind me. I stepped around the girl. I had thought she was one of the darker-skinned races, Indian, perhaps, but close up her coloration was dirt alone. She grabbed at my privates as I passed and I slapped her hand away. Buckles was moving like a locomotive. My bad leg throbbed as I tried to keep up.

We entered a room in which some men and women were huddled in a corner. Babies lay on a blanket on the floor. Two boys were engaged in a finger game on a bench. A man sat on a chair, scratching himself and staring at the wall. He had a bull neck and a dull look. Buckles stood in the doorway for a moment, then went directly to the man and put pincer fingers on his neck.

"On your feet, Thomas Tyler, I am taking you into custody."

"Let go. You got the wrong man. My name an't Tyler."

"In that case just step around to the station and you will receive our apologies."

Tyler got up suddenly, the chair scudding backward, jerking his head down to escape Buckles's fingers while jabbing back with his elbow.

It was done well and quickly but Buckles had anticipated him. The sergeant turned sideways to escape the elbow and then, with just the two fingers, snapped Tyler's head from side to side until the man raised his hand in submission. They walked toward the door.

"You'll never get me out of here."

I didn't see how he would, either, as I took up my position in back. We went through the courtyard without incident and through the first building and then, as we arrived at the yard through which we had first entered the circus, we were faced with a wall formed of the inhabitants of the Dials.

"Make way there," Buckles called out.

A man stepped forward. He was a gaunt man who looked attenuated from disease.

"You know me, John Buckles."

"I know you, Albert Camp."

"You can't take anybody out of here. This place is a sanctuary."

"Is it now. Consecrated and all?"

"It is for us, Sergeant. You'll not take him out."

"I'll take him, and anyone else who obstructs me. This man will stand trial. I never knew you to condone murder, Albert Camp. You're the finest screever I ever knew and I don't think you hold with murder, especially foul murder, as this man has done."

"What I don't hold with is the police coming in here. This is where we live, and we have a right to be as secure here as our betters in their castles."

"Don't stand up against me, Albert. Do you pine for Pentonville, or is it Millbank?"

"There's no fear of that. I've got no more than a week or two to live."

"I'm sorry to hear that, Albert."

"So I've got nothing to lose, you see."

"Is it the consumption like what your mother died of?"

"That it is."

"I'm truly sorry, Albert."

"So let him be now, Sergeant Buckles. Maybe one day you'll find him out in the streets."

"I can't let him go. You know that, Albert."

"We might have to do you in then, John."

Buckles shook his head sadly. "You know you can't do that either, Albert. First off, you know a man like me can't be done in; there's many has tried. Secondly, in the event that you do manage it—considering the quirks of fate and the mysterious workings involving the sparrow and all that—the entire Metro division would be here routing you out like rats. We're very sensitive about our policemen being molested in the line of duty. You might say it offends us deeply."

There were twenty or thirty men, and some women, lined up opposing us, and although none looked particularly stalwart, considering the damage done by poor food and unhealthy living, there was no way we could get past them if they were determined to stop us. The weakest of them could grab an ankle, and if you knocked a few down there were enough to take their places.

Buckles raised his voice, addressing the crowd. "Instead of impeding me—that's standing in my way—you should be backing me up and escorting me in style. This an't no bit faker or bludger or broadsman or bug hunter. He an't no beggar and he don't sell watches without insides. What he is is a murderer. And who did he murder? An old woman, an old woman like your mother or your grandmother. And for what? For a half crown, that's what. That's what her life was worth, a half crown. You know me. When I come in here it's after the perpetrator of something foul. You're family people. I respect your right to help each other. But not the murderer of an old woman."

As far as I could see, there was no change in the demeanor of those opposing us. Rather I sensed a certain tightening and a suspicion of forward inclination. I had been too interested in the unusual happenings and Buckles's maneuvering to get the full meaning of our position. But now I looked closer at the faces in front, and beginning to edge around me, and all were hostile and some were vicious and I was back at Inkerman, in front of me the Russian horde, and this time no British soldiers at my side.

"I know most of you," Buckles said, jabbing into the air with the forefinger of his free hand. "Dunster, you've a new baby, I hear. Mold. Pot. Clarence Juke. Sam Dandy—hair's grown back, has it? Flat—on the cockchafer for two months, I hear. Took the skin off, did it? I heard you were surly; they don't like them surly. Alfie Zook, what are you doing up front with the big boys? None of you, I take it, are currently employed? Therefore unable to feed yourself and your family. Therefore by the kindness of a gracious sovereign there has been provided for you space in the workhouse."

A soughing from the crowd, a faint moan.

"I see three, four dippers among you. What happens to your fingertips after you've been picking oakum for a week or two? Raw, bleeding, and useless is what they become. You'll have no trade left, you'll have to find honest work or learn to use a cosh on them's got no more in their pouge than you."

There was a faint smile here and there, and some uncertainty, and at that loosening Buckles suddenly roared, "Clear the way, Constable!" and I, fired by the unexpected command, set my

Muller cutdown firmly against my ears and, head down, rushed forward, arms out stiff, parting the mob like a Moses with Buckles and prisoner close behind. Had there been one voice as loud and authoritative as Buckles's they might have stood their ground, but their only leader was Albert Camp and he had been the first I had shoved out of the way (gently, though; I would not have wanted to hurt him).

In the street Buckles called upon a constable, who used his grogger to fetch a police van, and he took Tyler away.

"In celebration of your first day in this dirty world, Richard, I'll stand for your midday meal."

We went into an eating house and Buckles ordered two rum steaks. "You knew just what to do," I said. "How did you know to do that?"

"There was a ticket-of-leave man who told me where Tyler might be and all I had to do was go from room to room until I found the informer, who gave me the nod. I never set eyes on Tyler before, you see."

"I didn't think we'd get out of there," I said.

"You did well, Richard. I've seen probationers turn tail and run, faced with like circumstances."

"It looked bad," I said.

"The answer was authority. The English respond to authority. Like the Germans. I'll tell you what happened the other day. A man on an omnibus was threatening the driver and abusing the passengers, and the driver stopped the vehicle and said he wasn't continuing on until the troublemaker got off. Someone found a constable, who got on the bus and walked over to the miscreant. Now this constable had somehow slipped through the regulations, which call for a minimum height of five feet seven inches; he wasn't more than five-four and the other fellow topped him by at least five inches. This little man got right up against the other fellow's chest and raised his head—he had to—to look up at the man's eyes, and he said, with *unquestionable* authority, "You get off this bus now." And the big fellow just turned and went like a dog will jump at a command. Remember, he could have picked up the constable with one hand and thrown him through the window. It's being sure without question that you're going to be obeyed. Then it works."

"Always?"

"Of course not. That's why you were there, to bull through a path for me."

The steaks arrived, and after testing a tentative piece I began consuming mine in great chunks, forgetting my manners, but it had been a long time since I had been exposed to proper food. Buckles, noting my rate of progress, quietly gestured to the waiter to bring me another, along with potatoes and bread and a pint of bitter.

"That bit about the workhouse—" I said.

"Frightens them all."

"I thought the workhouses were established so that a man unable to fend for himself and his family is given something to eat and a place to sleep."

"Exactly right."

"Then—?"

"We have to take care of those unable to take care of themselves. That's the Christian way, isn't it? So we take care of the poor. The reason, the main reason, however, is that if we don't take care of the poor we're afraid the poor will take care of themselves and us too. We're afraid of them, you see."

"I don't understand," I said.

"No wonder. We Victorians mean what we say but will never say what we think. Most of us, that is."

"I never heard that before. Victorians, that is."

"That's what we call ourselves now. It's the first time Englishmen have ever called themselves anything but Englishmen. Not even under Elizabeth did we call ourselves Elizabethans."

"I noticed the first thing you did was take the mob and break it down. You used names, you made them individuals."

Buckles dipped some bread in gravy and put it in his mouth with finical precision. He chewed with his lips together. His manners were better than mine.

"You can pick up a brick easily and throw it, but when the bricks are formed into a wall—and withal I thought it a good sight, them standing together. Englishmen fighting for their rights."

"Criminals trying to protect a murderer."

"The poor, who have nothing to lose. That's what gives our rulers bad dreams."

After two steaks and the extras and the bitter I was beginning to feel better.

"A real tightener, eh, Richard?"

"I noticed it worried them when you mentioned the workhouse. Is it, then, worse than jail?"

"For some. Parliament passed a Poor Law to give relief to the needy, but the relief was designed to be just a step above starvation outside."

I noted that the parallel vertical lines in Buckles's face looked deeper, and his mouth opened and closed like a portcullis.

"It was not considered desirable that laymen in the workhouse do anything useful and thus compete with private businesses, so they are given senseless tasks—the men break stone and the women and children and the aged pick oakum. Young boys and girls who commit offenses are shut in the dead room, where they sleep upon the lids of coffins. Or sometimes they are shut away, naked, in a hole under the stairs for eight or ten days."

In an effort to lighten the air, I said, "Are you married, John?"

"I was for twelve months. She died giving birth, and the child with her."

I shook my head and Buckles, perceiving my distress at so blundering, smiled.

"Enough time has passed, there's little pain left. But I will not marry again. There's no sense to a policeman being married. I hope you haven't anything like that in mind."

"There's little chance of that. I know only one girl and she—"

"Unrequited love?" Buckles said.

"As ever was."

"Come, Richard, a woman's just a woman but a rum steak delights the soul. Now, not to mix up our waters, have a rum shrub with me. Will you have orange or lemon juice in yours?"

"Lemon." Thinking, if I could feel it on my teeth it might drive away the thought of Alethea which, stupidly, I had allowed to return.

Chapter Twelve

Dear Richard:

You can hardly imagine how dull it is here with both you and Peter away. I feel empty—and old! Sir James is crotchety and wants me attending on him all the time.

You write that you have joined the Police. I suppose that is a joke, ha ha. I would expect you to be in some fine profession by now, like the Law. I could just see you as a barrister. The wig would suit you, it would soften the fierceness of your face, I think. (Although it was your fierce looks which always appealed to me.) A girl likes to feel she is in the grip of someone a little dangerous. Not really dangerous, of course, although there were some occasions, especially when I teased you too much, when I was not sure what you might do. I did tease you, didn't I?

Peter is sowing his wild oats, I expect that you are doing the same. Sir James says a young man is entitled to crow and flap his wings before he settles down to a life in the barnyard. From what Peter says he has been doing, I would say there is more braying than crowing. What do you think of this kind of conduct, Richard? Oh, I forgot, you said you were in the Police, ha ha, so naturally you would disapprove.

Peter wrote he had to pay at the Derby assizes a fine of 100 pounds for common assault. He and Mowbray Blackstone and two other companions threw down a constable onto his back and painted him a bright red. As a policeman I doubt you would find that amusing. (What are you really doing, Richard?) I suppose if you met up with Peter you would have to arrest him, ha ha.

He also says he and his friends bought 200 sewer rats (ugh!) from a professional ratcatcher in Windmill Street and they carried them in sacks to the dancing room in Foley Street where young swells were dancing with—harlots was the word Peter used. They released the rats onto the dance floor and you can imagine the pandemonium. What they were doing, I suppose, is attempting to live up to the Regency tradition. Well, Richard,

I can't say I condone Peter's behavior, but when I read his last letter aloud to Sir James the old man roared with laughter. Richard, I can't see you doing anything like that because you've always been so serious! Would you do anything like that?

Peter says he sometimes goes on the town with a friend of his named Lord Waterford who really sounds a terrible fellow. He is heir to a vast fortune, which Peter is not, and I doubt that Sir James would find it all so amusing if it were Peter causing such expensive damage. For example, at Crockford's, Lord Waterford smashed a fine French clock on the staircase with his fist, and he sometimes amuses himself by using the eyes of his family portraits as targets for pistol practice. One of his exploits in which Peter shared, and which made Sir James laugh so hard that he turned quite red and I thought it was the end of him, was when they put anise seed on the hooves of a parson's horse and hunted the poor clergyman with bloodhounds.

Oh, Richard, what can I do to overcome this terrible boredom? If you were here I might—I might even—but what am I saying? This pen of mine runs on as if I have no control over it. How I envy you and Peter. A poor girl can do nothing but stay at home while her heroes are rampaging around the world. Do you think we three shall ever be together again? Were not those the best times of our lives? I close this now, dear Richard, secure in the knowledge that whatever you are doing (policeman, ha ha) your work will not be so demanding as not to allow you time to think occasionally of—

Alethea.

Her handwriting was even and formally correct in the way that young ladies of her class were taught. I sniffed the notepaper to recover the scent of her. I saw her eyes flash at a line of complaint, the languor of hand supporting her forehead as she spoke of boredom, the bottom lip caught up in those small teeth as she studied a recalcitrant phrase. There was too much, of course, devoted to Peter, but what did she mean that she might—even—if I were there? And how could her memories of me be so cheerful and pleasant when I could remember only misery? She said she had teased me. I remember crucifixion and betrayal. Yet if she appeared this instant with her arms out, was there a force in the world powerful enough to keep me from her?

If I caught Peter in one of his hilarious escapades would I arrest him? Ha, ha. If only it happened, and if only he resisted as I stated I was taking him into custody. I had to break the prisoner's arm, sir, he would not come quietly. Ha. Ha.

My work was dirty and demeaning and dangerous and often dull—and I liked it. A nod of approval from John Buckles was as much recognition as a man needed in this world. I was pushed to do more than I could, and did it, and was grateful that someone demanded it of me. I spent most of my time with criminals and I did not hate them all; some I liked and one or two I admired. The superior ones were not merely lazy men fattening themselves at the expense of the just. The effort and skill and patience, while misdirected, of a carefully planned and executed robbery was equal to any proper calling. With the higher class of criminals I was adversary, but I hoped for their respect as they had mine. This was not an attitude I cared to discuss with Inspector Criddle, or even Buckles. For the rest, for the vicious and corrupt, I was after them as I would be after any vermin, because most of their crimes were foul, and I followed Buckles in my horror of them.

I put my hands behind my head and dreamed about Alethea for a while, and then I put both the dreams and her letter aside for another time. I picked up a copy of the *Morning Herald* I had bought for fivepence and cut the leaves with a folding paper knife bought at the same newspaper seller's. I read about the young man riding along Rotten Row dangling a chignon at the end of a cane while every lady there clapped her hands to the back of her neck. Then I read about the *Flying Yorkshireman,* which had won the annual sailing race from China bringing in sou-chong, bo-hea, and pe-koe, winning an extra prize of ten shillings a ton and a bonus of one hundred pounds. A young girl had been taken by Mr. Ashcroft, secretary of the Refuge Aid Society, and placed in a refuge in Albert Street, Mile End, Newton. Simeon Fairweather, a pickpocket, had been taken to Bow Street Police Station and given two months in Westminster Bridewell. Prior to that he had been three months in Bridge Street, Bridewell. And before that, Coldbath Fields. He was obviously a dipper with little skill. Manderville Tate and his wife were presented to the Queen at St. James's palace. Mrs. Tate was dressed in a mantle of white imperial glacé, brocaded with white flowers and terry velvet, and trimmed with bouillons of tulle. Her petticoat was of white glacé silk with skirt bouillonée to the waist and tulle veil and corsage to match, trimmed with chatelaine of white lebanon flowers. Her headdress was a wreath of lebanon flowers with diamond ornaments in the center and diamond stars. Her necklace was of pearl and diamonds.

Almost six months of prowling London with John Buckles. That first criminal he had apprehended in St. Giles's was hanged to the accompaniment of the tolling bell of St. Sepulchre. The judge, black cap on his head, said, "Mercy to you would be cruelty to others."

Buckles and I attended the execution. Calcraft, the city executioner, whiskered, dressed in black like a parson, presented himself to the crowd like a lead player to cheers and boos. When the prisoner appeared there was a cry of "Hats off!" and every man uncovered.

"I take no pleasure in this," I said to Buckles.

"Nor do I."

"Then why are we here?"

"To see justice done."

"I would sooner be told when it is over."

"Are you squeamish then, Richard?"

"I have looked on death before. But this is death made demeaning; there is more dignity to a body stiffening at a bullet in the brain. And look about at these slavering devotees. Is a public hanging not meant to be a lesson and a deterrent?"

"It's an entertainment, Richard. One of the reasons I brought you here is to look upon a bit of history, since soon all this will be abolished. The wretches will shortly be done away with in secret."

Talking, I had been studying the crowd. "I see at least three dippers at work, John."

"I've taught you well. Let's nab a few."

I got one, clamping my hand down on his wrist as he reached inside the back pocket of a man so busy shouting encouragement he would not have felt the pressure of the most awkward pair of fingers. I knew the pickpocket. His name was Wells, a dandified man in his middle years who did not struggle, as much for fear of ruffling his attire as resignation. Buckles was hard after me, having collared a young boy in his apprenticeship. The boy began to cry, the tears streaking the dirt on his face.

"Stop sniveling," Buckles said. "Are you under fourteen?"

"Fifteen."

"Not for a year yet. Get yourself some clothes too big for you, and the most the judge will set for you is a whipping."

"What about me?" said Wells. "I'd settle for a whipping."

"You'll be sent where they're sure to smash up your fingers," Buckles said. "If a man has a few bob in his pocket because he's worked hard, it's not right that because you're too lazy to work yourself you relieve him of it. That is not the same as taking a swell's surplus, as you might if you were working the Strand. You're doing injury to the man's family as well as himself. That shakes me up, Wells. That shakes up my coadjutor too, right, Mister O'Boy?"

"Right," I said.

The chaplain read in a loud, clear voice—more for the benefit of the audience than the soul of the prisoner, who was hardly in a position to appreciate biblical comfort. Calcraft was strapping Thomas Tyler's legs together and pulling a nightcap over his face. Tyler's body began a quivering; you could trace the ascension through one thigh and then the other, then up into his arms. A woman screamed, "Dying you are, Thomas, and you never drilled me, just think what it might've been like," and broke into wheezing laughter.

I heard a veteran hanging-watcher tell a companion, "Always look at the crotch. This one's still holding it in."

Calcraft went down the steps and pulled the handle that worked the trap. The victim fell through but his neck did not break and he hung in dreadful contortions.

"Assist the man, for God's sake," somebody called out.

Someone else said, "Leave him be, Calcraft, leave him be."

The executioner heaved on the hanging man's legs until strangulation was complete.

I lay on my cot remembering the six months with John Buckles teaching me my new trade. The oddest sight was drinking pearl and watching a man called Tiger Tom take a man by the waistband of his trousers with his teeth and run around the room carrying him like a cat with a mouse. "The gentry never see anything like this," Buckles had said, setting his drink down on a table so black with dirt it could have been painted on. "Perhaps when

I retire I'll be a tour guide into the recesses of the Victorian netherworld. See the animals who used to be men. Marvel at the starving children, sample the women who will do your bidding for a farthing. All this under your unsuspecting feet in the same city of London."

"The smells, John," I said. "Don't forget to tell them about the smells."

One morning Inspector Criddle called us into his office.

"Well, John," he said, indicating me with his chin. "Will he do?"

"As well as any man we have, better'n most."

He had never said as much to me. I tried to look deserving. Criddle picked up a copy of the *Illustrated London News* and waved it in the air as if the space were suddenly infested with flies. "Have you seen this?"

Buckles and I shook our heads.

"They want to know where are the police. They want to know if we are paid to sleep while the citizens of London walk about in fear. And not long ago they were objecting to the presence of the police in the city streets. I want you and your protégé to put a stop to it."

"To what, the newspaper talk?"

"Don't be dense with me, man. I've had a bad night. I'm referring to the Garroters, of course."

"Just me and Richard here apprehending the villains has all London shaking in their slippers?"

"I want them stopped," Criddle said. "I want them in custody."

"Oh, well then," Buckles said. "Come along, Richard." As we walked he said, "What do you know about these garroting teams?"

"They're two or sometimes three. If they're three the third one keeps watch. The victim is attacked from behind while the second one goes through the pockets."

"Attacked from behind how?"

"With a rope or scarf or the side of the arm about the neck."

"No other weapons?"

"Sometimes they use a neddy."

"Learning the language, are we, Richard? Very good. The

first requirement in any new field is to learn the language. So a neddy is—?"

"A cosh."

"Which is used to—?"

"To kill or render impotent."

"How many shapes and sizes to a neddy?"

"Well—"

"It could be," Buckles said, "a short metal bar which can be carried up the sleeve, or some canvas stuffed with sand, or sometimes iron shot in a stocking. In short, anything that works."

"They don't," I said, "appear to want to kill."

"Happened once. Two weeks ago. A jeweler. His throat was crushed."

"But they don't seem to use the neddy on the head."

"Either they don't want to kill, as you said, skulls being made of thin stuff, or they can't depend on a fast submission, considering the protective nature of headgear."

"So they hit the upper arm or the shoulder or the thigh—"

"You've read the reports," Buckles said. "I don't see how you have the time, considering all those books you keep borrowing from Mudie's. Why not the old tried method of taking hold of the nose and pushing it flat toward the mouth so as almost to break the gristle, that takes away a man's senses nearly?"

"Identification. Garroting works from behind."

"Better and better. Yet I don't see where you get the time to keep abreast of it all."

"I sleep poorly."

"Alone?"

"Yes."

"Q.E.D."

If I said Alethea or no one—and there was no way it could be Alethea—did that have to mean I had opted for the priesthood, R.C. variety, and without even the succor of the church? My blood ran hot enough. The sight of an exposed ankle stepping up into a cab or the softness of profile or eyes fleetingly but imperishably linked to mine in the street or a restaurant was enough to fantasize on for half a night. Then there were the prostitutes I met in the course of my duties, some of whom I felt friendly toward, and any would gladly have served as initiation partner, and although I was often enough quickened and even eager, and although it was not a question of virtue or fear, I had so far resisted.

"I know a widow," Buckles said. "She is pear-shaped, and occasionally scented like a pear, fresh of course, after a rainfall, say. Once a week she comes to me and twice a week I go to her. I have carefully explained to her that I have determined never to marry again."

"You walk too fast for conversation," I said. "And it's about time I paid for your coffee." We went into a café and took seats near the window. "How can you do that?" I said. "You, an officer of the law."

"We are neither of us married."

"But it's fornication."

"Indeed, yes. And of a very high quality. Are you disturbed by my telling you, Richard?"

"You think this is condemnation in my eyes? It is closer to envy."

"Morality weighs heaviest on those in the middle," Buckles said. "The lords of our world take the women of their fancy with none to stay them and usually without guilt, since their spouses, if they already have three or four or more children, are quite content to be let alone. At the other end are the poor, the numberless poor—and we are getting to know them better and better, are we not?—being exposed to each other's bodies from childhood on, brothers and sisters sharing the same bed and often viewing each other unclothed; they cohabit early without shame or hindrance and the girl is no less free than her partner to choose or dissolve. No one waggles a finger or shuns them. So I, a policeman, classless as we have determined a policeman to be, find the example of the poor to my liking and worthy of emulation."

"She could have a child," I said.

"Ah, so you know that children often come from that type of activity, do you, Richard?"

"So I have heard."

"It is a problem, of course. When my wife was alive she often took a feather to herself—"

"Feather?"

"She was a Jew and that was mentioned in a book of theirs called the Talmud. I myself have tried the French letter, but it is a crude thing. With the widow now I practice Onan's method, or, if you will, the coitus interruptus."

"John—should I—not wait?"

"You are sure she will not have you?"

"She writes letters—"

"Is she betrothed?"

"She has not told me so."

"You're saving yourself as if you're some rare jewel. Keep away from Moorfields, Richard. The sodomites there will pounce on you like cats on a chicken."

I drank my coffee and stared out the window. I was a beginner at everything. I wondered when I would be fully formed.

"To business then, Richard."

"What is there more about the garroters, what is there that I do not know?"

"One, they have attacked Parliament in the person of Mr. Carruthers, M.P., as he was walking to his club in Pall Mall. The garroting was savage and he lost his voice for weeks. And then on the same night an old man named Thomas Barker was assaulted between St. James's and Bond Street. So long as crime kept to the rookeries no one cared overmuch. As Criddle said, when the police force began we were a threat to the public liberty, and now there is an outcry because we are not properly protecting their persons."

"You have a plan."

"They will not act out their infamy for us like a turn at the penny gaff, so if they will not stand still for us we will have to stand still for them."

"How's that, John?"

"I will walk those same streets at the same hour and invite an attack. Then you will come up and knock the malefactors' heads together."

"Why should you act the victim. Why not me?"

"You're too big. They prefer the old and the infirm."

"You don't look old or infirm to me. And were I a robber I would steer clear of such as you. There's a dangerous look to you, John, there's no gainsaying that. And besides you're known."

"I'm not known to everyone, and this is a new dodge. And as for looking dangerous, you watch me."

We then went to the Strand and he played sick while I played watchdog, but for each other alone. Not that I didn't enjoy Buckles's performance. I admired his halting and painful step, the artifice of his slouch. We tried Pall Mall and Regent Street before calling it a day. We went back for three nights running without success.

"Why not," I said, "put a sign across your back? 'I am an infirm man carrying a large sum of money.'"

"It took more than a day to form Rome."

"I am not discouraged," I said.

The next evening it was a little short of seven o'clock with Buckles out in front and myself a hundred yards behind when I saw him touch his hat, which was our signal, bringing to my attention a scruffy little fellow in a closed shop doorway who was looking up and down the street with more alertness than his lounging position called for. If he were lookout, then it was possible the ones we sought were between him and John Buckles.

I went a little faster but not fast enough to interfere with their purpose if they were going to appear. Then they did, coming out of the shadows like wolves, and one had Buckles around the neck, the other ready to go through his pockets. Then, so quickly that I had not yet broken into a run, Buckles perhaps struggling more than he had intended not to alarm them, one used his neddy against the sergeant's hat. It clanged, which gave away his identity, and off they fled with Buckles in pursuit.

At which point I discovered that the lookout was stationed not for the two ahead but for two behind, for at that moment, without my hearing a footstep, something soft was flung about my neck and immediately tightened so remorselessly that I felt panic. I flailed without design or skill and my knees bent under me and darkness settled.

When I could see again, which could have been a moment or an hour, there was John Buckles bending over me with an expression of such tender concern that it was like seeing a secret place in the man.

"How are you, lad?"

I started to speak and could not. I touched my throat. There was a soft thing still there and I pulled it away.

"A fine bit of silk. You can keep it as a souvenir." I gestured off to the distance and Buckles said, "I lost them. I'll be back in a moment."

I sat up, swallowing once, which turned into fire, and then, determining not to swallow again, found it impossible not to do so.

A group of swells passed, daintily avoiding me, one saying, "Gin's the curse of the workingman," and all laughing as they left. A hansom cab pulled up and Buckles got out. He helped me up and I saw the stars swoop down and go back again and, warning myself not to swallow, I swallowed and held my throat in anguish.

"Mercy Hospital," said Buckles to the driver, and as we rode off he said, "There was another pair who jumped you?"

I nodded.

"Two pair in the same street. The vermin are ruling London."

At the hospital, a doctor poked at me with indelicate fingers and pronounced me a lucky man since there were no broken bones, but the hyoid was well bruised and I was to keep my throat covered with wool cloths and take only warm broth. Buckles took me back to my room.

So I lay abed feeling slothful and guilty, while I spent the time reading to good advantage. Mrs. Gum nursed me in the time she could spare from the bakeshop. It occurred to me then that in time of stress I had been fortunate in women to take care of me—Mrs. Hitch in the army and Mrs. Gum now. I had no memory of being ill as a child, and hence no memory of being tended by my mother. Yet I could not have passed an entire childhood free of illness and it was worrisome that I could not remember ever being ministered to by my mother, as if I had buried the thought of it.

Mr. Gum spent hours trying to teach me finger conversation. He made no comment about the irony of my having come to his condition, except by his example to indicate that it was bearable. The soreness lessened but my voice did not return. It was, after all, a lesson in humility. My attacker, for all I knew, stood half as tall as I. On the eleventh day I recalled some history and was unable to tell it to anyone. September 2, 1752, was followed by September 14 in order to reform the calendar. It was felt by many that Parliament, by so decreeing, was shortening the life of every individual in the nation by eleven days.

I read *Oliver Twist* again and for the first time realized that

Charles Dickens was sparing the sensibilities of his readers. No matter how dreadful was the life he depicted of forsaken children in London, the reality, as I now knew it, was infinitely worse.

Buckles came, bringing along the surgeon who had determined I was unfit for police duty. His boots shone as brilliantly as I remembered. He took me to the window and looked down my throat by pulling out my tongue with his fingers. I could taste snuff. He felt my neck and said, "Who knows?"

"You're supposed to know," Buckles said. "You're a doctor, an't you?"

"My doctor's eyes and my doctor's fingers tell me there is nothing to account for Mr. O'Boy's not speaking. Perhaps he has been rendered speechless from shock."

"When does his voice come back?"

"I don't know. If ever."

If ever, I mouthed.

"Well, I didn't mean never, although—"

The doctor took his leave after cautioning me to keep my throat warm and not to force speech by attempting to yell but to practice whispering.

"Now I'll tell you," Buckles said. "We got the bastards. Both pair."

I grinned in approval and raised my eyebrows for more.

"Jeffries, Constable Jeffries, you remember him. He caught two just by being there. Evidently the lookout man wasn't looking out. Jeffries took the two down, having to use his persuader, I'm afraid."

"Well?" I said, as best I could.

"Well what?" Buckles said.

I shook my fist at him and he put up his hand placatingly.

"I took the other two."

Whom had he taken with him in my place? I mimed.

"Nobody," Buckles said.

I frowned.

"I wanted them for myself," Buckles said.

I looked disapproving.

"Of course I had to go out without my hat."

I looked horrified.

"They knew the hat, they'd never've come near. I got a tall top hat and dressed the rest of me like a countryman come into

London for a little depravity, begun by buying a hat here. The Strand appeared their favorite street, I walked it from Trafalgar Square to the Fleet and back, night after night."

I imitated what I thought he'd looked like, with every two steps a glance behind.

Buckles shook his head. "That would be writing Peeler across my back, wouldn't it? Anyway, I did not think anyone could creep up on me from behind if my ears were back there at attention. I walked far enough out from the hallways and I listened and sure enough I heard the steps, so when he jumped at me I had my arm up in front of my throat. The other one came around in front, and I had to dispose of the one quickly to snatch the other. I had this life preserver in the palm of my hand—this little ball, you know, attached to my wrist with a piece of gut—so I went for the one using the neckcloth—the silk was not as good as what you kept—and I needled him in the fork with that deadly piece of shot—he screamed like a pig at the butcher's—and the other one ran off. I would never have caught him, considering my age and stiffness in the joints, but fortunately he tripped and fell face down with myself a few yards behind. I jumped on top of him and to maintain my balance I'm afraid I had to fall on him straight-armed against the back of his head, which drove his face with some force into the roadbed. They've both been committed to Surrey Sessions, and the likelihood is they'll get ten years' penal servitude."

I nodded.

"Look pleased, man. Not that we've lowered much the level of crime in the streets; you put one away and two spring up to take their place. Maybe we ought to leave them alone so there'd be such a glut they'd have to begin wiping each other out. But it's conversation you want, not a monologue. Do what the doctor said, and I'll be in to see you in a day or two."

I saw him to the door and clapped him on the shoulder. I went back to bed and read until I was sick of reading and thought until I was sick of thinking. I went to bed too early and could not fall asleep.

The phantasmagoria of the Victorian other nation swirled and danced and reeked in the room. Was it true the Queen did not even know of its existence? Her knowledge of her subjects stopped with some small segment of the deserving poor. Her solution to the problem of the thousands who lived and died breaking her laws was not to be aware of them. I was aware of them.

I was sitting in a nethersken and, listening, was instructed.

He was probably not young, thin as a finger with a face so unremarkable that having looked and looked away you could not recall it. His companion was older, avuncular, reasonable.

"You're as good a flimp as ever was but you've got to stop nailing gentlemen's watches. Don't you understand you've got to get it to a jerry shop right away because while it's on you you can be nibbed? Now what you've got to learn to do is to go after a haybag's purse. You take what's inside and throw the purse away and you can go right back to work. You understand me?"

"I don't like to steal from women," said the faceless one. "That's not the way I been brought up."

Buckles had taken me to see the Hulks at Woolwich. They were shortly to be abandoned as prison ships, and Buckles said I ought to see it before that happened since it was something I would never see again. "Suppose you had a chance to see the Armada come sailing up the Thames but you were too busy feeding your pigs or fighting with your wife. Imagine missing a piece of history like that."

"Especially the Spanish Armada in the Thames."

"You know what I mean," said Buckles.

The shirts of the prisoners were hung out on the rigging. They looked as if sprinkled with black pepper. "Vermin," Buckles said.

My voice came back in the middle of the night while I was having a nightmare. I heard someone yelling no, no! and when I woke up I was clutching my bad leg, so I must have been dreaming about the surgeons at Scutari. I remembered hearing the voice. I tried it gently. I whispered yes, yes, yes and then my name, over and over, and I said "Queen Victoria" and "John Buckles." There was still a little hoarseness but no pain. I thanked God—not properly on my knees but in my mind, which I hoped He would find just as satisfactory—and not knowing the hour and seeing no glimmer of light out the window I tried to compose myself to fall asleep again. I felt strong. The loss of a faculty goes beyond itself to leave traces of unsureness, sowing doubt about the capacity of those faculties not affected. It had taken a long time for the rest of me to be assured that my leg would be neither anchor nor stumbling block.

Now that I felt whole again there was an increase of bodily joy, which was an increase of awareness in my nether parts, and I pictured Buckles's widow and went from there to Alethea, whom I saw now as Lilith rather than Eve, with a corresponding increase in carnal interest.

With the first light I got out of bed and clothed myself for the day. I practiced my voice, declaiming that part of Socrates' Defense which I had memorized for Mr. Fudd and which I had repeated to myself often enough at Varna and Balaclava: *To be afraid of death is only another form of thinking that one is wise when one is not; it is to think that one knows what one does not know. No one knows with regard to death whether it is not really the greatest blessing that can happen to a man, but people dread it as though they were certain that it is the greatest evil, and this ignorance, which thinks that it knows what it does not, must surely be ignorance most culpable.*

I spoke this in a reasonable voice to the inhabitants of the Gums' mews, who, I must confess, showed no interest, perhaps because there was a closed window between us; then, for those who were less classically informed, I sang "Gentle Annie" twice through and then a rousing verse of "John Bull and the Taxes."

There was no longer reason to play the invalid, and with my trousers on and shirt not yet donned, splashing water up from the basin, I was born again. Out the window there was as much grayness left from the night as brightness to come from the day. There was a knock at the door.

"Buckles?" There was no response and I said, "Who's knocking, then?"

"Jessie."

"Jessie?"

"Jessie Marsh."

"Who's Jessie Marsh?"

"You know me, sir. Please, let me in."

I opened the door. The dress was as ragged, but clean now, and her face had been washed, and she was looking at me with eyes so bright I had to turn away. I beckoned her inside.

"What are you doing here, and how did you know where I lived?"

"Roger told me."

"Roger?"

"You know, Roger."

"He hands out my address as he pleases?"

She looked around the room, nodding slowly as if reality had more than matched expectation. "It's like a palace here."

"Well?" I said.

"I came to give you this"—extending closed hand to drop in mine two coins, warm and moist from her palm. "Your two bob."

I pushed the money around with my forefinger and she watched as if there were significance in the way I did it.

"All this space. And one man alone."

"Where did you get the money? From some other victim? And didn't you think I might have forgotten it?"

"I saved it up. And you wouldna forgotten it."

"No, I would not have."

"Would not have," Jessie said. "I wouldn't be in your way, you know."

"What?"

"Who does for you?"

"I do for myself."

"Let me."

"I don't need anyone," I said.

"Oh, sir, don't ever say that."

"Ah," I said. "Perhaps not."

"I'd make your tea, a piece of fish. I don't take up much room. All I need's a corner."

"And what would your father say?"

"I've left him. I slept under Waterloo last night, but there were those who bothered me and I won't go back there. I won't go home either, no matter what. He's beat me for the last time."

I shook my head.

"There's lots of men say I'm pretty."

I shrugged.

"Twelve in that room and not as big as this one. But it's whatever you want. If it's just the cleaning and cooking, that's all right."

"Miss Marsh," I said, "you wouldn't do."

"*Why?*"

"Can you put a map of England together? Can you recite the dates of the kings? What do you know of mythology, plants, metals? Do you know any French, Italian? Can you sew, embroider, play the piano, curtsey? Can you sing in tune?"

"You got no piano. And I can do for you better than anybody."

"I'm a policeman. If you have no home I can see you get into the workhouse."

"Oh," Jessie said. "You are hard. Your heart's a rock. I'd never have thought it." And straightening her bonnet, head up and back erect, she went out the door.

I felt as I had when Maureen Rafferty, waiting for me, had to be told I had come out without a crumb in my pocket.

Chapter Thirteen

In the morning we picked up a constable's signal and found a dead girl on the upper floor of a fashionable house in St. John's Wood. She was lying in front of a gas fireplace.

"Her own hatpin," Buckles said, "so it wasn't prepared for, not malice prepense, you see."

"I see."

"And the next thing to observe is that the hatpin didn't kill her. It didn't go all the way in, you see. Just enough to drive her back and fall over the hearth guard and strike her head."

"I see that too."

It was an elegant room with a rosewood upright piano, Turkey carpet, gilded clock beneath a glass bell, and a gold-frame looking glass. In the bedroom was an enormous cheval glass angled toward the bed.

There was a commotion outside, and the constable on guard came in to explain the cause of it when the cause herself broke in. She had a pile of amazing red hair and she came in tottering on shoes too tight. At sight of the body she let out a shriek and put her fist in her mouth and looked at me and Buckles in horror. I wanted to tell her we had nothing to do with it.

"Who are you?" Buckles said.

"Aggie Norse."

"Who is she?"—pointing to the girl on the floor.

"Sybil Grey."

"Your friend?"

"My poor friend, yes." A wisp of accent, but in England you couldn't say that meant she was foreign; there were all sorts of ways in England of speaking English.

"Constable, take Miss Norse outside, we'll speak to her in a moment."

215

Sobbing, the girl was led out.

"Would you call this a foul one, John?"

"No. There are eighty thousand more tails out there, not counting the dolly-mops who do it for the price of dinner. So this one would not do what the man demanded, or her price was too high. Who knows and who cares?"

She lay on her back, eyes closed, as if in repose. I had not at first known her because what had been most notable about Maureen was the unblinking stare. Also, this face had been soaped clean under the layer of rouge—I had never seen Maureen's face unsmudged. She had grown up suddenly, too; her breasts were full and the cut of her expensive gown was not designed to conceal them.

"You're acting strange, Richard. You look as if you want to break something."

"I knew her, John."

"This one, the victim? From the streets?"

"From the farm where I lived. She was the daughter of the farm laborer who worked for my father."

"That's different, then. That makes it—"

"Foul," I said.

"Her name—?"

"Not Sybil, and not Grey. Maureen Rafferty. Her father thought she was in service."

"She may have been. It's a small step from miserable rocker to the easy money in the streets. At least your Maureen did well. She found a gentleman."

"How do you mean?"

"This part of town, these furnishings—a judy does not set herself up alone this way."

"He should not be hard to find, then."

I wondered that I felt so deeply over this death. There had been a sad-faced girl putting herself in my way for a scrap of food. What was the relationship between her and this poule deluxe? I stared down at the body and could find no trace of the little farm girl. The difference was more than brass-heeled shoes and paint on the face; one had not grown into the other; rather one life had stopped and another begun. And, I thought, I had never heard speech from either. Yes, I wanted this murderer. I wanted him in my hands.

Buckles said, "I don't like the look on your face."

"What look is that?"

"You will have to talk to people. You will have to use your winning manners to get them to confide in you. You will have to be a charmer. Most freeze before the police, and there are plenty to obstruct us just for the pleasure in it."

"I'll use my charm."

"Not with that face."

"How's this, then?"—taking a breath and letting it out and trying a smile.

"Now it's worse. Before, you looked fierce enough to kill, and now you look as if you'd enjoy it."

"It was up to her how she lived her life," I said. "Lord knows, there was no ease in it before—and as for them willing to pay for the warmth of her body, I hold nothing against them either. But the one man who hated her enough for this—how could anyone hate Maureen Rafferty?"

In the kitchen the larder was filled with breads and cheeses and a ham. There were four bottles of wine—Buckles assured me they were expensive. And sausage rolls and ginger cakes and a steak-and-kidney pie that had been picked over.

"Prepared for a siege," Buckles said.

"Maureen's doing. She was never going to be hungry again."

We went into the hall. Buckles said to the constable, "Where's the girl?"

"Girl?"

"The one you were holding here."

"Ah," the constable said, pointing to an empty chair.

"Chair. Yes. Very nice. Empty, I think."

"I left her sitting there, sobbing and crouched over, like. I was just stretching my legs down the other end"—which led to a window before which he probably had planted himself like a tree. Not his fault; constables were trained to stand that way.

"She appears to have left," Buckles said. "Along with your chances for improving yourself. Might I rely on you to stand guard so no one steals the body?"

"Sorry, sir. Yes, sir."

We went downstairs. The house, through accident or otherwise, was divided into two living quarters, both sharing the entrance and hallway.

"Name's MacPherson," Buckles said. "I'll fry his arse over this, but that won't bring the girl back. Who was she, d'you think?"

"A fellow practitioner."

"Yes. And sooner or later, with that hair, you ought to be able to find her."

"Eighty thousand of them, you said."

"You'll find her," Buckles said.

It was as if he had already accepted my primacy in this, that from now on no other task of mine could be as important.

Buckles knocked at the door downstairs, which was opened by a child in a maid's dress too large for her. She was bursting with the fascination of the event, bobbing in her version of a curtsey. She showed us into a drawing room. A woman turned to us from cooing into a bird cage. There were well-antimacassared Coburg chairs, bric-a-brac, and mementoes on the walls from, it looked like, all over the world. The woman was old with no flesh between bone and skin; she wore a wig as ill-fitting as a judge's.

"That will do, Poogie."

The girl's face showed disappointment. She bobbed and went to the door, hesitated just beyond the threshold.

"Poogie!" The girl left.

"Too much excitement," said the woman. "Too much—excitement."

"I am Sergeant John Buckles and this—"

The woman went back to the cage. "There are those who put out a linnet's eyes to make him sing better. I don't hold with that. I say a bird sings for those who feed it." She rustled some seed between her fingers but did not drop it into the cage. "A sweet note or two first, my pretty."

"Mrs.—" said Buckles.

"I am the widow of Colonel Ralph Prescott-Jones, late of the Twelfth Grenadiers. He returned from India to assume his retirement in peace, having served Her Majesty all his life—I have her personal note to him of thanks. He was killed under the wheels of an omnibus in the High Street, Kensington, as he left a tobacconist after purchasing half a dozen Trichinopoly cigars, of which he was fond."

"I'm sorry, ma'am," Buckles said.

"He could not see two feet in front of him. I wanted him

to wear spectacles but I am afraid he was a vain man."

Buckles solemnly pointed a finger upward.

Mrs. Prescott-Jones dusted the birdseed from her fingers. The linnet, I thought, cocked his head resentfully. "She was alone all day and I heard no sounds and I went up to knock on her door to see if anything was wrong." Her face was of pastrylike thinness, and she could not keep her large two front teeth covered by a short upper lip.

"Who?" Buckles said, pointing upward again.

"Sybil Grey. The fiancée of the young man. Sweet, his name is. Albert, isn't it? No, Alfred. She—Miss Grey—was companion to Lady—I can't recall her name now. She was going abroad, Lady—*why* can't I think of her name?—to stay with her daughter in Switzerland and, having no longer need of Miss Grey's services and Miss Grey being affianced, with the wedding, I understand, fairly imminent, the young man took advantage of my natural wish to help out the young and temporarily in need of shelter and so I agreed to let out the flat upstairs until the marriage, which, he said, would take place within a few months."

"Why," Buckles said, "did you say he took advantage."

"Not him. Oh, no. *Her.*"

"How's that?" I said.

"Because of the commotion. I thought she was a girl alone—perhaps like me, with no circle of friends in London—and yet there was always someone visiting, and often enough at strange hours of the night. Cousins, she told me, and once an uncle, mostly, she said, with a view to making plans for the wedding."

"This morning," I said, "you knocked on her door, to see if everything was all right. Were you in the habit of doing that? Taking care, for example, to see who her visitors were?"

"If you mean am I the sort of person to interfere with someone's privacy, the answer is of course I am not. And if I noted a visitor here and there it was because my door happened to be ajar now and again as they went upstairs—this is my house, you know. Also, one of the reasons I let the flat was that I did not care to be in this large house alone, except for Poogie, who needs more protection than she can give. We had many servants, of course, when the colonel was alive. All around the world. We had amahs and black ones and all sorts of oriental types. But when the colonel died and I came to settle here, I thought, why would I need a retinue, an old woman like myself with no thought of entertaining, whose ambition was to settle into a quiet life? So when this woman came to the door with Poogie in tow and asked if I could use her, I said to myself, why not? The mother was a strapping-looking woman who sold cabbages at Covent Garden—her own, she said, bringing them in every day from a small farm in Surrey—and she said her Poogie had ambitions to rise in the world and what better way than to be in service to a woman of quality—"

"This—Mr. Sweet," I said. "He left you his address?"

"Ah—no."

"How did he pay the rent? By post?"

"Came himself. Or sent a messenger. Quite promptly, I might add."

"Then you don't know where we might find him?"

"Unless you're here when he comes."

"He was prompt with the payments, you said," Buckles said. "Every week, was it?"

"Each Monday morning."

"How often did Sweet come to see Miss Grey?"

"Two, three times a week."

"This is Thursday. Should he appear next Monday would you let us know?"

"But the girl is dead," Mrs. Prescott-Jones said.

"Exactly," Buckles said, laying his finger alongside his nose like a conspirator. Mrs. Prescott-Jones nodded as if she followed him. I did not.

"Well, then," Buckles said. "Now if we can have a word with your small servant—"

"Of course, though I don't know what she can possibly tell you."

She signaled and Poogie appeared and Mrs. Prescott-Jones settled back in a chair to listen.

"If you don't mind," Buckles said.

"Yes?"

"If we could talk to the child alone—"

"Oh, I cannot permit that. She is in my care, you know."

Mrs. Prescott-Jones was immovable, and probably correct; Poogie was eager to begin the game, all but sniffing at each of us in turn.

Her pinafore was too large and her shoes had been made for a bigger pair of feet. Her brow furrowed as she strained to understand what was asked of her. She looked ten years old, but one could not tell with the children of the poor. The bodies developed slowly but their minds were older from having to cope, almost from birth, with the problem of keeping alive. This one was freckled and adenoidal and bright of eye. She put me in mind of Maureen at the farm and also of the girl who had cadged two shillings of me and returned them and had wanted to share my room. All somehow overlooked by those Societies formed to benefit the deserving poor, these girls, young enough for nurturing and humoring and proper food and minimal education. I thought of Alethea, in years at least of this sisterhood. She had never had to wheedle for survival, and for an instant I was annoyed that she had been so favored. Then I thought of Jessie Marsh and my anger turned toward myself because I had turned her away knowing she had no other place but beneath the arches of a bridge to stay.

"We have some questions of you, Poogie," Buckles said. "Poogie. What sort of name is that?"

"The only one I got."

"All right, Poogie. What do you know of"—pointing upward again—"Sybil Grey."

"I know she's dead."

"Did you ever talk to her?"

"She sent me out for sausage rolls a time or two. Let me have one all to myself."

"Did you ever see her fiancé?"

"Who?"

"The man who was going to marry her."

"Nobody was going to marry her. He just kept her here—" Poogie looked at Mrs. Prescott-Jones, who managed at the same time to look both encouraging and intimidating.

"Well, Poogie?" Buckles said.

Defiantly, for the game of it, Poogie said, "He just kept her here to have connection with her whenever he wanted."

"Poogie!" her mistress said.

Poogie shrugged.

"How long have you been here?" I said.

She looked upward, moving her lips, counting. "A fortnight?"

"Twice that," said Mrs. Prescott-Jones and, at Buckles's glance, "but no matter."

"How is it your mother left you here?"

"Mother?"

"The woman brought you here?"

One last look at Mrs. Prescott-Jones, and Poogie fixed her attention on Buckles and myself. Her position might be in danger, but frank speech to the detective was better sport.

"I never had no mother. Least that I remember. That was old Lis. Girls like us, she went around to sell us off."

"Poogie," said Mrs. Prescott-Jones, "you must not fib. Of course that was your mother, she said she was your mother."

"If you say so, ma'am."

"Why are you questioning my maid so? What has this to do with the unfortunate occurrence of last night?"

Buckles put up his hand. The gesture would have soothed a fidgety horse.

"This was the fifth house," Poogie said. "Old Lis said if the lay didn't take here we'd try another street tomorrow."

"You paid her a fee, Mrs. Prescott-Jones?"

"I gave her something, yes. Are you opposed to charity, young man?"

"And the girl, in addition to her—keep, is paid a salary?"

"I think," said Mrs. Prescott-Jones, "you are wandering far afield from seeking a miscreant for the crime upstairs. You may leave now."

"Just a question or two more," Buckles said politely. He smiled a little to show me what he meant about charm. He looked like an evil old man. "Poogie, did you often talk to—" The gesture with the finger upward again.

"I did but—" Poogie put her hands together and looked downward in a screamingly false version of piety. "I'm a good girl, least I try to be. Sometimes it's hard—"

"Of course it's hard, Poogie," Buckles said. "If being good was easy everybody'd be good, wouldn't they?"

Poogie grinned, pleased she had grasped the idea. "She sent me for things."

"Things to eat. Anything else?"

"Sometimes she sent me with a message—"

"To—?" It was suddenly difficult for me to breathe.

"Mr. Sweet."

"Ah," I said.

Buckles was more cautious. "To his home?"

"Oh, no," Poogie said. "To a public house."

"Called?"

Poogie shook her head.

"Now think. Where was this public house?"

Poogie gestured. She could have been referring to the dwelling next door or to an estate at the opposite end of the country.

"Could you find it again, Poogie?" I said. "Could you take us there?"

Poogie looked doubtful.

Mrs. Prescott-Jones said, "If you are quite finished with my maid, I need her services."

"Of course, madam," Buckles said, as courtly as you please. "Dr. Finny, whom you called and who pronounced Miss Grey dead, lives next door?"

"There is only one other house."

It was late Georgian, an influence the Victorians professed to dislike, so Buckles informed me as we walked up the drive, he being a repository of the kind of information which I was too young and inexperienced to have acquired. Or so he continued to tell me.

"Now this murder business, Richard, even one perpetrated in passion as this appears to have been—and we must always use the word, appears, until the truth is known for certain—murder, I say, is rarely direct, Euclidian, and solvable through application of logical principles."

"How, then?"

"This is not smash-and-grab, or an honest bit of jealousy. This one has a veil over it."

"I see no veil. I see Alfred Sweet."

"I hope you're right. To lift the veil, an inch at a time, and when it's stripped away to find there's nothing there but a shadow—that happens often enough. It might not be straightforward, Richard. Like that little Poogie leading us directly to the murderer. Don't depend on it."

Dr. Finny opened the door. He wore a brocaded velvet smoking jacket. He had a high shining glabrous head. He wore pebble glasses on the end of his nose, above which he peered inquisitively while sanding together long, thin, very white fingers.

"Sergeant Buckles and—"

"Of course. I have been expecting you."

He led us into the library. How, I wondered, could I ever afford this on a policeman's salary? There was a fat Burton which, given opportunity, would have easily turned me into a thief. The doctor bade us sit and offered us sherry, which we both accepted.

Finny said, "The wages of sin. Prostitutes are prone to this sort of violent end."

"Prostitutes," I said.

"Indeed," said the doctor.

Who was there to defend Maureen except myself? Who was there to deny what everyone knew her to be? "How did you know her to be a prostitute, sir?"

Finny frowned and looked at Buckles, who, in my defense, looked away. Dr. Finny made his eyes round and his eyebrows rose and I should have been cowed. He looked at Buckles again.

"How did I *know*?"

"Yes, sir," I said.

"A young girl like that, living alone. Dressed—did you see how she was dressed?"

"An income, perhaps? A wealthy indulgent father?"

"Men visiting at all hours—"

"A prostitute," I said, "as I understand it, is one who sells sexual favors. I am asking if you ever participated in such exchange or observed it happening with others."

"That's enough, young man," the doctor said.

Buckles looked at me and nodded slightly as if he, too, thought it was enough.

It had been a sad effort and I did not feel better.

Finny said, "If a creature has scales and swims in the water one is justified in calling it a fish."

"Of course," I said.

"Visitors," Buckles said. "Young, old, all hours?"

"Young and old and all hours."

"One special visitor?"

"I do not," Finny said, "spend all my time at the window—"

"We would be grateful for whatever you observed, doctor."

"One young man, notable because he did not slink. Most were surreptitious."

"The one free of guilt—would he be Alfred Sweet?"

"I would have no knowledge of his name."

"You do not know then that he rents the flat from Mrs. Prescott-Jones—"

"I barely talk to the woman. That in this respectable neighborhood she would allow such a person to live in her home—"

"You answered her call when she needed help."

"I must observe my oath as a doctor, although I have been retired for years."

"You're married, sir?"

"My wife died ten years ago."

"As a medical man," Buckles said, "I've heard it said that no other class of female is so free from general disease. The prostitute, I mean. Do you hold with that?"

"It is the general medical opinion, yes. It would appear to be the rule that prostitutes are endowed with iron bodies. So many of our notions of the nature of the occupation seem to go against the laws of nature. Take sewer men, dustmen—you would expect them to be sickly. Yet they are all healthy-looking, red-faced people. During the plague in London it was the dustmen who carried off the bodies and they did not contract any disease."

"There are differences," I said, "between classes of prostitutes, are there not?"

"As William Acton said, 'The greatest amount of income procurable with the least amount of exertion is with them, as with society, the grand gauge of position.'"

I felt proud of Maureen Rafferty for at least having come this far.

"And you cannot say," Buckles said, "if that one guiltless man visited next door last night."

"I could not say. I was engaged on my monograph. Whether gonorrhea is spontaneously generated by overindulgence."

"Is that your opinion?" said Buckles, interested.

"I think it likely. In my practice I found none suffering from that disease who was not a steady performer, regardless of his protestations otherwise."

Buckles thanked the doctor and we went out. I asked Buckles what we had learned.

"I learned," Buckles said, "that your mouth is as big as ever."

"Perhaps it was the doctor," I said. "He could have sneaked

across to see Maureen and then, worried that his visit might be discovered—"

"Now you're thinking like a policeman. Suspect everyone."

Poogie was out on an errand, so Mrs. Prescott-Jones told us when she answered the door to our knock.

"Will she be back soon then?" Buckles said.

"An ordinary servant might be back soon. With Poogie it's hard to tell. She gets distracted easily. A shopwindow, or an omnibus—"

"She delivered a note from Miss Grey to—someone. I would have her try to remember."

Mrs. Prescott-Jones shook her head tolerantly.

"A lie?"

"I don't think Poogie would know how to lie. It is just that the poor girl has such a bad head for remembering. If I want her to do a thing I must repeat it and repeat it and then stand over her to see it is done. Not a lazy girl, mind. But forgetful."

I though I heard her outside, her oversized shoes clip-clopping in the hall like a tired horse. I opened the door and she smiled at sight of us and it was very pleasant to see. Poogie might be forgetful but she had a sunny spirit.

"Are you ready," Buckles said, "to show us where you delivered the message to Mr. Sweet?"

Poogie looked confused.

"You remember, yesterday it was, Miss Grey gave you—"

"Oh," Poogie said. "Oh, it's not at all clear—" Then the fog cleared and she smiled. "Yes. I remember. I held the piece of paper in my hand like this"—making a fist, shaking it to show how firmly she had grasped it.

"With your leave then, ma'am, to borrow your servant for a while—"

"I'm sorry," said Mrs. Prescott-Jones. "Today is silver day. Then there is tea. She is not quick or apt, you see."

Buckles said sternly, "Is it that you do not want the apprehension of the villain who—" He pointed upstairs. "Shall we have murderers running about loose? A woman like yourself, living alone, would welcome the protection of the police, would she not? I should think cooperation with the law would be your first concern, Mrs. Prescott-Jones."

She bristled. She could not have been used to this tone from her subordinates when the Colonel held his command. "What is your inspector's name?"

"Criddle."

"I know Sir Barton Monks, who is well acquainted with one of the commissioners. Sir Barton served with my husband, the Colonel, in Calcutta. I suggest, Sergeant, you come back another day."

"Piddling," Buckles said. "What is all this piddling?"

"Sir?"

"I will have her back in an hour."

"I cannot spare her."

The constable who had been on duty upstairs came down and asked Buckles—the door was open—that since in our absence the body had been removed to the dead house could he go back to the station?

"Now I must have the flat scoured," said Mrs. Prescott-Jones. "Poogie, you will need a bucket and some soap and rags. How will I be able to find another tenant who would be willing to live where such a terrible event took place? And how can I be guaranteed a respectable lodger? Although Colonel Prescott-Jones left me well enough provided for, in these days of rising costs—"

"Come, Poogie," Buckles said. "You, MacPherson, fill out a report about the disappearance of Miss—"

"Norse," I said.

Poogie looked delighted at being promised a frolic while looking toward her mistress to be allowed off the leash.

"An hour, you say," said Mrs. Prescott-Jones. "Sixty minutes of lost industry. We cannot have that sort of thing, you know. It is why London is filled with beggars and other low types. Too idle and slothful to earn their daily bread. I myself am a member of the Female Aid Society and I support the Girls Laundry and Training Institution. I have promised my maid a morning off Thursday next, and if she wishes to use her time in that direction you may return and claim her."

"How unfortunate," said Buckles, "that we must ask you to come with us to the station house, Mrs. Prescott-Jones. I will notify Inspector Criddle to see your case immediately. The penalty might not be too harsh. A fine, perhaps."

"Fine? What fine? What are you talking about?"

"Constable, will you get a cab for—"

"Wait! How dare you imply that because I will not permit my servant to go gallivanting off with you I have broken some law. Who do you think you're hoodwinking, Sergeant whatever-your-name-is?"

"Who said anything about your servant?" Buckles said mildly.

"Then what—?"

"I was referring," said Buckles, "to the Common Lodging House Act of 1851. You must be aware of that."

"Lodging house?"

"Did you not have a lodger here?"

"I know nothing of any lodging house act."

"Do you recall the terms of that Act, Detective O'Boy?"

"Certainly, sir. First, it refers to standards of decency."

"Obviously those standards have not been maintained. Fines, at the very least. And we must take the lodging house keeper into custody. And is there more, Detective O'Boy?"

"Yes. The Act states a register of lodgers must be maintained."

"Mrs. Prescott-Jones, do you have listed such a register?"

"Certainly not. I do not run a lodging house. This is my own home and if I choose to rent out a flat that is my own affair."

"You will be permitted to consult your solicitor, of course. But I am afraid we must take you into custody."

"You are absolutely mad."

"I will permit you to get your coat and lock your domicile."

"Perhaps—" I said.

"Detective O'Boy?"

"Mrs. Prescott-Jones is certainly a law-abiding citizen—"

"I am indeed. I have always been."

"And Mrs. Prescott-Jones, as any law-abiding citizen, would obviously be willing to cooperate with the police—"

"Certainly. In any way that—if you wish to take Poogie with you for—did you say an hour?"

"Is it your recommendation, Detective O'Boy, that we overlook—"

"Under the circumstances—"

"Well, then. Come along, Poogie."

Outside, I asked Buckles if it had been necessary.

"Will we ever see the day when people approve of the police and assist them?"

"Are you sure Poogie won't be abused for this by her mistress?"

"No more than usual. Mrs. Prescott-Jones is a moral woman. She believes in the principle—as do most of our employers and schoolmasters—that the harder you are forced to work, the more tasks you are given to do, the less time for mischief. Especially a girl as young as Poogie, who would have plenty of mischief to consider were she not laden with sufficient chores."

"There are those not burdened with work whose taste does not turn to mischief."

"The rich, you mean? But then, you see, they are not criminally minded, as the poor are."

"Mr. Sweet—?"

"Rich, you think?"

"Could you rent such a flat for your mistress?"

"We must not anticipate, Richard. Take Lord Cardigan, your late military master. Having helped dispose of most of his Light Brigade, hearing of a vacancy occurring in the Order of the Garter, the highest of honors, he asked for it, being the first hero ever to request the honor for himself. He did not get it."

Poogie walked merrily between us. We went down Wellington Road and into Park Road and then into Regent Park. Buckles said, "We want you to do exactly as you did yesterday when you took Miss Grey's message. Do you understand, Poogie?"

"Oh, yes, sir."

In the park she stopped, linked hands behind her back, and looked up into the branches of a tree.

"This is what you did," Buckles said.

"I love trees. There is just something about trees."

"You took Miss Grey's message to be delivered to Mr. Sweet and then you came here and looked at a tree."

"It was bad of me, I know, but I look at trees every chance I get."

"We've been gulled," Buckles said. "Our bloodhound has taken us to a butcher shop."

"So then you didn't deliver the message after all, Poogie," I said.

"Oh, sir, of course I did. I just stayed here for a little while."

It appeared to be a plane tree of no particular distinction, the upper branches sibilant with starlings.

"What do you like about trees, Poogie?"

"They're strong and they're—proud. They're not told to do this and do that. And they're old and they got secrets and sometimes fairies live in them. Sometimes if you stand and look long enough, especially if you don't move much, you can see just the shadow of a fairy's wing. And if they get to know you, if they think you can stand still long enough, they can tell you some of their secrets."

"What secrets have they told you, Poogie?"

"Richard!" Buckles said. "It wouldn't be much of a secret if Poogie blabbed it to everybody."

"Sorry."

"Now where did you go, Poogie?" He was astoundingly patient. But then, so was I. We wanted a murderer and this child might be able to lead us to him, yet neither of us was moved to shake her into quicker action.

Buckles said, "Even without Poogie there's another way. Only one of her customers will not be returning."

"So then we have him, the one who does not appear."

"What next, Poogie?"

"Why, then I got into a fly. Miss Grey told me to, and gave me the money. Both there and back. She was an awful good person."

"Did you take a cab back, Poogie?"

" 'Course not. In order to pocket the fare, you see."

I started asking something else and Buckles put up his hand to stop me. "You got into a cab, then."

"Yes, sir."

"Now think, Poogie. What did you say to the driver?"

"Why, I just showed him the paper."

"And what was written on the paper?"

"How should I know? I can't read."

"Finished," I said. "We're finished, John."

"How many times have you been in a cab, Poogie?"

"This was the only—well, once before when old Lis took me out of the workhouse."

Buckles bent down before the girl and, taking her shoulders in his hands, put his face close to hers. "Now listen to me. I'm going to get a cab, we're all getting in, and we're going to have him take us to the same place, do you understand?"

"Yes, sir."

"And you will direct him, you must remember where the other driver went, you tell him where to turn, which streets to go on. Do you think you can do that?"

"I don't know. I'm not a very clever girl."

"Oh, but you are, Poogie. Isn't she, Richard?"

"Oh, my, yes."

"We went to a public house, I remember that. I asked for Mr. Sweet, and the man there said he would take the message."

"Fine, Poogie. Where did you get the fly?"

"Right at the corner there. And I remember he just kept going straight on."

"Lovely. You didn't put your head back and sleep, did you?"

"Oh, no. I looked out the window all the time."

We went to the corner where a cab was waiting. Poogie did not recognize the driver. We got in and Buckles told the cabman to go straight and he'd be told where to turn.

Poogie was having the time of her life. She bounced from side to side, sticking her head out the window. When at an intersection we slowed down, a street boy ran alongside with a tray of oranges. I bought one for Poogie. She thanked me and took a tremendous bite through the rind.

Buckles said, "Keep watching now. Never mind the orange—did you go straight on or did you turn?"

"There now, the two houses stuck together like one, that's where we turned."

"Right or left, Poogie?"

"She can't read, she doesn't know right from left. This way or that, Poogie?"

"This way"—bending her left hand at the wrist.

Buckles rapped on the trap with his hat and told the driver.

"Straight on here," Poogie said. And then she told us where to turn again, and then Poogie said, "There it is, right there."

"You're sure now."

"Of course," Poogie said, suddenly dignified. "I remember it because there was tumblers yesterday, one on top of the other and one on top of him. It was a sight, I tell you."

Buckles paid the driver and we got out. It was called the Jolly Bear; the animal on the sign looked like a cow and there was no sign of jollity in its expression. As we approached the entrance the door opened and a man in a striped apron, propelling a woman with hand on her arm, said, "Hook it smart, you bitch," and shoved her, letting go. She caught herself from falling by clutching Buckles and, mumbling to herself, went unsteadily up the street.

"Gentlemen, come in, sorry, gentlemen, she's been sitting here all morning without ordering anything, waiting for someone to take a fancy to her. Not very likely, wouldn't you say? Come in, come in."

Perhaps he was the jolly bear. He was a man as wide through as side to side and he had one full eyebrow while the other was a scar.

We went in and took a table. Buckles said, "Now you're sure this is the place, Poogie."

"Oh, yes, sir. I remember that man. I gave him the paper."

"That's not Mr. Sweet?"

"Oh, no. He said he would see that Mr. Sweet got it."

"You couldn't be mistaken, Poogie?"

"I *could* be mistaken, but I'm not."

"Believe her," I said.

"I do. How many sausage rolls do you think you can eat, Poogie?"

"How many?"

"If you could have as many as you wanted."

She shrugged one shoulder, hiding her head in it like a bird and smiling.

"She'll commence with three, then, and a meat pie for myself, and you, Richard?"

"Just a pint. I don't know if I'm ready yet for strong food."

After the waitress brought our orders, Buckles asked for the publican. He came, smiling, rasping his hands together.

"Do you remember this child?" Buckles said.

The publican looked uncertain.

"She came in here yesterday, bearing a message for Mr. Sweet. Do you know Mr. Sweet?"

The publican looked at Poogie and then at me and then he looked at Buckles, with all the workings in his head clear as he estimated the possible trouble in speaking the truth and the possible advantage in doling it out slowly. "What is it you wanted from the gentleman?"

"Do you know him or not?"

"I may—I'm not sure."

"Let's make you sure, then," Buckles said, standing up and reaching in his pocket to show his warrant card. "This is a police matter, you see"—the voice companionable—"but I would prefer the pleasantness of your cooperation rather than the official interrogation. What I mean to say is, we're just two people looking for an acquaintance. Nothing to do with whether your kitchen is clean enough to maintain your license. I'm not interested in that, you see."

"The girl do look a little familiar."

"And Mr. Sweet?"

"He do come in here sometimes."

"Is he here now?"

The publican shook his head.

"You did take a note from this girl and deliver it to him?"

"I can't be standing here all day answering questions. It's my busy time of day, you see."

Buckles nodded and tackled his pie. The publican, frowning, walked off.

"Oh, this is prime," Poogie said. She had a roll in each hand and was alternating bites.

The clerks of the neighborhood were coming in, their manner altering as they left their shops for the privileged surroundings of the public house, where men could loosen their neckcloths and tongues as they filled their bellies. Buckles finished his pie, delicately dabbed at his lips with his fingers, and stood up.

"Do you need me?"

"I think not, Richard."

Poogie was on her third sausage roll. Her eyes were beginning to look glassy, and perspiration stood out on her temples.

"You don't have to eat it all here," I said. "We'll wrap up what's left and you can take it home."

"Oh, they are prime."

Buckles came back and I wrapped the remaining sausage roll in a napkin. Buckles paid the bill and we went out. We would have put Poogie in a cab to go home by herself but her face was moist and she was beginning to look green. Before sending her into the house I went with her into the bushes and held her head while she heaved. When it was over she said it had been worth it.

"Well, John?"

"He has a ratting pit upstairs and they begin sometime after eight o'clock. Mr. Sweet will probably be there because he is an avid follower of the sport. Our friend will be happy to point him out to us."

"Did you have difficulty persuading him to be so friendly?"

"None at all," Buckles said.

I took Poogie to the door. "Maureen—Miss Grey—was she a happy person?"

"The happiest I ever seen. All she wanted to eat and the fanciest clothes. Nothing to do all day, either. I sometimes seen her still in bed at three in the afternoon. Why wouldn't she be happy?"

"Why not, indeed," I said.

Chapter Fourteen

Buckles and I went back to the public house at half past seven. The front of the long bar was crowded with men of all classes: costers, soldiers, coachmen, tradesmen, well-dressed bloods. There were some Frenchmen, keen to examine the English ways, and a taciturn German or two unhappy with the British beer but pleased at the prospect of free wagering. Some of the company carried small bulldogs, some bore Skyes; the most excitable were the little black and brown English terriers, struggling to get loose. All were smoking and drinking and discussing their animals. Waiters walked about shouting, "Give your orders, gentlemen!" The landlord had discarded his striped apron for long close-fitting black trousers and a frock coat and top hat. He went about the room exchanging greetings. There were dogs standing on the tables or tied to the legs or sleeping in their owners' arms. Prospective bettors examined the animals, stretching their limbs and looking into their mouths. Most of the dogs were well scarred from rat bites.

"Now, there is a dog. I've seen her kill a dozen rats almost as big as herself."

"What I don't hold with is the use of sewer rats. They give dogs cankers."

"We always rinse her mouth out well with peppermint and water."

Each time the publican's eyes went to our direction, the glance continued over our heads as if he had never seen us before. Buckles raised his head, then his finger, and finally went to stand directly in the man's way. Because of the crowding it happened that Buckles planted his foot high on the landlord's instep, causing him to howl and curse Buckles for a clumsy fool.

"I wondered about your memory," Buckles said, without apology. "Is it then so short, or have you trained it so?"

"Do I know you?"—lowering his head and staring as if he saw better from the tops of his eyes.

"I'm here to have you point out Alfred Sweet."

"The crusher, is it?" The publican looked quickly and carelessly around. "I don't see him. Looks like he an't coming tonight."

"Look again. I would have you make sure."

"And I would have you leave. It'd make my guests uncomfortable if they knew a crusher was in their midst."

"Ratting is against the law," Buckles said.

"It's overlooked, you know it's overlooked."

"I wouldn't stop your entertainment. Especially a man's so willing to cooperate in small matters. Like looking sharply for the man I want."

"I can't say he's here if he's not here."

"Keep looking," Buckles said.

I was taken with a fierce-looking terrier held in one arm by a man all in brown with a short pipe in his mouth.

"That's a fine-looking dog, sir," I said.

"Aye."

"What's his name?"

"Samson."

"Most appropriate. What does he weigh?"

"A full four pounds."

"Over the limit, then," I said, referring to a posted sign which restricted the entries to dogs with a maximum of three and three quarters pounds.

"I am matching Samson against Mr. Mullins's dog in a private match."

"Mullins—?"

"That's the landlord."

"I know nothing of ratting, but I might bet on your animal just from the resolute look of him."

"To tell you the truth, son," said the man in brown, confidentially lowering his voice, "you might not want to risk your money. This is Samson's first experience in a ring. Moreover, he's been trained with barn rats and I don't know what he might think of the sewer sort. He might be—fastidious"—smiling.

Buckles drew me aside. "The damned publican—"

"Mullins."

"Mullins?"

"That's his name."

"We have only his word for identification, and he'd just as soon not recognize Sweet, who could be standing next to us for all we know."

"He's all we have," I said.

Mullins stood on a chair with his hands up like a prizefighter who has just been judged victor. "Give your orders, gentlemen, drink up. The ratting pit will be open in five minutes."

"Shall we leave, Richard?"

"He might come in later."

"And you've never seen a ratting."

I tried to look as if it didn't matter to me.

"How do I explain to Criddle that we ought to be reimbursed for dropping a bob to see a ratting match?"

"A small price to catch a murderer," I said.

"I'll have you explain it then," Buckles said, leading me upstairs to where the landlord had preceded the company to stand in the doorway holding a box into which each dropped his shilling entrance fee.

A circular white-painted pit stood high in the center of the room like a cannibal's cauldron awaiting missionaries. Over the circus was arranged the branches of a gas lamp which brilliantly lit the white floor. The audience clambered upon tables and chairs or hung over the sides of the pit itself. The dogs were all now slavering and barking and struggling in the arms of their masters.

A man jumped into the pit and a rusty cage of rats was lowered to him. He pulled the rats out, laying hold of them by the tails and jerking them into the arena. While the rats were being counted, some ran around the floor and some huddled together and a few climbed up the man's trouser leg. He took them off, shouting, "Get out, you varmints!"

"Time!" A dog was dropped in. The rats skittered around the circus. The dog, a tired-looking black and tan, was not very anxious to kill, preferring to leave the rats to enjoy their lives. He had disposed of no more than a dozen when the timekeeper called an end to it. While the dead rats were being swept out for the next match Buckles suddenly jumped on a chair and in a parade-ground voice which echoed from the low ceiling said, "I'm looking for a man named Sweet. Is there a man here by the name of Alfred Sweet?"

There was a moment of curious silence; then someone said, "My name is Sid Lovely, would I do, Captain?" and another said, "Darling is my name," and another, "Ralph Delicious, at your service."

Buckles got off the chair in a dangerous mood, and the publican, who had been enjoying Buckles's discomfiture, made sure not to look in his direction. Buckles was so intent on something to kill I thought of suggesting he get into the pit with the rats, but I was fortunate enough to keep myself quiet. I watched as he took command of himself. He made himself still as a lake on a windless night and blinked once, like a salute to himself, and then he was as always.

"A stupid act, Richard, born of blind frustration. Not good police work at all."

"I understand the frustration."

"You will have to do it better, Richard."

That was the second time he was putting the case in my hands alone. I didn't ask why. I said, "How?"

"First, someone inconspicuous to hang about and listen for the name Sweet. Not an officer. Perhaps a boy."

"And second?"

"Too much hitty-missy so far. If we can't find Sweet from the outside, then we must reach for him from the inside."

"Which means?"

"The red-haired blower."

"I'm not at ease with women like that. I think they sense my—"

"Inexperience?"

"That too," I said.

"You're still saving yourself for—what's her name—Lysistrata?"

"Alethea. And I never said—"

"You're not—no, I know you're not."

"I'm not," I said.

"You wouldn't just ask her to marry you? She could say no, and you could then agree to forget her, with the assistance of several young ladies I know who would be delighted to—"

"I'm certainly not ready to take on a wife. And as for asking Alethea—" I could hear her laughter.

"Or," Buckles said, "you could walk up to the girl, put your phiz right into hers, and tell her it's time the two of you went to bed together."

"My God," I said, horrified.

"It's been known to work," Buckles said.

Mullins now requested that the gentlemen give their minds up to drinking, and the waiter walked about with his cry of "Give your orders, gentlemen." When the landlord was satisfied that no man's thirst had gone unquenched he announced the next dog to be tried. This one was so fat his belly barely cleared the ground, and the onlookers demanded of the owner why he did not feed the beast, and did you ever see such a scrawny one, and why was he limited to only five meals a day? Nevertheless the dog was a creditable rat killer that, without moving frantically, managed to dispose of rat after rat until he had exceeded the record for the day. That was pretense enough for Mr. Mullins to suspend proceedings while more drinks were ordered. Several gentlemen then protested that they had come for the ratting and not to drink Mr. Mullins's poison. Mr. Mullins chose to regard this slander humorously, saying he would be the first to drink any of his potions his customers would be good enough to buy for him, but there were expressions of like irritation that he was delaying the entertainment, so he announced he was now pitting his own animal against the bull terrier of Mr. Caster—who was the gentleman in brown—for a private wager of two guineas. I would have ventured a shilling on the bull but there were no takers for that amount, some of those present betting as much as five pounds.

The dead rats were gathered up by their tails and flung into a corner and the floor was swept and then a big flat basket with an iron top was brought. Mullins and Caster tossed to see whose animal would go first and the proprietor won. Mullins went into the pit, put his hand inside the rat cage, and stirred up the living mass with his fingers. Fifty rats were counted and flung into the pit. They gathered into a mound. They were all sewer and water-ditch rats, and the odor that rose from them was like that from a hot drain. Mullins offered them the lighted end of his cigar. Some of them sniffed and singed their noses. There were cries of "Blow on them" from the spectators, which Mullins obligingly did and which caused the rats to flutter about like feathers.

Time was called and the publican's dog was dropped into the pit. He was an old dog, well scarred, and the damage to his ears, the side of his neck, and haunches looked the product of disagreement with his own species.

The dog rushed at the rats, sinking his nose in until he brought out one in his mouth. In a short time a dozen lay bleeding on the floor, the white paint of the pit reddened. Then the dog had a rat hanging from his nose. He could not get rid of it until he dashed it against the side, leaving there a patch of his own blood. When time was called he had dispatched two dozen rats, which was considered fair enough, if hardly a record.

The ring was cleared again and the man in brown jumped down into the seconds' circle and a new batch of fifty rats was lowered and dumped. Samson was dropped in. The dog's nose wrinkled at the mephitis and he stood still for a moment, no doubt comparing the distasteful urban rodents with the clean barn rats of his acquaintance. "Go about it, Samson," said Caster. Samson began cracking the skulls of rats and tossing them aside without worrying them, getting on with the next one. He had the grim efficiency of a destruction machine. At the final count he had dispatched thirty-two. Mullins, with ill grace, paid up his bet while all around us wagers were being collected; Buckles and I had to pretend temporary blindness, considering the anti-gaming laws.

We stood at the door watching the gamesters depart. "Any one might be him," Buckles said.

"In the storybooks," I said, "an urchin will now appear, tug at your coattail, and say, 'Sweet? Is it Sweet you want? I know where to find him, just follow me, sir.' "

"You're taking this all very lightly, Richard."

"I was thinking of the rats."

"What is there to think of about rats?"

"I was thinking if there was a parallel between what we witnessed tonight and the Christians in the Roman arenas."

"Rats are ugly, they smell bad, and they do no good that I can think of."

"That's what they said about the Christians."

"Richard, I've got something to tell you."

"I hate hearing that. It never means anything good is coming."

"You'll be looking for Sweet by yourself."

"Why?"

"Saturday morning I'm off to Paris. Edgar Hammer, the eminent snoozer, has decided to take a vacation from our London hotels and is reported to be sampling the hostelries of Paris. They've asked for someone who can identify him."

"How long will you be gone?"

"Until they apprehend him. Or, if that seems unlikely, until Criddle demands my return. He says he can't spare me, but the commissioners like to encourage these international exchanges."

"You'll like it."

"I'm anxious to see the difference between the French gendarme and the British bobby. They began by putting their soldiers in the streets, that's what the word means. Our British public was afraid we were going to do the same thing."

"Won't somebody be replacing you—working with me, I mean?"

"Criddle, on my recommendation, says you're to work alone."

"Thanks."

"I was appointed your instructor, not your permanent associate."

I felt sad. At the corner where his home and mine lay in opposite directions I said, "How will it go, John?"

"Murder will out, as old Chaucer said."

"I want him," I said.

"London may not be his home. This may have been a temporary playground for him, and his association with your Maureen one of his city indulgences."

"Are you saying he could be lost to us?"

"I am saying there will be no anguished outcry in the newspapers as there was during the garrotings. I am saying that the commissioners will not be demanding daily reports. I am saying that Inspector Criddle will not approve of your spending all your time on this case alone."

"Because a girl like that is expected to come to a bad end."

"I'm saying that no one cares if she does."

"Is the law then not for all?"

"Justice is equal for all, but there are grades of justice."

241

"What would you have me do, John?"

"Find him," Buckles said.

In the morning Inspector Criddle called me in and said I was to see about a complaint of a robbery in Covent Garden.

"Yes, sir," I said. "But—"

"But?"

"That murder in St. John's Wood—"

"Yes, some prostitute or other, wasn't it? I saw Buckles's report. What about it?"

"I was planning to—"

Criddle looked at me with those cold blue eyes of his. "Some ponce was putting her up, was that it? And then she insulted him—they're quite sensitive, aren't they—and he was stupid enough to abrogate his means of livelihood. That's about it, wouldn't you say?"

"No, sir. Gentleman lover, it looks like."

"Ah. Well. Handle it as you see fit, then, so long as it doesn't take up all your time. Now off to Covent Garden, the man is screaming as if he's lost his life's savings."

"Yes, sir," I said.

When I was at the door he said, "Detective O'Boy—"

"Sir?"

"This girl who was killed—she was as much a subject of Her Majesty as you or I. Station in life is no criterion for the manner in which we do our work. You follow me."

"Yes, sir," I said, not following him.

"Prostitute or lady-in-waiting, it's not up to us to make judgments about the value of a life; we do the Lord's work. Thou shalt not kill, He said."

I looked at the inspector closely. This didn't sound like him.

"That's all, O'Boy."

"Yes, sir."

He stopped me again, with his hand out this time. "I expect results from you, but not miracles. Do a responsible job, but don't be wasting all your time at it. Do you follow me?"

"Yes, sir."

"Damn," he said, half turning away so he could see out the window but still keep me in sight. Criddle never turned his back on anyone. "Buckles said you knew the girl."

242

"Yes, sir."

"If we had the number of men to fit one officer to one crime we'd need a force of millions. Do you know what I'm trying to say?"

"You're asking me to be fair," I said.

There was certainly nothing unfair in stopping by the Jolly Bear on my way to Covent Garden. Mullins had stood up against Buckles; I could hardly hope to do better alone. But I had a stronger reason than Buckles to put my hands on Sweet. It was unthinkable that the publican, able to guide me to Sweet, would refuse. He was behind the bar, polishing glasses with a dirty rag.

"You again. He an't been in."

"Am I wrong? You seem in a more agreeable mood, Mr. Mullins."

He smiled with teeth the color of corn. "I had an agreeable night."

I said hurriedly, for fear he would tell me about it, "Describe Mr. Sweet."

"I told you. A toff, middle height, fine clothes—"

"His face."

Mullins used his hands to shape clay in the air between us. He pulled the face down, extruded the chin, put a cleft in it.

"Small, straight nose," I said.

"You know him, then?"

"I will know him when I see him."

A dandy came out of a back room. His chin was deep in his collar and hat brim low over his eyes. He sidled out. Mullins looked too blank, too uninterested.

"Him?" I said.

If the faint movement of Mullins's chin was a nod you could not have held him to it. I went out and followed the man. He was a hundred feet ahead, a darter, slipping through crowds like water. He did not look behind, but I thought he moved like a man escaping. I could not narrow the gap between us, although despite the strain on my poor leg it did not widen, either.

Something squashed against the side of my face. I picked off the remnants of a tomato and another hit me. Some passersby looked at me curiously. I took out my handkerchief and wiped my face. It was impossible to determine where it had been thrown from. In front of me appeared the costermonger Pearly, with one of his friends.

My quarry, if he had ever been that, was gone.

"How awful, the man just happened to be standing under a falling piece of rotten fruit."

I took his kingsman from about his neck and wiped my face and, wadding the handkerchief into a ball, dropped it on the ground.

"Hey, that's my best wipe. That's a miltonian for you, they got no manners." He was blocking my way and I would not walk around him. He said, "You've insulted me. Bert, you're a witness, he insulted me."

"He did that," Bert said.

"I demand satisfaction," Pearly said.

"Pearly," I said, "I'm a patient man. I was patient the last time we met and I'm patient still, but there's a limit to patience, as there's a limit to brains. Which, as you will agree, is a limit you reached long ago."

"What does he mean, Bert, is he calling me stupid?"

"Sounds that way to me," Bert said.

This kind of situation had not been covered in my instructions. Was a policeman different from a civilian? Could he accept this kind of personal challenge? More important, what happened if he did not accept it?

Pearly said, "Do the honors, Bert."

Bert said in a cheerful voice, "I charge you that my friend here, Pearly, has been mortally insulted and stricken by your behavior and he demands satisfaction so I ask you, sir, as a gentleman, are you prepared to offer such to him?"

"What weapons?" I said.

"Fists," Pearly said.

"Done," I said, thinking the only way out of this was to fight my way out, leaving the arts of diplomacy and public guardianship to those better able to deal with them than I. Pearly looked pleased with himself. His reputation among his fellows would be well secured if he could legitimately knock down a policeman.

"Lead on, then," I said.

They took me to a place where the coster wagons were stored, much like the courtyard into which I had first gone with Buckles when he introduced me to St. Giles. The word had gone out ahead of us, and there were fifteen or twenty costers waiting to cheer Pearly and jeer at me. A circle was formed and Pearly removed his jacket and shirt. I did the same, but slowly, because I wanted to gauge what he looked like under his clothes. What I saw did not fill me with optimism. He was rich with muscle from neck to shoulders, his chest was deep, and there was no fat across his abdomen. Although I had been trained by my father, that was a long time ago and I had not fought anyone since, while this coster had fought frequently, it being their practice.

For the first time the thought occurred to me that I might be humiliatingly beaten instead of being the gracious victor buying the police some respect.

Taking off my hat I said, "Will it be safe now? Can I depend on you not to toy with it?"

"I'll guard it myself," Bert said. "We takes our prizefighting serious. There's not a man here would use this occasion for sport of his own."

We squared off, Pearly smiling in anticipation, I determined to teach him a lesson without seriously injuring him. I peppered him three times with my left and I did not dislodge his smile. Suddenly he closed with me, head down, and brought it up sharply into my chin. I tasted my own blood and there was a grittiness as from chipped teeth, and for a moment more than one Pearly was circling me.

"Don't finish him so quick, Pearly."

"Slice him up a bit first."

"He has to know he's fighting a coster boy and not some poor gonoph afraid of the law."

I thought how fine I looked, head up, standing straight, hands extended in the proper position. I hit out at Pearly and he grabbed my left hand in both of his and bit down hard at the base of my thumb.

The pain was punishing. His friends cheered at the brilliance of his move. I backhanded him hard on the bridge of his nose to make him let go. My bitten hand dangled, almost useless. Pain was a mist before my eyes. How fine I looked, and how stupid. This was a fight, not an exercise, with my opponent out to maim me, not to score well in a contest. I had learned nothing from my father to have prepared me for this.

Having scored with his head and teeth, Pearly now came in

feet first. As slow as I had been to learn the nature of our combat I knew now the prize ring, despite its brutal battering, was a model of gentlemanly conduct by comparison. It was not that I regretted the absence of rules but that I had been savaged so through ignorance. So now as Pearly came at me with raised foot to render me forever impotent, I hooked his leg in mine and as he went down hit him with the side of my fist in that terribly vulnerable spot where the back of the head meets neck, and he crashed face down without hand or arm for cushion.

He lay bleeding from nose and mouth and no one came to touch him, because that would have signified the end of the match. Instead he was berated for lying there and at the same time exhorted to stand up to the pig, who, despite one lucky blow, could barely keep himself standing up.

Which was true. And as I stood swaying over him, Pearly, with some residual bit of costermonger pride heeding the pleas of his fellows, got slowly to his feet, his nose mashed and lips split, and struck out at the air beside me. So not in anger but in need of conclusion I measured him and struck as hard as I could and he went down like a sheep in the slaughterhouse and none of his friends begged him to stand again.

My thumb hurt where it had been bitten; it was a wonder he had not taken it clean off. Each beat of my heart hammered madly on a drum in my head. I discovered the helplessness of a one-armed man trying to get a shirt on. Nor did any step forward to assist me. If I had thought to buy at least some suspension of hostility by agreeing to fight, it looked as if I had mistaken my own pride for exigency.

Then they shut me away from them, all puckering in their own tongue. They fetched bucket and towels and began ministering to Pearly. Soon he was groaning, which was a relief to me; I had not wanted him dead. I got my shirt on after a fashion and did not want to remain there while I struggled with my jacket, so I took it and my hat in hand and walked out to the street.

They must have been following me with all the skill of James Fenimore Cooper's Indians because I didn't notice any of them until they converged on me in an alley off Monmouth Street. There were ten or twelve of them, all costers, all with the kingsman proudly knotted, all out to avenge Pearly's defeat.

I backed into a wall and, gesturing with the hand that held

my coat, said, "There's no end to it. If you're after me because I licked him then I have to be after you when this is over—it doesn't stop, do you understand?—and anyway Pearly and I fought man to man but now you're breaking the law and I'll be coming after you with constables, do you understand?"

I was gabbling to ears without interest in listening and mouths unwilling to talk, and that began to frighten me. They should be taunting me; it was a pleasure to them to mock the police. They were too grimly, coldly quiet.

I dropped my coat and hat and waited. I could use elbow and forearm for protection in my left arm, but if the thumb were struck—

One by one they darted in. Slash and run. After which, if I were sufficiently weakened, they would probably close en masse and stomp my brains out. Some had knives and some coshes. It occurred to me that I would be dead soon.

Which made me angry. This wasn't my idea of dying well, pounded to death by a mob of young costermongers.

Run, then. Break through and be in the street. There's no shame in running when there is no other way to save your life. Are you too vainglorious to run from a band of boys?

One came in cutting and I sidestepped him. He was not quick enough to recover out of my reach and I hit him on the side of his head, a glancing blow but enough to remove him from the company. It wasn't pride then, it was arithmetic. Subtraction.

Oh, I was still standing proudly. But not for long. I would be no match for geese or puppy dogs if they were in sufficient number and bent on destroying me. Soon I would be on the ground, huddled with arms over my head so that I could stay alive another moment or two.

A neddy landed on the knee of my bad leg. *No*, I screamed to myself. My hand was in someone's hair and I banged him on the ground. Two of them out of it. While I did the subtraction, the knife of another slashed my shirt. Only my shirt, I thought, yet how is it that a shirt can bleed?

Up to now I had been as silent as my attackers. There could be a constable within cry. Was I afraid to use my throat, so recently healed? But there was a simpler, more stupid answer. I did not know how to ask for help. I had never learned.

Then suddenly appeared a banshee with a stick like the sword of Saint George. Flailing at a leg, an arm, a head, but more devastating was the condemnation and outrage of her shrieking—so alarming was its denunciation that I felt guilty myself. And unbelievably, as I tottered, my assailants slunk away and only my benefactor remained. Her dress was torn, her hair would have been in place in a cornfield, she was solicitous and triumphant.

And she began to cry.

"What is it, Jessie? Are you hurt?"

"No."

"What then?"

"Nothing."

"But you're wonderful. You saved my life."

More tears.

"But why?" I said.

"Now you see I'm not a lady," she said.

"Thank God," I said.

She wiped her nose on her wrist (time to change that habit later, I thought) and said, "Let's go, then."

I could not walk easily and leaned upon her as we went to the corner, where she hailed a cab. Two scarecrows such as we appeared might not perhaps so easily have found transportation, but no driver could have passed by the imperiousness of her gesture. My room was so close that conversation was unnecessary. We went through the mews and she helped me upstairs. She took my clothes off and laid me on the bed, and I did not wonder that she had the strength to handle my large body since she had just demonstrated the annihilative power of a battalion. I lay with eyes closed as she bandaged and stanched and applied cooling compresses. She covered me and I fell asleep.

I awakened to candlelight and a figure heating something over a gas flame.

"You're still here," I said.

I could see her back stiffen. She straightened up and went to the door. "For Christ's sake," I said.

"Don't blaspheme," she said.

"I've heard you say worse than that."

"I guess you can take care of yourself now."

"All I said was, you're still here. I didn't mean you're still here, that's bad. I meant you're still here, that's good."

"I never know what you mean," she said. "You might as well drink this."

She brought a bowl to the bed and spooned hot broth into me.

I could tell time from the sound of the vehicles in Oxford Street. The day's flux had diminished but it wasn't yet the stillness of the night.

"There's nothing too bad," she said. "Bumps and scratches, mainly. Your thumb is swole but the skin an't tore. How did you get that?"

"I was fighting a coster who bit me."

"That's why, then. You licked him, and they hates to lose to a crusher. Lucky he didn't get in too deep. Costers' teeth are more filled with poison than a snake."

"I will buy you a new dress," I said.

"No need."

"You saved my life."

"Did I?" She tried to hold it back but the smile broke free. "I did, didn't I?"

After the broth I was hungry. I moved to get up and she said, "Stay where you are, what do you think you're doing?"

"You said I was all right."

"What I meant was there wasn't anything a little rest wouldn't cure. That doesn't mean you can go hopping about."

"How do you know so much about it?"

"I raised ten brothers and sisters, didn't I?"

"There's little food here, I have to get some."

"I'll get what's needed."

"I have another reason for getting up."

"I'll bring you a pot."

"You certainly will not. Get me my trousers."

I went down to the privy, sternly admonishing her not to follow. I was not worried about my thumb or my knifings but the thought of the blow to my bad leg turned my blood to water. I put as little weight on that side as possible while I followed the strain in my head, anticipating the stress on sinew and bone and praying it would all hold together.

She was waiting at the foot of the stairs and I gratefully let her help me back to the bed.

"Here's some money," I said. "Would some chops and a potato please you?"

"Please me?"

"I expect you to join me."

"All right, then. I'll go to Charlie's, he carries the best and he doesn't try to rob you."

"Get bread and cake downstairs. Is there tea enough?"

"There's tea."

"Then run along," I said, making my tongue rough.

"And you," she said, mimicking the roughness. "Lie still and don't go hopping about."

I insisted on getting out of bed for supper. Sitting across from her at my small table, the candles between us, I saw that she had managed to wash her face and comb her hair, which, pulled away from her face and helped by the soft glow, made her look astoundingly pretty and not so young that I had to speak to her with the heavy condescending humor of the older man (there were, perhaps, three years between us), except that the pattern of that was set and would take some effort to undo.

"How did you happen to be there?" I said.

"I been watching over you," she said.

"Have you. Yet the last time, I said unforgivable things. Not that I meant them—"

"Oh, yes, you did, and don't get soft and mushy because I did you a good turn. I'm all the things you said. I have no eddication and I don't usually keep myself clean enough—"

"That's true enough."

"I have all my teeth," she said, putting fingers in each corner of her mouth and making a tragic mask.

"I see you have."

"And my nose an't crooked."

"No, it's not. A bit long, perhaps."

"Is it?" She measured with thumb and forefinger and put her fingers out to the light to study the distance.

"If you put it to the grindstone, it gets smaller. Reading and writing will do that."

"I can read. I can read every street sign there is."

Her tears caught the candlelight.

"Stop that. I was teasing. Your nose is perfect."

"I'm not crying about my nose."

"Then what are you crying about?"

She shook her head.

"I didn't mean to hurt your feelings."

She shook her head, fiercely this time.

"What are you crying about then?" I said, annoyed.

"There you go. You're sharp with me again."

"I'm not sharp. Just tell my why you're crying."

"You're grateful 'cause I helped you."

"Of course I am."

"I did as good as any man, didn't I."

"That you did, and better."

"That's what I mean." A sob now followed the tears.

"I don't understand," I said.

"A lady wouldna."

"Ah."

"Well, would she?"

"No, I guess not."

Alethea would have screamed and hid her eyes. What lady would not have?

"I thought we passed by that," I said.

"I saved your skin, is all. Sitting quietly like this, just the two of us, you can't be glad I'm not a lady."

"This is getting complicated. What I mean to say—"

"Say it," she said.

"I'm—I'm glad you're here," I said.

"Do you mean that?"

"Well, yes," I said, becoming irritable. "Can't we stop this?"

"I can put it on, if that's what you like," Jessie said. "I can say what I don't mean. I can say what I think you want me to say. I can do those things, just like a lady, if that's what you want."

"That's hardly the definition of a lady."

At which she shut me off, like pulling down a blind. She stopped talking and her face went still. She put the dishes away and she put on her shoes—I had not noticed that she had taken them off—and she went to the door. "Thanks for the supper."

"You're welcome."

And she was gone, without hesitating at the threshold for remonstrance.

I pushed back the table, which fell over, and went stumbling to the door, favoring the bad leg. She was halfway down the stairs. "Come back!" I yelled.

She kept going.

"Come back, damn you!"

At the very last step she hesitated.

"What for?" she said.

"Because I want you to."

"You thanked me already."

"It's more than that."

"More?"

"I need you."

"To do for you?"

"Yes."

"Like I wanted to before and you wouldn't let me?"

"Yes."

She came slowly up the stairs. She said, at the door, "I might give it a trial, just a trial, mind."

"Thank you," I said.

"You might start to bleed or something in the middle of the night and you oughtn't to be alone."

"Exactly," I said.

I went to bed while she made herself some kind of palliasse on the floor. In the middle of the night I woke up frightened; I saw the shape of her across the room and felt reassured.

Then later I was sitting up in bed and talking and I did not know dream from reality. It seemed as though I were going through life seeking the cause of my distress, yet I had not known of my own unhappiness. Then I slept, and then the experience was repeated, and this time Jessie was sitting in a chair beside the bed.

She said, "Alethea. Is that your own true love?"

"She's not mine."

"A person can go through his whole life with his love un— unrec—"

"Unrequited."

"That's it. And never be able to look at another girl."

"And always be alone?" I said.

"That's the tradegy of it."

"Tradegy" made me feel better.

"He couldn't even be able to look at another girl who would be better for him in every way."

"Don't go away, Jessie."

I was inside a dream again, and talking; I knew Jessie was there and for some reason I wanted her to understand all about me.

"If she's what you want, you just got to go and take her," Jessie said. "You can't spend the rest of your life just mewing about it."

"Buckles said that too."

"Buckles?"

"Never mind. I'm a lucky man, I have no lack of advice. Just take her and put her in a room like this, is that it?"

"I like it here," Jessie said.

I slept and unslept.

Jessie said, "You're afraid your mother hasn't found peace, is that it?"

"I never wept for her. I wept for my father but I never wept for her."

"But you took her name," Jessie said.

I was a ball bouncing in and out of the past. Alethea and Peter. Maureen Rafferty and Balaclava. Peregrine and John Buckles. And Alfred Sweet. That's when I began to fight, and it made my contest with Pearly less than the sparring bouts with my father. Jessie tried to hold me down. Once I flung her so violently she spun across the room and crashed into the wall. In horror I was out of bed and beside her, taking her in my arms, patting her to see if I had hurt her.

"No bones broken," she said.

"I'm sorry, Jessie. I would never do you harm."

"Back to bed," she said firmly.

"You haven't said you forgive me."

"For that and more," she said.

"More?"

"To come."

She tucked me in like a mother, fingers soothing on my forehead.

"You're a strong one," she said.

"Richard. You haven't used my name."

"Richard."

"I took her name, as you said. But that was an accident."

"Was it?"

"A mistake made by the recruiting sergeant."

"You didn't weep for her but you took her name."

"Was that enough?"

"For then."

"I don't know if I loved her, Jessie."

"Of course you loved her."

"How can you know that?"

"She was your mother."

"You don't have to love your mother, especially if she doesn't love you."

"I see the whole thing now," said Jessie. Enough light came in from the window to show her in profile, nodding.

"What do you see?"

"It was easy for you to weep for your father because you're not him. You're her. You couldn't weep for your mother because you would have been weeping for yourself. She was cold, and you are cold. That's the whole thing, right there."

I could feel her scratching at the truth. "Are you a witch, then, Jessie?"

"There's witches in my family. I had a great-aunt, Hetty, she used to be able to turn milk sour."

The morning held more promise than any I could remember. I was aching, but alive. Jessie had opened the window to air the room, she was dressed and looked fresh, she had found some pins for her torn dress.

I said, "There are two matters for you to attend to this morning. First you go out and buy yourself a proper dress, and two you find Roger—you know him, you said, the boy who's so poor at stealing handkerchiefs—and send him to me."

"That's not first," she said. "That's second and third. First is breakfast."

She brought me a mug of hot tea and then began to fry some bacon.

"Where did you get that?"

"I been out."

"Where'd you get the money?"

"Enough was left from last night."

A king, I thought, must live like this. I washed my face and dressed. I squatted to test my leg and was pleased at the soreness, which was better than pain.

Chapter Fifteen

"Ah," I said. "Roger."

He was just as ragged and dirty and with the same uneven smile that made you listen, without rancor, to his lies.

"Will you have some tea?"

"I had my breakfast, but I will take a cup."

"And some bacon?"

"Just a collop."

"A sweet roll? Baked downstairs an hour ago."

"Just one, then."

He did not eat like a boy who had just had his breakfast. Jessie slapped his fingers as he reached for a third piece of bacon.

"You're a prime cook, Jessie."

"This is Mr. O'Boy's food."

"You're welcome to eat as much as there is, Roger."

Jessie looked heavenward, shook her head, resumed her work at the window. Having been washed to invisibility, it was now being polished like royal silver. In the brief time since we had agreed that Jessie could stay she had become frenzied housekeeper, cook, and, as with Roger, protector of the larder.

"How have you been keeping, Roger?"

"I been busy."

"At what?"

"This and that."

"Are you too busy to do a job for me?"

Roger hastily swallowed the rest of his bacon and sat up straight.

"You get a basket and go to W. A. Hargreaves in Covent Garden and buy some apples or whatever else you think you can sell from a basket. I am suggesting Hargreaves because if you mention my name I think he will do well by you. Then I want

255

you to station yourself in front of the Jolly Bear on Compton Street. Do you know where that is?"

"I know Compton Street and I know the Jolly Bear. I know every public house there is."

"You sell your wares. And you listen to everyone going in and coming out. What you listen for is the name Sweet. Have you got that? Sweet."

"Sweet," he said, nodding hard.

"If you hear the name Sweet, you will mark who uses it, and you will follow that person to where he lives, and you will come tell me. Do you understand?"

Roger nodded, looking doubtful.

"Let me talk to him," Jessie said. "You're an innercent chavy. You stand at the gattering but no griddling, no cause to be chased off by the owner—if you see him you mizzle right smart, not to lose your place, you see."

"What I want," I said, "is to find the man named Sweet, or find a man who knows him."

I gave Roger some money and he left.

I was off duty until the evening, when I had been assigned to go to a night house in Panton Street which was known to be frequented by a navy lieutenant named Singleton who had had a warrant sworn out against him by a tobacconist named Chervil who, upon informing Lieutenant Singleton that Chervil was out of Russian cigarettes, had at first been verbally assaulted by the sailor and then several showcases had been torn down and finally the proprietor had suffered a broken arm. Lieutenant Singleton had then informed Mr. Chervil that not only had he no intention of paying for the damages but that the lieutenant would break the man's other arm if he persisted in molesting him.

Jessie had prepared a tea as elaborate as my limited utensils would allow. I watched her eat until she flushed and put her hand up to shield her mouth.

"Byron," I said, "said a woman should never be seen eating."

"No wonder, if you're going to stare right past her teeth."

"I didn't mean to do that."

"I heard of Byron."

"He could have been referring to you. Were you never told not to speak with a full mouth?"

She swallowed.

256

"I didn't mean you weren't to chew. What do you know about Byron?"

"He was a Lord and drank wine from a skull."

"How did you know that?"

"When I was a step girl once they let me in for a cup of tea. I heard the lady of the house talking about it to a choker was visiting."

She took a tiny bite of bread and ate it, mincing it like a mouse.

"Jessie, we'll have to find you a bed."

"I don't want a bed."

"You can't prefer to sleep on the floor."

"If there's going to be money spent on this room I would rather see a sideboard so we could get some more dishes and a small rug, perhaps, and a chair—I mean a place for you to sit and put your head back and I could take your shoes off for you, maybe a Coburg. I'd rather see those things ahead of a bed for myself, and anyway another bed in here would make it look like a lodging house stead of a proper bed-sitter." She shook her head, lips together. Then she said, so softly I had to strain to hear, "One bed in a house is enough unless there be children.

I decided not to pursue it. Jessie cleared the table and rinsed the dishes. The luxury of having someone to do that for me was pleasant. She moved with grace, I thought. Even in the fracas she had not looked awkward.

"Jessie—outside of those street signs—do you read at all?"

"No need to."

Was she right? I wasn't sure. If reading was learning, how to convince anyone that learning mattered? To be able to quote another man's thoughts instead of your own? Jessie was watching me for rebuttal, and I didn't think anything I could say would be convincing. If you never expected to be a lawyer or a Member of Parliament, was it not enough to be able to scratch your name and read a butcher's prices?

"I'd read if you wanted me to, sir."

"Richard."

"It's hard to use your name."

"Why?"

"Because you're always stern to me."

"It's the coldness," I said.

"It's there," Jessie said.

"A man said reading and writing was no more education than a knife and fork is a good dinner."

Jessie shrugged. "Anybody'd know that."

"Where did you learn to read?"

"I went to a ragged school. They didn't like me there I was so dirty."

"Yes, I remember."

"That wasn't dirty. That was clean compared to what I was when I went to school. My father was a coal heaver at the docks, and when he came home he was all over black with the dust of it and he spread it all through the house. They told me in school I had to clean myself up, even though there was those there hadn't been out of their clothes for months on end. Everybody knew what was crawling on them, but it wasn't as easy to see as the dust of the coal was on me."

"We might try looking at the paper," I said.

"I'd as soon be working on some of your buttons."

"That can wait. Here we are, a proclamation from our Queen. Take it up now, and let me hear you."

Jessie took the paper and held it out and looked at it from the top of her eyes and then from the bottom.

"Is there anything wrong with your eyes?"

"I can see a crawler way off there in the corner"—jumping up with the paper and rolling it and swatting.

"Read," I said when she came back.

She cleared her throat. " 'We, Victoria Regina; considering very seriously and very religiously that it is our indispensable duty to apply ourselves above all things to maintain and augment the service of Almighty God, as also to discourage and suppress all vice, profane practice, debauchery and immorality—' "

Some stumbling and some hesitancy but with more facility than I had imagined.

"More, Jessie."

"I don't understand more than a word here and there. If she's got something to say to people like me, don't you think she ought to say it in a way that it'd be clear?"

"I want to hear more, Jessie."

" 'We do prohibit and forbid by these presents all our faithful subjects of what condition or quality soever, to play on the Lord's day, at dice, cards, or any other game whatsoever, in public or private habitations, or elsewhere, wherever it may be, and by these presents we require and command each and every one of them to attend, with decency and reverence, at divine service on every Lord's day.' "

"You absolute faker," I said.

"The Queen?"

"You."

"Any street girl knows how to use fakement."

"You didn't learn to read like that in any ragged school."

"You can't know everything about a person in the little time we've had."

"Tell me, then."

"After I was a step girl I was brought inside to be a rocker. While I was soothing the baby there'd be someone reading to the young master, who was about as old as me, and I would listen; what else was there to do?"

"You did more than listen."

"Well, when they was through, I would pick up the book and give it a going over."

"Why, Jessie?"

"Why?"

"Why did you want to?" Since I could not think why it was needful for her to be educated, perhaps she could tell me.

"You been to Hyde Park in the afternoon?" she said.

"Yes."

"And you seen the boys and girls riding their ponies alongside their father's horse?"

"I've seen that."

"I wanted to be like them."

"Above your station, you mean."

"Yes." Head down and subservient. And false.

She was, I thought, deeper than I, more subtle, and perhaps more intelligent.

"Fakement," I said.

She smiled a little, just enough to have me see inside, but only a glance's worth.

"Read this to me, from the *Chronicle*, a critic's view of a celebrated female vocalist."

She took the paper and looked at it, then to me, then back.

"'For our part, being moderate men, adverse from any violent measures, and lovers in all things of gentle counsels, we should incline to adopt Handel's method of making performers sensible of their faults. In the days of Handel, if a singer gave offense he used to take her by the waist and throw her out the window.'"

I sat back in enjoyment.

"Is that what it really says?" Jessie said.

"You're the one's reading it."

Shaking her head, Jessie read on. "'This was a laudable practice and should be revived. In those days, a man had some chance of hearing tolerable music, when such judicious means were taken to perfect the performers. If they gave themselves airs, away they went into the street. If they were out of time or tune one moment, they were out of the window the next. This was the true concert pitch.'"

Jessie looked at me for guidance. I nodded. She smiled uncertainly.

"'We conceive that sore throats, coughs and colds, and hoarseness were very scarce in those exceedingly good old times. Those airings from windows must have hardened the constitutions and braced the nerves finely. We would feign see something of the kind revived. The idea of throwing them out of windows would seem just the thing. Until some plan of this sort is adopted, we shall have nothing but apologies and disappointments. One decent tumble would cure all the sickness and sulkiness even of the opera company.'"

"I wouldn't have believed it," Jessie said. "In the newspaper."

"So there you have been," I said, "knife and fork poised and starving to death."

"He doesn't mean it," Jessie said. "Does he?"

"It's called satire. But sometimes that's just a word writers hide behind when they mean exactly what they say."

"Of course I didn't understand most of it."

"You know how to read yet you do not read. You know that's one of the deadly sins?"

"I read it like a parrot. I don't know enough words."

"You'll write down the ones you don't understand and we'll talk about them."

"You'll be my schoolmaster."

"Yes. And I'll take a stick to you if you're stupid."

She smiled as if I had promised her a golden reward. Then, thinking of her performance in the melee, I decided not to use a stick.

That evening Constable Jeffries called to accompany me to the night house. As I was leaving, Jessie asked when I would return.

Which presented a problem. Sharing my room, she was entitled to know. Yet I had granted her no entry into my life; she was neither wife nor paramour. She solved it herself by adding quickly, "I'm only asking because if I hear someone at the door late at night I'm liable to open it with a cudgel in my hand."

"If I don't tell you it's me strike out."

Constable Jeffries, in uniform, would remain outside the house in case of need while I went inside. Jeffries said, as we walked along, "I'll be kicking my feet together to ward off the frost and you'll be sitting at a table with a glass and perhaps a little female companionship and do you call that fair, Detective O'Boy?"

"I don't call it fair but I certainly call it enjoyable."

"I like the uniform, that's my trouble."

"Look alert," I said. "If you hear my whistle come running."

"Just remember, O'Boy, the regulations say no spiritous liquors can be drunk while on duty. Nothing but water, now."

I went upstairs and took a table and had no sooner ordered a glass of white satin—certainly it looked like water—when a man appeared at my elbow asking permission to join me. He was tipsy, at the stage where its sole manifestation is a slight loosening of manner.

"Justin Newcastle"—extending his hand. I took it, muttering "O'Boy," and although I did not welcome company I realized that a companion in his state would take away any odor I had of policeman.

"Heeding the call of nature, are you, O'Boy?" he said, beckoning to the waiter. "The male rut, as in the rut of all evil." He guffawed, slapping me on the shoulder.

A man wearing a naval officer's uniform came in and took a table nearby. I should have confronted him at once, asking if he were Singleton and identifying myself and then taking him into custody. I was not there for any other purpose. But it was pleasant to sit with a glass listening to the gabble of a stranger. I could take Singleton any time I chose—I had no intention of taking my eyes from him—and what could be the harm in only a few moments' delay?

(Forgive me, Maureen, for not yet having taken into custody your murderer. I will have him, I promise you. But I must attend to this and that, else the Inspector will take back my warrant card. So be patient, I will never forget the foulness done to you.)

Singleton did not look anything but serene and gentlemanly, a slight man with rust-colored hair and an air of independence.

"O'Boy, is it? What's your first name?" Newcastle said.

"Richard."

"Well, Richard, do you consider yourself a man of experience?"

"In what area?" I said.

"In the area of women."

"I was brought up on a farm. I know the way things work."

Newcastle laughed. "You're not here to meet a sheep, I hope."

I didn't smile.

He said nervously, "No offense, of course."

I nodded, sipping gin and keeping an eye on Lieutenant Singleton, whose identity was now established because the proprietor, a man in a glistening mauve waistcoat, had addressed the sailor by name, going from table to table with an air of cordiality. He knew my companion too, saying, "Well, Mr. Newcastle, are you looking for something rare this evening or something comfortable?"

"Has that oriental girl been in?"

"Mary Lee. She should drop in later. She likes a negus on these chilly evenings. I'll tell her you been asking for her."

"Unless something more interesting appears first."

"There's always that chance, Mr. Newcastle."

I thought now of taking the lieutenant out before the room crowded up, but I was filled with a not unpleasant inertia and I sat on, listening to Newcastle.

"If you're not above taking some advice," he was saying.

"In what area?"

"The same area, the only area worth exploring, the fixed and yet infinitely variable slit between a woman's legs that from the beginning has caused all the trouble in the world and all the pleasure and glory."

"And why would I need advice in that area?" I said.

"I was not implying—"

"On the other hand, who can know it all?"

Newcastle called the waiter and ordered a dog's nose, a combination of gin and beer. "Appropriately named for the occasion, eh, Richard?"

I sat thinking I should rise now and get myself over to Singleton before sipping further from my glass, yet loath to force myself to my feet.

"I'll tell you how to get round a woman," Newcastle said.

I nodded, keeping an eye on Singleton and thinking there was no harm in more learning.

Newcastle put his hand out palm down, patting the air as if to make room for a syllogism. "To get over a girl, never flurry her till her belly's full of meat and wine; let the grub work—it's sure to make a woman randy at some time. Talk a little quiet smut to make her think of bawdy things. Show her your prick as soon as you can, it's a great persuader; once they have seen it they can't forget it."

A waiter brought a tray with brandy and soda to Singleton's table. A woman with a very large extended crinoline went up to him. It was amazing how much of a room a woman could fill with a flounce of starched garments. Two or three ladies, and an average-sized room was taken up. She appeared to be at about the same level of tipsiness as my own table mate. She asked Singleton for something to drink. He said he was waiting for a friend. And, he offered, she had already had enough.

Newcastle said, "She's big. I like big women. I should like to tickle up her legs."

"A small gin is what I need," said the woman to the lieutenant.

"Go home," he said. "And make sure you sleep alone, else you'll wake up with your flower gone without remembering how it happened. I'm making a grand assumption, you see, that you still retain it. No gentleman can assume less"—hand on heart and bowing slightly in his seat.

She leaned over and picked up his glass and threw it against the wall. While doing so her crinoline flew up, and Singleton put out his hand to keep it down.

She turned and screamed, "How dare you take such liberties!" And she began to strike him in the chest with her fists. Singleton held on to her hands and had to push her down into a chair.

At my table Newcastle said loudly, "Hardly the sort of thing a gentleman would do, wouldn't you say? More likely the behavior of a cad, I would think."

Singleton, ignoring him, called a waiter and asked that the woman be removed. The waiter pulled her to her feet and she struck him and scratched his face. Another waiter came, and between the two of them they managed to turn her out.

Then Newcastle stood up and said, "Damn plucky thing, by Jove, to strike a woman," and went up to the lieutenant, pulled him from his chair, and knocked him down.

And what were the forces of law and order, as represented by myself, doing during all this? Nothing. I was watching as if it were an entertainment. The two waiters had run up and seized Newcastle, and while he was being held, Singleton smashed him in the face. Then Newcastle broke free and knocked Singleton over a table, jumped after him, seized his head, and began knocking it against the floor. The door porters were called and they ran in and took hold of Newcastle. Singleton got up and pulled him loose, grabbed Newcastle by the collar and one leg and onto a long table set for a large party, pulled him along the table, driving everything before him—glasses, dishes, candles—and cast him away to fall stunned and bleeding into a corner. Then Singleton, head down, charged through the porters and waiters, throwing them right and left, and dashed out into the street.

I had been standing by as effectual as a doorpost. I had forgotten to signal Jeffries. I ran out to the street and called, "Didn't you see him?"

"Who, sir?"

"The lieutenant."

"Someone in uniform came tearing out, but I didn't know who it was and I had received no signal to stop him."

"Did he say anything?"

"Well, he did. He was shouting that he'd be damned if he'd have anything more to do with the swell side of the city and he was going to find some honest sailors to be with. What happened up there, O'Boy?"

"What happened is that I sat like an ass watching a gentlemanly fracas and forgetting what I was there for."

"Criddle won't be pleased," Jeffries said.

"Thanks for reminding me."

"What now, then?"

"The docks," I said. "What else?"

"Useless, wouldn't you say?"

"I would at that."

"You'd need an army."

"At the least."

"You're in charge," Jeffries said.

"You'd best go home, Tom. Get some sleep."

"He'll show up."

"Right you are, Tom. Good night."

Constables were mainly for preventing crime and politely answering the questions of visitors to the metropolis. They were solid manifestations of the might of the law and were designed to make peaceful citizens feel safe and hooligans change their ways. Detectives were different. Detectives were designed to look like all men while tracking down and apprehending lawbreakers. Detectives who failed through inaction (stupidity, cowardice) should consider other means of gaining a livelihood.

London had six main docks and each was a great port of its own. Thousands were employed in loading and unloading cargo from ships come from all over the world. Sailors poured into the city for the carousing they had dreamed of through months of female deprivation. Enterprising, public-minded businessmen, in order to prevent a plague of starved international mariners in the city itself, established near dockside sufficient dance halls, brothels, and lodging houses to contain the seamen, limiting fecundation to the neighborhood of the sea. The containment, it was hoped, would apply to stabbings and gougings, thievery and drunkenness, raping and roistering. For this public service it was not too much to ask that the sailors contribute their accumulated pay.

It was not a place to be visited by the pure, but it was no more perilous than Spital Fields, or the Holy Land, or Brick Lane and Whitechapel, or Ratcliffe's Highway and Jacob's Island, or Bermondsey, or the Jamaica Road. There were enough violent men in London to destroy it, but happily they were content to pound on each other, or the occasional innocent, or threaten the self-doubting fledgling detective whose alternative was to go home and eat on his liver and anticipate Inspector Criddle's corruscating tongue in the morning.

To which of these seafarer's delights of rest and recreation would Lieutenant Singleton now be repairing?

The fog came in from the river yellow and choking and rendering the ordinary mysterious by cloaking the unpleasant and softening the harshness of glaring gaslight. One could not see where the feet were placed. The mist swirled over boot tops so that there was the illusion of treading on cotton batting until the jolt of stepping into a hole between the cobblestones or the squish into a pool of mud—one hoped it was mud. The fog muffled sound so the clatter of horses' hooves and iron cab wheels seemed to come from a distance until the swinging lantern suddenly appeared with no warning and one more step might mean being run down.

London's beauty often depended upon its being shrouded. Other cities had to depend on their filth's being covered by snow. London's fog was omnipresent. Even as you knew what it concealed, the mystery beckoned. The diseased prostitute showed a flash of white teeth and painted mouth. A girl's rags were a gauzy covering. A mean dwelling was tremulant in its poor rushlight.

I walked through Shadwell. Foreign visitors said it was meaner than the worst sections of Marseilles or Antwerp or Paris. The houses squatted along wretched streets leading down to the river. One could hear music from the gin cellars. If there was not entertainment enough within, the crowds spilled into the street to watch the women fighting—those who were not busy sorting out the rubbish dumps for rags and bones.

At the docks I went down the hundred steps in the unsteady light of the gas jets. The walls ran with water. There were shops so small and hidden one wondered that customers knew of their existence. On impulse I walked into one, intrigued by the colored flagons in the window. There were bottles and flasks and vials on shelves along both sides, all different shapes, all different in color. The proprietor was a hunchback.

"Perfumes from all over the world, sir. India, Araby, Persia. Do you seek something to please a woman?"

"A girl, yes."

"Myrrh, incense, balm of Gilead?"

"Why are you here?" I said. "Why are you not on Oxford Street, teasing the gentry?"

His eyes were bright, beady. Another one in the ratting pit, I thought, waiting for the jaws of the terrier.

"What makes you think they do not seek me out here?"

"Something small," I said.

"The most expensive essence in the shop is the smallest."

"Perfume water—for a girl."

"Not for a princess, is that it?"

I would not have him diminish my gift. "She is worth more than I can afford to please her."

"Here, then"—a vial, cunningly cut, its facets gleaming. "Eau de cologne, would this please her?"

"It would please her, if the price would please me."

"Is a sovereign too much?"

"Yes."

"A crown?"

"More than I can spend."

"A shilling, then?"

"I can afford that."

"Then you can have it for a shilling."

"I have determined the price, not you?" I said.

"It's my shop. I indulge myself as I wish. Is she beautiful?"

"No," I said.

He was forced by his infirmity to carry his head on one side, forever inquisitive. "The city of Cologne is famous for its perfume water. Yet it is the most stinking city of Europe."

I could not think of anything to say to that.

I went into the basements of the low lodging houses to examine the sailors in stupor on the penny hangs—ropes breast high on which they were suspended in lieu of beds. Lieutenant Singleton was not among them.

In the eating houses I found sailors gobbling anything that was green. At sea they had developed spongy gums and aching muscles from weeks of salt beef after the limes and lemons had run out and the biscuits had spoiled and the water was slimy in the casks. Who would be a sailor? I thought. As they might have said, who would be a detective?

I went to the dancing rooms, through a bar of a public house, and up a flight of stairs into a long room well lighted by gas. There were benches along the walls and musicians on a dais playing: a fiddle and a cornet and two fifes. They played mostly polkas. The women were sprightly and held up their skirts with one hand, the other on their partners' shoulders. There was an amazing amount of decorum.

In an alley I saw two men supporting themselves on a wall, rough men, not sailors, and they had been well bruised. Farther along was a chandler's shop, and through the window I saw the proprietor and a boy putting things to rights. It looked as if a strong wind had been a vicious visitor. I went in and asked the cause.

"A wild man," said the owner. "Asked for Jamaican segars and we don't stock them."

I saw Lieutenant Singleton at dawn sitting on a piling, listening to the sounds of creaking capstans and sailors scraping the hulls of their ships.

"I'm Detective O'Boy and I'm here to take you into custody on the warrant of one Chervil for having done damage to his person and his place of business."

Singleton looked up at me without interest.

I smelled the sea and the warehouses—spices and hides and leather and fats and oils.

"Are you going to come quietly?" I said.

He sucked in his upper lip and considered me. I braced myself. He said, "What if I don't?"

"I would call some men and have you carted through the streets on a board."

He sighed. "I wouldn't like that. Not that you could, you know."

I wasn't sure I could, either.

"I don't like it here. On land, you know."

"I was wondering about that," I said.

"Well," he said. "I do have to get some sleep."

"We'll accommodate you," I said.

She wasn't there. There was just the one door and the one room, no place to hide. I felt something I could not explain—a tug at the heart, a fear, a weight. Desolation? I had no right to have expected her to be there. That I had given her lodging for the night was no contract. There was nothing binding in allow-ing her a roof. She was free to go as she wished, to work or to steal, to remain in London or seek a new life elsewhere. Nor had she changed my life by appearing in it for so brief a time. Had she not? How, then? That she had made breakfast and tea and washed the window?

I took off my jacket and shirt, hoping that the other one was clean, and not remembering. It was not only clean but freshly pressed and neatly put on a shelf. Although I had scoured the room upon moving in, I had not been so resolute in its maintenance. Now the room shone.

Did I miss her because of that? Was she indispensable because she kept my room clean? Would not any woman have been able to do that?

When first I saw her she was dirty of face and dress, so whence the training at cleanliness? Of herself too, because she had become neat and scrubbed and—pretty. I could say it, it meant nothing. She was pretty.

At home there had been ten children and a brutish father. She had been a servant there. Had she been anything other than that with me? But a servant gives notice of departure.

She came in then, bringing in the outdoors as if the air and the sun had a reason for clinging to her. "There you are," she said.

"And there you are," I said.

"You were out all night."

"And so were you."

"No—I went out to buy you this." She brought out a neckerchief bright enough with colors intermixed to tie to a mast and guide a ship through the blackest of waters.

"Thanks," I said. "But why didn't you go to bed?"

"Don't you like your present?"

"Of course—"

"You think it's too bright. But you're supposed to wear things like that today. It's Derby Day."

"Ah, so it is," I said.

"And I'm sewing all of this to my bonnet"—taking out bows and artificial flowers with colors never known to nature. "But you haven't slept."

"Nor you," I said. And then, sternly, "You didn't stay up waiting for me, did you?"

"I was too frightened to sleep."

"Frightened?"

"You told me to read so I was, and every time I heard a sound my hair stood up."

"What were you reading?" I said, looking at the books on my shelf, none calculated to induce that kind of reaction except maybe the Sykes murder and that was far along in the book.

Jessie picked up a pamphlet with a startling cover from the table, "Sweeny Todd, the Mad Barber of Fleet Street."

"I got it at the news seller. It was hard to decide between that and 'The Ranger of the Tomb, or The Gypsy's Prophesy,' and then there was 'Varney the Vampire, or The Feast of Blood.' "

"I'll have to read this," I said.

"If you like to have your blood chilled."

I took the kerchief and knotted it around my neck. "And I have something for you, Jessie." I brought out the bottle which the hunchback had wrapped in some colored paper and handed it to Jessie. She opened it slowly and her eyes filled.

"I'm sorry," I said. "I thought girls liked things like that."

"Of course I like it."

"Then why—?"

"Because nobody ever—"

"It's a no-reason present."

Jessie pulled out the stopper and sniffed cautiously and looked upward. "Oh, my," she said, giving the vial to me to smell.

I drew back. "I'd just as soon smell it on you and be surprised it came from a bottle."

She seized my hand and kissed it. I pulled back in horror.

"Don't do that. I'm not the pope or a king."

"You're mean," she said.

"Mean?"

"Not to let me thank you."

"I hate anything soppy."

"Yes, Richard."

"About Derby Day—"

She shed ten years while not letting hope in too far. Jessie could be any age she wanted.

"So long as it's Derby Day, shouldn't we go to Epsom?"

"Oh, Richard, could we?"

I nodded, magnanimous as an emperor.

"The bonnet. I must fix the bonnet."

While she sewed I lay down and closed my eyes. Then, just short of sleep, I realized that Jessie would not awaken me, and I forced myself to sit up.

"Maybe you'd best rest for a while," Jessie said. "Epsom can wait."

"I can't. Let's go"—taking her by the wrist and pulling her toward the door.

She hung back. "Just one minute, please." She took the eau de cologne and appeared to pour a quantity into her cupped hand.

"Not like that, Jessie. Ladies don't use it like that. Just a drop on your handkerchief."

"You've seen ladies do that, I suppose."

"I read about it," I said.

In the streets there were already carts and carriages on the way to Epsom Downs, the vehicles gaily decorated, the drivers and their ladies in bright finery. A gypsy wagon came along and I signaled it. The dark, mustachioed man hauled up on the reins as if he had spotted a ten-pound note in my hand.

"Epsom?" I said.

"You want to come?"

Jessie was already clambering up and I jumped in after her. Seated beside the driver, his wife, plump and bandanna'd, with large gold earrings spinning as she turned her head, smiled a welcome at Jessie. It occurred to me then that anyone would. It was extraordinary how she had changed, how lovely she had become. She was, I thought, in her way as attractive as Alethea, but Alethea was as remote as the crown jewels under glass. No one in the space of one day could turn so suddenly from begrimed gamin to comely young woman. Was it myself, then, who had learned how to look at her?

"You and him, you jumped the budget?" the woman said.

Jessie shook her head and sighed. The woman laughed.

"What's that?" I said. "Jumped what?"

"It's just a gypsy saying," Jessie said.

"What does it mean?"

"It's how they get married. They jump over a string."

"That's marriage, jumping over a string?"

"It's their way," Jessie said, sounding as if I were too dense to pursue it further.

The man and his wife began to talk in a jargon. I asked Jessie if she understood it; she shook her head. I asked the woman. She said it was Romany talk, Shelta.

There were three children in back with us on the straw-covered bottom of the wagon, all in equivalent voluminous patchwork gowns. One, I thought, was a boy although there were no outward differences. Jessie's hand crept into mine and I thought it a natural thing that I hold on to it. She brought it up, linked, to my face to smell the eau de cologne which lingered there, and without thinking I kissed one of her fingers.

She said, "Nor am I pope or king."

"Some things are proper and some things are not."

The gypsy driver said, "What are you going to Epsom for, the betting?"

"Just for the outing," I said.

"My wife tell fortune if you want."

"Not me. You, Jessie?"

"I know mine," she said, smiling to herself.

"I go wherever there's a fair," said the man. "I'm a tinker. Except Bath, no more I go to Bath."

"Landsdown Hill," said the woman, looking grim.

"It's outside of Bath," I said. "What of it?"

"Every year the big sheep, cattle fair—" He spoke in his own dialect to the woman, who said, "He think my English better. You know Bath?"

"Never been there. You been there, Jessie?"

"I never been out of London."

"Bath full of great buildings and in back the poor live like pigs."

"Like London," I said.

"Worse. At night, after the fair, a big mob come out, a lady the leader."

"Lady?"

"Woman," said Jessie, impatient for the story.

"Very bad lady. They break wagons looking for whiskey, they break our wagon. They hit Lazlo with stick and break his arm"— touching the driver above the elbow.

"They were paid back good," Lazlo said. "The fairmen took them to the bottom of Landsdown Hill and tied them up and pulled them this way and that through the pond there, and then they tied them to wheels and hit them with whips."

"We not go back there," the woman said.

One of the children—the boy, I suspected—hit another in the eye and there was a great howling, the injured sister joining in, and Jessie picked up the injured one and rocked her in her arms. The woman smiled in approval and I said, "She has ten like that at home," and the woman said, "Ten is good, but not for one so young."

Jessie looked at me in hauteur, having changed into a woman of breeding unfortunately exposed to the lowly. "Don't you take on so," she said to the squalling child.

Jessie began to sing her "The Ballad of the Female Cabin Boy." The pleasant monotony of Jessie's voice and the pitching of the wagon joined my sleepless night and my chin dropped to my chest and I dozed. When I awoke we were in a vast press of traffic. There were buses and wagonettes and coaches with red-coated guards tooting on polished brass horns, rich and poor all united in one joyous procession. There were gentry in long frock coats and shiny top hats with their racing colors. There were schoolboys in toppers and soldiers in pillbox hats and scarlet tunics and workingmen in their brightest colors and loudest checks.

Finally, after barely moving for half an hour, our driver took his wagon out of the road into a field and said he would remain there and eat and let the children relieve themselves and rest until the road cleared up. Jessie and I jumped out. I offered the driver some coins which, with dignity, he refused. Jessie pulling my hand with excitement, we continued alongside the road until we got to the downs from which one could see the racecourse for the Derby stakes.

Jessie's eyes moved continuously from sight to sight in the impossibility of seeing all there was. Though I played at greater sophistication, it was all as strange and exciting to me as to her. Some thimblemen had set up their tables and were pattering for customers. We stood and watched. The pea went so obviously under one thimble and remained there that I reached for a copper to bet. Jessie stayed my hand.

"You think you're smarter than they are. They'll let you win a farthing and take a crown back."

"But I see where it is."

"All you see is what they want you to see," Jessie said.

A cadaverous man, made longer and thinner by the extension of his black stovepipe, carrying a banner calling for repentance, harangued us for being sinners. "Christ will take you in," he told us. "It is not too late. The choice is yours. Rivers of hellfire or the kingdom of heaven."

"I'll take the kingdom," Jessie said.

"Kneel then, child, and take the pledge."

"No need," Jessie said. "I'm as pure as the snow."

I saw pickpockets working like ants in the throng. This was my holiday and I ignored them, taking out my own wallet and keeping it in the waistband of my trousers. There were carts piled high with steaming pies and bottles of ale and I bought a pie, Jessie and I eating it mouth to mouth, I letting her have most of it while I stared at her white teeth and red lips and wondered again at the change in me that the cadging street girl I had rejected had become someone precious. I decided it was Jessie had done it, Jessie Marsh the sorcerer.

"Oh, Richard, you've let me eat more than my share."

"Not to worry. There's enough left on your chin and nose to make another meal."

She began to use the back of her hand and I handed her the handkerchief she had bought for me.

"Not on your pretty wipe."

"There are so many colors in it already who can see the difference." I cleaned her while she stood docile and again a child. She shimmered so one could not hold onto any image of her too long.

We watched the acrobats in white tights, proving that man need not remain earthbound. There were fire eaters and jugglers, tumblers, and comedians with red noses. Drunkards relieved themselves at people's carts while the female occupants shouted indignantly or covered their eyes with their hands. All part of the show. Humanity, vulgarity, and elegance. On the heights servants catering to the wealthy from vats of vintage champagnes. Beneath the grandstands an army of cooks preparing lamb and beef, lobsters and oysters, eggs and spring chickens, pigeon pies and lettuces. We watched the tableaux—the death of Nelson and Aphrodite rising from the sea. Then everything stopped as the race began, the pickpockets taking advantage of that universal moment of concentration. We picked our horses and cheered them on. And ate. And went from booth to booth, and there was no point at which we had seen it all, and finally fell into a carriage about to be taken by a drunken tradesman and his stuporous wife, and so back home.

"I'll never forget this day," Jessie said.

I was already on the bed, too much trouble to take off clothes, vaguely aware that she was making up her palliasse for herself on the floor.

Sometime in the night I awakened. Jessie was at the window, outlined by the moon, wearing a thin nightdress through which her form was limned.

"You'll freeze," I said.

"Warm me, then."

I said nothing. How was it possible to be on fire without its melting the coldness?

"It's that girl," she said. "Alethea."

I could not deny it.

Chapter Sixteen

The cage hung in the same place, the linnet was gone. "He never sung a note, not a note. Despite the cost of the cage and the bird and all the feed I had to buy—and then there's the cleaning of the cage each morning. I never heard a note of song. I want my money back, all of it, and I want that villain charged—wait, you are a policeman. I want you to charge that man."

"Did you buy the bird from a shop?"

"A shop? No. He was on the street, carrying the bird. A songbird, he said. Would you believe that? A songbird."

"Do you know his name?"

"I never asked his name, what did I want with his name? Police, indeed. You haven't found the murderer of that poor girl upstairs, have you? Can you at least find that bird seller? No, I expect not. Not one note of song from that miserable creature. Dead this morning, just like that girl. This house has a curse on it, that's what."

"Mr. Sweet, now, has he returned?"

"Not a sign of him."

"After all this time, perhaps you can remember something of how he looked, something distinguishing, perhaps."

"I told you, nothing. Young and handsome, he was." She shrugged. Why, after all, should she have taken notice of a handsome young man?

She called Poogie to see me out. "You'll find that thieving bird seller, see he returns my money?"

"I'll do my best, ma'am."

Poogie came in, coughing, unable to catch her breath.

"Poogie!"

"Sorry—mum"—her face red. I slapped her back.

"Do you have pain in the chest, Poogie?" I said. "Fever?"

"No, sir, it's just the dust."

"Dust!" said Mrs. Prescott-Jones.

"Where I sleep," Poogie said. Under the stairs is where Mrs. Prescott-Jones put her.

Poogie and I went to the door and I handed her the bag of peppermint wafers that Jessie had suggsted I bring, because Jessie remembered her own fondness for them. Poogie examined the contents and squealed. "Oh, thank you, sir."

"But if you were out by yourself in the street, Poogie, and a stranger, a man, offered you something like this, would you accept it?"

"I sure would."

"Without knowing what he wanted of you?"

"Oh, I'd know what he wanted. What he would get is the toe of my boot in his wishbone. I'd keep the sweets, of course, rather than his giving them to some poor girl not knowing how to take care of herself."

"I'm happy to know you have no need of a protector, Poogie. But should you ever need one you call upon me. My name is O'Boy, you remember that, and if you need me you go to the Palace Yard and you ask for me."

"If I'm in trouble or anything?"

"Or just if you need a friend."

Poogie gave me a lovely smile and offered me one of the candies. With a glance behind her to see that she was unobserved, she took one herself and we shared our delight in the confection for a moment before I winked at her and left.

I was no closer to Sweet than I had been. Although I had eliminated Mullins himself. Handsome, Mrs. Prescott-Jones had said.

Roger reported no success except in the business he had done with the contents of his basket. He had gone back and refilled at W. A. Hargreaves', who said the first accommodation had been to the detective but from now on the charges would be the same as to anybody else. The only avenue open, then, was to find Aggie Norse, the friend of Maureen, who, according to Buckles, had to be a member of the same profession.

I decided to start at the bottom with the park women. I went to Hyde Park, shortly after five, and had barely begun strolling down a path when a girl approached who looked little older than

Poogie. Hands on immature hips, she piped, "Do you want some company?"

"No, thank you. I'm looking for a girl named Aggie Norse, a girl with red hair. Do you know her?"

"You like red hair, I could get some red hair for you."

"Never mind," I said.

"I'm ready to do anything."

"Thank you just the same."

"Not looking for a boy, are you?"

"No. I'm looking for Aggie."

"Please," she said. "I an't had a customer in two days."

"I'm sorry, I can't help you."

There were thousands of children like her taken to whoring. London seethed with girls. Although she couldn't earn more than three shillings by drudgery from morning to night in so-called respectable employment, I wondered if this were an easier life.

From out of the shadows came a rough-looking man with a navvy's kerchief about his neck and a greasy cap.

"Hey—you been making up to my sister?"

"Hardly," I said.

"It won't do, it won't do at all."

"I'm a policeman," I said, not bothering with the warrant card. "If you don't want to be taken into custody, hook it, the both of you."

"Policeman, is it," said the girl's bully. "Come into the park to take advantage of a young girl, is it—threatening her to do as you want else you'll take her in? Did he tickle you up, lass?"

"He was just about to do it when, thank God, you came along."

Two working-class youths came along and stopped. The ponce appealed to them. "Says he's a detective. Thinks he can tickle up young girls without paying."

"It was her virtue concerned you a moment ago," I said.

I had made a mistake in identifying myself; it had been neither necessary nor helpful. Nor could I expect any aid from the two young men, who would probably themselves have no reason for liking the police. I was surprised then, and grateful too, to hear one of them say, "They're trying to bear you up, chum. Like they did to Alf last week, you remember, Charlie?"

"Waited until his trousers was down," Charlie said, "and they lambasted him and took his week's wages. Maybe it was the same cove, what do you think?"

"Could have been," said the other slowly.

The bully then, calculating his chances, muttered to the girl, "Let's be off."

Charlie said, "You're not really a jack, are you?"

I made a gesture that was half affirmation, half denial.

"Hate ponces," said Charlie's friend. "You makes your terms with a girl and it's between the two of you and that ought to be good enough. Come along, Charlie, let's try our luck."

A few moments after which a woman approached who could have been the first girl's grandmother. She had been dragging herself along when, at the sight of me, she called on reserves of recalled youth, lifting her head and trying to put life into her waist.

"Looking for me, are you?"

"I'm looking for a girl named Aggie Norse, a girl with red hair. You know her?"

"Aggie—?"

"Norse. Red-haired."

"Is she something special? I could do whatever she could do."

"It's not like that. I—"

"Aggie," the woman said, taking my arm. "Aggie, you said"— pulling me close to her. Whatever she had doused herself with was a far cry from Jessie's eau de cologne. I disengaged myself. "What's so special about her?"

I shook my head and went on. The woman said something coarse. I did not blame her.

I had perhaps fifteen such encounters, and no one had heard of Aggie Norse. I went home and slept for what was left of the night and in the morning I reported to the Inspector. He asked about my progress.

"None," I said.

"Which leaves you only the rest of London."

"The woman is there, she can be found."

"Even if you have to talk to every whore in the city."

"You could bring them in, twenty or thirty at a time, in police vans and I could talk to them here."

"Are you serious, O'Boy?"

"No, sir."

"This red-haired woman you seek, by now she could be black or white or green. They change the color of their hair at their whim, and so with their names too. How much more time do you think I can give you?"

"As long as it takes to catch a murderer," I said.

"There are murders being committed in London every day. Buckles is still away, I have no more than thirty-five, forty men in the detectives. I commend you on your diligence, O'Boy, but I have to station my men where results are more likely."

"There is still the chance that Roger, the boy I have put outside the public house, will hear something."

"About as likely as the killer walking in here himself and giving himself up."

"I don't know what else to do, sir."

"If I asked you," said Inspector Criddle, "to stop wasting further time on this investigation, would you heed me?"

"Asked me or ordered me?"

"Ordered you, then?"

"Then," I said, "I would either have to obey or quit my position."

"And would there be a question of which you would do?"

"Yes, sir."

"Then I will not so propound it. Yet there is a limit to how long I can afford to let you continue."

"I understand, sir."

I next went to the night houses—Mott's, Roseburton's, Jack Percival's, and Kate Hamilton's. If Aggie Norse was not as low as the park women, was she as high in her profession as those in these rooms, drinking champagne, none who were not attractive and well dressed?

I frequented the Café Royal, Lizzie Davis's, and the Café Riche. After a while I was pointed out. The madman looking for one prostitute out of thousands.

If she were neither high nor low would she be an inhabitant of one of the brothels? I went to the squalid ones at Lambeth and Whitechapel, Spital Field and Wapping, Ratcliffe Highway and Waterloo Road. No one had heard of her. I went to the expensive ones in King's Place, St. James's, Oxenden Street, and Curzon Street.

I walked at night in the gaiety of Regent Street and the Haymarket, brilliantly illuminated with the gaslights from the shops and cafés. There were street whores and courtesans, the latter deserving the prettier title because they rustled in silks and satins and laces. They wore black silk cloaks or light gray mantles, with silk paletots and wide skirts extended by crinolines, looking like pyramids with the apex terminating at black or white bonnets trimmed with ribbons and flowers. Only the fact they were not escorted by men distinguished them from women of quality. Everywhere I asked for Aggie Norse.

I talked to French girls in Tichbourne Street and Great Windmill Street. I talked to prostitutes near All Souls' Church, in Langham Place and Portland Place, down Regent Street to Waterloo Place and Pall Mall. I talked to women in Soho—in Dean Street and Gerrard Street, King Street and Church Street.

Returning home in the early morning, my head spun with the notion that surely every woman in London was a prostitute. I had ceased to look at faces. It was enough that they walked where streetwalkers abounded, that there was more than the usual brightness of shawl, that the walk was not demure.

Aggie Norse, the red-haired. Do you know Aggie Norse?

Now I understood what I had read and dismissed: England—a small, select aristocracy, born booted and spurred to ride; a large dim mass born saddled and bridled. The men were out making selections like women prodding fish at Billingsgate.

"I wish," said Jessie one morning, "that you'd make an end to it."

"I too. I have had enough of women. If a man were to wish to remain virtuous he has but to do what has occupied me all these weeks. They cry, Take me; no, me—yet they are all alike."

"None different—?"

"Oh, they label themselves according to their station and their price. Some I have seen are beautiful, which is fully as sad as the pocked and sagging faces in the alleys."

"You don't smile any more," Jessie said.

"Mr. Pusey and I. The one helped found the Oxford Movement. He took a vow he would never smile again—except at children."

Jessie put out her arms and made herself very young. I laughed and embraced her, at once letting her go.

"Do any of them tempt you, Richard?"

"Many."

"And have you not fallen?"

"Perhaps a stumble, nothing more."

Knowing nothing of Aggie Norse, I had to look in on the houses of strange practices. There was a flagellation parlor run by the "Abbess." I went to places where twisted men could be stimulated only through humiliation, and there was one loft which was a facsimile of a farm tended by field girls where one paid a fee to become a foreman exercising seigneurial privileges.

Somebody had to know Aggie Norse. Didn't prostitutes talk to one another? By now I tried posing as the girl's brother come to bring her home because her mother was dying. Prostitutes were sentimental, and they tried to help. They couldn't tell me where Aggie Norse was but they suggested other places to look. Like the coffeehouse on Wellington Street on the Covent Garden side of the Lyceum Theatre. The police could not interfere because it was a coffeehouse and not a brothel. If a man came with a woman and asked for a bedroom they could be travelers, according to the proprietor. I waited downstairs to talk to the women. One told me she knew a red-haired prostitute, but it turned out she was fifty-five years old and had become the owner of a brothel herself.

London was the most densely populated city in the world. The more people, the more women. Lacking even the smallest success I had become short of temper. I could not explode at those I sought information from, and I could not be anything but respectful to Inspector Criddle. The one left was Jessie.

"It's not worth it," she said. "Maybe there are some things we're not supposed to know."

"Now you're a philosopher."

"I know what I know."

"What did you ever persevere in?" I said.

I thought that a girl grateful for my largesse and eager not to alienate me would have meekly bowed her head and accepted my disapproval. What Jessie did was to set her chin and look me in the eye.

"Maybe," she said, "your precious Maureen was no great loss."

I raised my hand to her.

"It even says so in the Bible," Jessie said, unafraid.
"What do you know about the Bible?"
"I know it says thou shalt not suffer a bitch to live."
"Witch," I said weakly.
"Try it in a different way," Jessie said.
"What way would that be?"
"All you're doing is wearing down your feet—you're going to be my size in no time." She put out her hand level with her head. "I shouldn't like that at all. Why not just walk the Haymarket? If Aggie's alive and still working, one day that's where she'll be."
"I've been there."
Jessie said, "Are you still—"
"Resisting?"
"Yes."
"Yes."
"You're good at that," Jessie said.

The street women told me about places their sisters practiced I had not known about. Like the Burlington Arcade between three and five in the afternoon—a friendly bonnet shop the stairs of which led to upper chambers. A drawing-room floor in Queen Street. A house off Langham Place, looking so respectable except that there were always clients in its bedrooms.

"You're getting to know them all, aren't you?" Jessie said.
"I am."
"I could have been one, you know."
"Really?"
"It wasn't the idea of sin that stopped me."
"Oh?"
"Tell me what they tell you—about what sort of life theirs is."
"A typical one? Goes something like this: She gets up about four o'clock, dresses, walks the streets, picks up someone if she's fortunate. After that she goes, say, to the Holborn and dances a little and if anyone likes her she takes him home. If not, she goes to the Haymarket, wanders from one café to another, from Sally's to the Carlton, from Barn's to Sam's, and if she hasn't found anyone else by then perhaps she goes to the Divans. She

says she likes the Grand Turkish best, but as a rule you don't find good men in any of the Divans. The other day, she tells me, a friend of hers met a gentleman at Sam's and yesterday morning they were married at St. George's, Hanover Square. The gentleman, she said, has lots of money."

"It don't sound like a bad life," Jessie said.

"Try it, then," I said.

"Richard!"

"An appropriate emotion for them might be pity—never envy. Remember, they take on anyone with a few shillings in his pocket. They take on disease and violence and sickness of the mind as well. One told me a customer wanted to use a knife instead of his doodle. If there are some who choose it as a way of life, most come to it because of hunger. Mayhew—the writer—was investigating prostitution among the needlewomen. He convened a meeting, and a thousand women came to protest their miserable pay and excuse those among them who turned to prostitution in consequence. Into the meeting, unannounced and unexpected, came Lord Ashley and Mr. Sidney Herbert. Lord Ashley addressed the assemblage, stating his opinion that the only remedy for their distress was emigration to the colonies. And Mr. Herbert got up and said that there were five hundred thousand surplus females in England and Wales and—could you see the hand of Providence in this?—there were exactly five hundred thousand too few females in the colonies."

"I think," Jessie said, "that Lord Ashley and Mr. Herbert ought to go to the colonies since we have a surplus of them here."

"Jessie, I didn't mean that you—"

"I know you didn't mean to say it. But you've become a hard man to be with, Richard."

"Look," I said, "I'm smiling."

"Am I your friend?"

"Yes."

"There's a difference between a friend and a whipping boy."

"Let me tell you about Jeffries. He was called to a man in serious condition who had to be taken to a hospital after trying to shoot himself."

"Why did he want to shoot himself?"

"I don't know. What difference does that make? The main two reasons are women and money. Why don't you let me tell the story without being interrupted?"

"I just like to keep things straight. Go ahead, I'm listening."

"He was a man loved buttered muffins but could not eat them because they disagreed with his stomach. When he resolved to shoot himself—for whatever reason, Jessie—he ate three buttered muffins beforehand, knowing that whatever he would be troubled with it would not be indigestion. And now, having bungled the job—he had not even placed the pistol head on—he was complaining bitterly that his stomach hurt."

"He should not have tried to kill himself," Jessie said. "There's always something worth living for."

"I'll try again, Jessie. There was a man loved buttered muffins but—"

"I understand all that," Jessie said. "I just didn't think it as humorous as you did."

"Back to my whores," I said.

Sometimes, when they were convinced I had no business interest in them, and if they had made connection already and were disposed to rest themselves for a bit, they would talk of how they were driven to their lives. "It was my brother's good friend," said one, "he was often in my house, joking with my mother and father. So, innocently, I accepted his invitation to go to Simpson's Hotel on the Strand, where we had dinner. Then he took me to the opera, and after that to Scott's supper room in the Haymarket. After that we walked up and down the Haymarket and he took me to several cafés where we had wine and refreshment, and about four o'clock in the morning he called a hansom and drove me to his house and there he seduced me by violence in spite of my resistance."

It was an axiom among those who cared to account for their station that they had been deflowered by force and were consequently barred from decent society.

No one could direct me to Aggie Norse. Occasionally I saw a red-haired woman, but it was the wrong shade of red or the face did not match. I thought I was becoming hardened to street life until one evening, in a mean street, a woman offered herself to me while holding an infant obviously drugged into stupefaction by Godfrey's Cordial or some other concoction of opium and treacle. I was suddenly sickened by misery and went home.

Jessie was reading the newspaper to Roger. " 'J. Hansen, Chimney Sweep, Tower Street, begs respectfully to inform the gentry and inhabitants of the vicinity that he has commenced the above profession and hopes by his unremitting attention to merit their liberal support. Small boys and clean clothes upon the most reasonable terms. Beware of strollers.' "

"He's right about that," Roger said. "Strollers is dangerous."

"Why is that, Roger?" I said.

"Oh, Richard," said Jessie, getting up from the chair. Roger remained on the floor. I went to the bed and started pulling off my boots. Jessie took over.

"What about the strollers, Roger?"

"Those flue fakers can get into a house as quick as a squirrel and silent as snow, and when you wake up your valuables is gone."

"How do you know about that, Roger?"

"Because I used to be a snakesman myself."

"Reformed, I hope," I said, hardly believing him.

"I was apprentice to somebody like your Mr. J. Hansen. He made me suffer something fierce."

"How did he make you suffer?" said Jessie.

"Because they has to make the flesh hard, you see, they takes your elbows and knees and they rub in brine. You got to stand close to a hot fire while they're doing it. Then when you can't hardly stand no more they stands over you with a cane to make you stand a few more rubs."

"Poor Roger," Jessie said.

"I used to come home with my arms and knees streaming blood, specially the knees, and what do you think they'd do for it? They had to be rubbed with brine again. Oh, it was proper horrible, it was."

"How old were you then, Roger?" I said.

He could not handle questions involving numbers. He shrugged. "Just a baby, I was."

"Then what did you do?"

"I got big. I got big overnight. I couldn't fit into the chimneys no more. But I'm still able to jump on back of a carriage like I did this afternoon."

"You could get hurt doing that," Jessie said.

"I couldn't worry about that when I'm doing something like what Mr. O'Boy told me to do."

"Which is what, Roger?" I said, taking pleasure in wiggling my toes. I remembered the story of the man who refused to pay his bill at the bootmaker's, whereupon the bootmaker filled the man's shoes with wax and helped the customer on with them. As the welsher wore them the wax hardened, and when he came to remove his boots off came the skin too. I wiggled my toes some more and sat back with hands clasped behind my head, considering my good fortune in having a place of my own in which to wiggle my wax-free toes.

"I had to jump on the back of the carriage, you see, having no vehicle of my own with which to follow him."

"Follow who?" I said.

"Follow the man who knew Mr. Sweet," Roger said.

I leaped up and grabbed him and stood him up against the wall. He was shaking with fear of me, so I let him go and said as gently as I could, "From the beginning, Roger. Don't leave anything out."

"You hurt my head," Roger said.

"I didn't mean to. Now get to it."

"Well, I was out in front of the Jolly Bear, selling my apples, and I was doing good business, too. I was down to my last two—"

"Roger," I said quietly.

"You don't want me to leave anything out."

I swallowed. "All right, at your own speed, then."

"These two swells come out and one buys an apple and I was down to the last one, you see."

"I am going to kill a boy," I said to Jessie. "If you can't stand the sight of blood, turn away."

Roger began to blubber; real or feigned did not matter because it all made for delay.

"Richard," said Jessie.

"Well?"

"You don't know how you look. I'm frightened of you myself."

Jessie offered Roger a crust left over from breakfast and he chewed it, sobbing. Unfortunately that made me think of Maureen. I wanted to squeeze the information from him like juice from a lemon, but I kept myself quiet and waited. When he had finished the piece of bread and wiped his eyes with his knuckles, he said, "I mean to tell you just the way it was, sir."

"Good," I said.

"There was these two swells, see, and the one who bought my apple he says, And what name does my friend select for his little adventure? Alfred Sweet. And then they both laughed."

"Friend? He said his—friend?"

"That's what he said, all right."

"Go on."

"That's all there was."

"He didn't say anything else?"

"He said the apple was mealy and he had a mind to ask for his money back."

"What else, Roger? What *else?*"

"Well, I was ready to make a dash for it if he was serious—about asking for his money back."

"What else did either of them say?"

"Well, nothing. Except good-bye, of course. And then he got into a carriage and you told me I had to follow him and I got on the back."

"And where did the carriage take him, Roger?"

"Why, to the Clarendon."

"Of course," I said. "The Clarendon. A swell, you said?"

"Gray coat fitted him like it was poured on, and buttons—looked like gold they did."

"Now, Roger," I said, "look at me." I took his face between my hands. "I want you to remember. They said good-bye. The other one, not the one bought your apple, he said good-bye to the man whose friend was Alfred Sweet."

"Yes, sir."

"He said good-bye—what? He had to use a name."

Roger frowned. The act of remembering was painful.

"Think, now. He said good-bye and the other man said good-bye—"

"Good-bye, Lord Waterford," Roger said.

"Oh, yes," I said. "Oh, yes. Thank you, Roger."

I reached for my boots. Jessie said, "You're not going out again?"

"I have to. I have half the noose now, Jessie. Now to put the other half to it. I must find Aggie Norse."

"What can you do now that you haven't done before?"

"I'll stop every woman in the Haymarket, if need be. Someone has to know her."

I walked a hundred yards and was approached by a hundred streetwalkers. I asked for Aggie Norse and no one knew her and

I asked twenty more. I was driven; I could see the rope about the murderer's neck. The face was in shadow but the lineaments were beginning to come. And then the angel in charge of retribution decided he had toyed with me long enough, because a girl in black with a white throat and a face powdered pale—as if necrophiliacs also came seeking street wares—said to me, "I know Aggie."

"I must talk to her."

"She's been sick."

"Where is she?"

The girl hesitated. I offered her money and she shook her head. "You wouldn't be looking to do her harm?"

"No harm, I swear on my mother." Which was odd, I thought; I had never invoked my mother before.

She gave me the address and I ran, hardly limping. A running man in a city catches all eyes, and there were some who stood uncertainly to block me but there was no one behind shouting stop thief.

Aggie Norse lay in a low room in a low dwelling and she had left the door unlatched not to have to get out of bed for callers. I thought that if these were the wages of sin, then better to remain a seamstress.

I said I was Richard O'Boy and she smiled and bade me welcome because I was male. She lay in bed with a yellow silk peignoir clutched to her throat with one hand, and her remarkable hair was hers alone unless, even in illness, she remained bewigged. She was racked with a cough that came with every fifth or sixth word, and her eyes were glazed with fever. I asked if I could call a doctor.

"I won't be bled or purged and I won't be put to sleep because I don't like my dreams. If this is the bad one I won't live much longer, doctor or no, and if it isn't I'll get better, doctor or no. So, Mr. O'Boy, seeing that my condition is what it is I cannot offer you my best, but if you wish to climb in you may do so, sir."

"I didn't come for that, Aggie."

"No? I don't recognize your face. Mostly I remember faces from my back. I think you've never stared down into mine."

"No, never. I'm a detective and I've come to ask you about Sybil—Maureen."

"Christ," she said. "That poor child. Not that it doesn't happen often enough in our business. We don't care whose mind is bent so long as his shillings are straight. Do you like the way I express myself, Mr. O'Boy?"

"I do indeed."

"For a time I stayed with a literary man. Metaphors, he used to tell me. Juice up your language with metaphors."

At once, then. "Do you know who killed Maureen?"

"No."

"Tell me what you know about her."

"There's one thing that helps this cough and my memory," Aggie said. "That's geneva, and I'm out."

"I'll take care of that."

When I returned, having stopped at the chemist as well as the gin shop, I found Aggie out of bed, the coverlet drawn up, some semblance of order in her hair, and a touch of color on her lips and cheeks.

"Shouldn't you have remained in bed?"

"This is a dismal enough place at best. Maybe the customers I bring here don't care what it looks like, but a gentleman caller, that's another thing." She settled herself in a chair with a careful arrangement of gown. The sperm-oil lamp reeked. I was in a frenzy to get on with it, and at the same time I was holding back. She was all I had. If she had nothing for me, then Maureen would be forever unavenged.

I took the bottle of gin from my pocket. "I brought this, too, spirits of sweet nitre. They say it's good for colds."

"Gin's better."

She pointed to some glasses on a shelf and I brought them down and poured for both of us.

"First, why did you run off like that?"

"I saw no profit in getting mixed up with the police."

She had a directness of gaze and manner that was removed from the artifice that I connected with her profession. Her features were well assembled, and her speech was not a product of the London streets.

"You like me," she said. "You're looking at me as if you like me."

"Well, I do," I said.

"Would you pay to go to bed with me?"

"No."

"Would you pay to go to bed with anybody?"

"No."

"All right, then. You're thinking that I don't remind you of the kind of whores you know."

"That's right."

"It's this hair. What can you do with hair like this? You could go on the stage, and I had no feeling for that. But you couldn't just be somebody's wife or sweetheart. No man wants to carry a blazing torch on his arm wherever he goes. He might say he'd like that, but he wouldn't. After a while he'd be sick of it. So I did the only thing was natural."

She picked up the implication in my looking around the room. "You're thinking I wasn't very successful at it if I have to live like this. Well, I was—and am—if you want to believe it. Because this"—she waved her hand—"is success for a street whore. You want finer surroundings, you have to be a whore to the gentry or the royal family. By the time I pay the ponces and the keepers of the accommodation houses and the dressmaker—and you know how many girls there are out there?"

"I know."

"I've seen them take a man's arm, one on each side, and you'd think they were going to rip him apart—but you wanted to talk about Maureen."

"You knew her by that name."

"It was I changed it to Sybil. I was soliciting then for a quite respectable milliner—your wife would know her name—she let out rooms above her shop to certain gentlemen who wanted young ones fresh out of the country. At that time, it being slow in my own line of work, I would go to the inns where the coaches came in and look for those come here to seek their fortunes."

"You turned Maureen into a whore, then."

"Maybe I did, maybe I didn't. Maybe she was one before she came here. There was some things she said led me to believe that. But I don't care about your opinion of me, Mr. O'Boy. You can leave right now if you like, and I thank you for the gin and the medicine."

"I need your help," I said.

"All I said to your Maureen—with the country in her face and all her belongings in her neckerchief—all I said to her was

291

if she didn't get a position in service, which is what she said she came for, and if she found herself in such straits she didn't know where to turn, then she should come and see me—that's all I told her. I didn't tell her about the riches and other delights in making a fortune on her back. I left the choice in her hands."

"So she came to you."

"So she did."

"And you took her to the millinery lady."

"I did that."

"And then?"

"I was sitting having tea with the milliner while Maureen was upstairs with her first customer. She comes running down the stairs and out to the street. I followed her and finally got her into a coffee shop, where she told me she was going back home, this was not what she had come for."

Aggie drank half a glass of gin and raised her glass to mine, and I drank a sip or two and she finished hers and added more.

"Maureen wasn't that simple to talk to. Getting words out of her was like—"

"Pulling teeth," I said.

Aggie shook her head. "The literary man I lived with wouldn't let me use old phrases like that. Getting Maureen to talk was more like—say, digging out coal. I spent a night with a miner once, he told me all about it."

I had never known Maureen to talk at all.

"So after she ate a few cakes and drank some coffee she said that she went upstairs and there was an elderly man there—of course, when Maureen said elderly he could have been thirty-five or seventy-five—and the man asked was she a good girl and she said she was, and he asked her what she liked to eat and she said especially steak-and-kidney pie, and he promised her as many as she wanted. Then he asked if she knew how to soothe the back of his head for aching and she said she could do that, and he told her to, and then he asked her to do the same to his back."

I did not want details. Aggie was pulling them out reflectively as if she were examining her own life. If I stopped her I might lose the one piece of information I had come for. I apologized to Maureen.

"She stopped talking. She just sat looking down at her mug of tea without even blinking her eyes."

"I know how she could do that," I said.

"She was somewhere else. In the middle of talking to you she would seem to move away even though she was sitting right there. She had done this before so I just waited. Then I said, 'Well, Maureen, will you tell me the rest of it?' And then she said the man took off his clothes and he was the fattest man she had ever seen, not only in front but in back and had chins and chins. And then it came down to what the man wanted. All he wanted was to have Maureen frig him, and she ran away. She couldn't touch him, you see."

"I suppose that is to her credit, isn't it?"

"You're a whore or you're not. I told Maureen the life wasn't for her. She said she didn't object to the life, she objected to the ugliness of that one man. I said the ugly ones need us more than the handsome ones do. I said that she had given up a good thing, all the man wanted was a little frigging, and she was still virgo intacto—"

"From your literary friend?"

"Of course."

"And was she—?"

"No."

"How did you know?"

"She told me."

"And then?"

"I didn't see her for a while and I heard she was sailing on her own bottom, and then I heard she had met somebody who was setting her up in a smart flat. Which would be a dream come true for any of us."

"Did you know who the man was?"

"No, I never saw him. Maureen asked me in a few times to tea. She was always alone."

"But Maureen had a number of men come to her—"

"Those weren't Maureen's visitors, they were mine."

"I don't understand."

"Well, after Maureen was established in that flat in St. John's Wood I used to visit her, and she said that if I needed a place I could bring a man to her flat and save myself the price of the accommodation house. This could take place only when the man keeping Maureen was not in London. He had a home in the country, and when he was visiting there is when I used Maureen's flat."

Aggie had been coughing little during this discourse, and we both agreed it was because of the curative properties of the gin. The bottle was now nearly empty and Aggie said she could not talk dry so I went out for another. I wondered whether there was anything more to be gotten from her, and whether it justified another purchase. Gin was the cheapest anodyne but it was not freely available, and I wondered what Inspector Criddle would say if I asked for recompense for two bottles of gin expended in official business leading to the apprehension of a murderer.

Roger had given me a name and a hotel. If Aggie could add to that then I would be sure. Not enough perhaps for Criddle, or the courts, but sure enough for myself.

("How much of the spirits did you consume yourself, O'Boy?" "Enough to show a sociable interest in the problem, sir.")

"You're a dear man," said Aggie Norse, as I opened the fresh bottle and added to her glass. "Are you sure there is nothing I can do for you? As you see my cough is almost gone and I feel perfectly well enough to return to my work."

"Tell me more about Maureen and the man, Alfred Sweet."

"There's nothing more to tell."

"There has to be something."

"You keep saying his name was Alfred Sweet. That's not the name she used for him."

"What name did she use for him?"

"She called him Peter," Aggie said.

Chapter Seventeen

Avengers are happy because they move in their obsession with no deviation for family worries, or illness, or food, or ambition in other directions. So for the first half of the ride to Clamford I was happy. I wanted nothing but to have Peter in my hands. That I was an officer of the law, that he had to be delivered safely and impartially tried—I was not concerned with that. I had him now: Peter the humiliator, Peter whose lies had forced me into a war, Peter who had had me whipped. Perhaps, I thought, he might resist me. In my authority I might take whatever means necessary to subdue a suspect. Oh, Peter, do not come willingly.

The poorly sprung coach met a declivity in the road and I was thrown against the other occupant, an apple of a man wearing the neckcloth of a clergyman. I feared I had flattened him. When the coach lurched forward and I was able to get myself upright, I reached to retrieve my fellow passenger from the corner of the seat, into which he had been pressed as into a mold. He shook himself and I pulled him here and there and finally between the two of us we patted him back into shape.

"I beg your pardon," I said.

"It was certainly not your fault, sir, although the experience was something like being under a falling tree."

"We'll be there soon," I said, "that is, if the wheels don't snap off."

"I am not a happy traveler. If I had my way I would live and die in the same house and in the same village in which I was born."

"I take it then the Church will not leave you stationary."

"I have been a curate here and there, and now I go to Clamford as prebendary to Mr. Davenport. Do you know him?"

"I have never met him. I hear he is a stern man."

The clergyman sighed. "So they have all been." He used the second and third fingers of his right hand to stroke his temple three times. I took it as his personal calmative. "And what manner of town is it?"

"It is a market town and hence it thrives on Fridays and falls asleep during the week."

"The living is larger than any in which I have yet served. I suppose one must go out into the world if one has any hope of rising in it. And you, sir, I take it, are a city man."

"Is it these clothes that tell you so?"

"The apparel oft proclaimeth—but more than that there is an air about you."

I felt flattered. Had I, then, covered over the country lad?

"My name is Duckins."

"O'Boy."

"I am what I am, obvious to all. And you, sir?"

"I'm a policeman."

"Fascinating," Duckins said.

We hit some obstacle in the road and this time the jolting was upward and I, the taller, banged my head against the roof. I leaned out the window and demanded of the driver if he received the same fee for delivering bones as live passengers. He called back, his voice whipped by the wind, that he did not build the roads nor had he guaranteed his passengers' comfort.

"Is this insane celerity necessary?" Duckins said. "If you rush through life you but meet the grave the sooner. Do you agree with that, sir?"

"For what I am about I would as soon get it done quickly."

"Of course, justice. It must be swift. What does the Magna Carta state? No merchant shall be filched of his merchandise, and no villein deprived of his agricultural implements—"

I put my head back and closed my eyes to terminate the conversation. I tried to recapture the pleasure of contemplating the task ahead of me.

"I consider you a fortunate man," said Mr. Duckins.

"Eh?" I said, opening my eyes.

"In your choice of profession, I mean to say."

"How is that?"

"Every sane man hates injustice. You are in a position to do something about it. That must be a source of satisfaction to you."

"Indeed," I said.

Had I been concerned with justice? Or even Maureen?

Somehow my well-being had left. I fell into a sadness. Peter had been contemptuous and arrogant, he had mocked and derided me, but it was all to remind me of the difference in our station—I must not disregard that, even as we played together. We were not equal.

Peter had been raised to be aware of his natural superiority. I seemed the only one to have doubts about the inevitability of birthright. Yet were not the virtues of those childhood days greater than the harm? Had there not been times that we played together as friends? Was there not warmth in being with him? And, above all, had he not given me Alethea?

Was that, however, to his credit, or more slyly destructive than even the whipping he had demanded that I receive at Balaclava? Alethea, who had teased and provoked me, who had swollen my loins and my heart and had relieved neither. As the clacking wheels of the coach brought me closer to that earlier time, I wondered if I need see her. Perhaps I might scoop up Peter and take him back to the city with no one knowing I had come and gone.

I played the scene in my mind:

"I am come to take you into custody, Peter Nott-Playsaunt, for the willful murder of Maureen Rafferty."

"You, Richard? Are your actions now determined by your fantasies?"

He laughed. But Peter's laughter at my expense was never free. His eyes, at least, were always wary of me.

I showed him my warrant card.

He shook his head. "Even so. Did you really believe I would go with you?"

"I could, if you prefer, call up some constables from the village and have you strapped to a board and carried to a coach."

"Ridiculous," he said.

But he had not the somewhat demented sureness of Lieutenant Singleton when presented with the same alternative. I had believed Singleton.

"But I would not subject you to that, Peter."

"Oh?"

"I would not call for help," I said. "I would take you myself, Peter, in one way or another. Perhaps with a rope around your neck to drag you through the fields, to accustom you beforehand to the noose. . . ."

"In your work in London—most of it, I assume, among the criminal classes—" Duckins said.
"Yes."
"And the poor."
"Yes."
"I wonder, do they attend church?"
"None that I know."
"But there are many great organizations to further church attendance, to see that worship is kept alive—"
"Where the poor live there are not many churches."
"Yet they need the comfort only religion can provide."
"It would provide more comfort if they were fed."
"We're past the time of loaves and fishes. The food we offer is forever and ever."
"When I was a child in Dire-Toombley, each Sunday after the service the poor were fed."
We dropped into silence. Then Duckins said, "One rides in a carriage with a stranger and I doubt we shall meet again. So one can speak of matters usually unsaid. I have been sitting here thinking that I shall never be more than what I am. At my previous post my superior took to wearing caftans—sewed up for him by a lady of the village—because, he said, those were the garments worn by the first followers of our Lord. Eventually he was served with a writ of *de lunatico inquirendo* and relieved of his post. Yet he may have felt some evangelical conviction, who is to say? The living was taken over by a relative who brought his own curates with him and I was—dropped." Duckins clasped his hands in his lap and looked down at them. "I have never felt personal revelation in my life."

I said nothing. If he was seeking spiritual comfort, I was not the one to supply it.

"What is my work to be before me? I will keep records and go on errands to those parishioners not important enough to be visited by the Reverend himself. Sometimes, on unimportant occasions, when he is away I might be permitted a sermon. Do you consider that being in the service of God, Mr. O'Boy?"

"I have no opinion about that," I said.

"A stern man, you said he was. As you are, Mr. O'Boy. I envy a man who never doubts himself."

From Clamford I hired a trap to take me to Dire-Toombley, and I was let off at the bottom of the hill leading to the manor house. This time I decided not to look in on Rafferty. He had had his daughter's body to bury and I did not know what story had gone along with it. I had no wish to talk to him of her, to reveal or conceal what she had been. Nor did I wish to tell him why I had come—I needed no choleric Irishman to interfere with my taking Peter. I went up toward the house of the Squire.

I had come home once before to find my mother and father had died, the farm out of the family hands, my small inheritance eaten into by the arithmetic of Sir James. Now I was a man to be feared, come on a terrible errand that could destroy the Squire's house.

So I told myself as I climbed, my city boots squishing in the country earth.

Soon I could make out some figures in front of the house, and then I was close enough to determine that a lawn party was in progress. Closer still and I could see gentlemen in elegantly casual dress, and women in flimsy-appearing but solidly opaque garments, wearing enormous hats. I could see the servants gliding with such unobtrusive skill that no guest had to do more than turn his head to have at his elbow a choice of cakes on a tray, sweetened fruit drinks out of silver ewers, wines and whisky.

I saw Sir James sitting at an umbrella'd table, his foot up on a stool. Here and there was a glance in my direction, not openly curious in the way of those not so well bred, but sent over from the brim of a glass being raised or the shoulder of a person being spoken to. I was obviously not of the company or the servants, while the awfulness of the power I represented could not be apparent.

I knew what I was. Even if for a moment I held my head stiffly, looking neither right nor left, as if to overcome through purposefulness of bearing the inferiority, in that company, of being my father's son. And it was true that for that instant inferior I felt, with the weight of class and place overcoming me as it would have pressed on my father. I would never learn to wear clothes with the assurance of the gentlemen around me, or be able to converse so lightly with the female guests. Because neither bumpkin nor sophisticate, intellectual nor clod, but simply ill born, my presence was unwelcome. Suddenly I yearned for the company of the whores and villains, the costermongers and tradesmen, that had become my world. However, my discomfiture lasted only for a breath, because I knew I represented what was greater than class, and beyond security of position. There was one law for everyone in England, and I was representative of that law. If any here were to breach it despite wealth and family, I, a farmer's son, could apprehend them. My father had consigned me to the same place he occupied, tugging his forelock and bending his knee (though he called himself free), but I had found a place of my own where justice was the same for all.

Sir James saw me and beckoned. It was not imperious, it might even have been friendly.

"Richard Ramsey, have you come home then?"

"This is not my home."

"Ah, yes, the farm. Have you come to contest Rafferty's right to it? He runs it well enough, although hardly up to the standards of your father."

"I am no farmer."

"What are you then, boy? What have you made of yourself since last you were here?"

I could not say right out what I was. I looked about for Peter in the groups of his lisping peers and could not see him. "Where is your son, Sir James?"

"Of course, you came to see Peter."

Sir James looked better than he had the last time I had seen him. There was color in his face unconnected with the distension of his veins. His foot, though propped, was not so heavily bandaged. He looked more like the Squire who had judged me and, out of regard for my father, sentenced me to the army rather than jail.

"Is he here?"—thinking how stupid it would be if Peter were still in London. I had inquired at the Clarendon and had been told he had gone back to the country, but he could have changed his mind.

"He went out for a ride this morning, despite all his friends gathering in his honor. Peter is headstrong, as you know. I'm sure he would be happy to see you, Richard, on some other occasion."

"I must see him now," I said.

"Must," Sir James said.

"Must," I said, watching the Squire's eye go to one of the nearer larger footmen.

"I have become," I said, "a policeman."

"Have you now," said Sir James, smiling.

There was no help for it. In Sir James's world I must be subservient; he knew to whom I had been born. Hence, in reaction, I had to be loud and bumptious, which in turn could only reinforce his opinion of me. My yanking out my warrant card was a desperate act.

"Very nice indeed," Sir James said. "So our safety is now in the hands of our farmers' children." Said smiling, barbless, a small avuncular remark.

"And so," I said, "if you could be somewhat more precise, Sir James, and tell me when Peter will be here."

"Can you predict the wind, Richard?" He nodded in appreciation of his own phrasing. "Peter is his own master. If the spirit took him and the horse was willing he could be on his way to the north country and he might not come back until tomorrow. But tell me, is it as a *policeman* that you seek my son?"

"Yes," I said.

"What has he done; has he been seen watering the bushes in Hyde Park?" At which, choking with laughter, his face turned purple, and for an instant I thought I would sit unmoving and watch him die. Then he put out a hand to me and I took it and pumped it up and down. His breath returned. "Why are you here? Out with it, Ramsey."

"To see Peter."

"To—arrest him?"

I said nothing.

"You could not have the gall. What is his offense?"

I wanted to tell him, I wanted to tell him his son had killed a young girl. But I wanted Peter to hear it first from myself.

Sir James gestured and a whisky was set before him. He did not ask me to join him. He drank a little, then he dipped two fingers in his glass and flicked them in my face.

I stood up, feeling—delighted.

"You poor foolish farmer's lad. Don't you know you have no jurisdiction here? That card of yours is worthless. Don't you know that? Didn't they teach you anything, boy?"

"That useless card, Sir James, can secure for me a sufficient number of local constables to take whomever I choose into custody."

He was getting apoplectic again and I turned from him.

"Damn it, man, what did he do?"

"He's your son. Is there anything you can be sure he is not capable of?" I would have told him what it was, for the pleasure of flinging the word in his face as he had flicked the whisky in mine.

I walked away.

Two women in their middle years and a girl were seated at a table. One of the women, humped like a dowager, was saying, "I hear you will be going first to the Greek isles, then to Venice? I can never forget when I—never mind. But when you come home and settle in and become accustomed to the care of your grand new house you may want to give some time to good works. I myself have found much satisfaction in distributing tracts for the Reformatory and Refuge Union."

"I," said the other woman, "prefer to work for the Society of the Refuge for Young Women and Children. We have eleven homes throughout London. How the deserving poor look to us for their solace."

The girl looked up and saw me and let out what appeared to be an honest cry of joy. She excused herself and came up to me.

"Oh, Richard, is it you?"

Not touching, it was as if we embraced. The women were staring.

"Oh, Richard, it is good to see you." Spoken aloud the words were no more than politeness. Whispered, politeness became intimacy. I moved her out of earshot of the charity workers.

"What are you doing here?"

"My job."

"In the law?"

"Yes."

"Are you then handling some cases for Sir James? How wonderful of him to see that you—"

"I am not a lawyer."

"What then?"

"A policeman," I said. "Ha, ha."

She smiled. "If you want to keep that up—have you tried those tarts?"

"I haven't tried anything. Could I have some?"

With a gesture Alethea produced a tray at my side. I ate three or four in quick succession.

"You're still a child, Richard."

The cakes, I thought, were not as good as Mr. Gum's.

"Now, tell me, what are you really doing here."

I looked upon the golden scene, the sweet-smelling garden party, the laughter and security and peace. I was an intruder, the bearer of ill tidings, the farm boy with dung on his boots marching into the parlor.

"I am come," I said, "to arrest Peter for the murder of Maureen Rafferty."

She frowned, but that was all. Should there not have been a whitening of face, hand clutched to throat—fainting, tottering, hand on my shoulder for support?

"You're playing a game, is that it?"

"Like the games we used to play, Alethea? Let's see if we can get the farm boy killed, let's put him in uniform."

"You fought for your country, does that make you ashamed? Peter went, no one forced him to."

"*Est modus in rebus.*" I took another cake. No question, Mr. Gum was by far the superior baker.

It was not as I had planned, or dreamed.

"The truth, Richard?"

I handed her my warrant card and she studied it for a long time as if the language were not native to her. When she handed it back her fingers trembled slightly and I was relieved that she could feel.

She took me down a path and around a bend where we could not be seen. She took my arm. She was as close then as any of the prostitutes in their solicitation. "If this is a game it is a horrid one."

"No game, Alethea."

"Peter? Maureen?"

"He paid for her flat in London, where he visited her just as he did here when we were younger."

"It cannot be, Richard. You must know it cannot be."

"Let him prove otherwise, then."

"He's out riding. I don't know when he will return."

"Sir James said this gathering was for Peter—"

"And for me. We are to be married tomorrow."

It was my turn to show surprise, but I was as outwardly calm as she had been. "*You* and *Peter?*"

"Do you find that strange? Were you not aware that even as children—it has always been understood between Sir James and my father."

"It did not seem to me that Peter took it for granted. Rather did he act as if he were completely free to do as he wished."

"You mean he and Maureen in that bower you discovered?"

"You knew about that?"

"Yes."

"And it made no difference?"

"It meant nothing to Peter, and our marriage was arranged long before that, and a boy has to—"

"Has to—?"

"Learn about such things."

Peter and Alethea.

"I think you owe me a wedding gift."

"Of course," I said.

"Good. Then I ask that you leave Peter alone. You must know he did not do anything to Maureen, he could not."

"Could not?"

"He did not," Alethea said.

"He could, and did, and I am taking him back to London."

I watched the thoughts go chasing one after the other across her face. Finally:

"Are there others besides you who think he did so terrible a thing?"

"No one else knows yet."

"Is it really so important, Richard?"

"One useless girl."

"Perhaps too useful."

"A whore," I said.

She nodded.

"Yet protected by the law the same as the rest of us."

"You intend to arrest Peter."

"Yes."

"What will it take to change your mind?"

"A bribe?"

"An—inducement."

"You could always have your own way with me, could you not, Alethea. But we are no longer children."

"Then the—inducement—must be greater."

The wild thought came into my mind and I banished it and it came back. Alethea was standing with hands cupped at her sides, head down, the perfect virgin selected for sacrifice.

Granted that Alethea loved paradox, that her special delight had always been to make me hop to her command for the sake of some small reward, usually imagined, a touch of her hand or a chaste kiss, and then withhold it, smiling as I squirmed. Granted that she was a source of torment to me in my bachelor bed. Granted that and more, and despite the excitement of having her close, there could be only one perverse and inescapable reaction. I laughed.

"Sir!"

"So formal? Was not your suggestion more intimate?"

"Is it that your feeling for me has vanished?"

"It is stronger than ever," I said.

"Well?"

"You want an answer? Whether I accept the quid pro quo? And you think Maureen's method different?"

At that how could she do otherwise than scornfully depart? Yet she stayed, and I was not proud of myself.

She said quietly, "How insufferable you have become. The old Richard was never like this."

"Does that mean the offer is withdrawn?"

"You're such a fool," she said.

"Is that better or worse than insufferable?"

"Is it not what you have always wanted?"

"Tomorrow you marry. You offer the farmer's boy the droit de seigneur?"

"Go to your home and wait for me."

"I have no home here."

"Your father's house. The Raffertys wanted to move in but Sir James would not allow them to."

She left.

I walked slowly toward the farm, bending to touch furze and bracken, reaching down for a handful of earth to crumble and sift through my fingers. There were no noxious smells, no sounds save those made by the wind and the farm animals in the distance. Yet I had no feeling for this life any more. I was no farmer. I had decided on life in the midst of tumult.

The house was untenanted and unmolested. I walked about like a dog sniffing corners for memories. This time I was moved to go into my mother's room. I sat in her chair. Back and forth I rocked as she had done evening after evening until I could feel her presence descending on me.

Your coldness is my coldness, unmelted even by death. Had you warmed me, Mother, would I be different?

Peace. The only important thing is peace.

Have I denied you that, Mother?

You have withheld your tears.

What was my father, that I was able to weep for him?

A strong and simple man, I answered myself, the English yeoman content with his place in the world.

My mother was frozen and alien, denying her bed to her husband and maternal comfort to her son.

One tear, she said. Can you not spare one tear?

Her place was not my father's place. She belonged to some distant village in France where the language was not something painfully learned and uncertain on her tongue, where she felt pride in country and easement with family and friends. Here she had never stopped being a stranger.

Was I not the same? Had I not, at the garden party, borne the suspicious glances of the guests and the supercilious servants?

It was always like that for me, she said.

But your husband loved you. You could have let him warm you. Your son needed you; you could have warmed him.

The fault was mine.

You say that?

Of course. Where I am now there is nothing but truth. I loved you and I loved your father. But the love was kept in a cold place. Will you forgive me?

Yes.

Will you then weep for me?

Yes.

I rocked back and forth and wept for my mother.

Then I went outside and there was a figure approaching,

skipping from rise to rise with the lightness of a mountain animal. She came up to me openly and joyously. She carried a small hamper, handing it to me and saying, "We will need food."

"Did you put in some of those cakes?"

"Of course," she said, laughing.

"You're here," I said.

"You didn't believe me."

"No."

"Peter had the wildness in him this morning. You know how he used to get when he would plan a race, the course he selected would always be the roughest. Today he would have ridden until the fever was out of him and then he might stay at whatever friend was nearest and come back in the morning spent and once more as agreeable as only Peter can be. You do admit there were times when he was most agreeable."

"I remember."

"And so, having come on this detestable business of yours, you must have felt some sadness."

"Yes. It's like a man and a rat stranded together, the only two living beings on some island. The rat will eat from the man's hand and they will become great friends, except that once in a while the rat will have to bite the man because it is his nature. Having recovered from the bite, if he does recover, the man will remember the charming times they had together."

"He has bitten me too," Alethea said.

"Yet you will marry him."

"He is heir to his father."

"Honestly said," I said.

She looked at me in surprise. "I have always been honest with you."

We remained outside watching the sun fall. We did not touch. The sun painted the clouds above the valley. Alethea shivered.

"I'll go in to light a candle," I said.

She came in after me, small and dainty and taking short steps like a filly on a strange turf.

"So this is where you lived."

"Hardly the sort of grand place you were used to."

"Oh, Richard, you are really such a fool. You know nothing about me. I was always the poor relation, the daughter of Sir James's younger brother. My father sent me to live at the manor in the hope that my cousin might find me suitable as a wife."

"Which he has."

"My father was a younger son. You know what that means according to English law and custom. He shared in none of the estate. He had no prospect except to marry a girl with money. Instead he married the daughter of a clergyman whose living barely supported his own family. Finally Sir James, not out of the goodness of his heart but because he was afraid my father might disgrace him, gave him a small allowance. So I am far from being a great lady, Richard, and the fact that I am here proves me no lady at all."

"The little rich girl, so far above me in station I barely had enough courage to speak to her."

"I played the part well, did I not?"

Chapter Eighteen

Alethea removed her bonnet and did something atop her head and her hair fell. She shook her head once but did not use her hands to smooth it. In the light of the single candle she was mysterious, peering out from the thicket more sprite than girl.

"You dreamed of me, Richard."

"Often."

"In your dreams, Richard, what did I do?"

"You reached for me."

"Like this?"—coming close and putting out her arms.

"Yes."

"And what else did I do?"

"You put your arms around me."

"Like this?"

"Yes."

She kissed me. In the past it had happened once or twice, a pressing of lips to lips with hardly more significance than the pressing of palm to palm. This now was an engulfing roaring wave with something live and quivering and wet in the center and I did not know what to do with her. She pulled away and said, "Richard, I think you've broken my back."

"I'm sorry."

"Don't be sorry, be gentle."

With coolness, as if in her own boudoir, Alethea began to undress, divesting layer after layer as I looked away, and back out of the corners of my eyes, and away again. I had seen statues and thought myself prepared, but not for this warmth, this triangulated copse, this defenseless innateness.

"You have never," she said, "seen a woman naked?"

"No," I said.

"Come, then, see it closer, judge me."

She turned slowly, hands behind her neck. "Is this what you expected?"

"I cannot speak."

"Off with your garments, while we make an Eden of this house."

I followed her to the bed and I touched her, afraid that she would break in my hands. She was, she told me, made more durable than that. She guided me, and although I had known how it was done I had known nothing, no one to tell me of the feelings surpassing every sense. I was afraid that I would rive her so she grappled me and counted with moans instead of numbers until I was shattered, bits and pieces up to this star and that. She did not let me rest long. The moment I was whole again we resumed, more slowly now, with infinite exploration.

"Was your fantasy better than this, Richard?"

"This is fantasy," I said.

I lay exhausted, yet without fatigue, and I thought of my life, as they say one does in the moment before dying, and I knew that what I was experiencing was—exorcism.

We slept and resumed and slept again. The light was just beginning outside to touch the darkness when I awakened to feel a melancholy as from a burden put down which, having been so long borne, had been conceived to be part of the flesh. It changed to lightness which was still as much ache as relief. I had no need, I thought, ever to think of Alethea again.

She stirred. "Richard?"—reaching for me.

I held her, but in farewell. I got out of bed and began to dress.

"You're going for Peter."

"Yes."

"You had never meant to balance this against that."

"No."

"Then you must know," Alethea said, "that it was I, not Peter, who was responsible for Maureen's death."

I made myself feel surprise, yet all along there had been the fretting question: How could Peter, or any man, have used a hatpin in anger?

While I mulled that she said, "I found out about the flat in St. John's Wood. I was afraid that Peter might prefer Maureen to me. I offered her money. She laughed, saying Peter had more money than I. That was true and I—it was more to frighten her than otherwise. It was not murder. You do not think it was murder, Richard?"

"No."

She sighed with relief and said, "Then you will not arrest me?" and it was at once the teasing of old with something new. She was not sure what I would do. I liked her not being sure. She had descended far—so far she was now on a level with me, and no better than the poor girl whose death she had caused. I considered the sadness of her, invoking privilege to perfume defect.

I delayed my answer. How often had I waited for her to answer me and heard only silence, or a laugh.

"Let me be lenient," I said. "As lenient as you were when you testified falsely to Sir James, as lenient as he was when he sentenced me."

She was brave, she was not going to beg.

"I need not take you into custody, Alethea. I leave that to Peter. Go now, it's your wedding day."

I left that house and went to my home, where a pretty girl, scrubbed and neat, hearing my step had put the kettle on. She came to look up at me and then, smiling, prepared the tea.